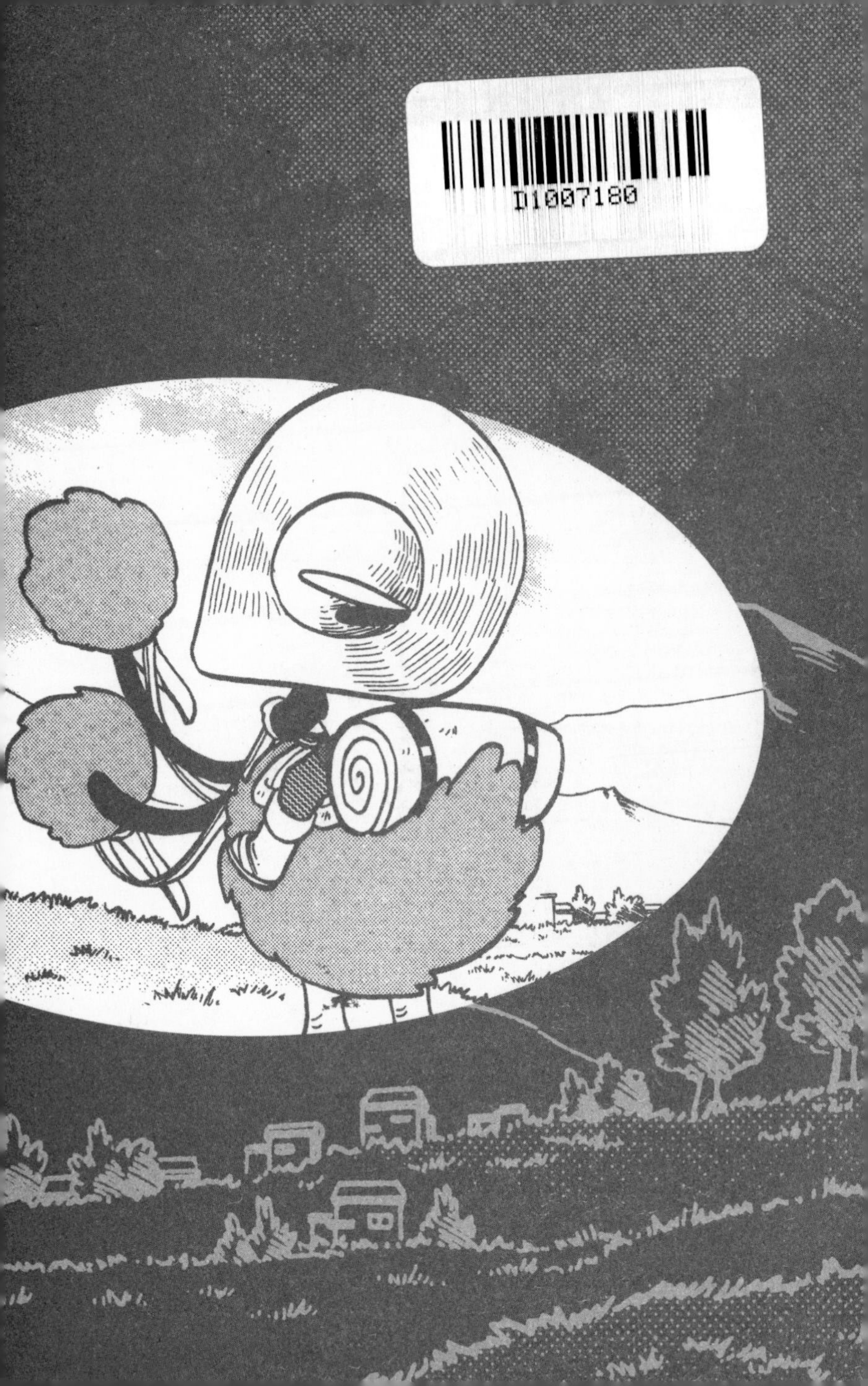

THE BEST OF
POKÉMON
ADVENTURES

YELLOW
VIZ Kids Edition

Story by **Hidenori Kusaka**
Art by **Mato**

From VIZ Graphic Novels *Pokémon Adventures* Vol.4-Vol.7 published by VIZ Media.

[1st Edition]
Translation/Kaori Inoue
Touch-Up & Lettering/Dan Nakrosis
Graphic Design/Carolina Ugalde
Editor/William Flanagan

[VIZ Kids Edition]
Cover & Graphic Design/Izumi Hirayama

Editor in Chief, Books/Alvin Lu
Editor in Chief, Magazines/Marc Weidenbaum
VP of Publishing Licensing/Rika Inouye
VP of Sales/Gonzalo Ferreyra
Sr. VP of Marketing/Liza Coppola
Publisher/Hyoe Narita

Printed in the U.S.A.

Published by VIZ Media, LLC
P.O. Box 77064
San Francisco, CA 94107

VIZ Kids Edition
10 9 8 7 6
First printing, December 2006
Sixth printing, August 2007

For advertising rates or media kit, e-mail advertising@viz.com

store.viz.com

VIZ media

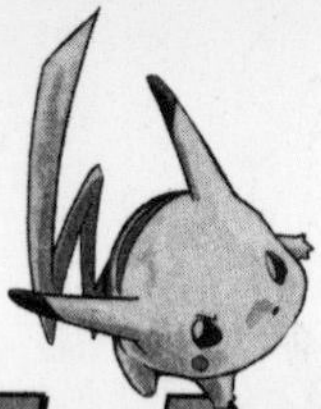

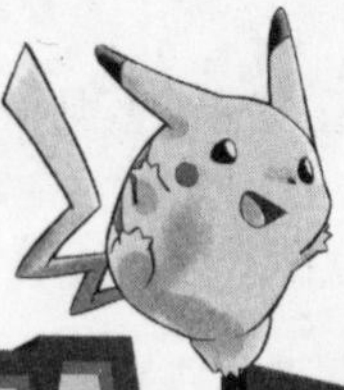

The Best of Pokémon Adventures®

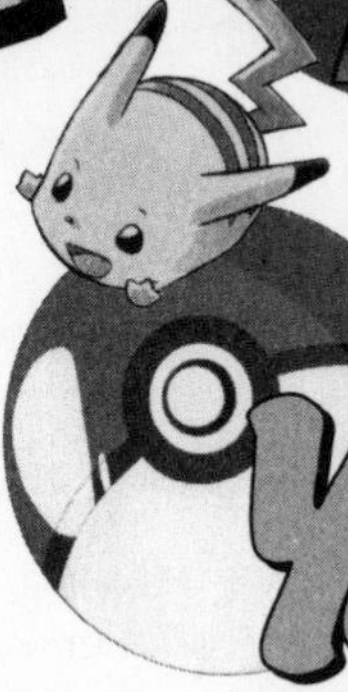

Yellow

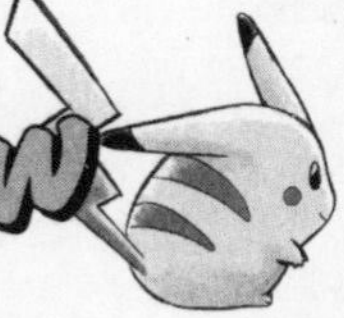

VIZ Kids Edition

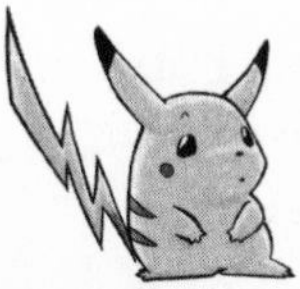

Story by Hidenori Kusaka

Art by Mato

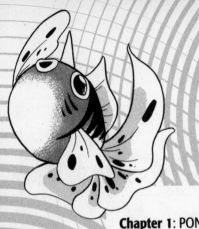

CONTENTS

CHAPTER 1

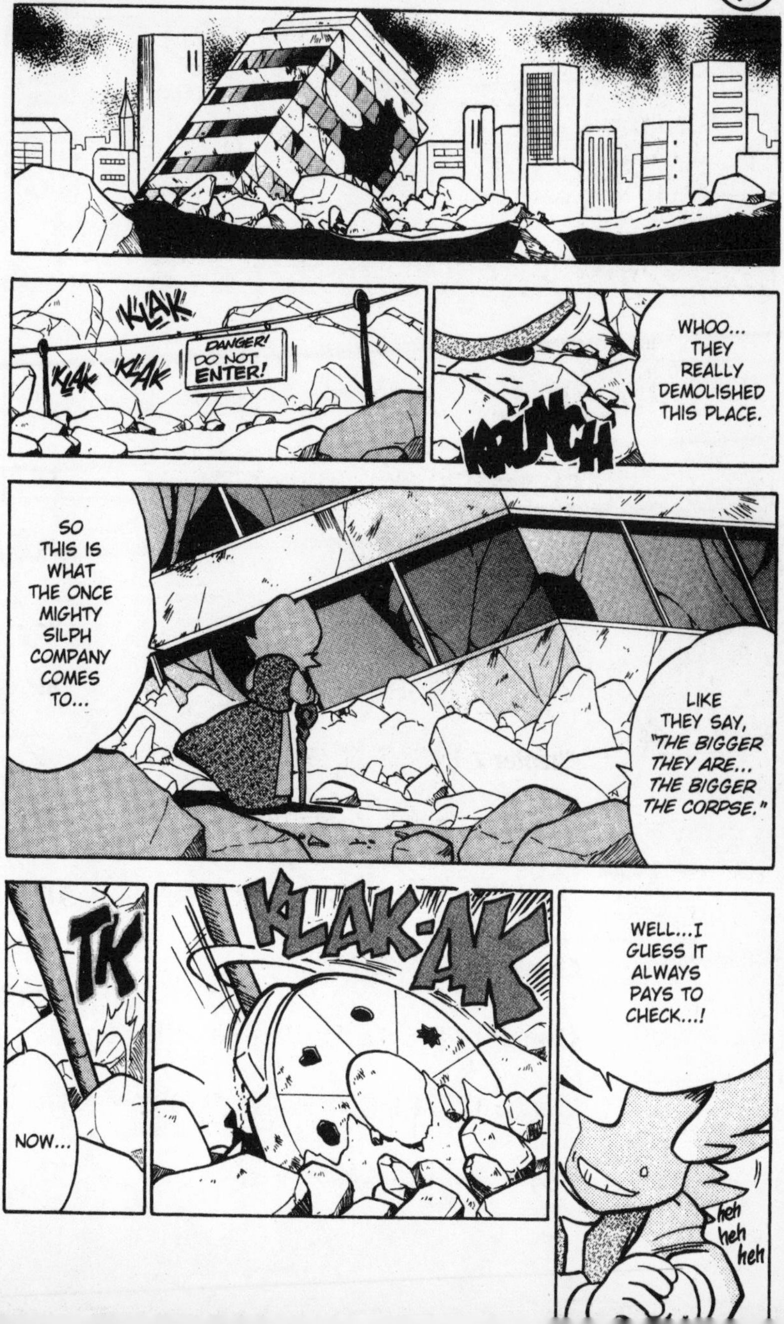

KLAK
KLAK
KLAK
DANGER! DO NOT ENTER!
WHOO... THEY REALLY DEMOLISHED THIS PLACE.
KRUNCH
SO THIS IS WHAT THE ONCE MIGHTY SILPH COMPANY COMES TO...
LIKE THEY SAY, "THE BIGGER THEY ARE... THE BIGGER THE CORPSE."
TK
NOW...
KLAK-AK
WELL...I GUESS IT ALWAYS PAYS TO CHECK...!
heh heh heh

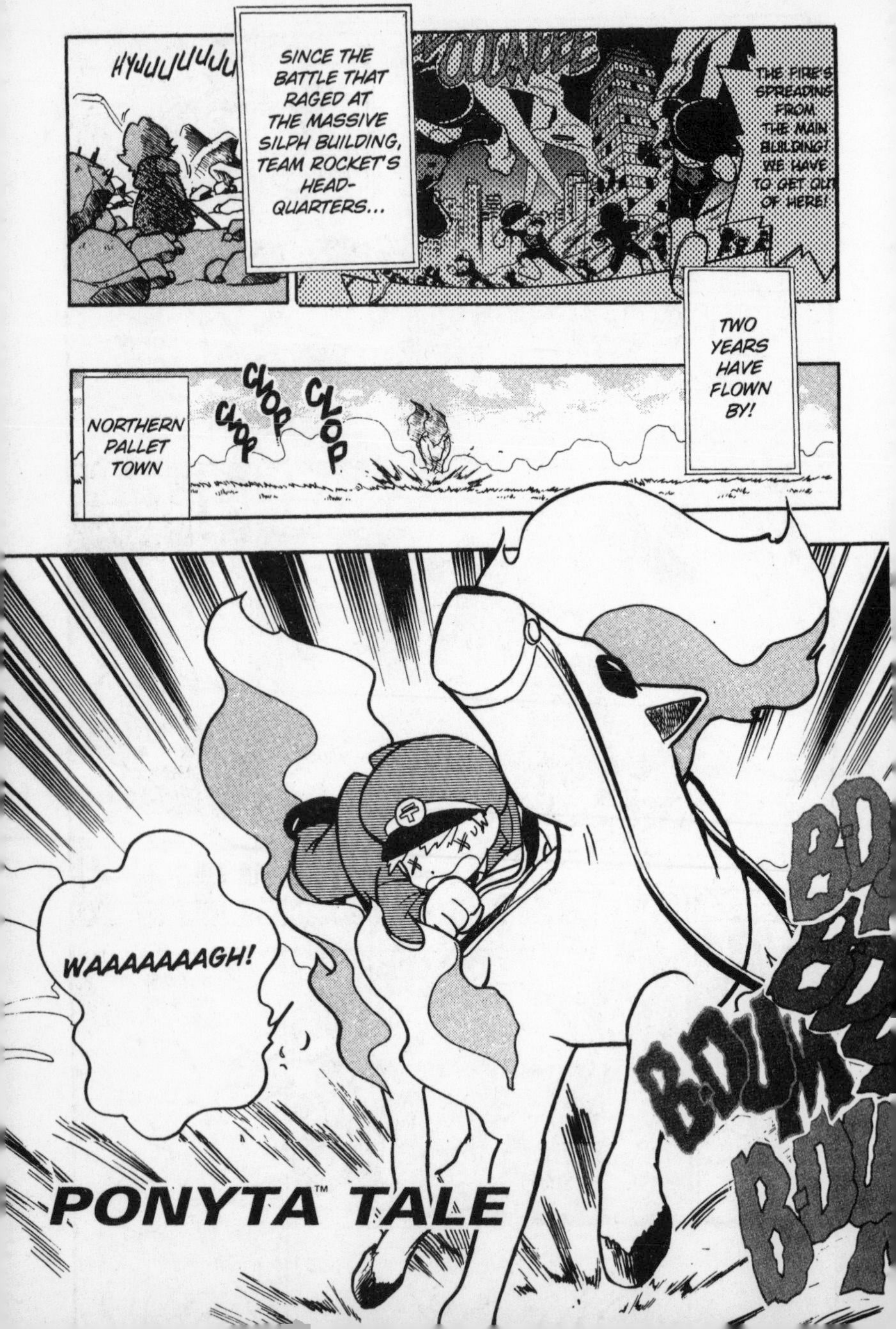
HYUUUUUUU
SINCE THE BATTLE THAT RAGED AT THE MASSIVE SILPH BUILDING, TEAM ROCKET'S HEAD-QUARTERS...
THE FIRE'S SPREADING FROM THE MAIN BUILDING! WE HAVE TO GET OUT OF HERE!
TWO YEARS HAVE FLOWN BY!
NORTHERN PALLET TOWN
CLOP
CLOP
CLOP
WAAAAAAAGH!
B-DUM
PONYTA™ TALE

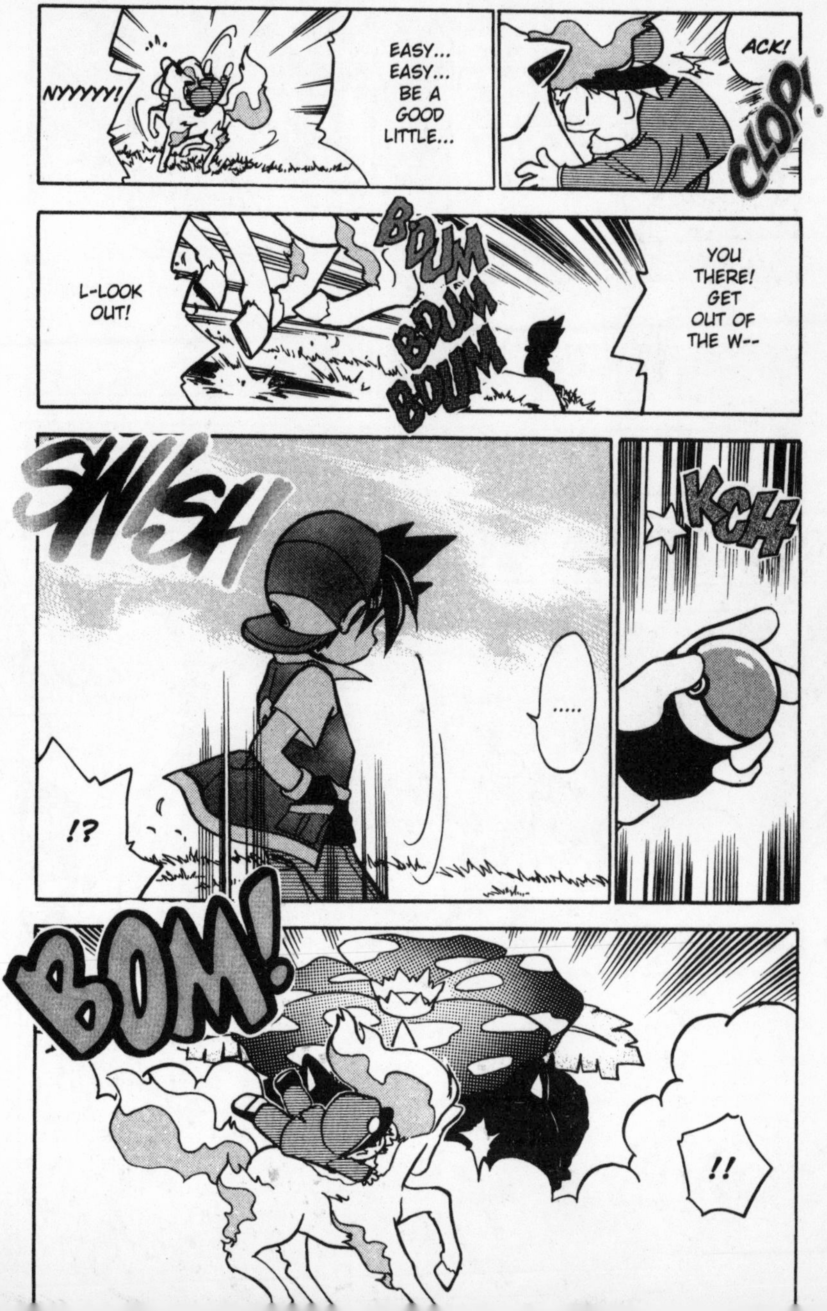
NYYYYY!
EASY... EASY... BE A GOOD LITTLE...
ACK!
CLOP!
L-LOOK OUT!
B'DUM
B'DUM
B'DUM
YOU THERE! GET OUT OF THE W--
SWISH
!?
.....
KCH
BOM!
!!

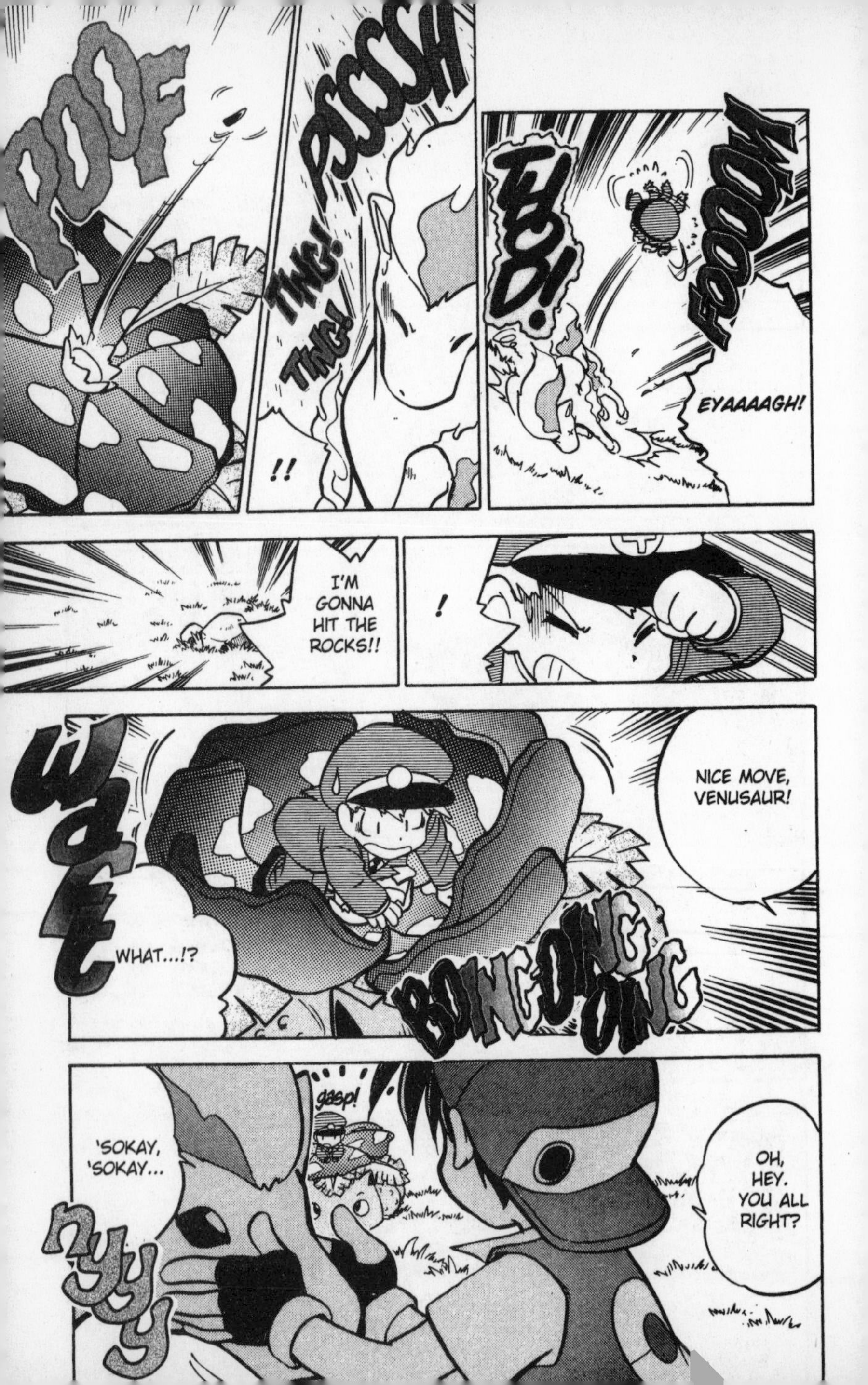

POOF
PSSSH
TING! TING!
!!
FOOOM
TEDD!
EYAAAAGH!
I'M GONNA HIT THE ROCKS!!
!
WHAP
WHAT...!?
NICE MOVE, VENUSAUR!
BOING OING OING
gasp!
OH, HEY. YOU ALL RIGHT?
'SOKAY, 'SOKAY...
nyyy

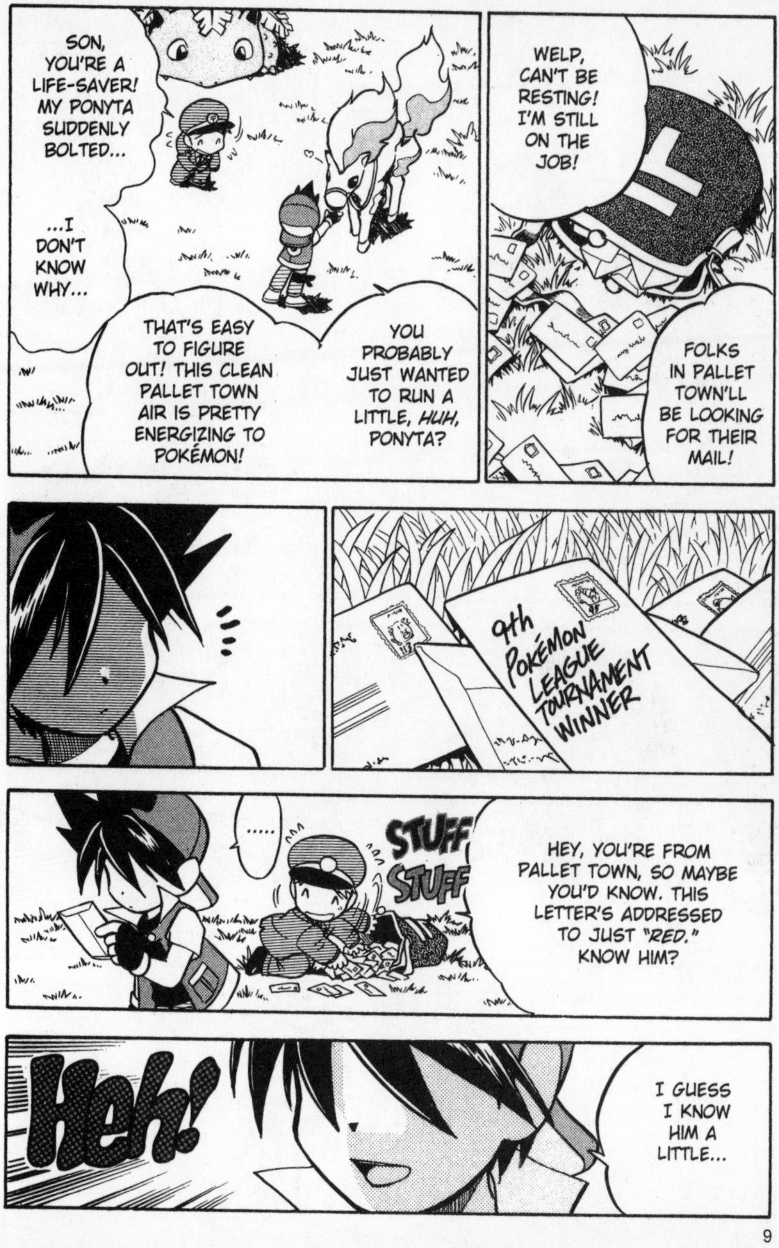
SON, YOU'RE A LIFE-SAVER! MY PONYTA SUDDENLY BOLTED...
...I DON'T KNOW WHY...
THAT'S EASY TO FIGURE OUT! THIS CLEAN PALLET TOWN AIR IS PRETTY ENERGIZING TO POKÉMON!
YOU PROBABLY JUST WANTED TO RUN A LITTLE, *HUH*, PONYTA?
WELP, CAN'T BE RESTING! I'M STILL ON THE JOB!
FOLKS IN PALLET TOWN'LL BE LOOKING FOR THEIR MAIL!
9th POKÉMON LEAGUE TOURNAMENT WINNER
.....
STUFF
STUFF
HEY, YOU'RE FROM PALLET TOWN, SO MAYBE YOU'D KNOW. THIS LETTER'S ADDRESSED TO JUST "*RED.*" KNOW HIM?
Heh!
I GUESS I KNOW HIM A LITTLE...

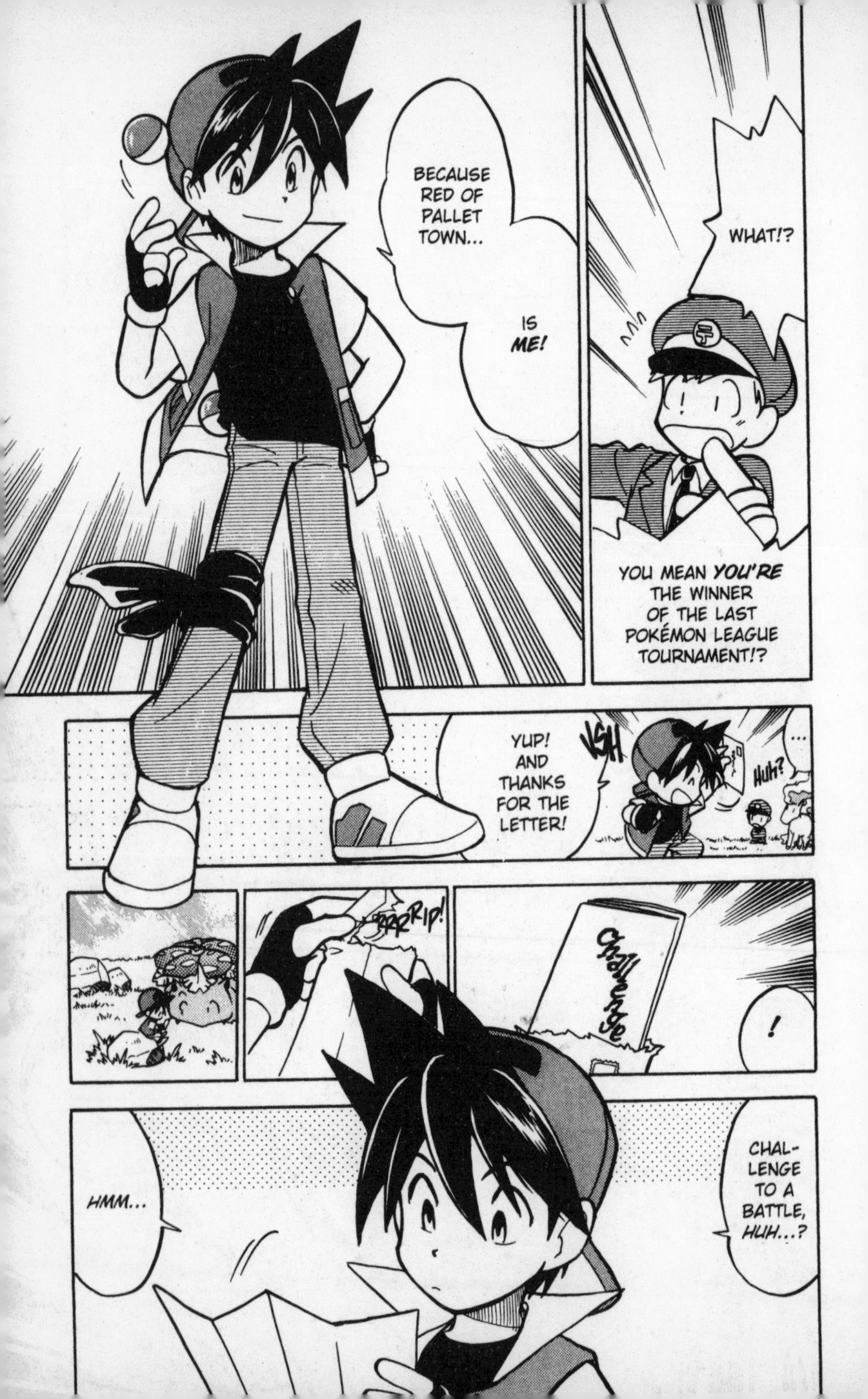
BECAUSE RED OF PALLET TOWN...
IS *ME!*
WHAT!?
YOU MEAN *YOU'RE* THE WINNER OF THE LAST POKÉMON LEAGUE TOURNAMENT!?
YUP! AND THANKS FOR THE LETTER!
VSH
...
HUH?
RRRRIP!
Challenge
!
CHAL-LENGE TO A BATTLE, *HUH...?*
HMM...

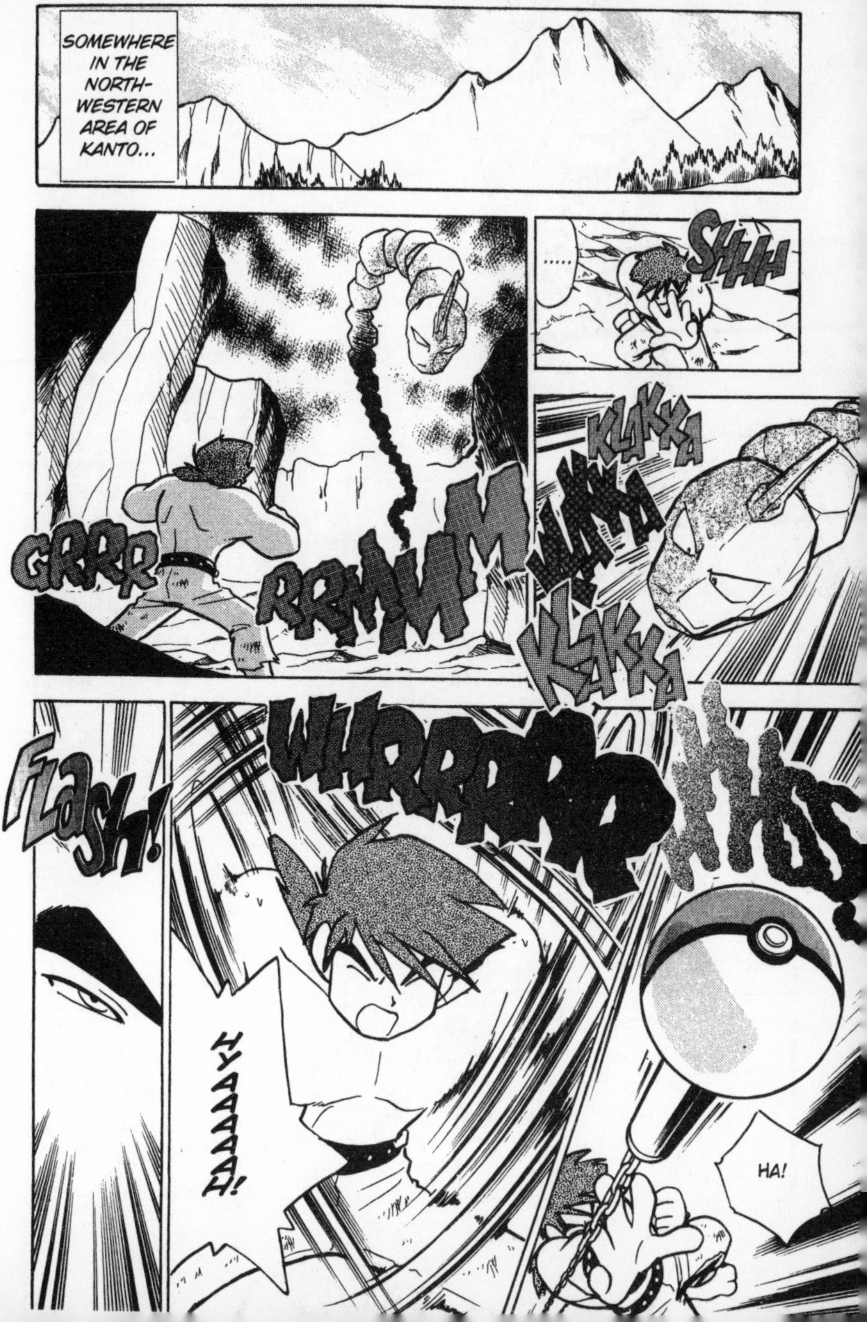
SOMEWHERE IN THE NORTH-WESTERN AREA OF KANTO...
......
SHHH
KLAKKA
KLAKKA
RRMMMM
GRRR
HA!
WHRRRRR
FLASH!
HYAAAAAAH!

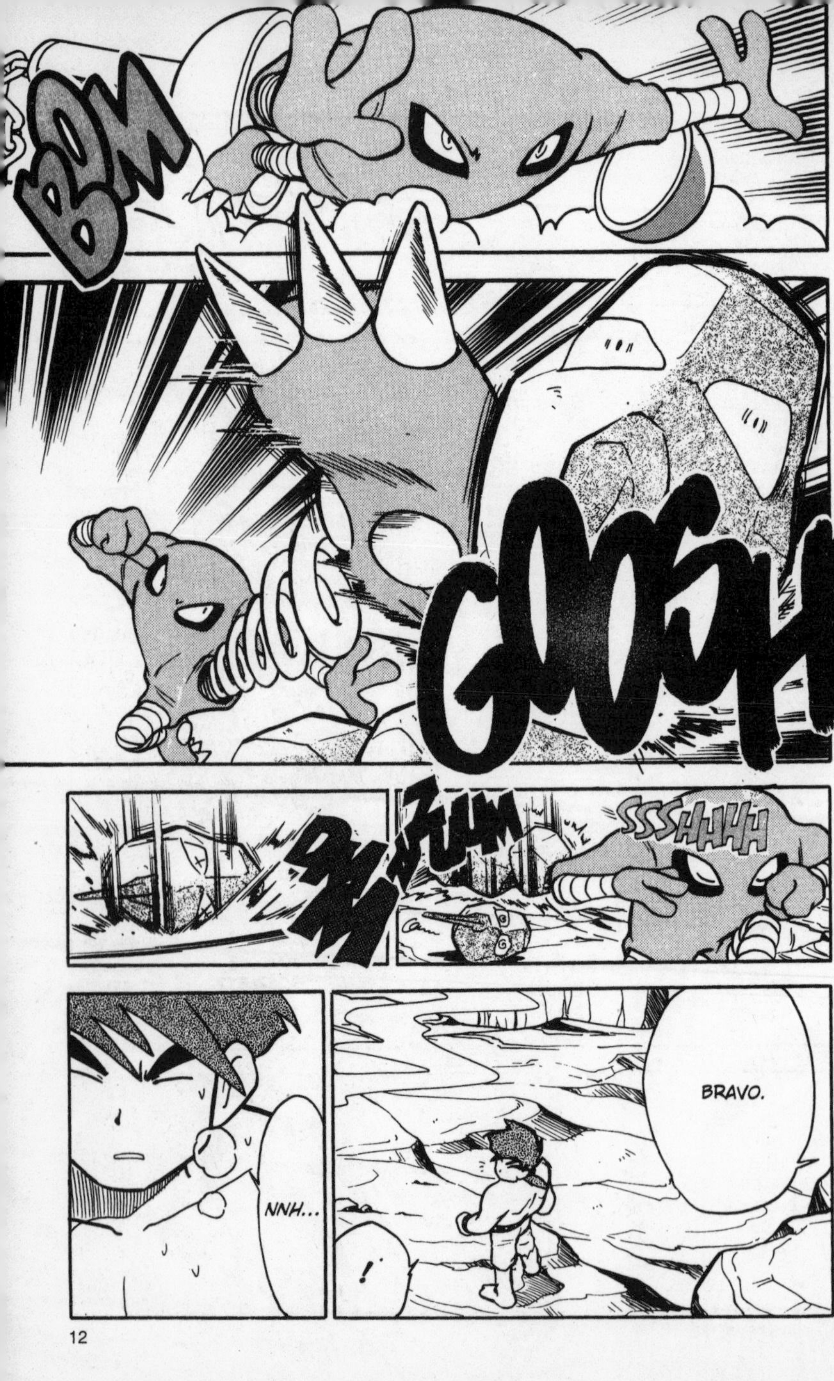
BOM
GOOSH
DWM
ZUUM
SSSHHHH
NNH...
BRAVO.
!

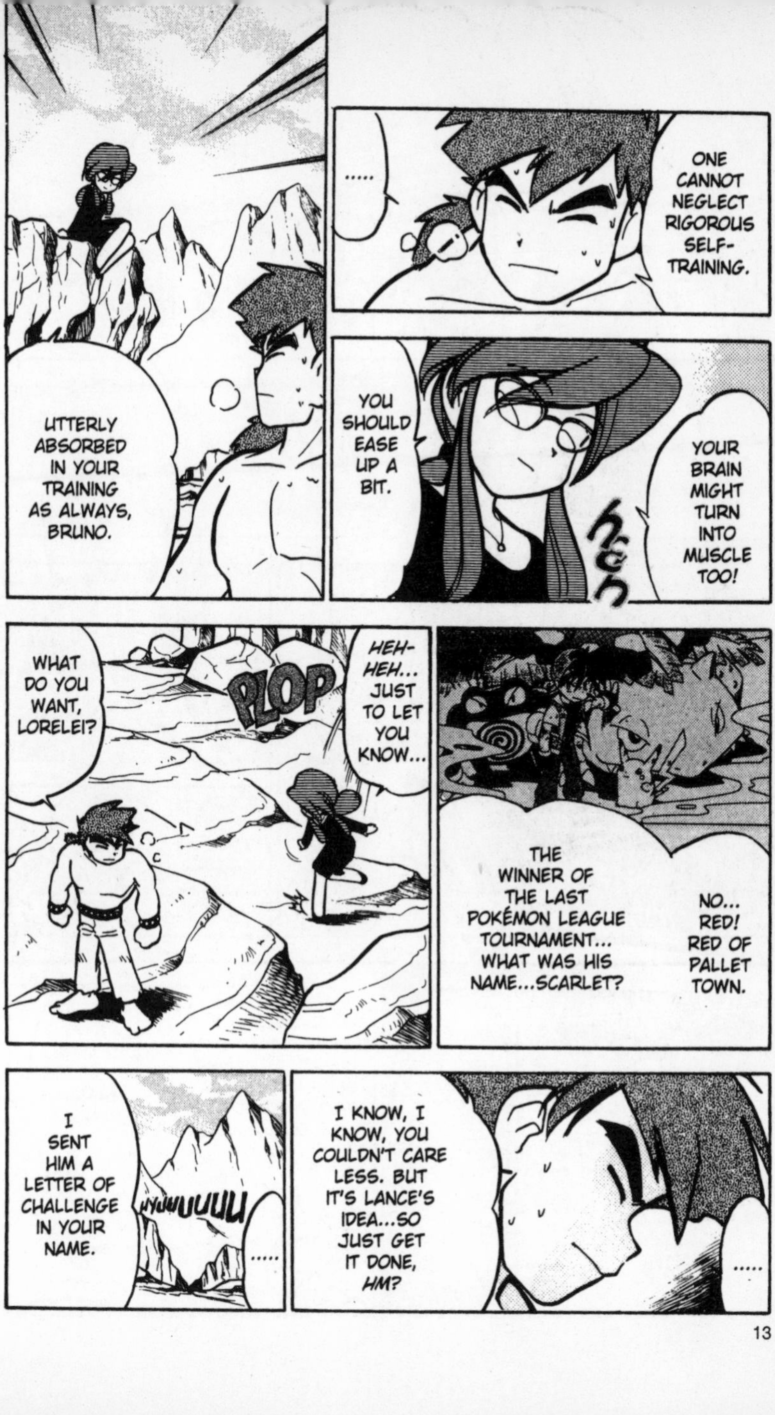
UTTERLY ABSORBED IN YOUR TRAINING AS ALWAYS, BRUNO.
.....
ONE CANNOT NEGLECT RIGOROUS SELF-TRAINING.
YOU SHOULD EASE UP A BIT.
YOUR BRAIN MIGHT TURN INTO MUSCLE TOO!
WHAT DO YOU WANT, LORELEI?
PLOP
HEH-HEH... JUST TO LET YOU KNOW...
THE WINNER OF THE LAST POKÉMON LEAGUE TOURNAMENT... WHAT WAS HIS NAME...SCARLET?
NO... RED! RED OF PALLET TOWN.
I SENT HIM A LETTER OF CHALLENGE IN YOUR NAME.
.....
I KNOW, I KNOW, YOU COULDN'T CARE LESS. BUT IT'S LANCE'S IDEA...SO JUST GET IT DONE, HM?
.....

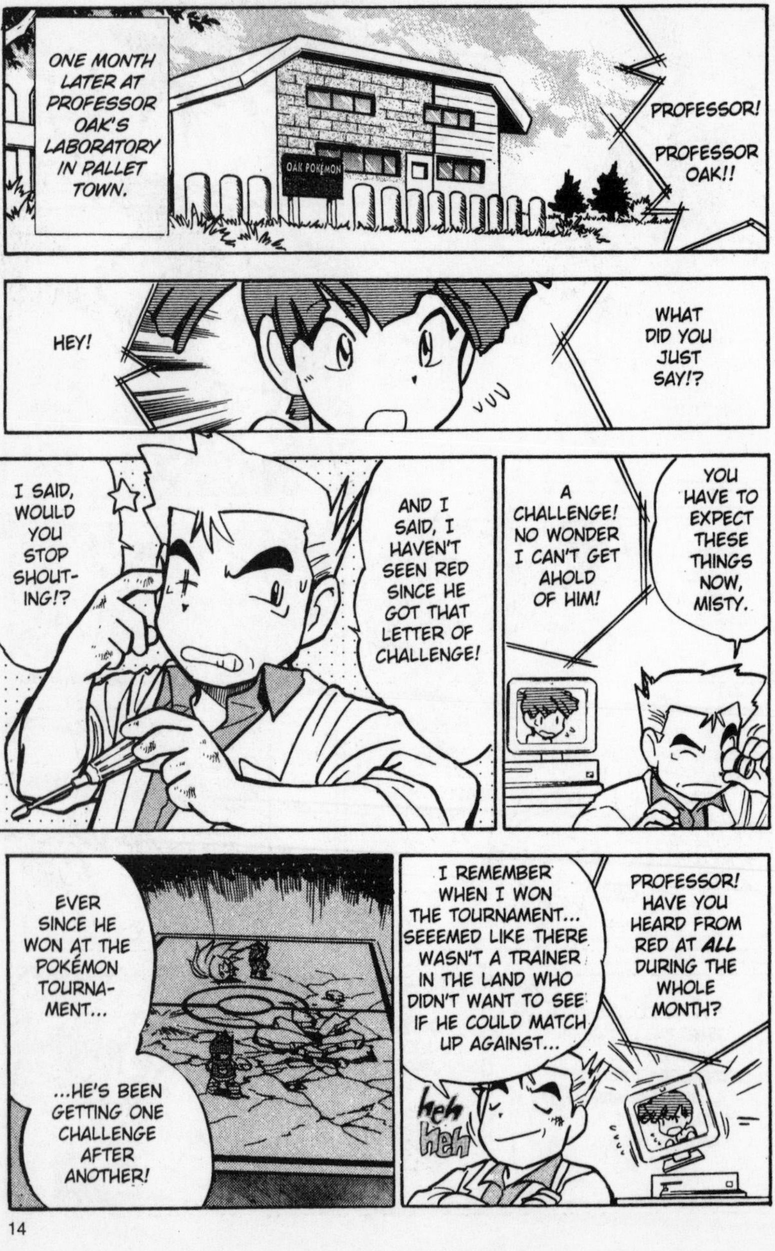
ONE MONTH LATER AT PROFESSOR OAK'S LABORATORY IN PALLET TOWN.
OAK POKÉMON
PROFESSOR!
PROFESSOR OAK!!
WHAT DID YOU JUST SAY!?
HEY!
I SAID, WOULD YOU STOP SHOUT-ING!?
AND I SAID, I HAVEN'T SEEN RED SINCE HE GOT THAT LETTER OF CHALLENGE!
A CHALLENGE! NO WONDER I CAN'T GET AHOLD OF HIM!
YOU HAVE TO EXPECT THESE THINGS NOW, MISTY.
EVER SINCE HE WON AT THE POKÉMON TOURNA-MENT...
...HE'S BEEN GETTING ONE CHALLENGE AFTER ANOTHER!
PROFESSOR! HAVE YOU HEARD FROM RED AT ALL DURING THE WHOLE MONTH?
I REMEMBER WHEN I WON THE TOURNAMENT... SEEEMED LIKE THERE WASN'T A TRAINER IN THE LAND WHO DIDN'T WANT TO SEE IF HE COULD MATCH UP AGAINST...
heh heh

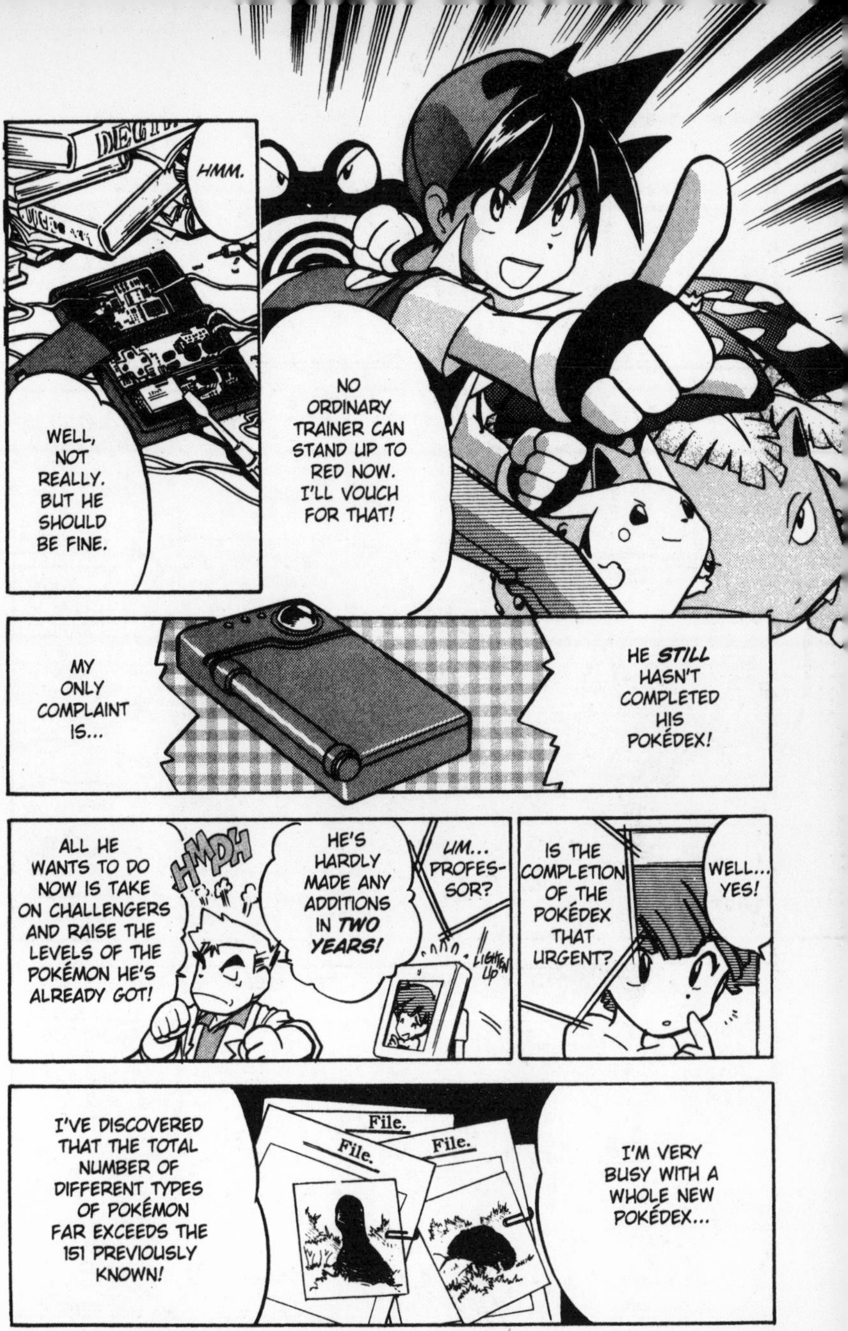
HMM.
WELL, NOT REALLY. BUT HE SHOULD BE FINE.
NO ORDINARY TRAINER CAN STAND UP TO RED NOW. I'LL VOUCH FOR THAT!
MY ONLY COMPLAINT IS...
HE STILL HASN'T COMPLETED HIS POKÉDEX!
ALL HE WANTS TO DO NOW IS TAKE ON CHALLENGERS AND RAISE THE LEVELS OF THE POKÉMON HE'S ALREADY GOT!
HMPH
HE'S HARDLY MADE ANY ADDITIONS IN TWO YEARS!
UM... PROFES-SOR?
LIGHTEN UP
IS THE COMPLETION OF THE POKÉDEX THAT URGENT?
WELL... YES!
I'VE DISCOVERED THAT THE TOTAL NUMBER OF DIFFERENT TYPES OF POKÉMON FAR EXCEEDS THE 151 PREVIOUSLY KNOWN!
File.
File.
File.
I'M VERY BUSY WITH A WHOLE NEW POKÉDEX...

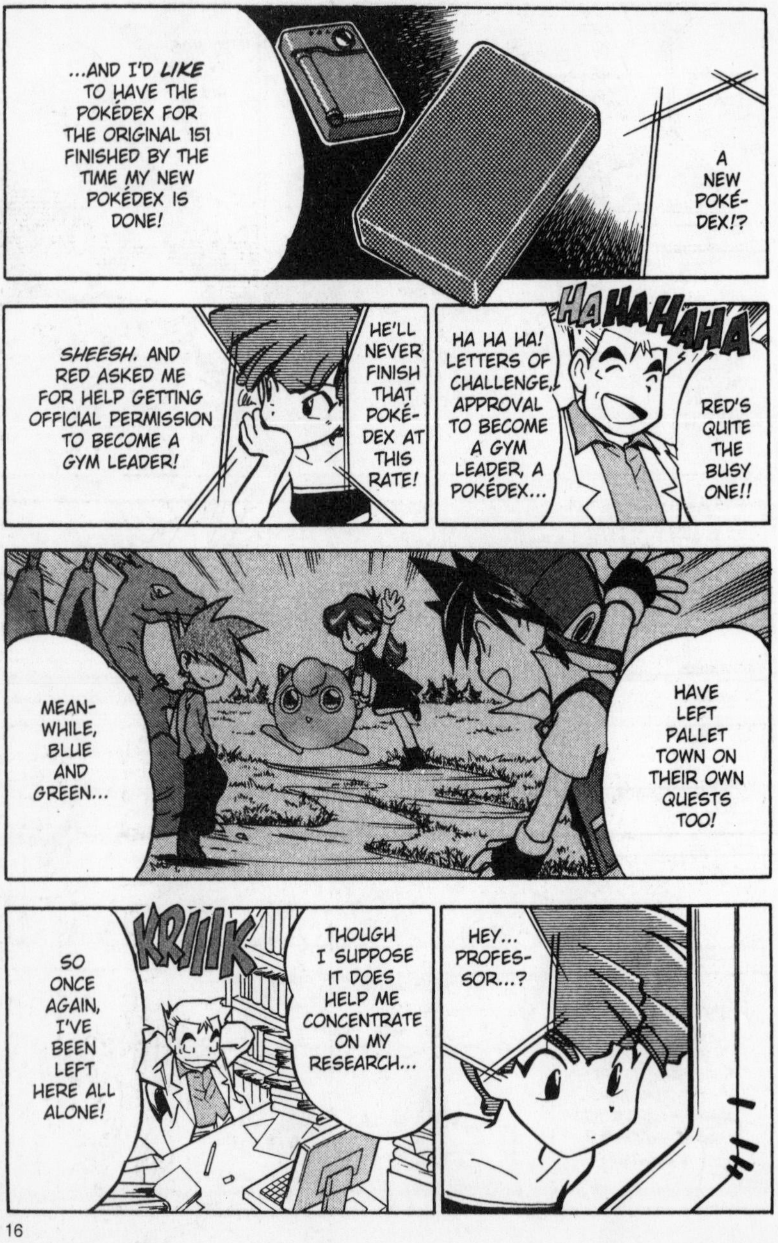
...AND I'D *LIKE* TO HAVE THE POKÉDEX FOR THE ORIGINAL 151 FINISHED BY THE TIME MY NEW POKÉDEX IS DONE!
A NEW POKÉ-DEX!?
SHEESH. AND RED ASKED ME FOR HELP GETTING OFFICIAL PERMISSION TO BECOME A GYM LEADER!
HE'LL NEVER FINISH THAT POKÉ-DEX AT THIS RATE!
HAHAHAHAHA
HA HA HA! LETTERS OF CHALLENGE, APPROVAL TO BECOME A GYM LEADER, A POKÉDEX...
RED'S QUITE THE BUSY ONE!!
MEAN-WHILE, BLUE AND GREEN...
HAVE LEFT PALLET TOWN ON THEIR OWN QUESTS TOO!
KRIIK
SO ONCE AGAIN, I'VE BEEN LEFT HERE ALL ALONE!
THOUGH I SUPPOSE IT DOES HELP ME CONCENTRATE ON MY RESEARCH...
HEY... PROFES-SOR...?

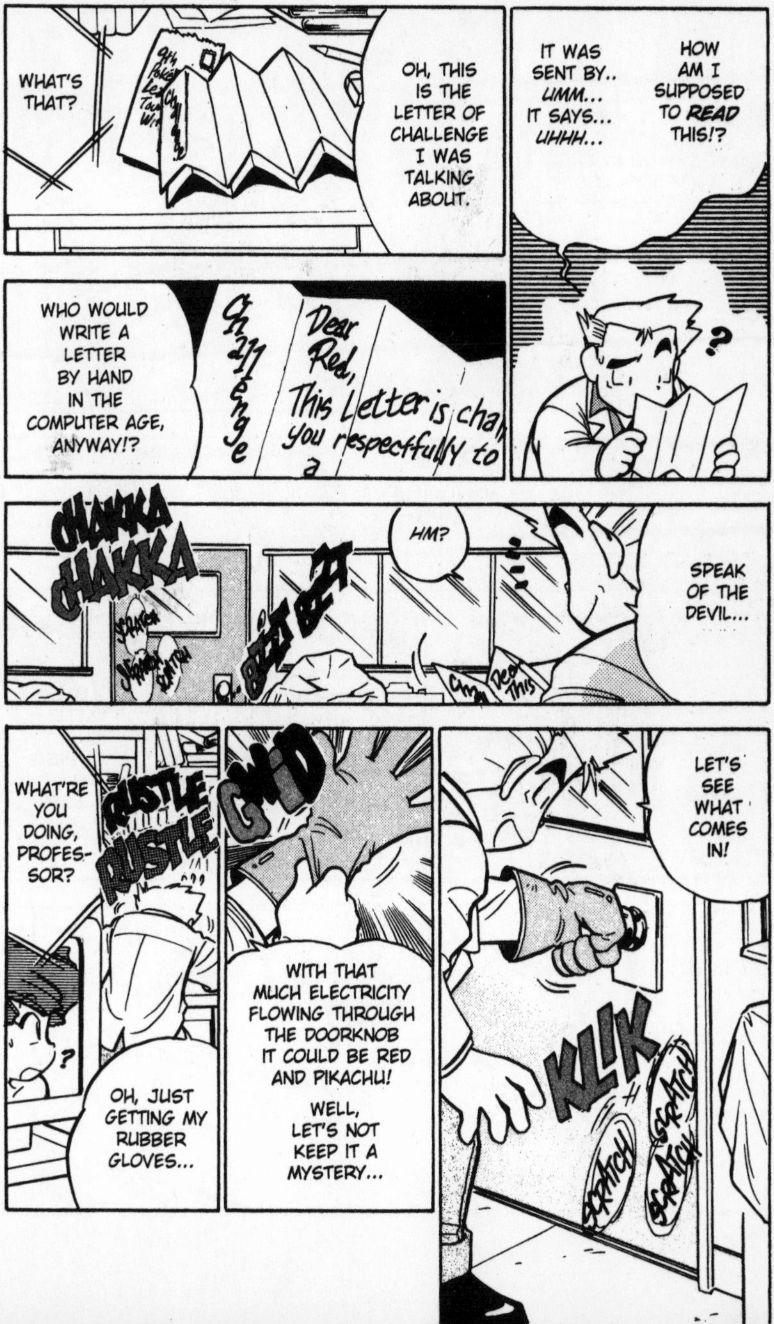

WHAT'S THAT?
OH, THIS IS THE LETTER OF CHALLENGE I WAS TALKING ABOUT.
IT WAS SENT BY.. *UMM...* IT SAYS... *UHHH...*
HOW AM I SUPPOSED TO ***READ*** THIS!?
WHO WOULD WRITE A LETTER BY HAND IN THE COMPUTER AGE, ANYWAY!?
Challenge
Dear Red,
This Letter is cha
you respectfully to
?
CHAKKA CHAKKA
HM?
BZZT BZZT
SPEAK OF THE DEVIL...
WHAT'RE YOU DOING, PROFES-SOR?
RUSTLE RUSTLE
OH, JUST GETTING MY RUBBER GLOVES...
GWID
WITH THAT MUCH ELECTRICITY FLOWING THROUGH THE DOORKNOB IT COULD BE RED AND PIKACHU!
WELL, LET'S NOT KEEP IT A MYSTERY...
LET'S SEE WHAT COMES IN!
KLIK
SCRATCH SCRATCH
SCRATCH SCRATCH

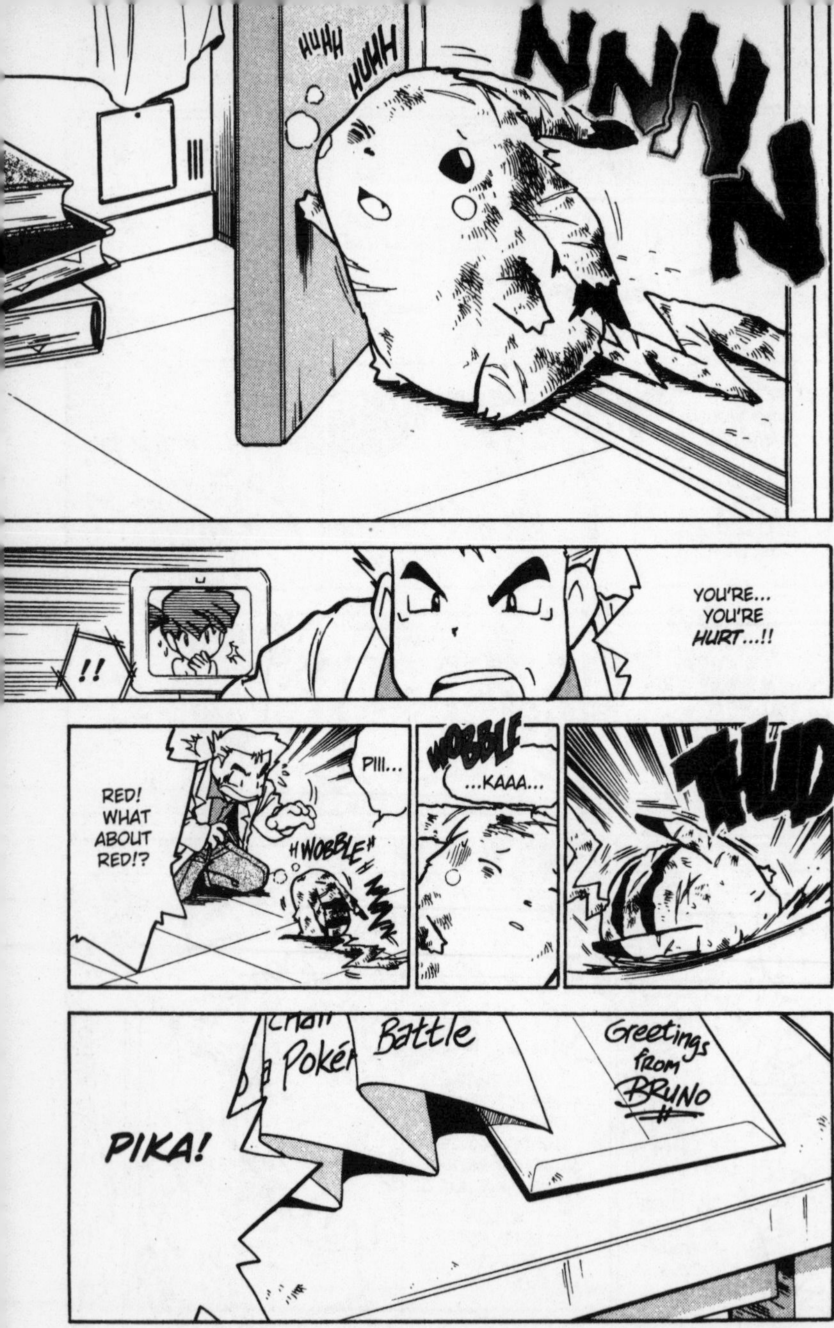
NNNN
HUHH HUHH
YOU'RE... YOU'RE HURT...!!
!!
RED! WHAT ABOUT RED!?
PIII...
WOBBLE WOBBLE
...KAAA...
WOBBLE
THUD
PIKA!
Battle
Poké
Greetings from BRUNO

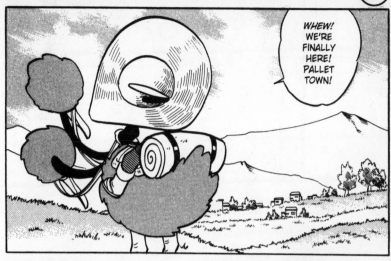

WHEW! WE'RE FINALLY HERE! PALLET TOWN!

HEY! YOU THERE!

I NEED SOME INFORMATION! I'M LOOKING FOR...

HERE...

SKWIK SKWIK

YEAH... NOT BAD...

Electric Mouse

Attacks.. Thunderbolt, Thundershock

DO YOU KNOW THIS POKÉMON!?

19

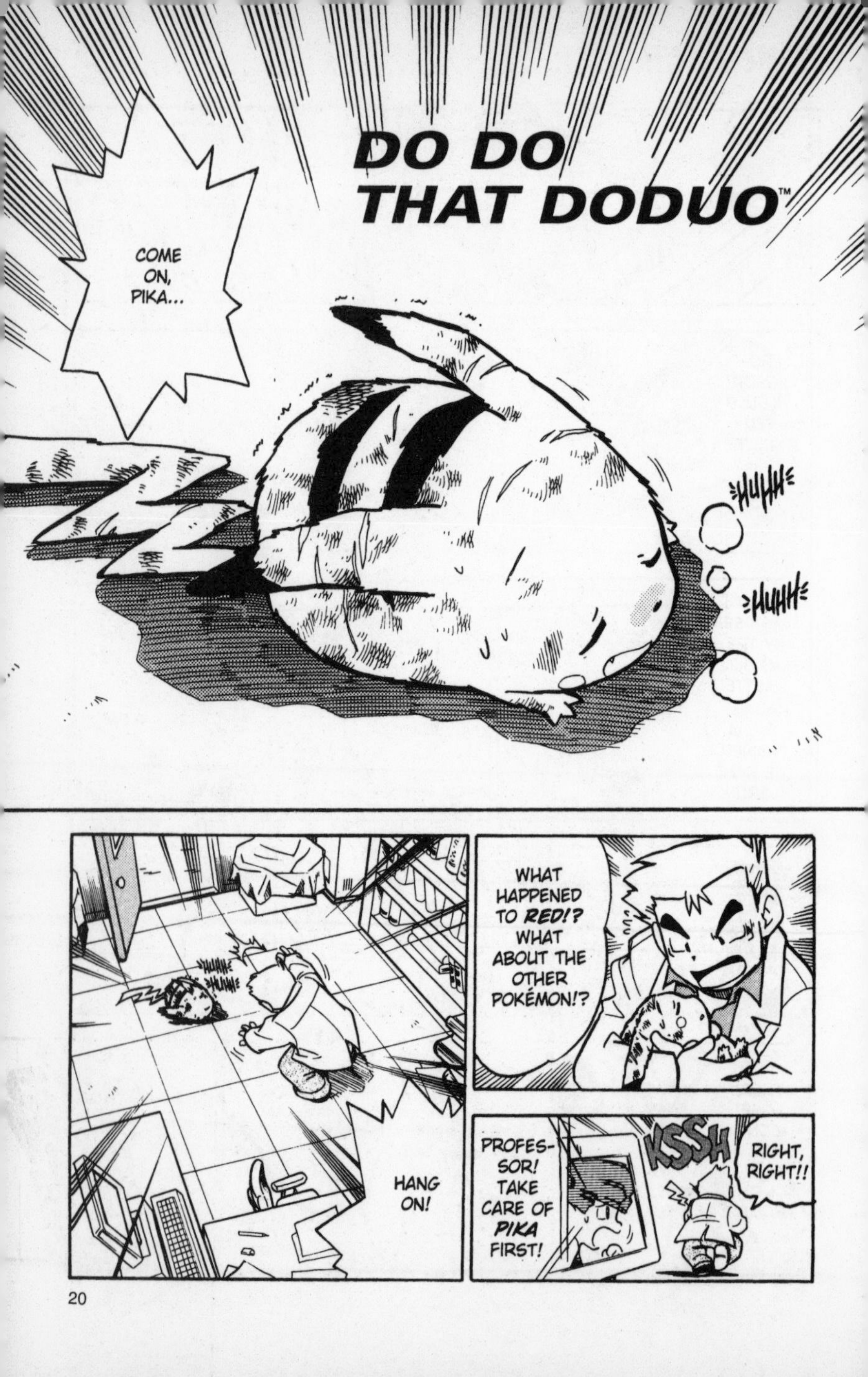
DO DO THAT DODUO™
COME ON, PIKA...
HUHH
HUHH
HANG ON!
WHAT HAPPENED TO RED!? WHAT ABOUT THE OTHER POKÉMON!?
PROFES-SOR! TAKE CARE OF PIKA FIRST!
KSSH
RIGHT, RIGHT!!

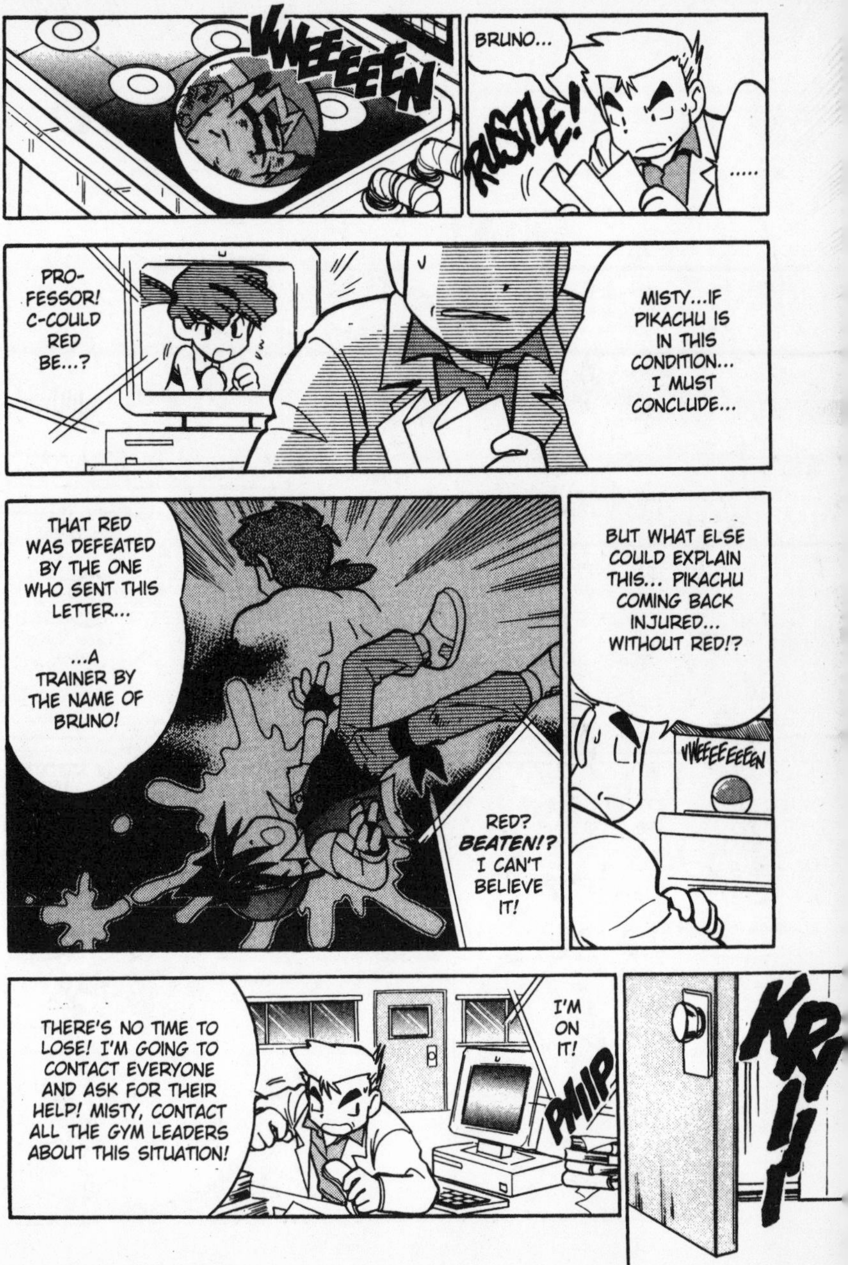
VWEEEEEEN
BRUNO...
RUSTLE!
.....
PRO-FESSOR! C-COULD RED BE...?
MISTY...IF PIKACHU IS IN THIS CONDITION... I MUST CONCLUDE...
THAT RED WAS DEFEATED BY THE ONE WHO SENT THIS LETTER...
...A TRAINER BY THE NAME OF BRUNO!
RED? BEATEN!? I CAN'T BELIEVE IT!
BUT WHAT ELSE COULD EXPLAIN THIS... PIKACHU COMING BACK INJURED... WITHOUT RED!?
VWEEEEEEEN
THERE'S NO TIME TO LOSE! I'M GOING TO CONTACT EVERYONE AND ASK FOR THEIR HELP! MISTY, CONTACT ALL THE GYM LEADERS ABOUT THIS SITUATION!
I'M ON IT!
PHIP
KR

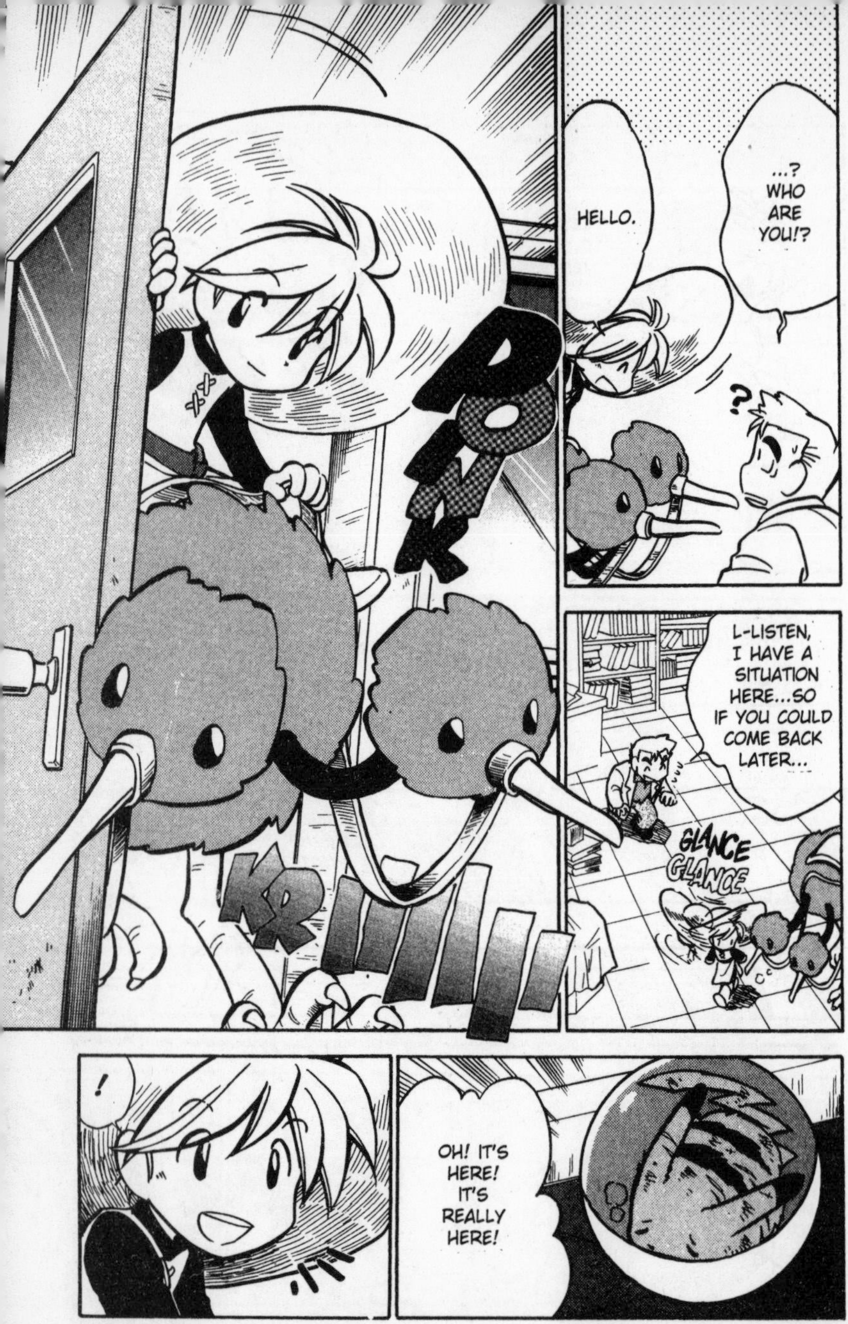
BOK
KRIIIIII
HELLO.
...? WHO ARE YOU!?
L-LISTEN, I HAVE A SITUATION HERE...SO IF YOU COULD COME BACK LATER...
GLANCE
GLANCE
!
OH! IT'S HERE! IT'S REALLY HERE!

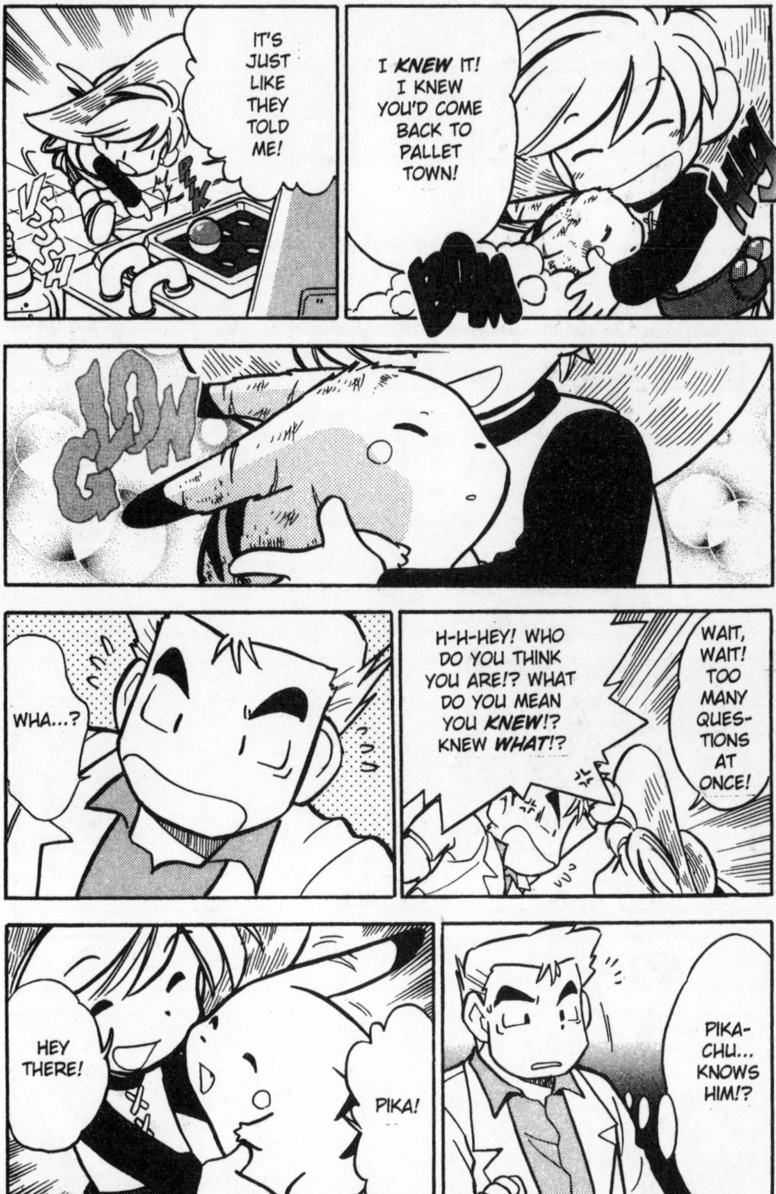
IT'S JUST LIKE THEY TOLD ME!
I *KNEW* IT! I KNEW YOU'D COME BACK TO PALLET TOWN!
HUG
GLOW
WHA...?
H-H-HEY! WHO DO YOU THINK YOU ARE!? WHAT DO YOU MEAN YOU *KNEW*!? KNEW *WHAT*!?
WAIT, WAIT! TOO MANY QUES-TIONS AT ONCE!
HEY THERE!
PIKA!
PIKA-CHU... KNOWS HIM!?

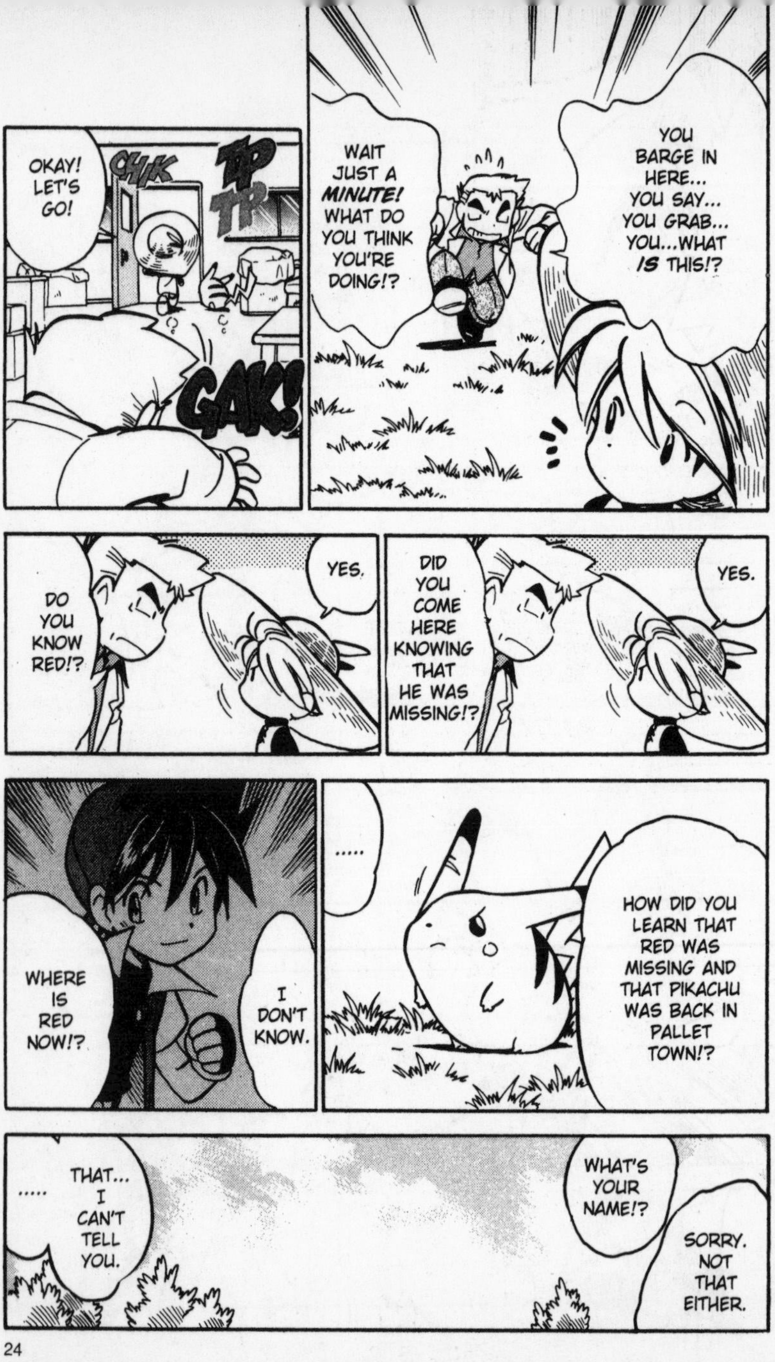
OKAY! LET'S GO!
CHIK
TP TP
GAK!
WAIT JUST A MINUTE! WHAT DO YOU THINK YOU'RE DOING!?
YOU BARGE IN HERE... YOU SAY... YOU GRAB... YOU...WHAT IS THIS!?
DO YOU KNOW RED!?
YES.
DID YOU COME HERE KNOWING THAT HE WAS MISSING!?
YES.
WHERE IS RED NOW!?
I DON'T KNOW.
.....
HOW DID YOU LEARN THAT RED WAS MISSING AND THAT PIKACHU WAS BACK IN PALLET TOWN!?
.....
THAT... I CAN'T TELL YOU.
WHAT'S YOUR NAME!?
SORRY. NOT THAT EITHER.

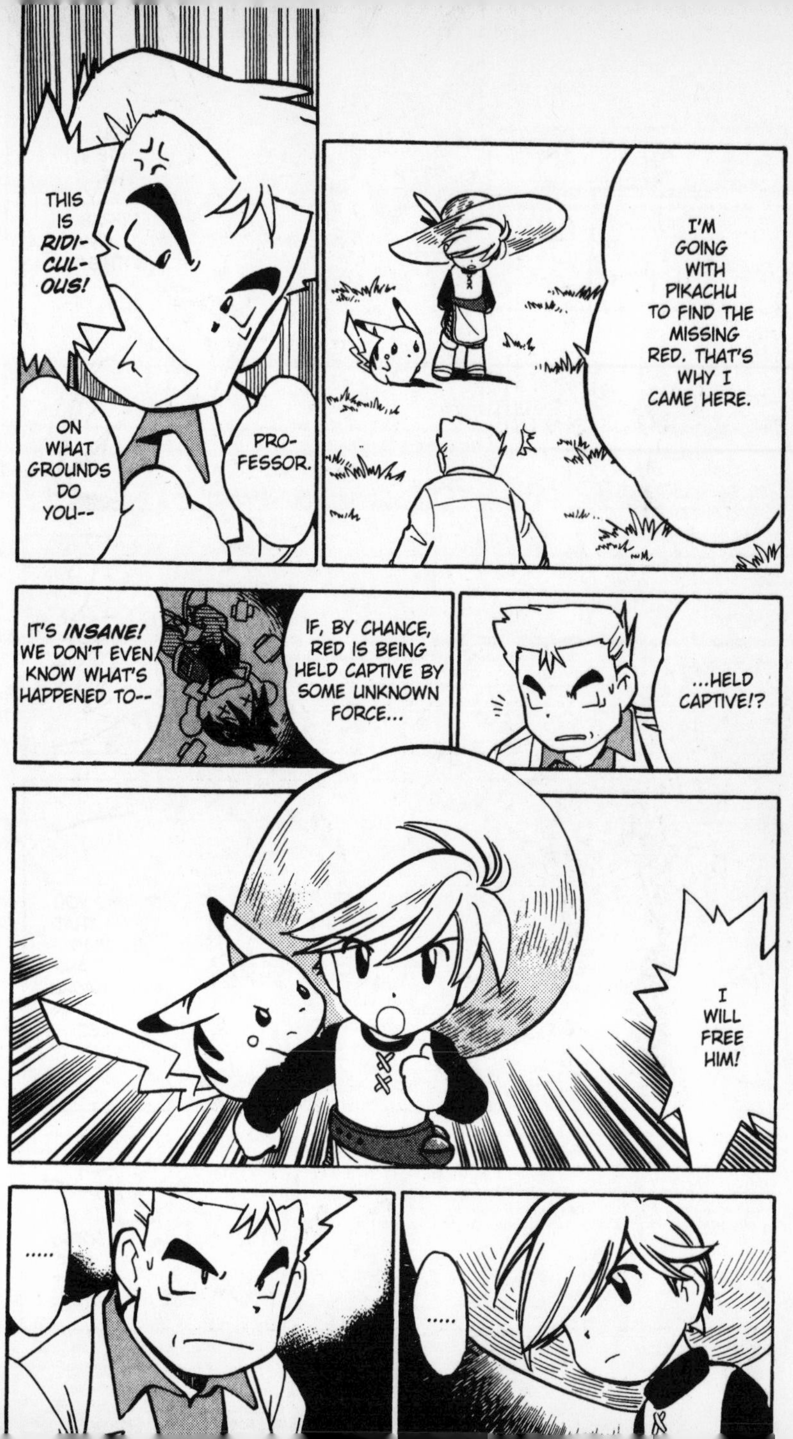
I'M GOING WITH PIKACHU TO FIND THE MISSING RED. THAT'S WHY I CAME HERE.
THIS IS RIDICULOUS!
ON WHAT GROUNDS DO YOU--
PROFESSOR.
IT'S INSANE! WE DON'T EVEN KNOW WHAT'S HAPPENED TO--
IF, BY CHANCE, RED IS BEING HELD CAPTIVE BY SOME UNKNOWN FORCE...
...HELD CAPTIVE!?
I WILL FREE HIM!
.....
.....

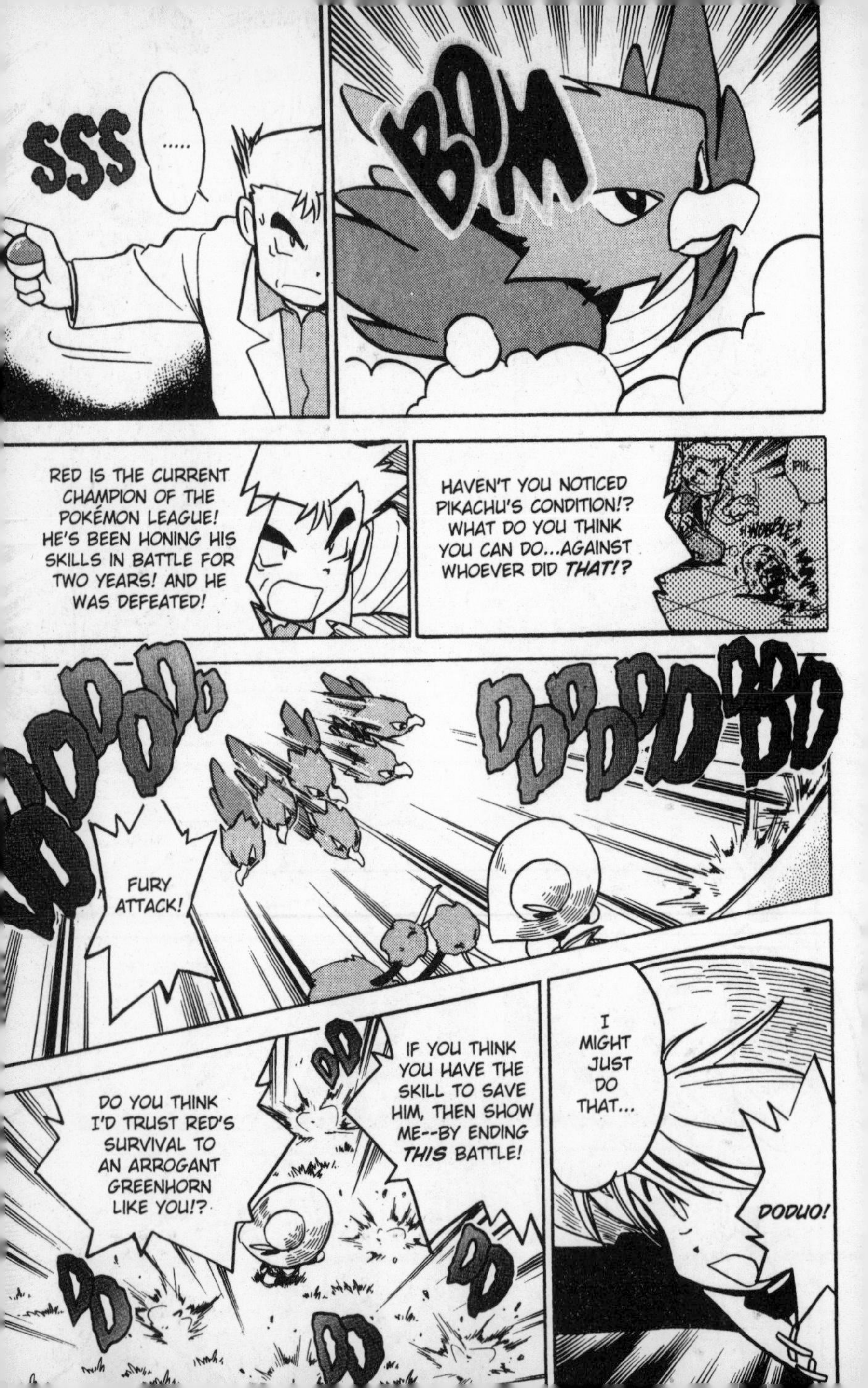
SSS
.....
BOOM
RED IS THE CURRENT CHAMPION OF THE POKÉMON LEAGUE! HE'S BEEN HONING HIS SKILLS IN BATTLE FOR TWO YEARS! AND HE WAS DEFEATED!
HAVEN'T YOU NOTICED PIKACHU'S CONDITION!? WHAT DO YOU THINK YOU CAN DO...AGAINST WHOEVER DID THAT!?
DDDDDD
DDDDDDDDD
FURY ATTACK!
DO YOU THINK I'D TRUST RED'S SURVIVAL TO AN ARROGANT GREENHORN LIKE YOU!?
DD
IF YOU THINK YOU HAVE THE SKILL TO SAVE HIM, THEN SHOW ME--BY ENDING THIS BATTLE!
DD
DD
DD
I MIGHT JUST DO THAT...
DODUO!

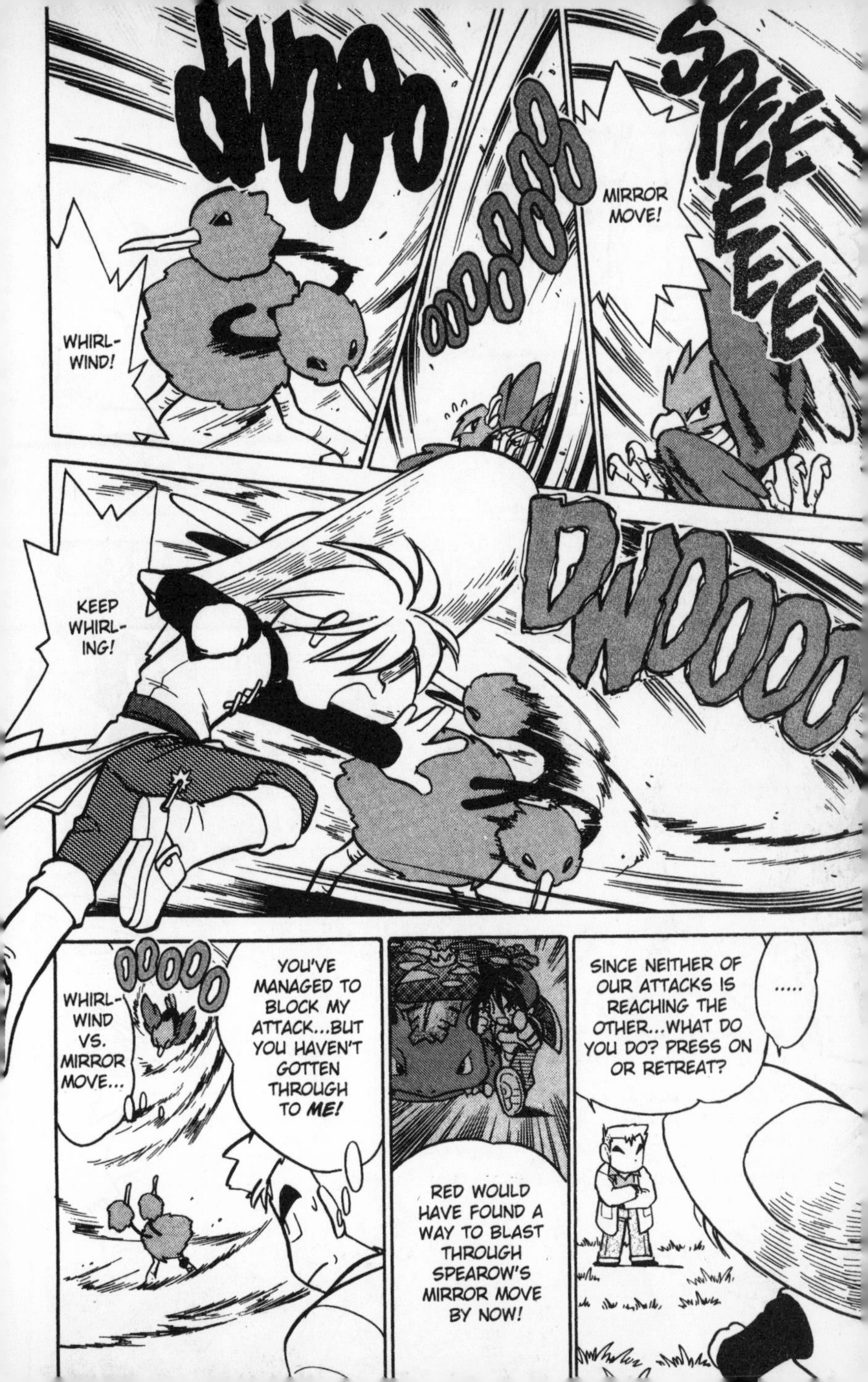
dwoo
SPEE
MIRROR MOVE!
WHIRL-WIND!
KEEP WHIRL-ING!
DWOOOO
WHIRL-WIND VS. MIRROR MOVE...
YOU'VE MANAGED TO BLOCK MY ATTACK...BUT YOU HAVEN'T GOTTEN THROUGH TO *ME!*
RED WOULD HAVE FOUND A WAY TO BLAST THROUGH SPEAROW'S MIRROR MOVE BY NOW!
SINCE NEITHER OF OUR ATTACKS IS REACHING THE OTHER...WHAT DO YOU DO? PRESS ON OR RETREAT?
.....

PHOOOOOO

IS IT FAIR TO SAY... THAT YOUR HANDS ARE TIED?

I DON'T DOUBT THAT YOU HEARD SOMETHING ABOUT RED... AND PROBABLY THINK YOU CAN SAVE HIM...

BUT IF THIS IS YOUR BEST, YOU'RE BETTER OFF STAYING OUT OF THE WAY!

.....

DODUO!

PASA

USSH

!

VWIP

?

TMTMTM

USSH

SKRK

VWRP!

KD

?

?

BUYING SOME TIME...?

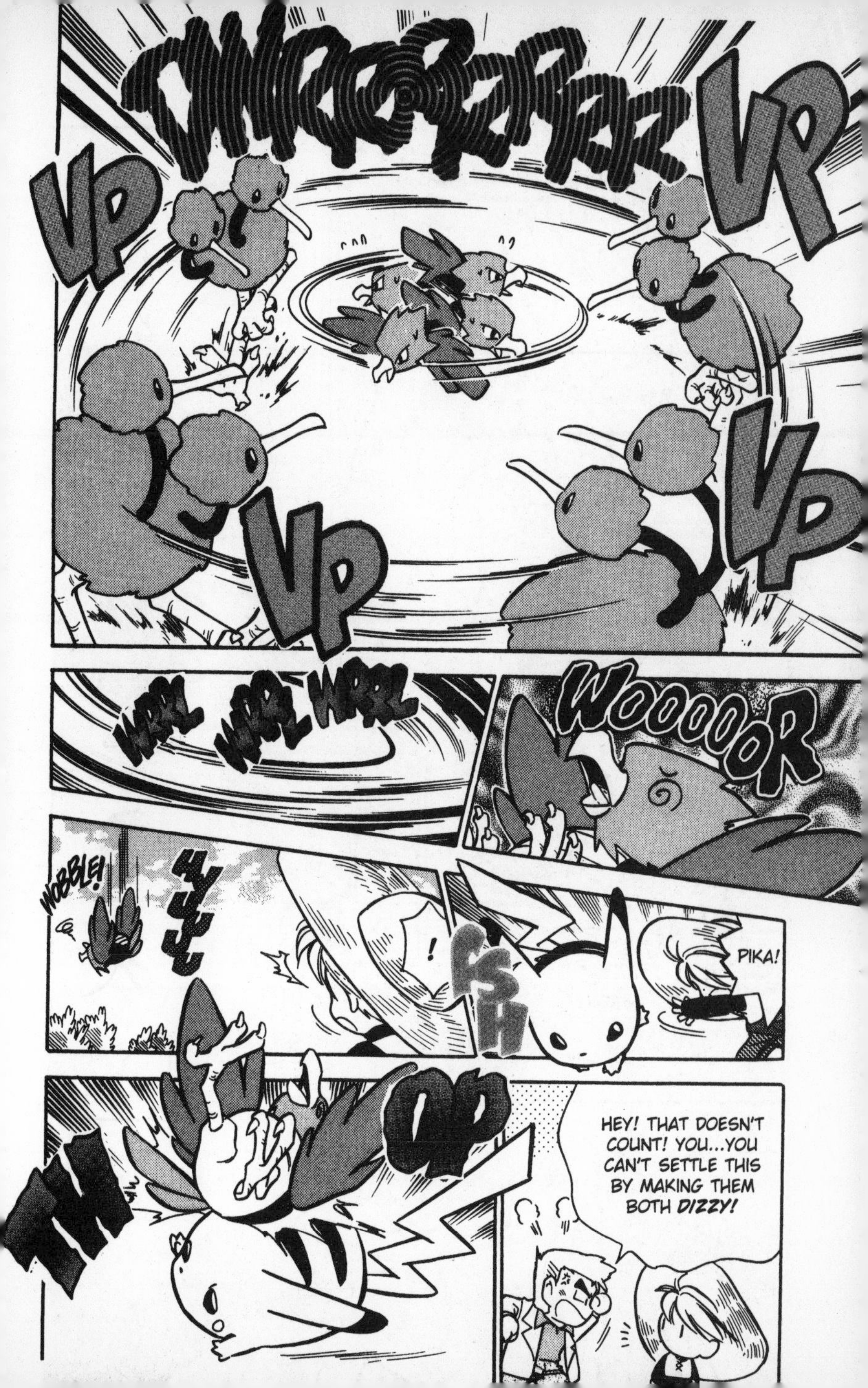
WOOOOOR
WOBBLE!
PIKA!
HEY! THAT DOESN'T COUNT! YOU...YOU CAN'T SETTLE THIS BY MAKING THEM BOTH *DIZZY!*

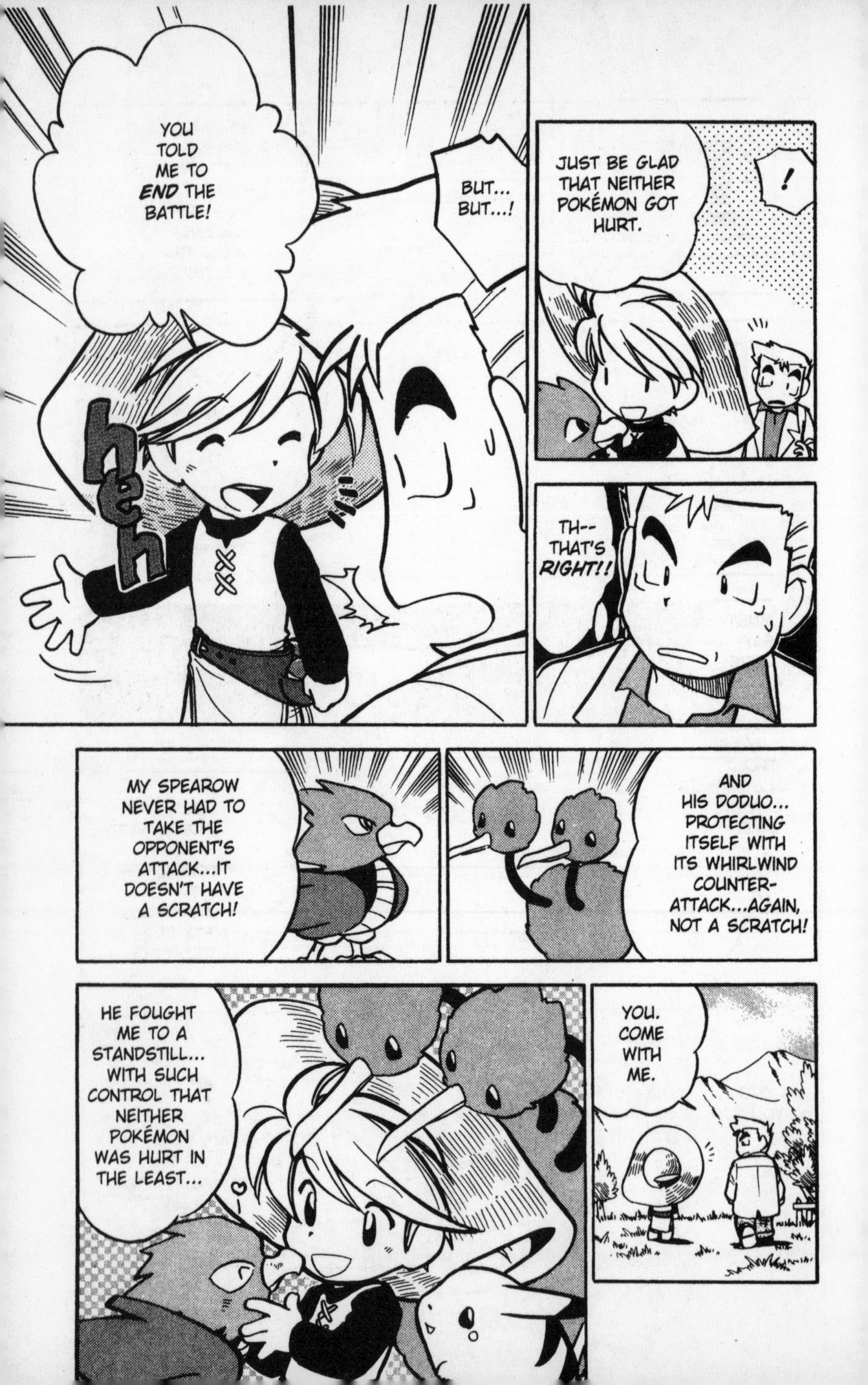
YOU TOLD ME TO END THE BATTLE!
heh
BUT... BUT...!
JUST BE GLAD THAT NEITHER POKÉMON GOT HURT.
!
TH-- THAT'S RIGHT!!
MY SPEAROW NEVER HAD TO TAKE THE OPPONENT'S ATTACK...IT DOESN'T HAVE A SCRATCH!
AND HIS DODUO... PROTECTING ITSELF WITH ITS WHIRLWIND COUNTER-ATTACK...AGAIN, NOT A SCRATCH!
HE FOUGHT ME TO A STANDSTILL... WITH SUCH CONTROL THAT NEITHER POKÉMON WAS HURT IN THE LEAST...
YOU. COME WITH ME.

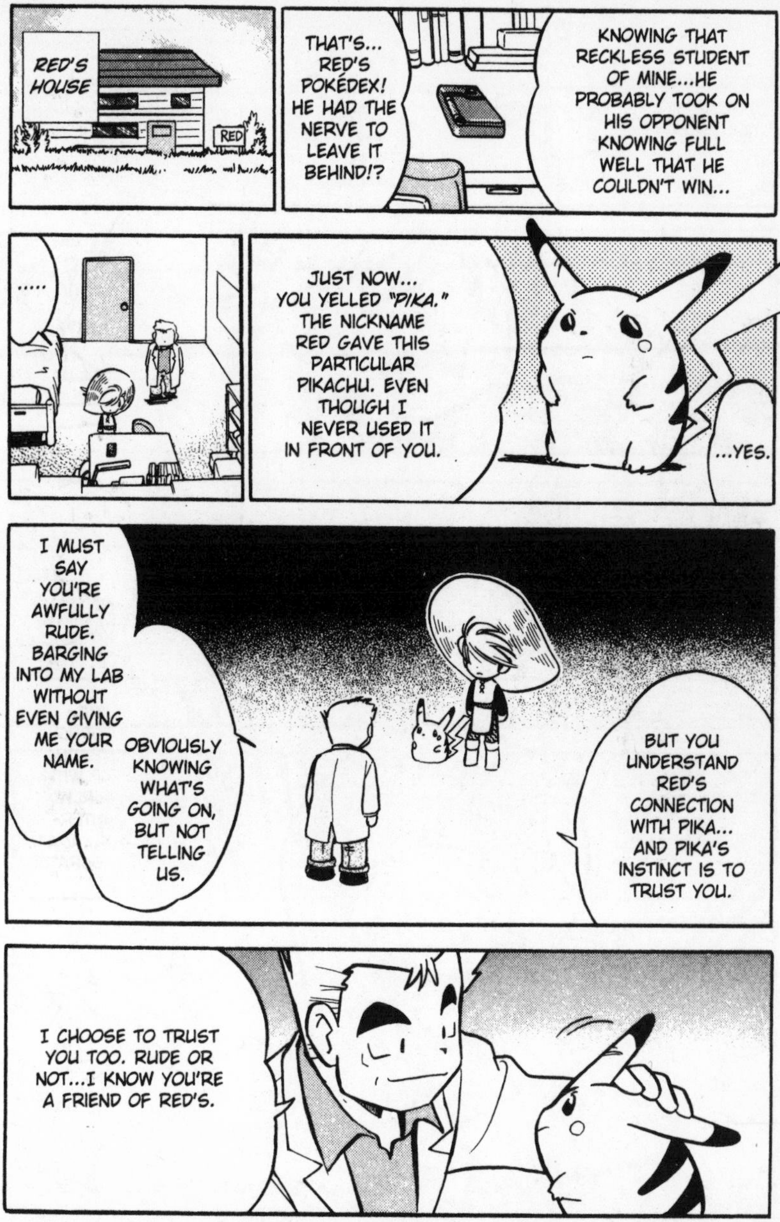
RED'S HOUSE
RED
THAT'S... RED'S POKÉDEX! HE HAD THE NERVE TO LEAVE IT BEHIND!?
KNOWING THAT RECKLESS STUDENT OF MINE...HE PROBABLY TOOK ON HIS OPPONENT KNOWING FULL WELL THAT HE COULDN'T WIN...
.....
JUST NOW... YOU YELLED "PIKA." THE NICKNAME RED GAVE THIS PARTICULAR PIKACHU. EVEN THOUGH I NEVER USED IT IN FRONT OF YOU.
...YES.
I MUST SAY YOU'RE AWFULLY RUDE. BARGING INTO MY LAB WITHOUT EVEN GIVING ME YOUR NAME.
OBVIOUSLY KNOWING WHAT'S GOING ON, BUT NOT TELLING US.
BUT YOU UNDERSTAND RED'S CONNECTION WITH PIKA... AND PIKA'S INSTINCT IS TO TRUST YOU.
I CHOOSE TO TRUST YOU TOO. RUDE OR NOT...I KNOW YOU'RE A FRIEND OF RED'S.

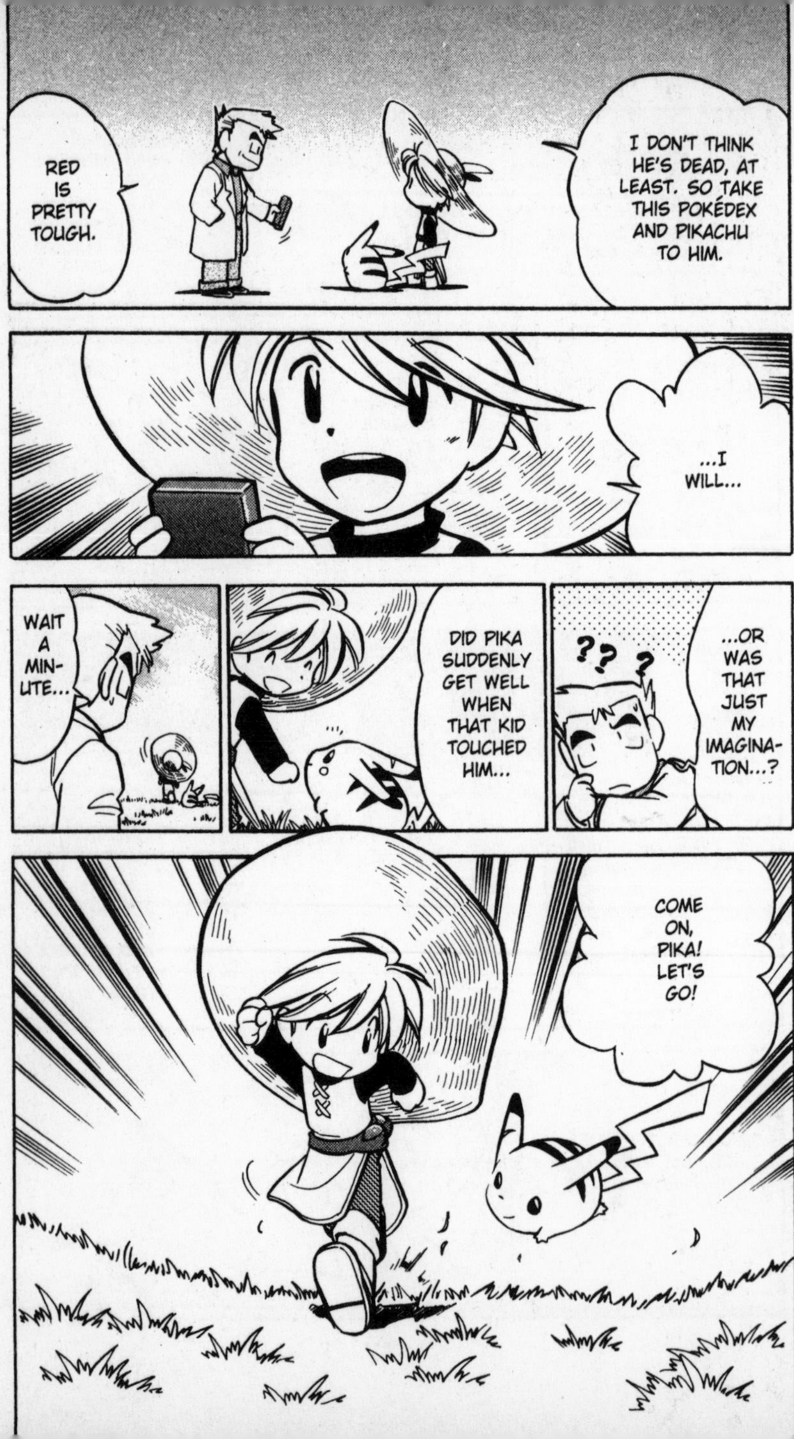
I DON'T THINK HE'S DEAD, AT LEAST. SO TAKE THIS POKÉDEX AND PIKACHU TO HIM.
RED IS PRETTY TOUGH.
...I WILL...
...OR WAS THAT JUST MY IMAGINATION...?
??
?
DID PIKA SUDDENLY GET WELL WHEN THAT KID TOUCHED HIM...
WAIT A MIN-UTE...
COME ON, PIKA! LET'S GO!

CHAPTER 3

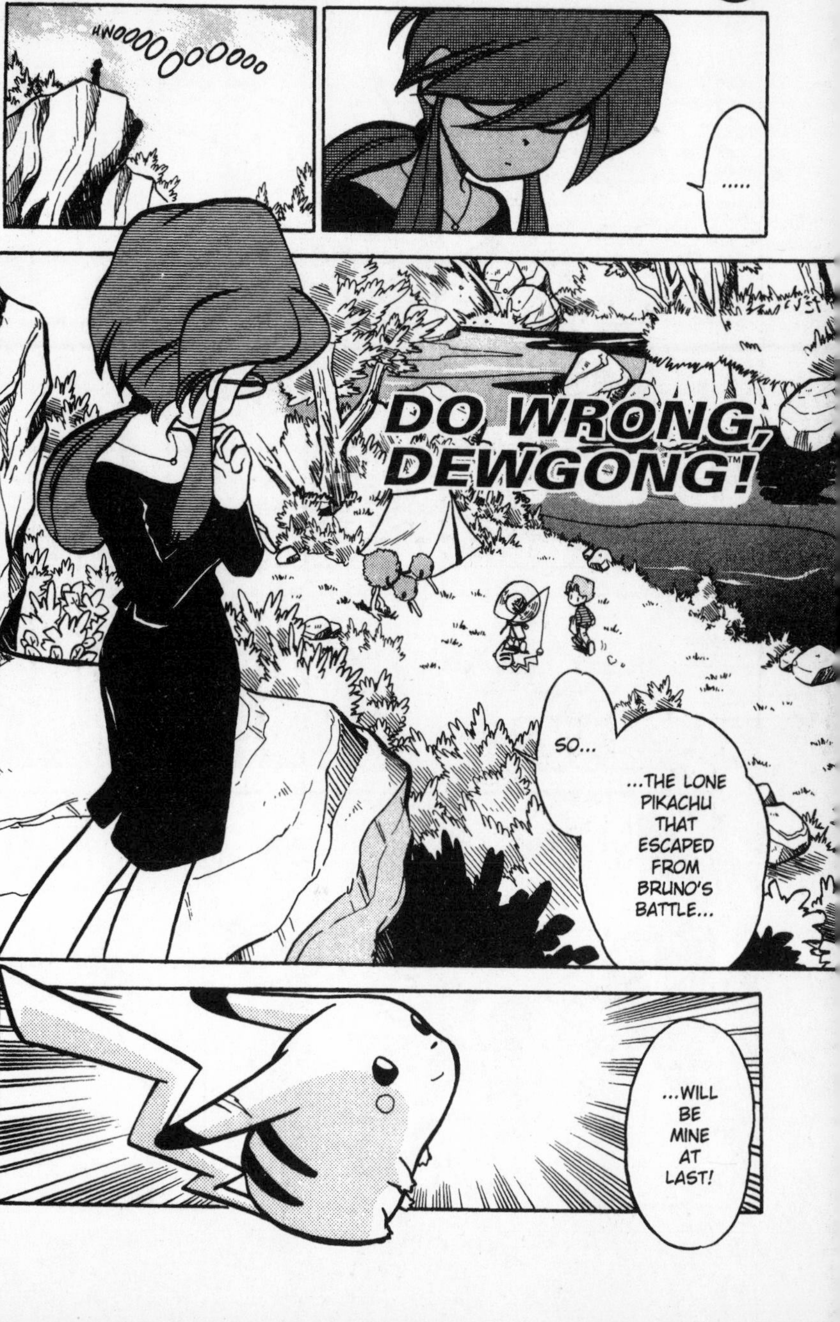
HWOOOOOOOOOO
.....
DO WRONG, DEWGONG!™
SO...
...THE LONE PIKACHU THAT ESCAPED FROM BRUNO'S BATTLE...
...WILL BE MINE AT LAST!

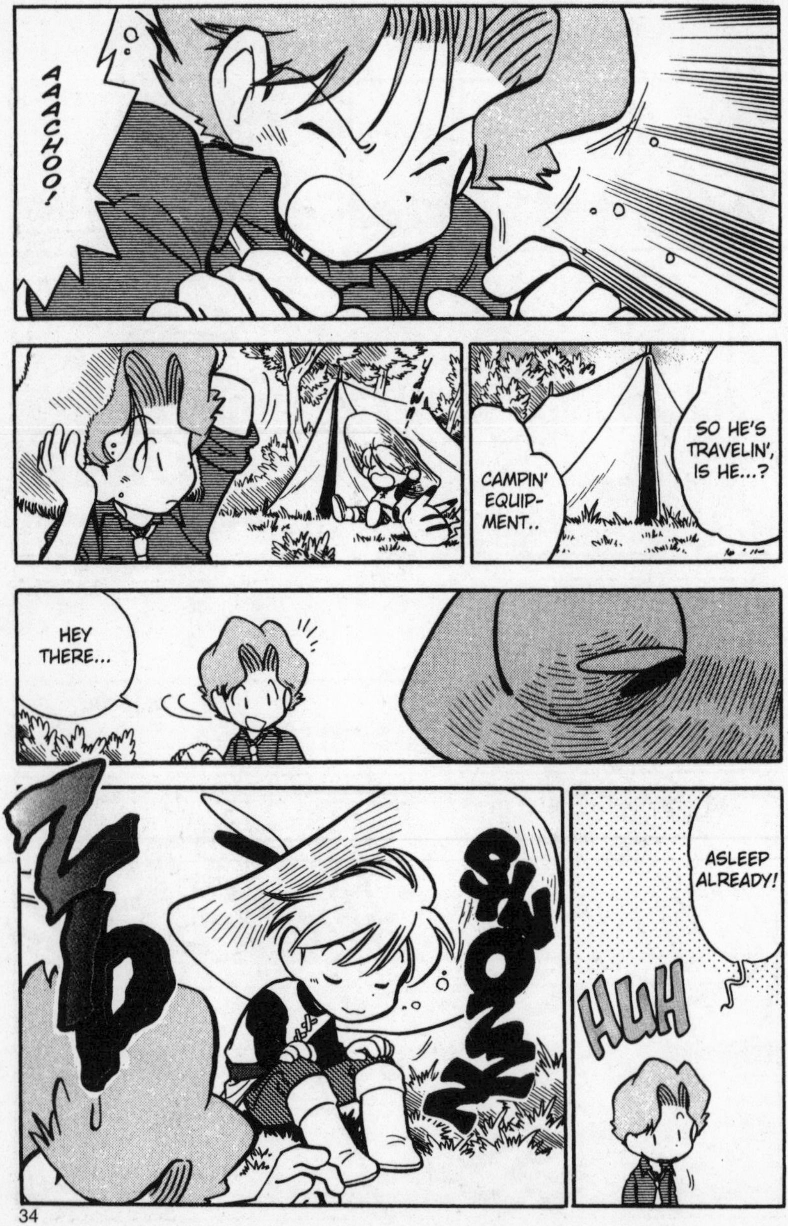
AAACHOO!
YAWN!
CAMPIN' EQUIP-MENT..
SO HE'S TRAVELIN', IS HE...?
HEY THERE...
ASLEEP ALREADY!
HUH

tappatappatappa

HE CALLED YA "PIKA"...

HMMM...

SURE LOOKS LIKE IT *COULD* BE RED'S PIKA... BUT THERE COULD BE TWO WITH THE SAME NICKNAME...

HEY, PIKA. IT'S ME, BILL. REMEMBER ME!?

hey!

.....

BZZZ!...

ZZAK!

GAH!!

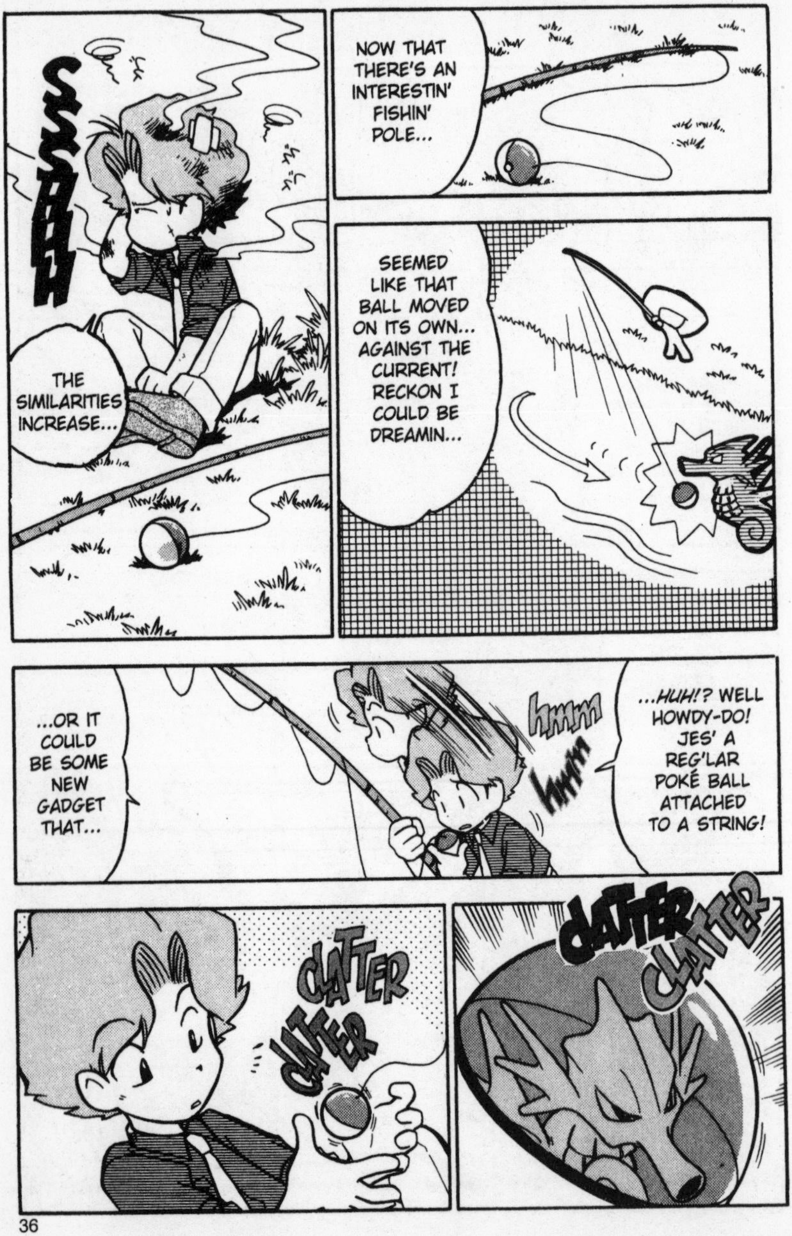
THE SIMILARITIES INCREASE...
NOW THAT THERE'S AN INTERESTIN' FISHIN' POLE...
SEEMED LIKE THAT BALL MOVED ON ITS OWN... AGAINST THE CURRENT! RECKON I COULD BE DREAMIN...
...OR IT COULD BE SOME NEW GADGET THAT...
hmm
hmm
...HUH!? WELL HOWDY-DO! JES' A REG'LAR POKÉ BALL ATTACHED TO A STRING!
CLATTER
CLATTER
CLATTER
CLATTER

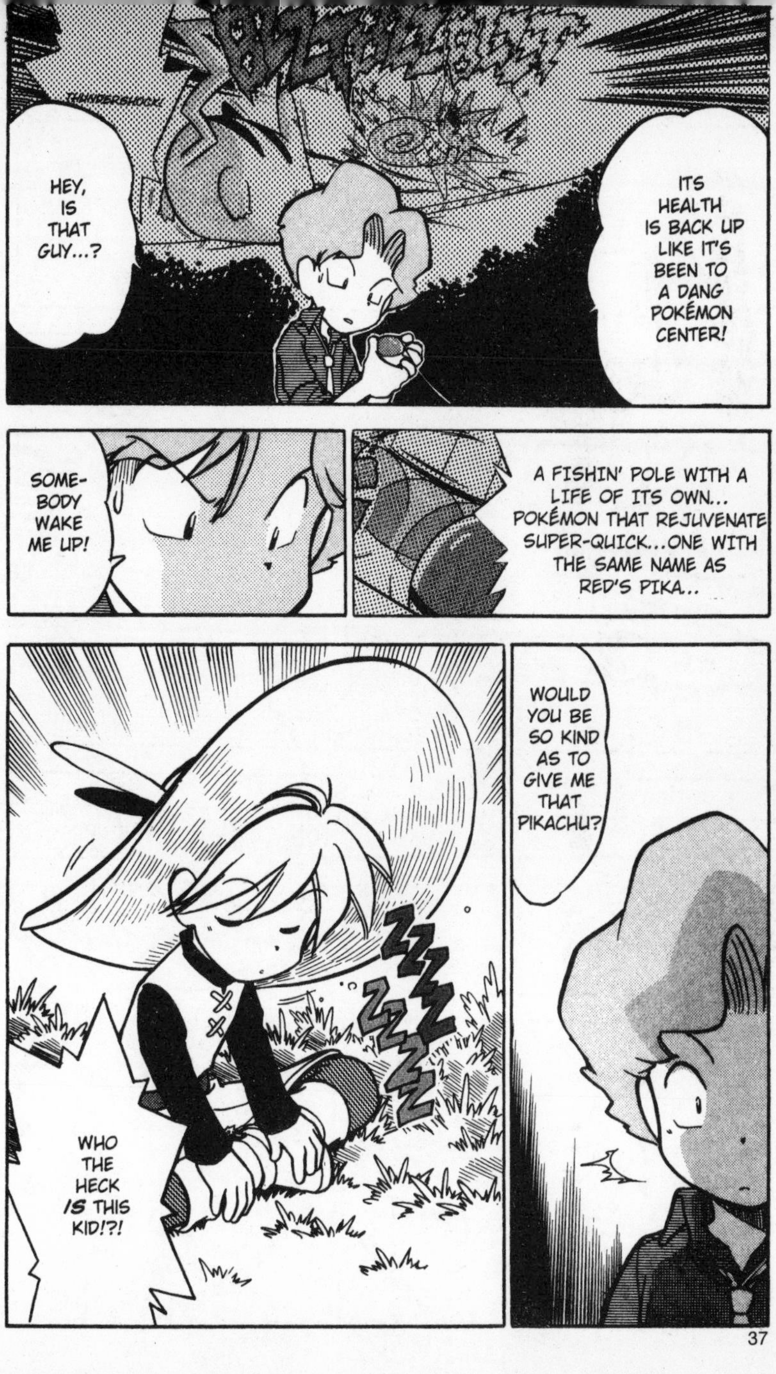
THUNDERSHOCK!
ITS HEALTH IS BACK UP LIKE IT'S BEEN TO A DANG POKÉMON CENTER!
HEY, IS THAT GUY...?
A FISHIN' POLE WITH A LIFE OF ITS OWN... POKÉMON THAT REJUVENATE SUPER-QUICK...ONE WITH THE SAME NAME AS RED'S PIKA...
SOME-BODY WAKE ME UP!
WOULD YOU BE SO KIND AS TO GIVE ME THAT PIKACHU?
WHO THE HECK *IS* THIS KID!?!

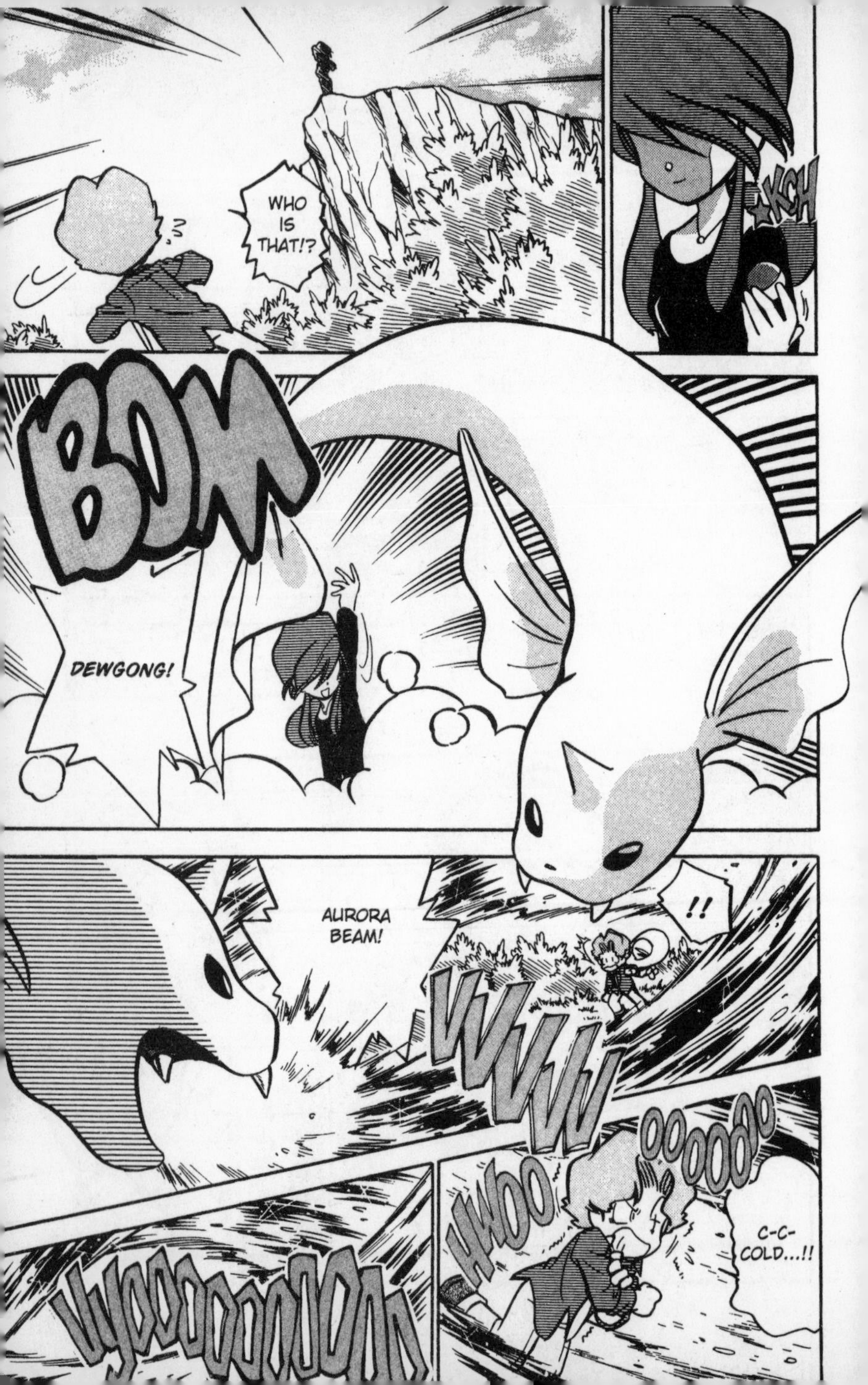
WHO IS THAT!?
KCH
BOM
DEWGONG!
AURORA BEAM!
!!
C-C-COLD...!!
HWOOOOOOOO

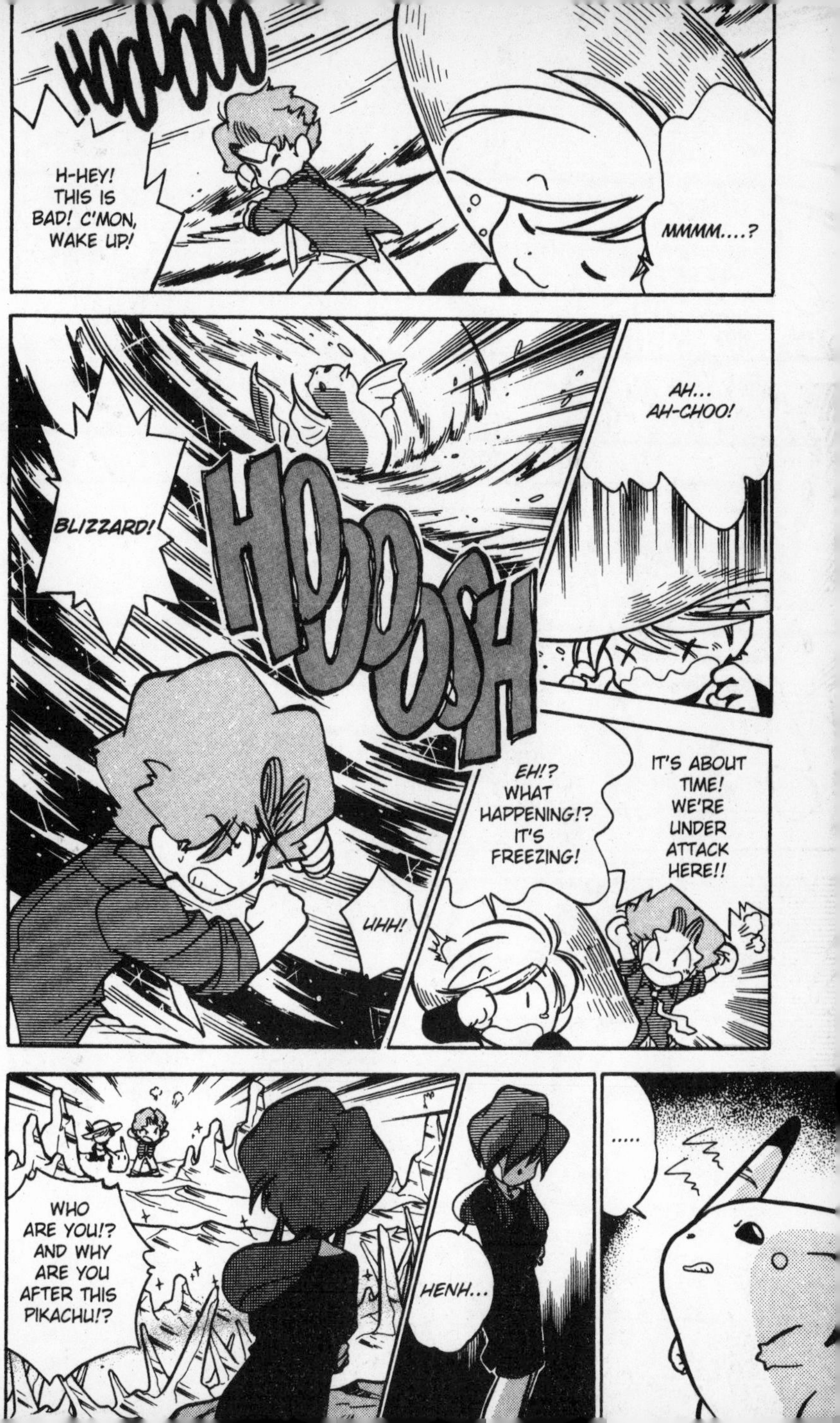
HOOOOO
H-HEY! THIS IS BAD! C'MON, WAKE UP!
MMMM....?
BLIZZARD!
HOOOOSH
AH... AH-CHOO!
UHH!
EH!? WHAT HAPPENING!? IT'S FREEZING!
IT'S ABOUT TIME! WE'RE UNDER ATTACK HERE!!
WHO ARE YOU!? AND WHY ARE YOU AFTER THIS PIKACHU!?
HENH...
.....

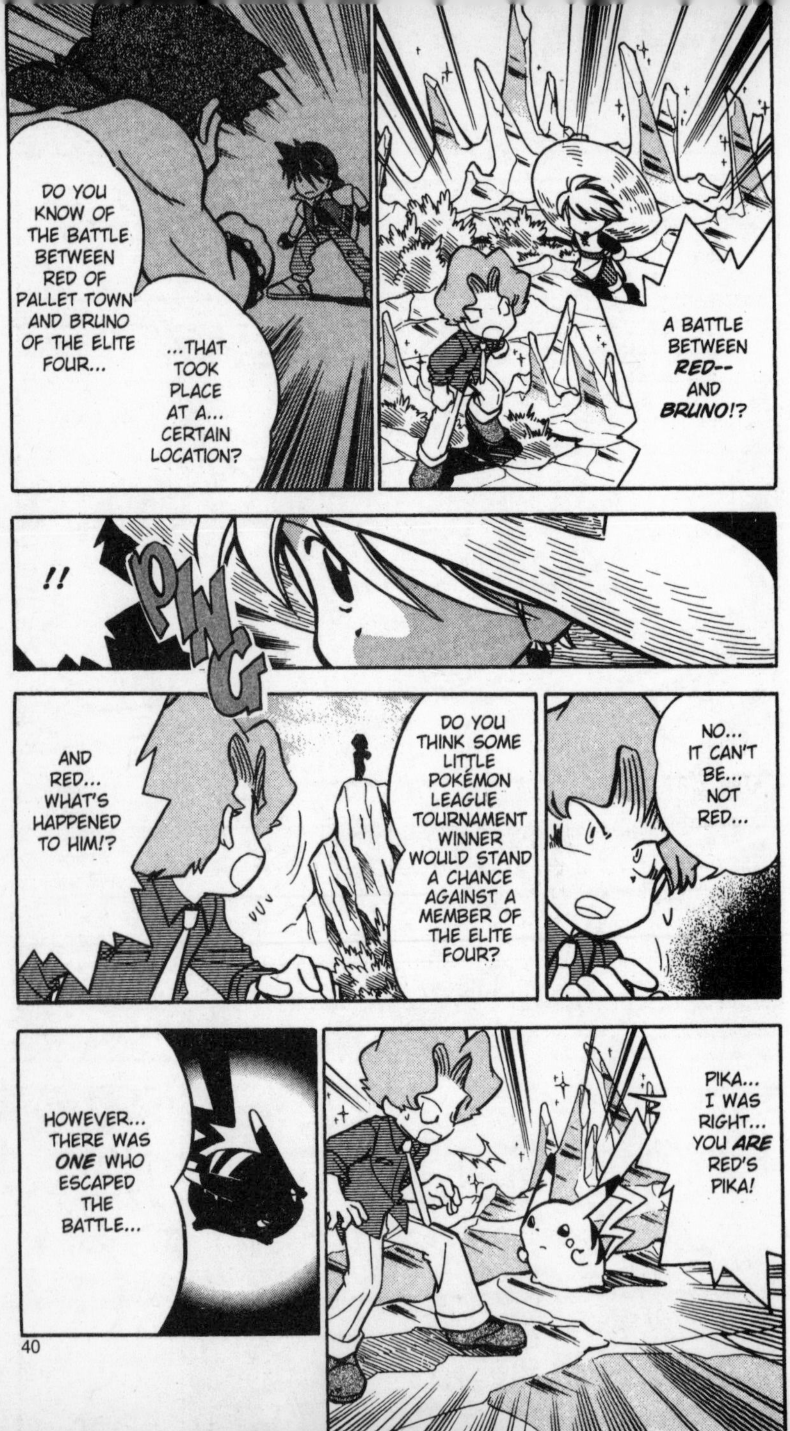

DO YOU KNOW OF THE BATTLE BETWEEN RED OF PALLET TOWN AND BRUNO OF THE ELITE FOUR...
...THAT TOOK PLACE AT A... CERTAIN LOCATION?
A BATTLE BETWEEN *RED--* AND *BRUNO*!?
!!
PING
AND RED... WHAT'S HAPPENED TO HIM!?
DO YOU THINK SOME LITTLE POKÉMON LEAGUE TOURNAMENT WINNER WOULD STAND A CHANCE AGAINST A MEMBER OF THE ELITE FOUR?
NO... IT CAN'T BE... NOT RED...
HOWEVER... THERE WAS *ONE* WHO ESCAPED THE BATTLE...
PIKA... I WAS RIGHT... YOU *ARE* RED'S PIKA!

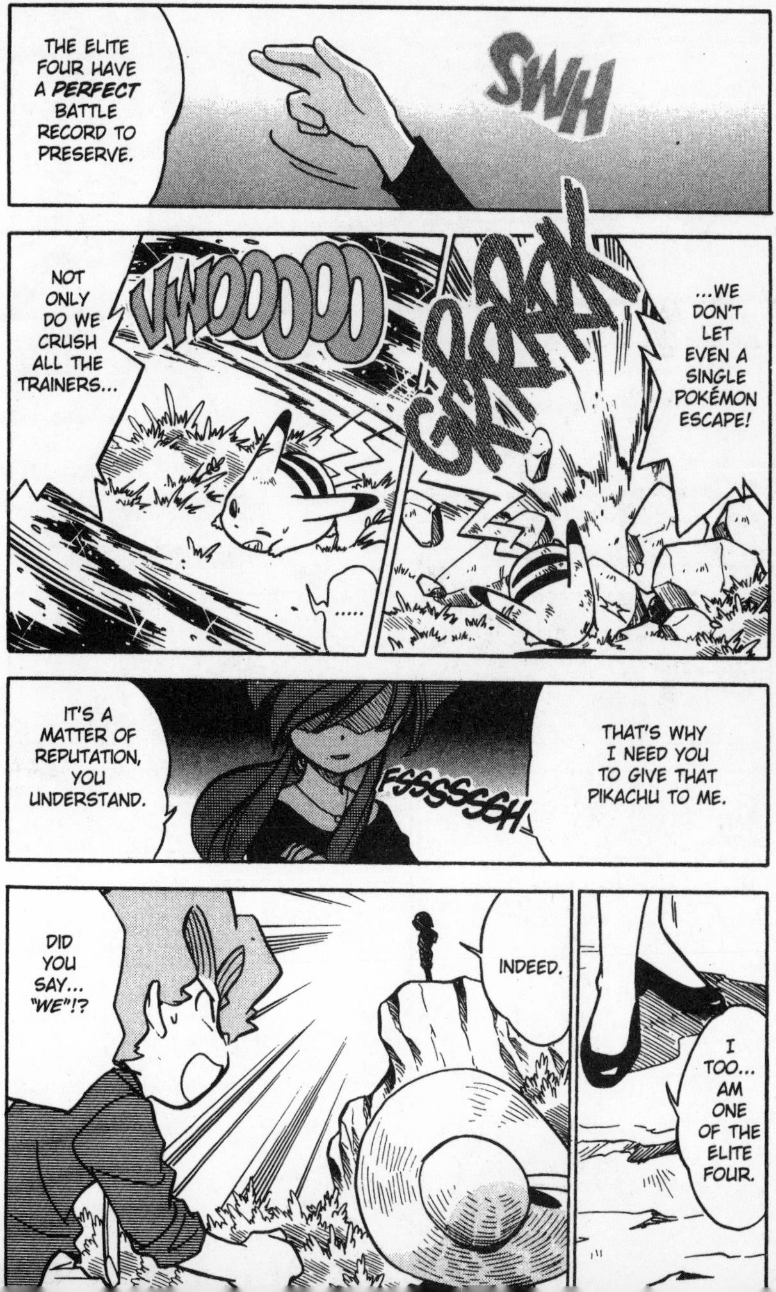
THE ELITE FOUR HAVE A PERFECT BATTLE RECORD TO PRESERVE.
SWH
NOT ONLY DO WE CRUSH ALL THE TRAINERS...
VWOOOOOO
.....
GKRRRK
...WE DON'T LET EVEN A SINGLE POKÉMON ESCAPE!
IT'S A MATTER OF REPUTATION, YOU UNDERSTAND.
FSSSSSSGH
THAT'S WHY I NEED YOU TO GIVE THAT PIKACHU TO ME.
DID YOU SAY... "WE"!?
INDEED.
I TOO... AM ONE OF THE ELITE FOUR.

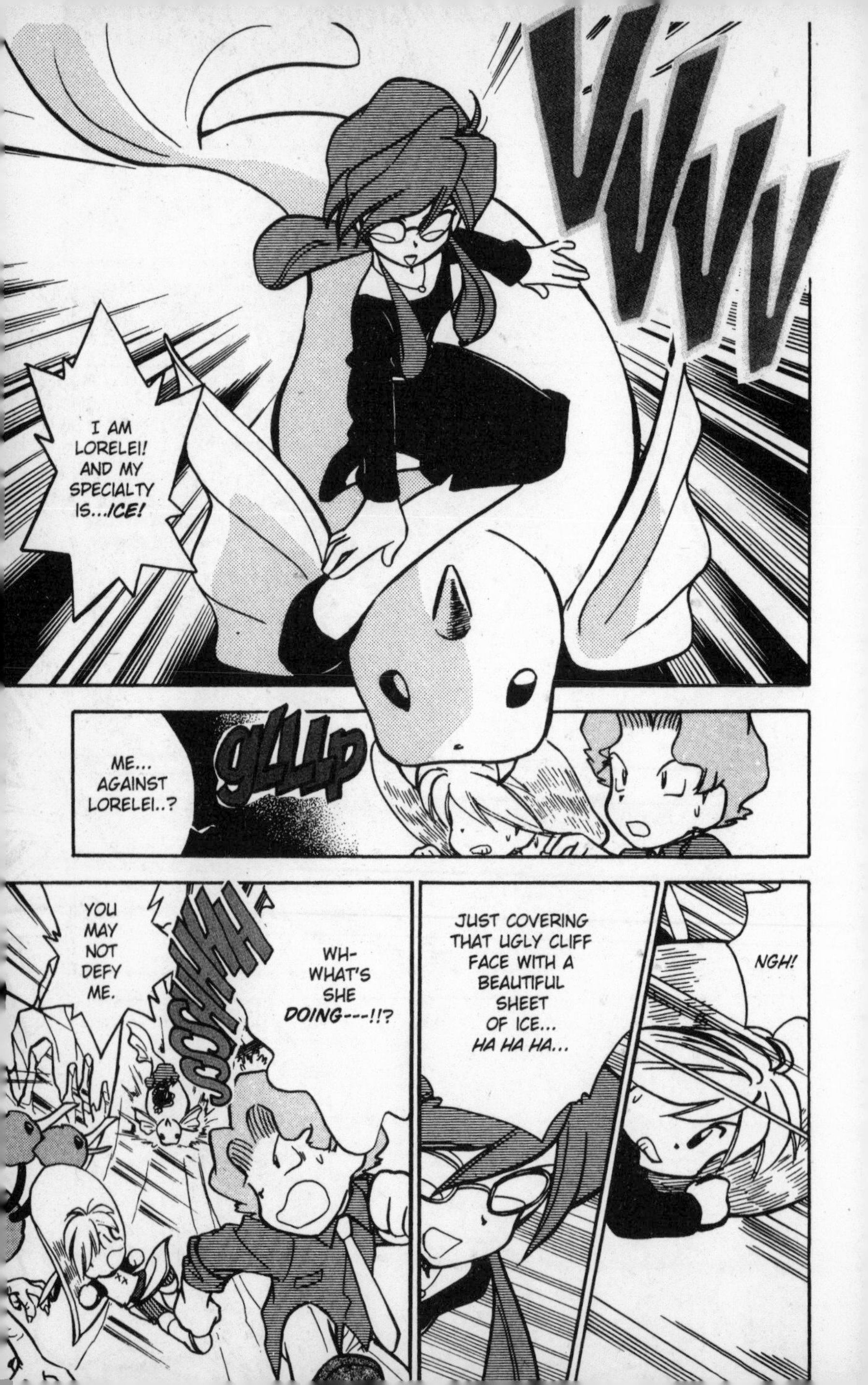
I AM LORELEI! AND MY SPECIALTY IS...ICE!
ME... AGAINST LORELEI..?
YOU MAY NOT DEFY ME.
WH-WHAT'S SHE DOING---!!?
JUST COVERING THAT UGLY CLIFF FACE WITH A BEAUTIFUL SHEET OF ICE... HA HA HA...
NGH!

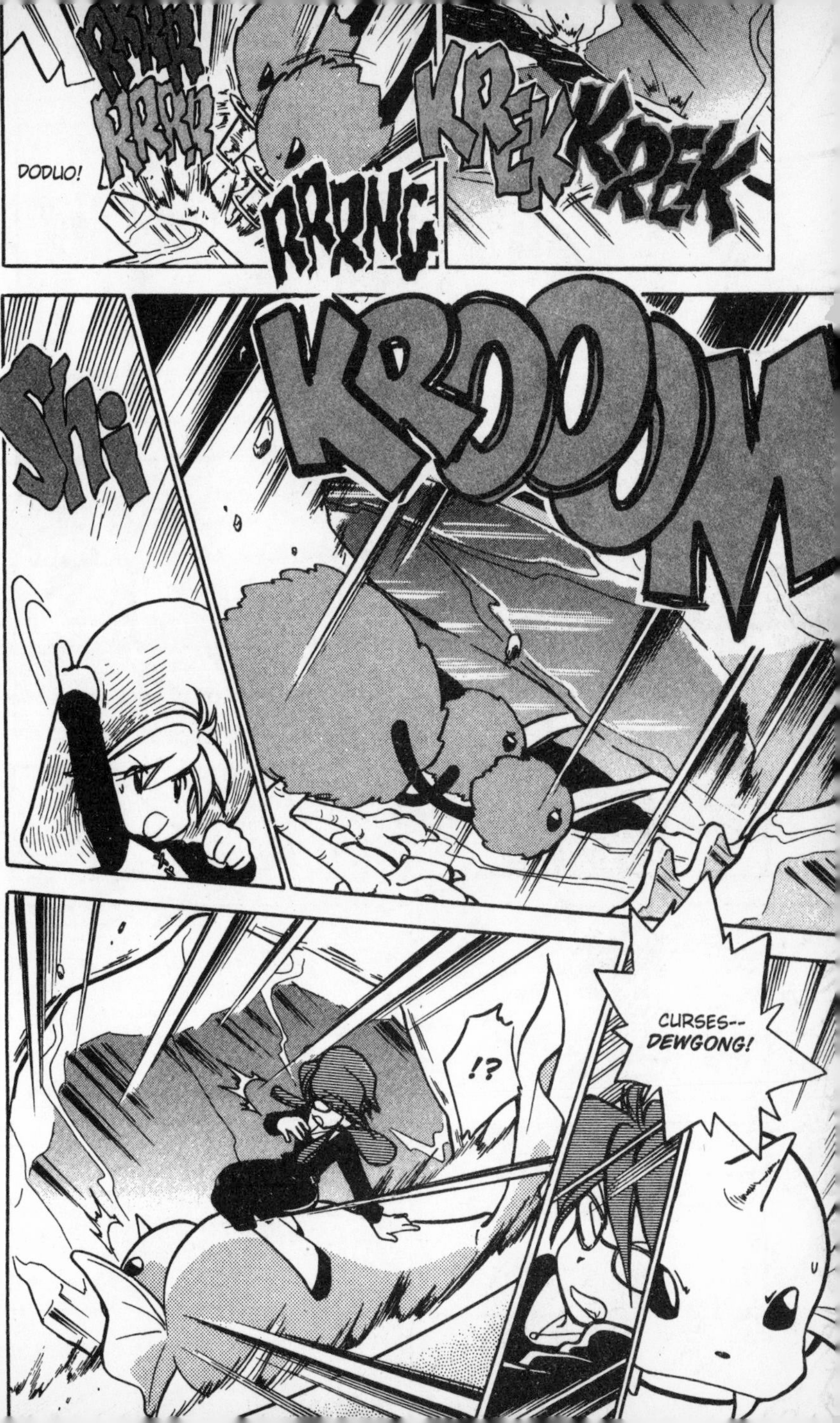
KREK KREK
RRRNG
DODUO!
KROOOM
SHI
CURSES-- DEWGONG!
!?

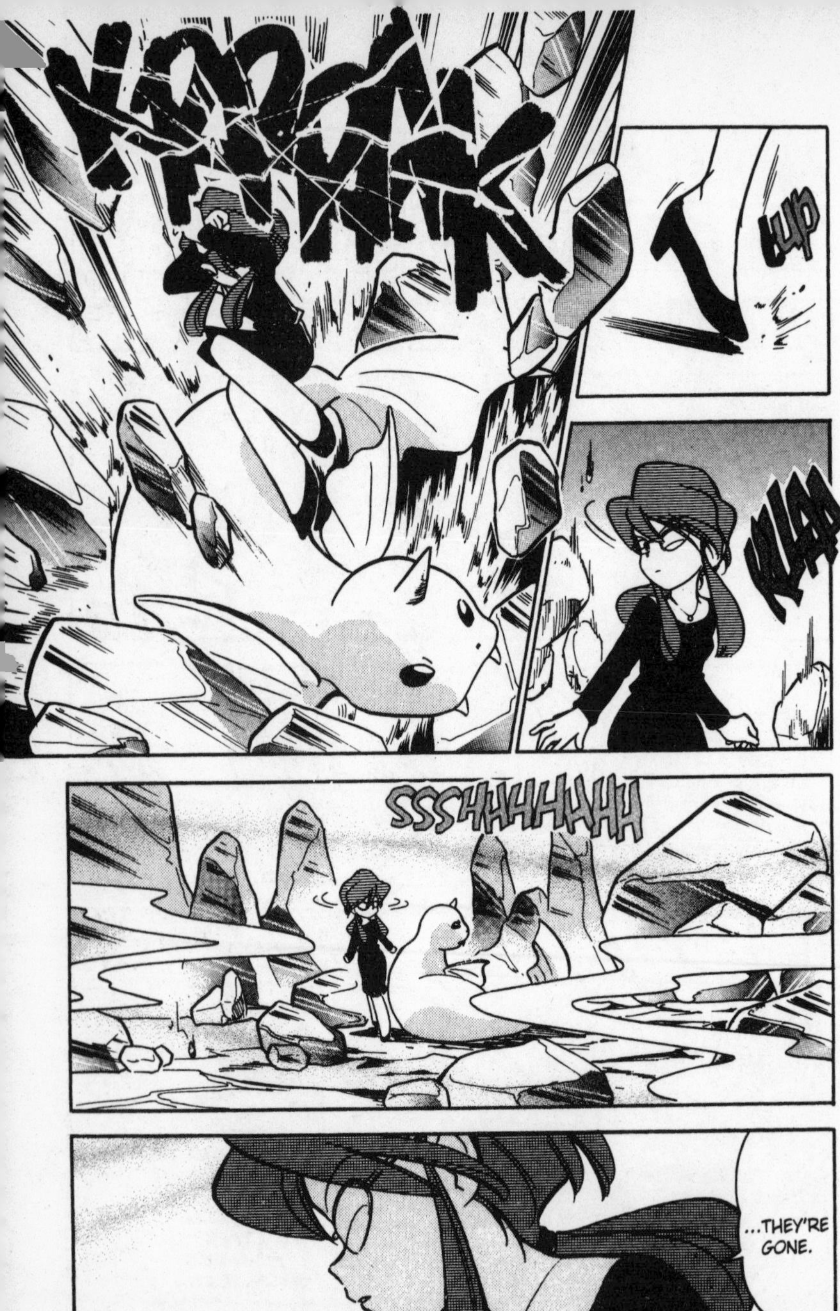
KA-BOOM
UP
KLAAA
SSSHHHHAHH
...THEY'RE GONE.

MAN, I HATE DAYS LIKE THIS...!

SO WHAT THAT GAL WAS JUST SAYIN'...

IT'S ALL TRUE, YES.

PIIII... KAAA...

WHEN RED WAS LAST SEEN, HE WAS GOING OFF TO ANSWER A LETTER OF CHALLENGE. HE PROBABLY THOUGHT IT WAS FROM JUST ANOTHER TRAINER...

...BUT IT WAS REALLY FROM *THEM*...

SQUEEZE

...AND ONLY PIKA CAME BACK ALIVE...

I CAN'T BE-LIEVE IT!

THERE'S AN ENEMY NOT EVEN THE POKÉMON LEAGUE CHAMPION CAN BEAT...

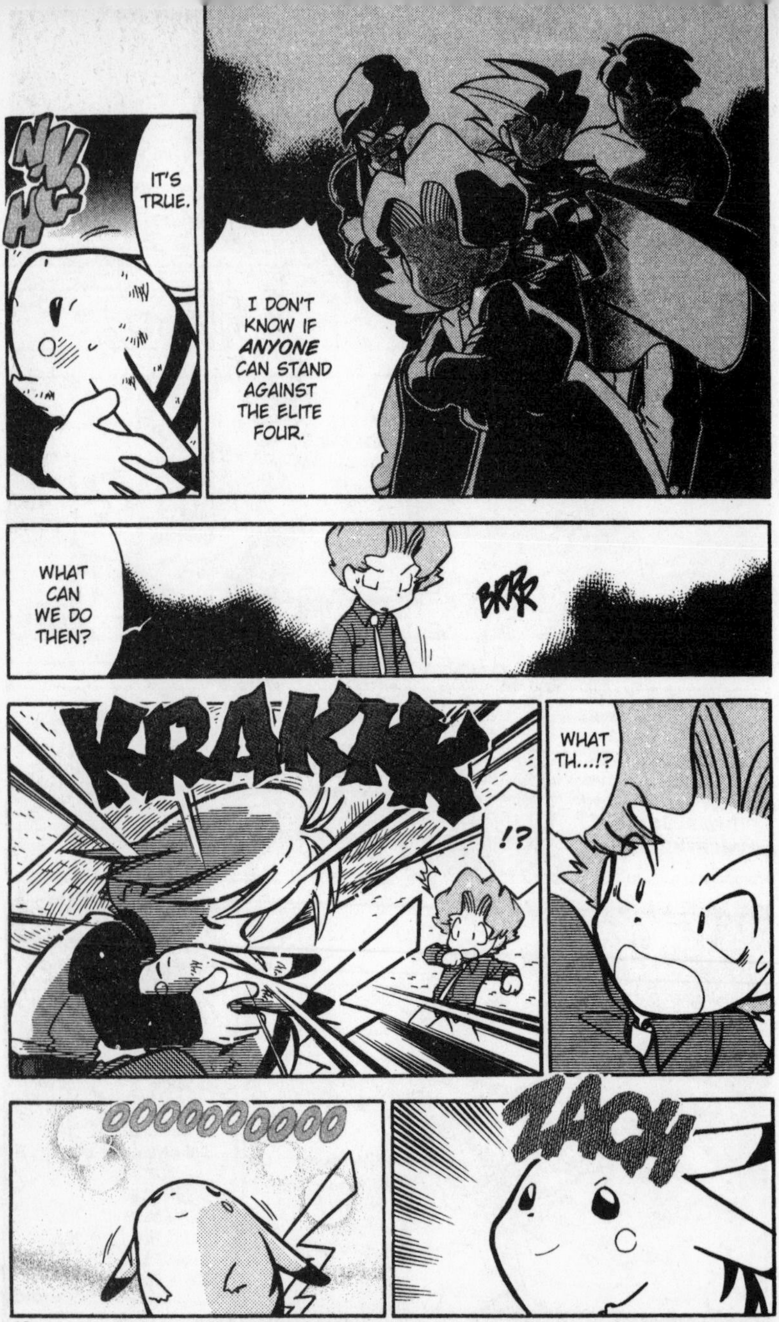
NNHG
IT'S TRUE.
I DON'T KNOW IF ANYONE CAN STAND AGAINST THE ELITE FOUR.
WHAT CAN WE DO THEN?
BRRR
KRAKK
!?
WHAT TH...!?
OOOOOOOOOO
ZACH

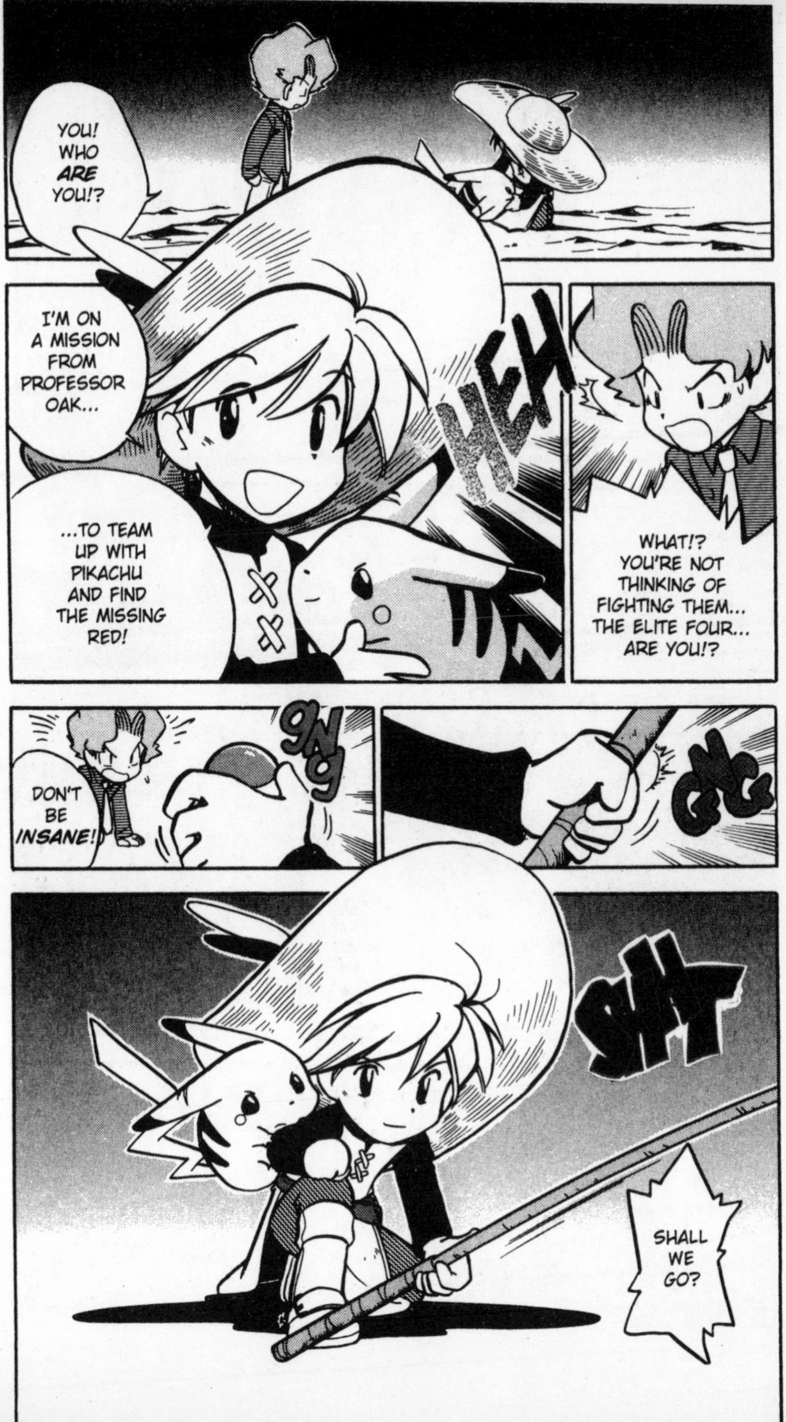
YOU! WHO ARE YOU!?
I'M ON A MISSION FROM PROFESSOR OAK...
...TO TEAM UP WITH PIKACHU AND FIND THE MISSING RED!
HEH
WHAT!? YOU'RE NOT THINKING OF FIGHTING THEM... THE ELITE FOUR... ARE YOU!?
DON'T BE INSANE!
gng
GNG
SHALL WE GO?

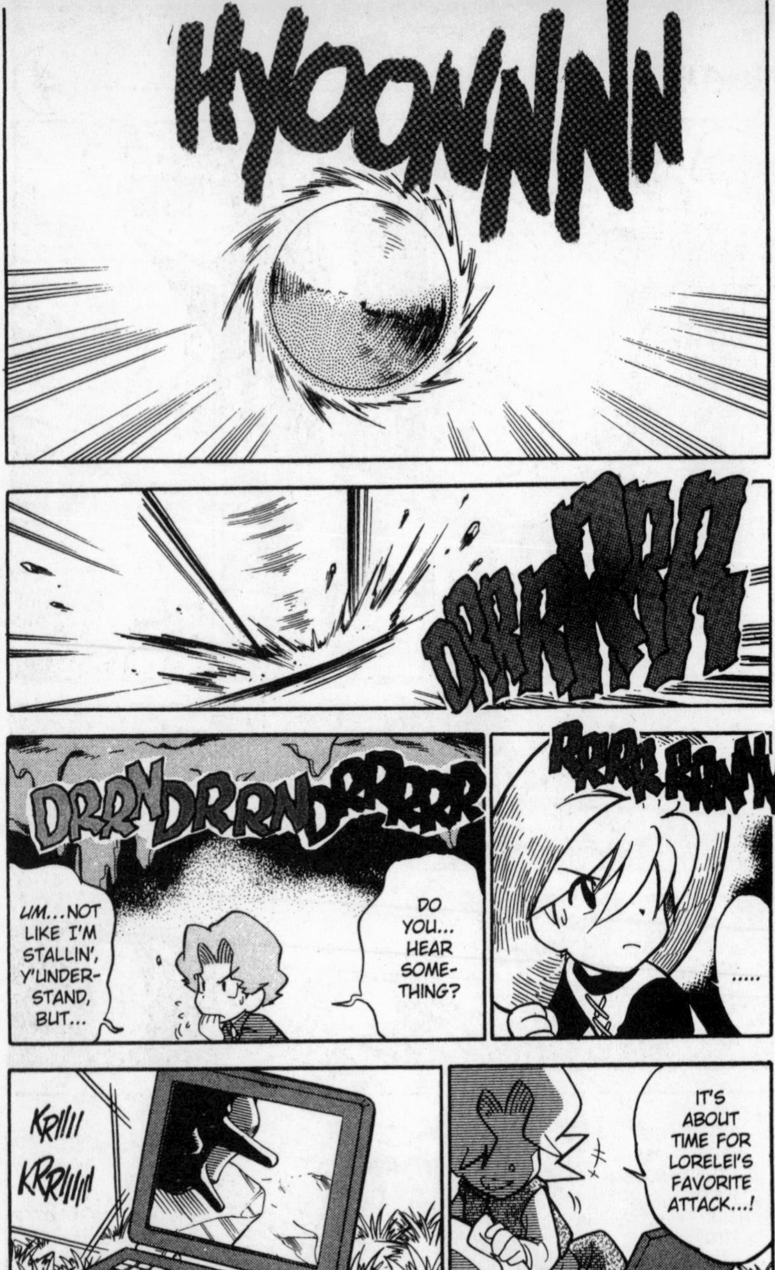
KYOOWNNN
DRRRNRR
DRRN DRRN DRRRRRR
DO YOU... HEAR SOME-THING?
UM...NOT LIKE I'M STALLIN', Y'UNDER-STAND, BUT...
RRRR RRNN
.....
IT'S ABOUT TIME FOR LORELEI'S FAVORITE ATTACK...!
KRIIII
KRRIIIII

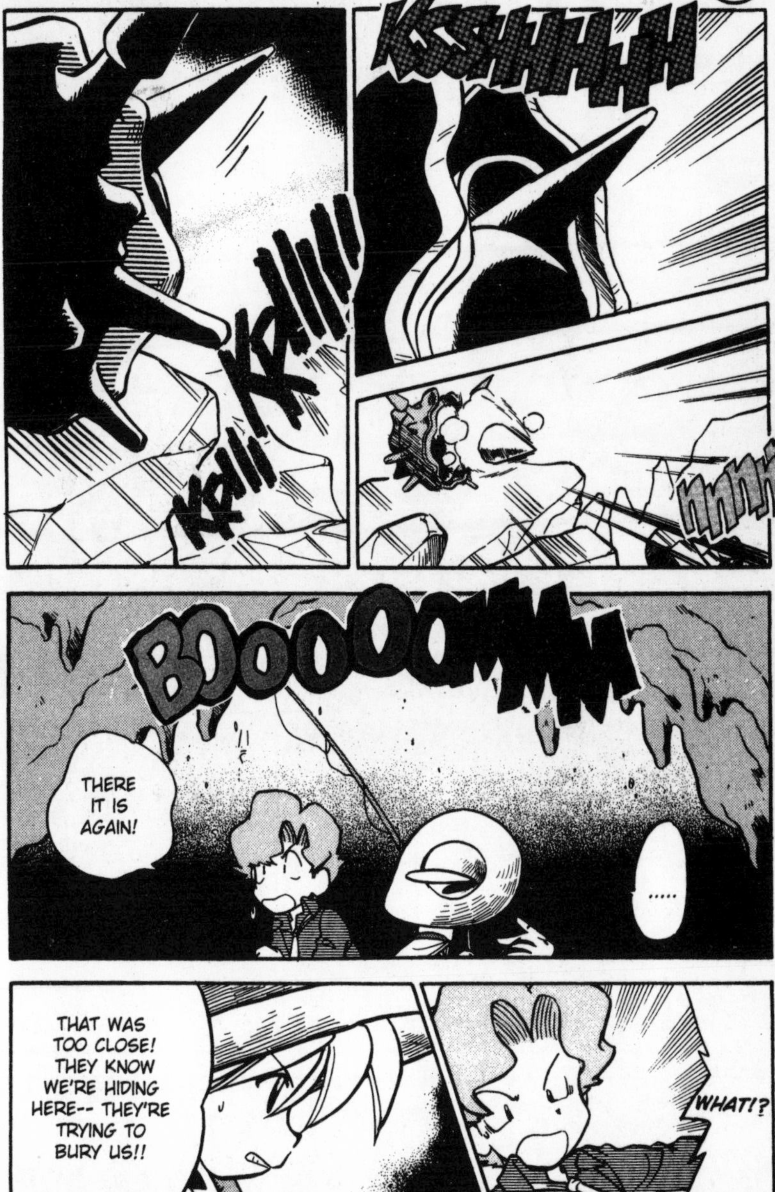
BOOOOOMMM
THERE IT IS AGAIN!
.....
THAT WAS TOO CLOSE! THEY KNOW WE'RE HIDING HERE-- THEY'RE TRYING TO BURY US!!
WHAT!?

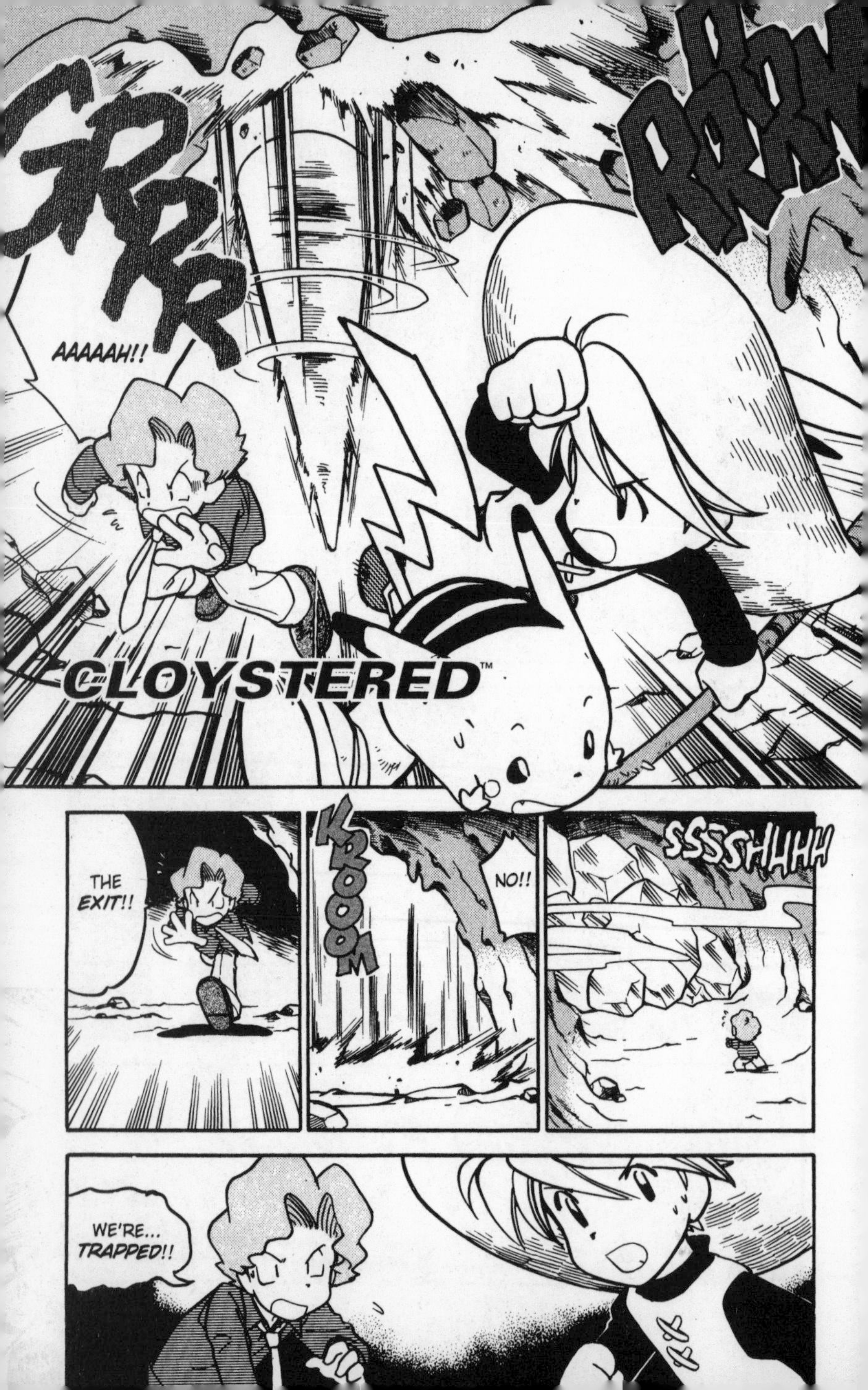
GRRR
DOOOM
AAAAAH!!
CLOYSTERED™
THE EXIT!!
KROOOOM
NO!!
SSSSHHHH
WE'RE... TRAPPED!!

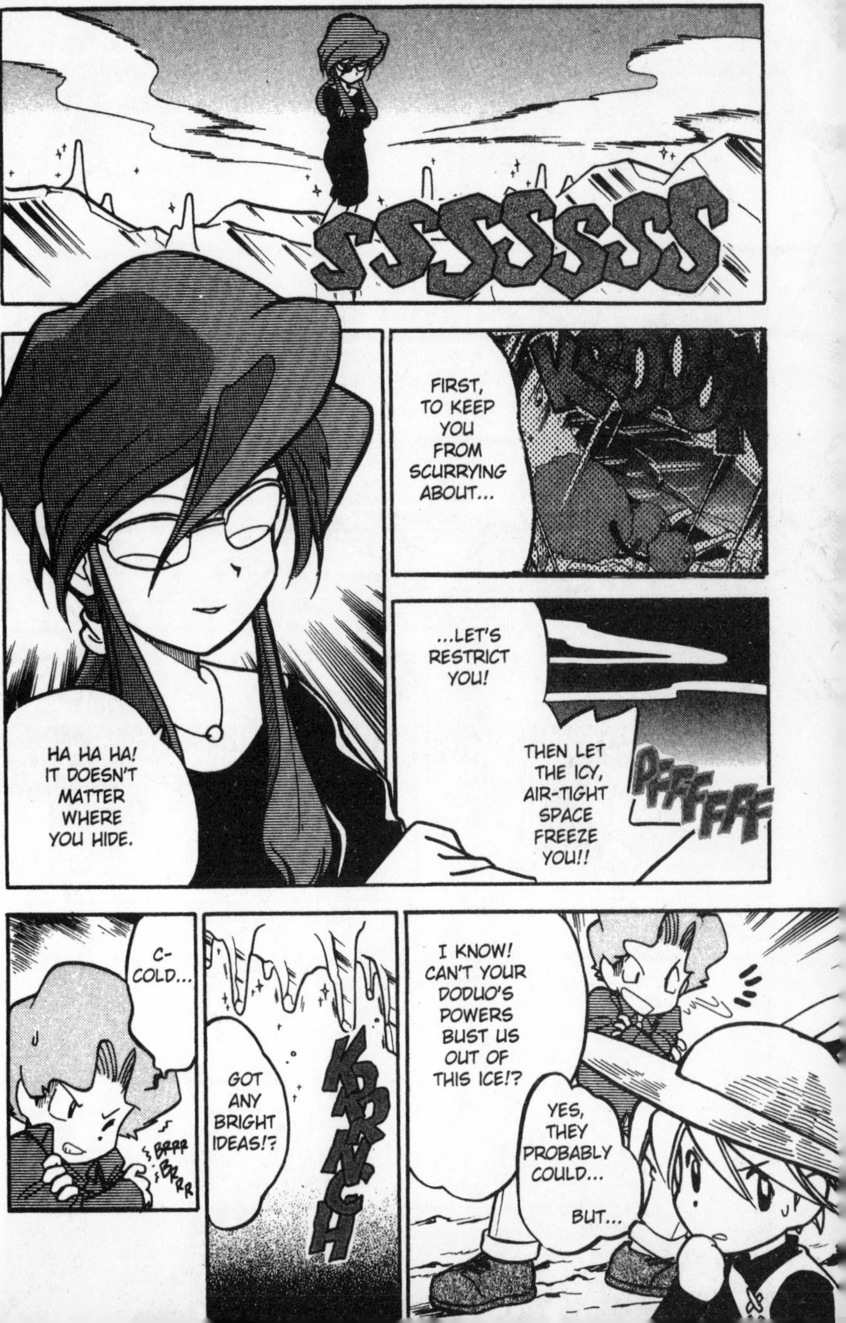
SSSSSSS
HA HA HA! IT DOESN'T MATTER WHERE YOU HIDE.
FIRST, TO KEEP YOU FROM SCURRYING ABOUT...
...LET'S RESTRICT YOU!
THEN LET THE ICY, AIR-TIGHT SPACE FREEZE YOU!!
C-COLD...
BRRR BRRR
GOT ANY BRIGHT IDEAS!?
KRNCH
I KNOW! CAN'T YOUR DODUO'S POWERS BUST US OUT OF THIS ICE!?
YES, THEY PROBABLY COULD...
BUT...

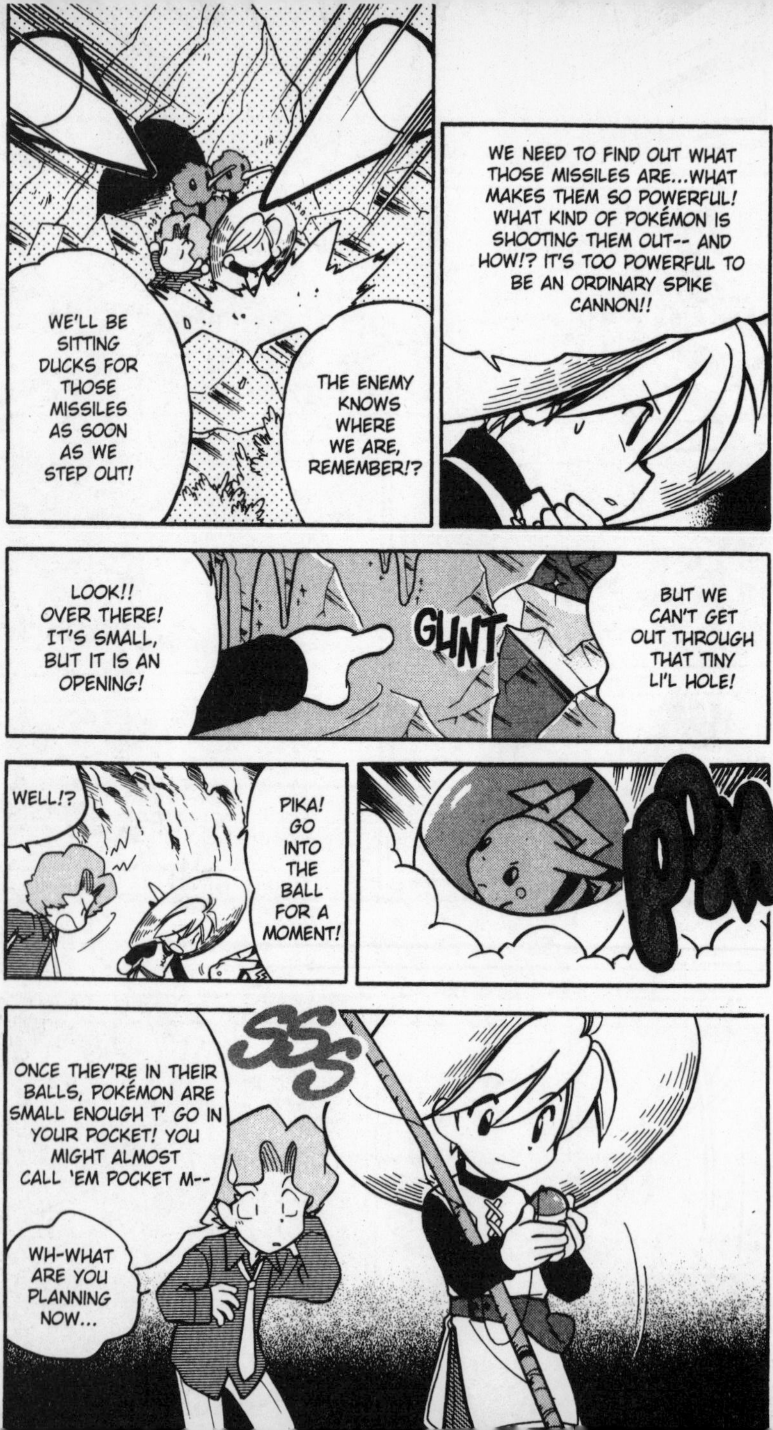
WE NEED TO FIND OUT WHAT THOSE MISSILES ARE...WHAT MAKES THEM SO POWERFUL! WHAT KIND OF POKÉMON IS SHOOTING THEM OUT-- AND HOW!? IT'S TOO POWERFUL TO BE AN ORDINARY SPIKE CANNON!!
THE ENEMY KNOWS WHERE WE ARE, REMEMBER!?
WE'LL BE SITTING DUCKS FOR THOSE MISSILES AS SOON AS WE STEP OUT!
BUT WE CAN'T GET OUT THROUGH THAT TINY LI'L HOLE!
GLINT
LOOK!! OVER THERE! IT'S SMALL, BUT IT IS AN OPENING!
POM
PIKA! GO INTO THE BALL FOR A MOMENT!
WELL!?
SSS
ONCE THEY'RE IN THEIR BALLS, POKÉMON ARE SMALL ENOUGH T' GO IN YOUR POCKET! YOU MIGHT ALMOST CALL 'EM POCKET M--
WH-WHAT ARE YOU PLANNING NOW...

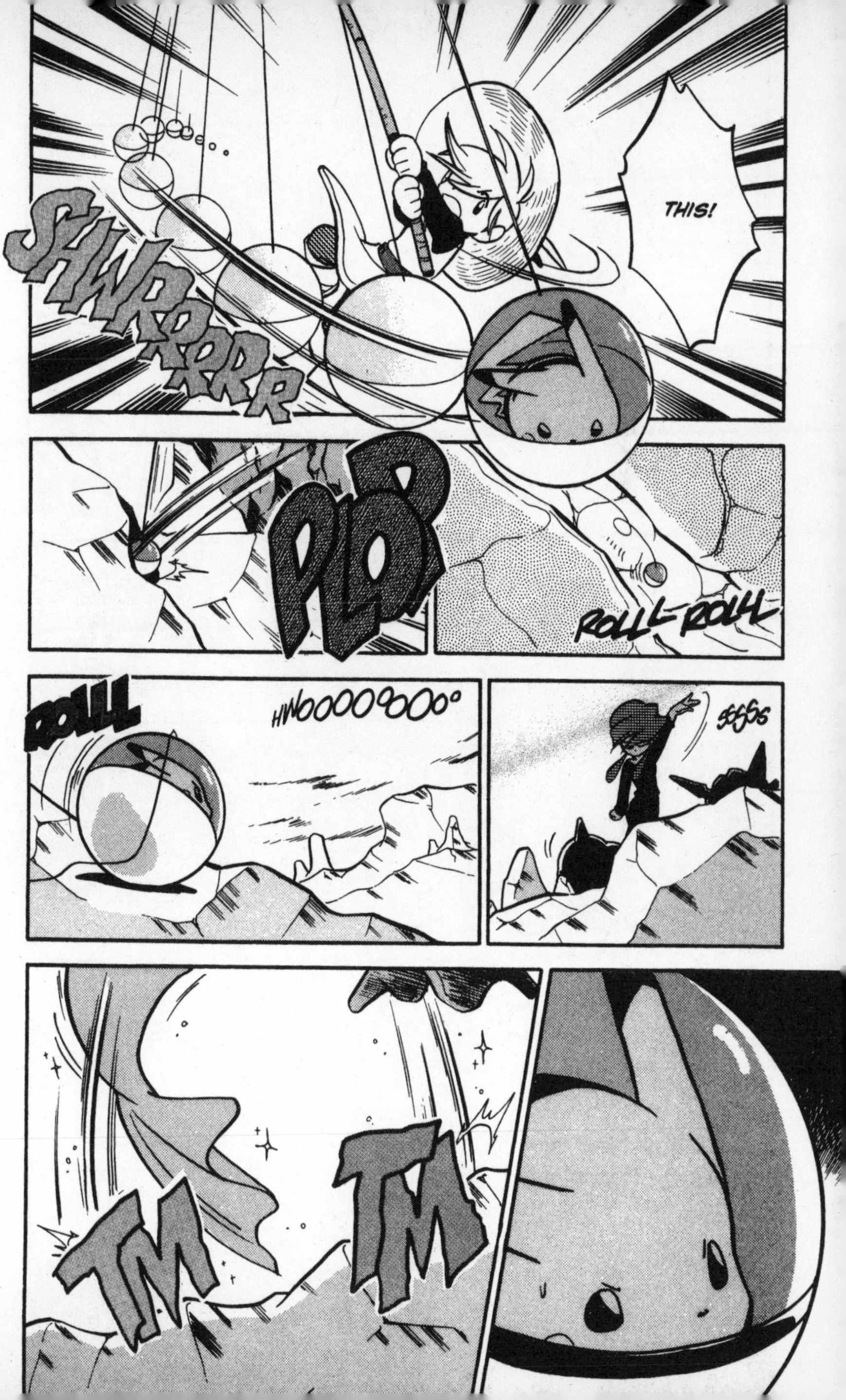
THIS!
SHWRRRRRR
PLOP
ROLL ROLL
ROLL
HWOOOOOOOO
SSSSS
TM
TM

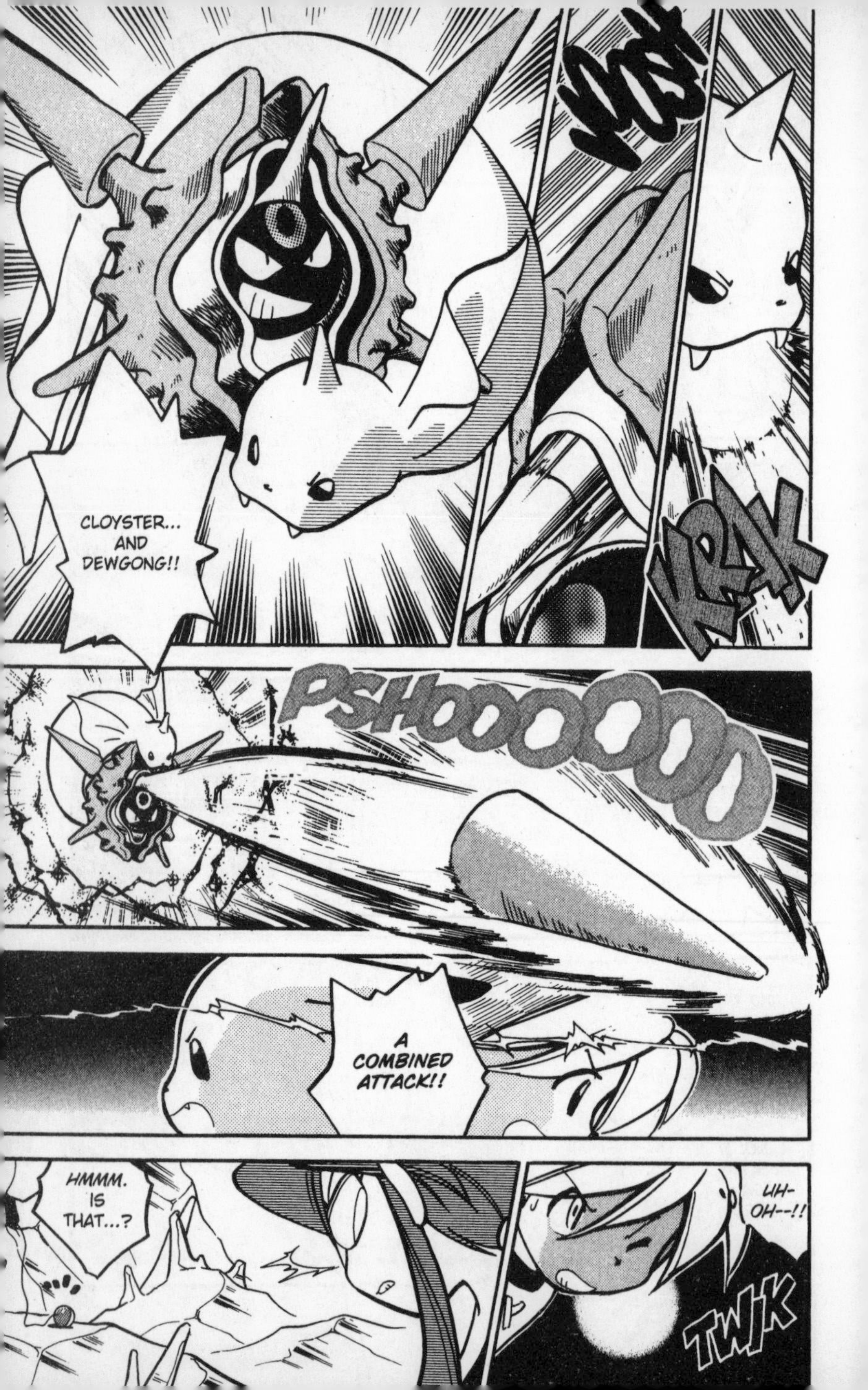
WOSH
CLOYSTER... AND DEWGONG!!
KRAK
PSHOOOOOOO
A COMBINED ATTACK!!
UH-OH--!!
HMMM. IS THAT...?
TWIK

GH.

TUG

VIP

DRRRRMMMM

YES. THAT WAS OUR TARGET...

PIKACHU!! TRAPPING THEM IN THE ICE WASN'T ENOUGH...

SSSSSSSSSSSS

DID I DEFEAT IT...?

NO! IT ESCAPED AGAIN... BARELY!

NEXT TIME IT COMES OUT I'LL BE WAITING!!

ROLL

HUF HUF

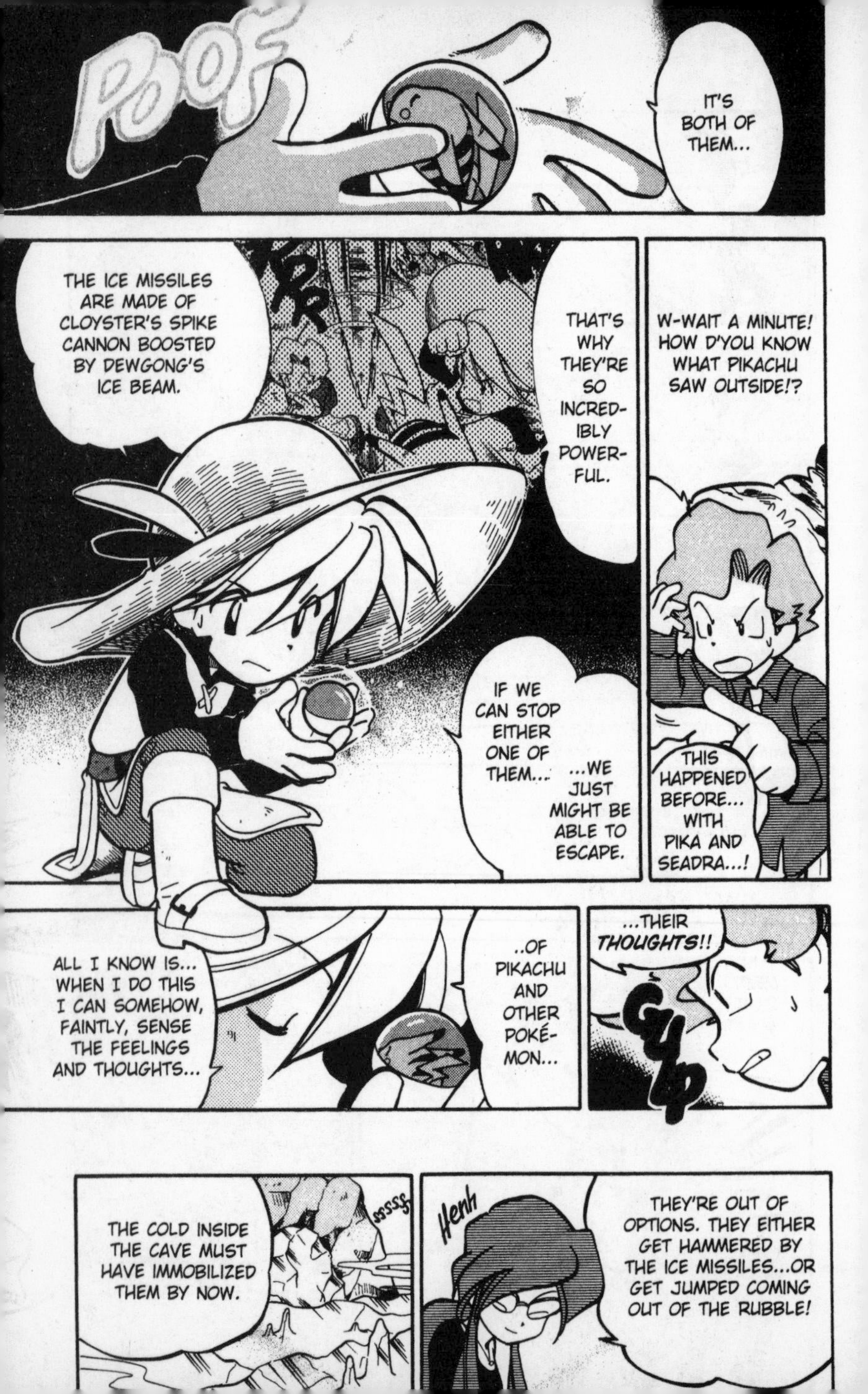
POOF
IT'S BOTH OF THEM...
THE ICE MISSILES ARE MADE OF CLOYSTER'S SPIKE CANNON BOOSTED BY DEWGONG'S ICE BEAM.
THAT'S WHY THEY'RE SO INCRED-IBLY POWER-FUL.
W-WAIT A MINUTE! HOW D'YOU KNOW WHAT PIKACHU SAW OUTSIDE!?
IF WE CAN STOP EITHER ONE OF THEM...
...WE JUST MIGHT BE ABLE TO ESCAPE.
THIS HAPPENED BEFORE... WITH PIKA AND SEADRA...!
ALL I KNOW IS... WHEN I DO THIS I CAN SOMEHOW, FAINTLY, SENSE THE FEELINGS AND THOUGHTS...
..OF PIKACHU AND OTHER POKÉ-MON...
...THEIR THOUGHTS!!
GULP
THE COLD INSIDE THE CAVE MUST HAVE IMMOBILIZED THEM BY NOW.
SSSSS
Henh
THEY'RE OUT OF OPTIONS. THEY EITHER GET HAMMERED BY THE ICE MISSILES...OR GET JUMPED COMING OUT OF THE RUBBLE!

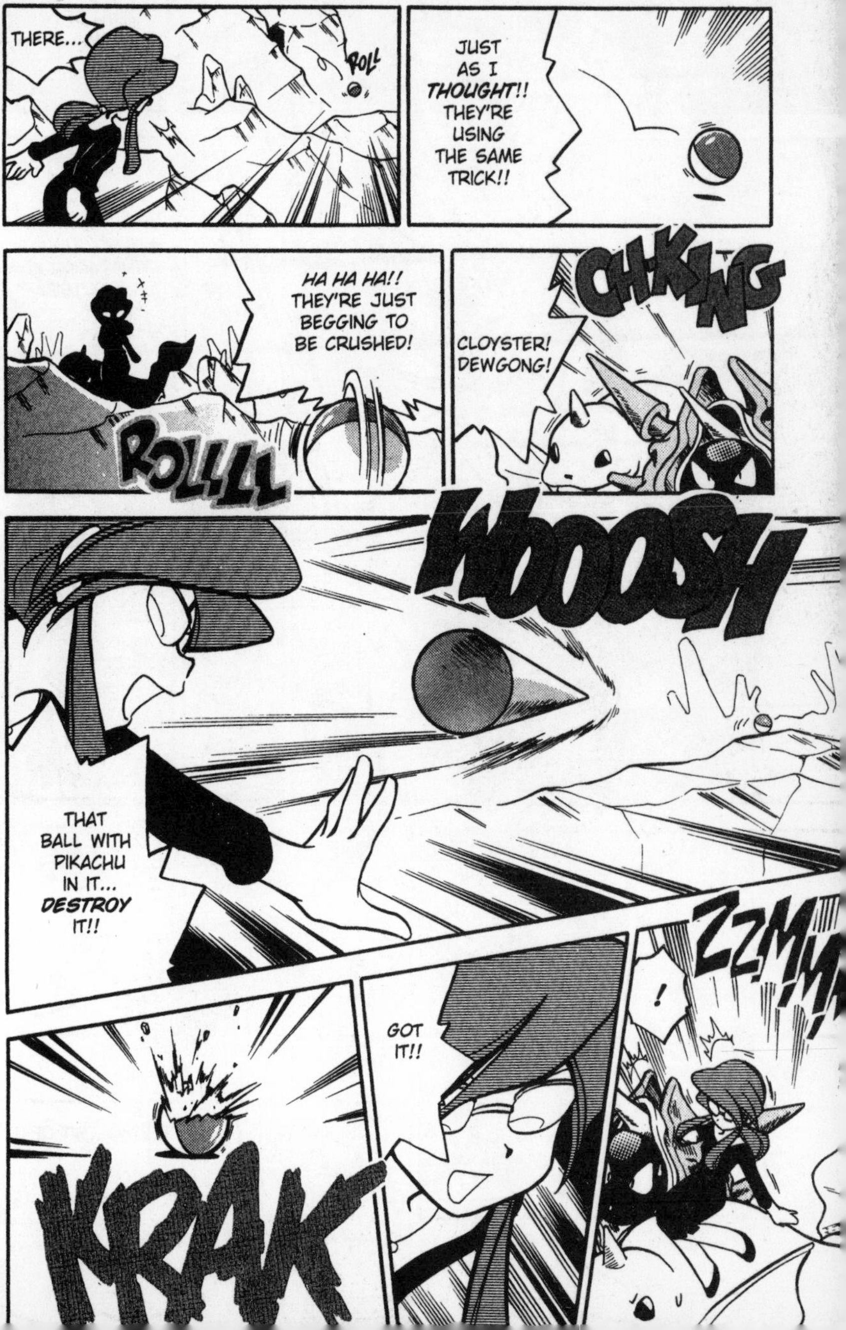
THERE...
ROLL
JUST AS I *THOUGHT*!! THEY'RE USING THE SAME TRICK!!
HA HA HA!! THEY'RE JUST BEGGING TO BE CRUSHED!
ROLLLL
CH-KING
CLOYSTER! DEWGONG!
WOOOSH
THAT BALL WITH PIKACHU IN IT... *DESTROY* IT!!
ZZMMM
GOT IT!!
!
KRAK

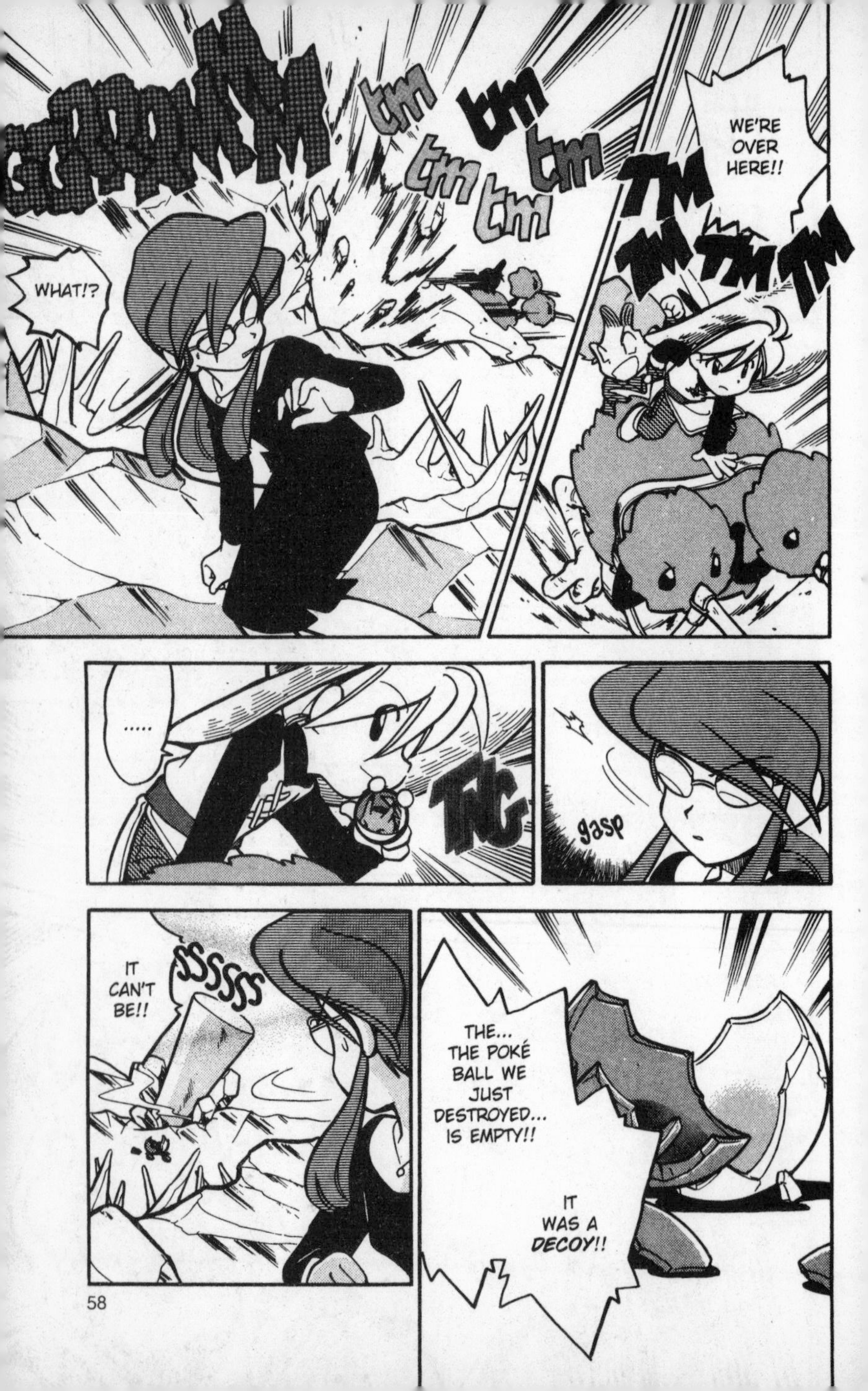
WHAT!?
WE'RE OVER HERE!!
.....
gasp
IT CAN'T BE!!
THE... THE POKÉ BALL WE JUST DESTROYED... IS EMPTY!!
IT WAS A DECOY!!

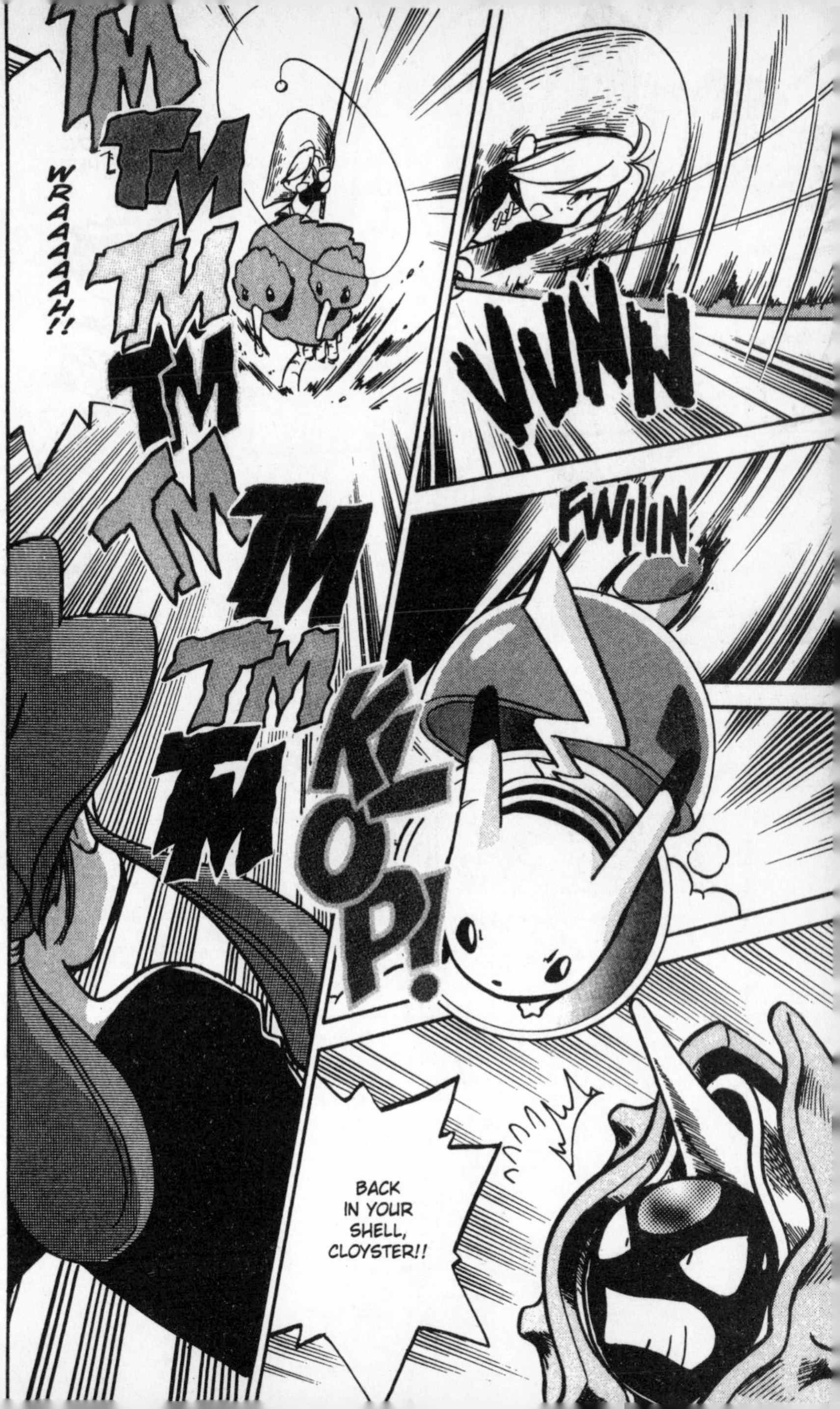
VUNN
TM TM TM TM TM TM TM TM
WRAAAAAH!!
FWIIIN
KLOP!
BACK IN YOUR SHELL, CLOYSTER!!

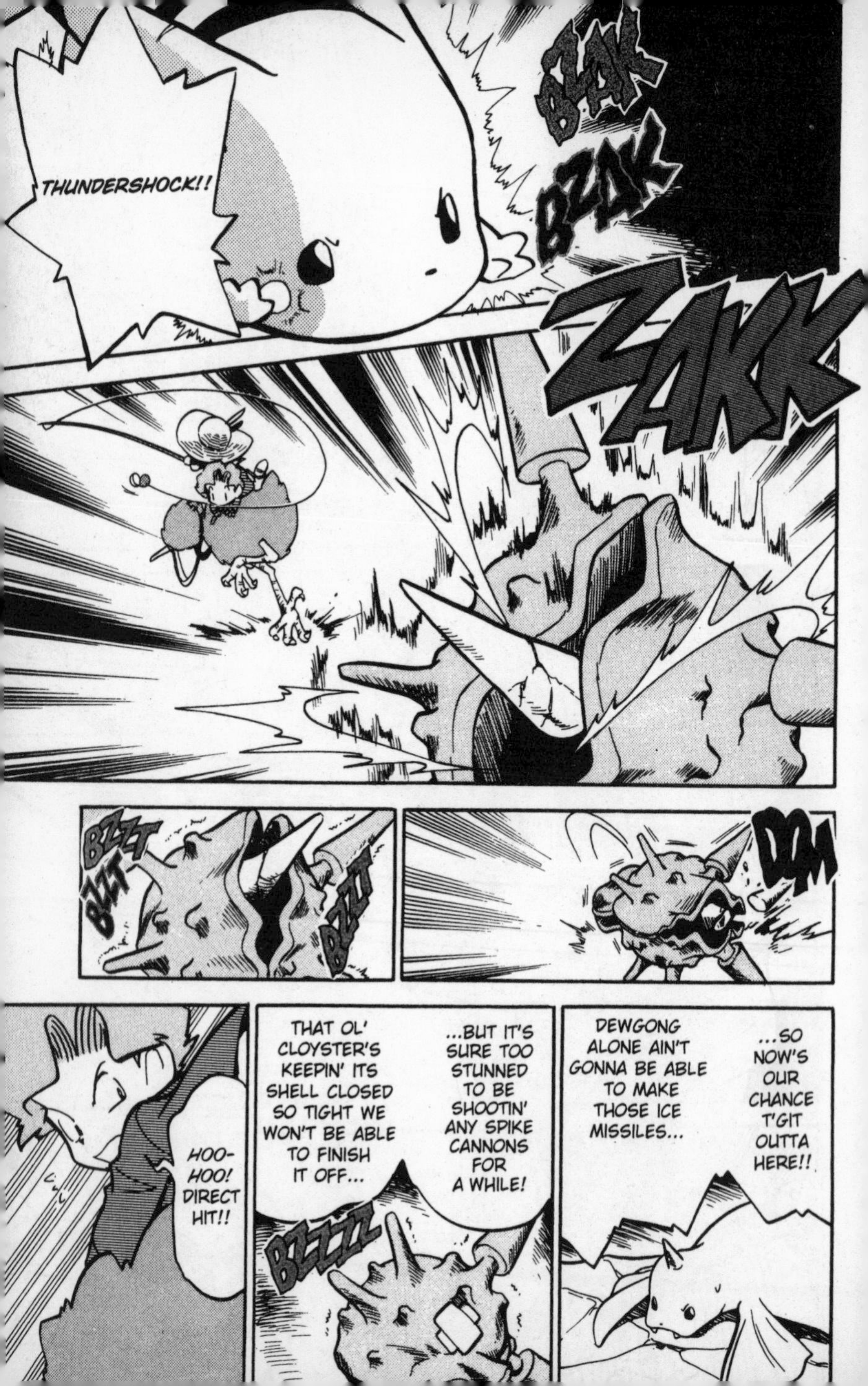
THUNDERSHOCK!!
BZAK
BZAK
ZAKK
BZZZT
BZZZT
BZZZT
DOM
HOO-HOO! DIRECT HIT!!
THAT OL' CLOYSTER'S KEEPIN' ITS SHELL CLOSED SO TIGHT WE WON'T BE ABLE TO FINISH IT OFF...
...BUT IT'S SURE TOO STUNNED TO BE SHOOTIN' ANY SPIKE CANNONS FOR A WHILE!
BZZZZ
DEWGONG ALONE AIN'T GONNA BE ABLE TO MAKE THOSE ICE MISSILES...
...SO NOW'S OUR CHANCE T'GIT OUTTA HERE!!

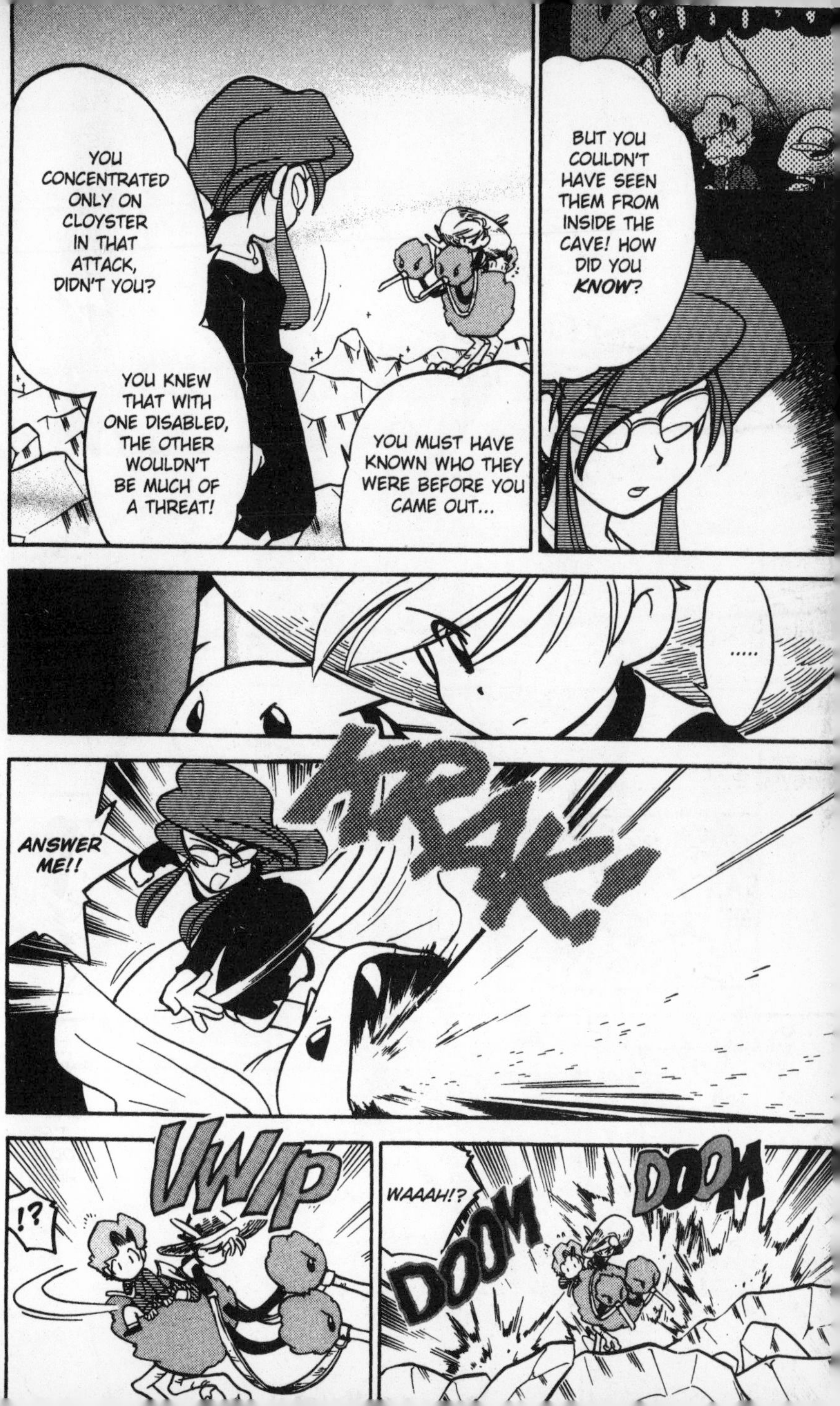
BUT YOU COULDN'T HAVE SEEN THEM FROM INSIDE THE CAVE! HOW DID YOU KNOW?
YOU CONCENTRATED ONLY ON CLOYSTER IN THAT ATTACK, DIDN'T YOU?
YOU KNEW THAT WITH ONE DISABLED, THE OTHER WOULDN'T BE MUCH OF A THREAT!
YOU MUST HAVE KNOWN WHO THEY WERE BEFORE YOU CAME OUT...
.....
KRAK!
ANSWER ME!!
WAAAH!?
DOOM
DOOM
VWIP
!?

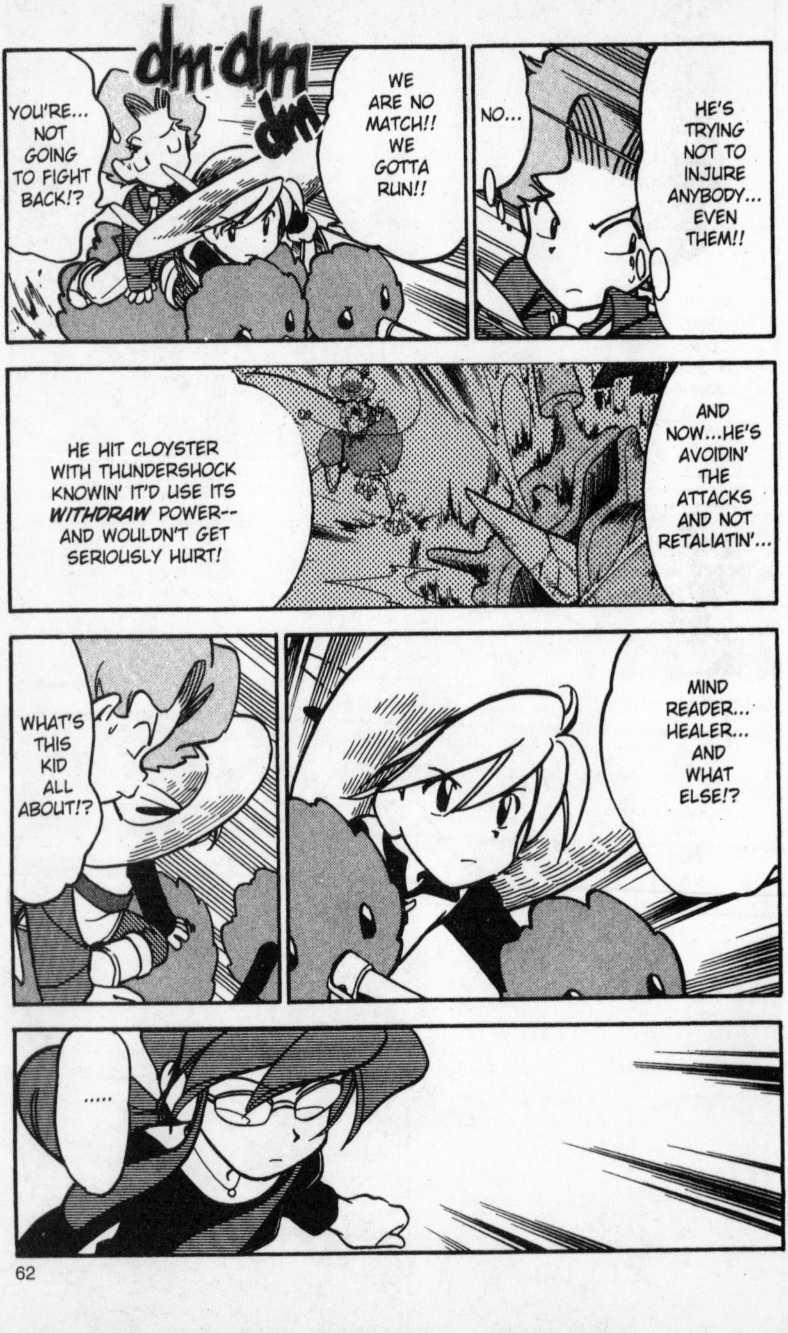
dm dm dm
YOU'RE... NOT GOING TO FIGHT BACK!?
WE ARE NO MATCH!! WE GOTTA RUN!!
NO...
HE'S TRYING NOT TO INJURE ANYBODY... EVEN THEM!!
HE HIT CLOYSTER WITH THUNDERSHOCK KNOWIN' IT'D USE ITS WITHDRAW POWER-- AND WOULDN'T GET SERIOUSLY HURT!
AND NOW...HE'S AVOIDIN' THE ATTACKS AND NOT RETALIATIN'...
WHAT'S THIS KID ALL ABOUT!?
MIND READER... HEALER... AND WHAT ELSE!?
.....

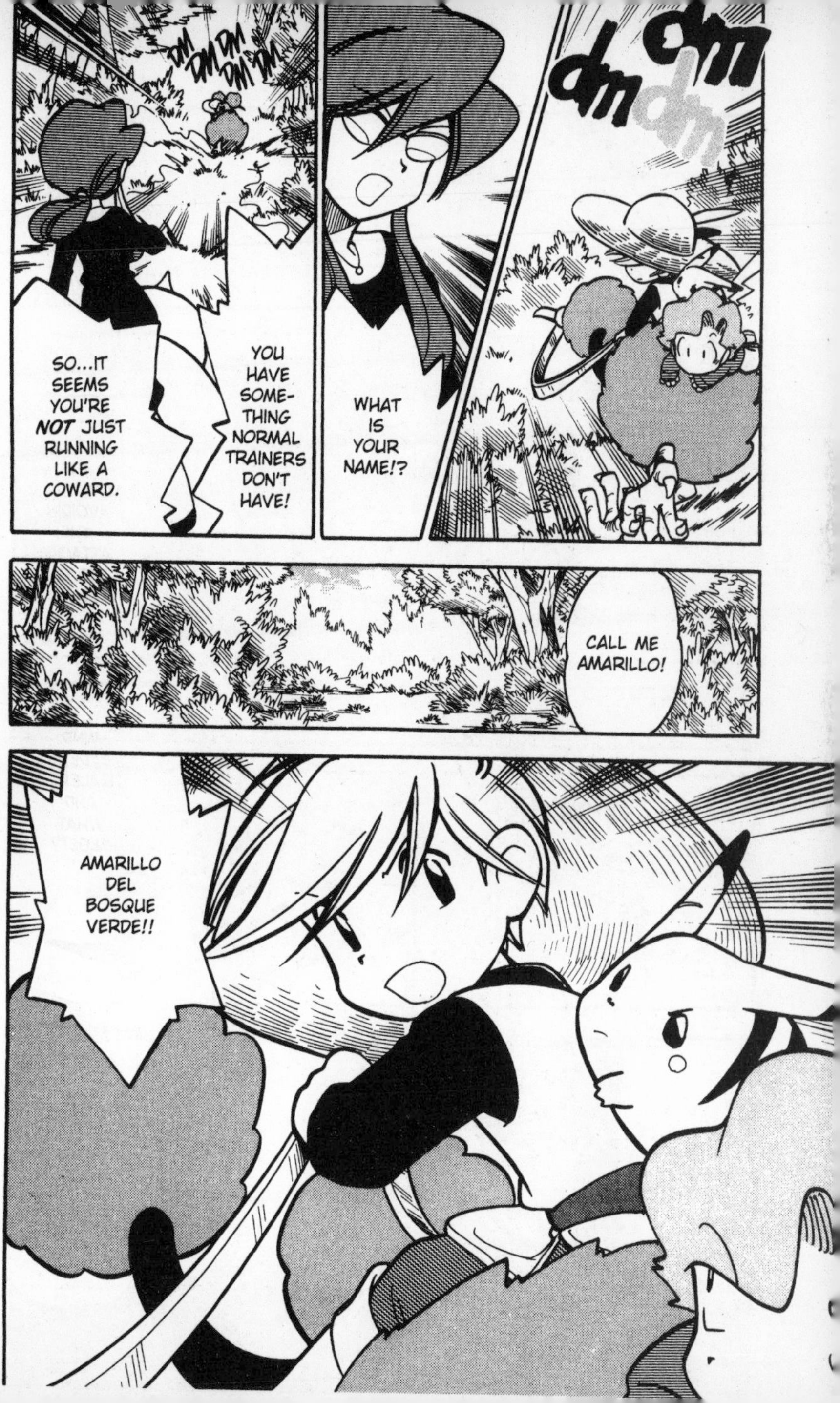

DM DM DM DM DM
SO...IT SEEMS YOU'RE *NOT* JUST RUNNING LIKE A COWARD.
YOU HAVE SOME-THING NORMAL TRAINERS DON'T HAVE!
WHAT IS YOUR NAME!?
dm dm dm dm
CALL ME AMARILLO!
AMARILLO DEL BOSQUE VERDE!!

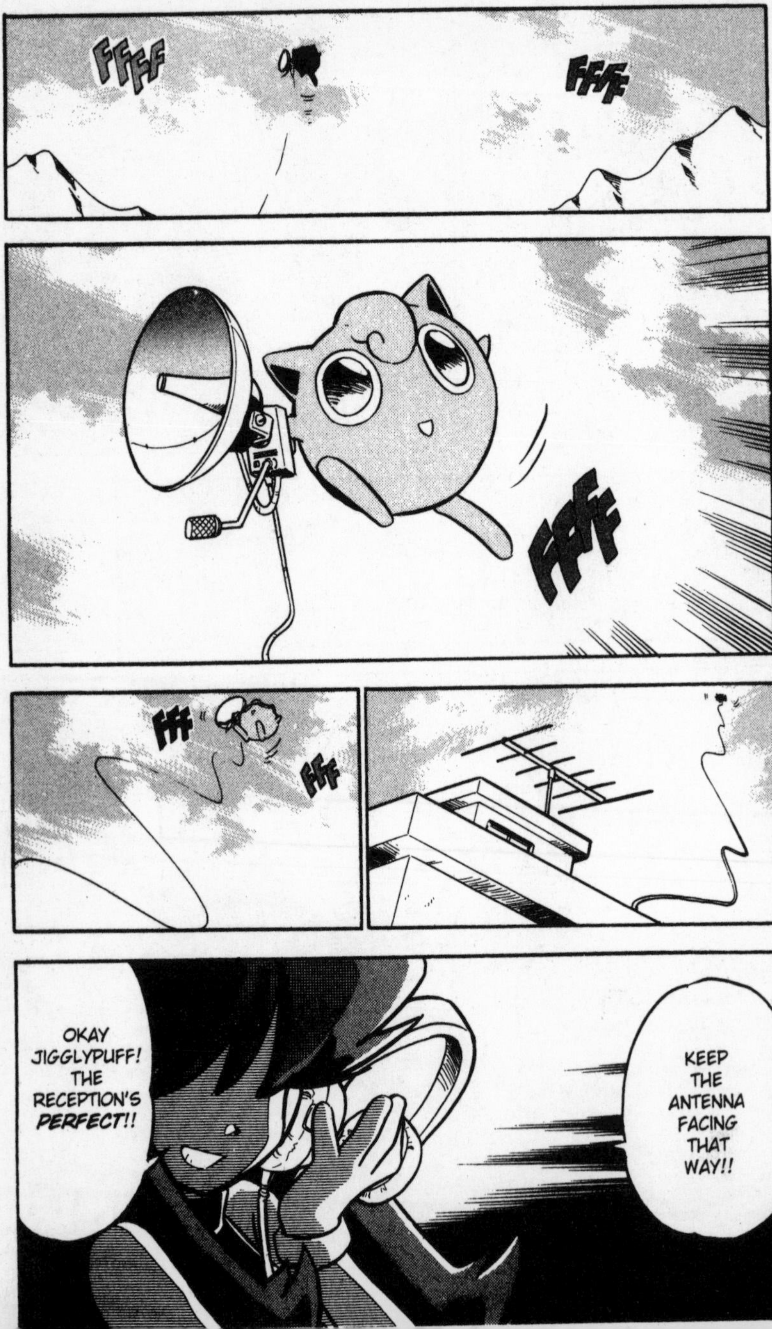
FFFF
FFFF
FFFF
FFF
FFF
OKAY JIGGLYPUFF! THE RECEPTION'S *PERFECT*!!
KEEP THE ANTENNA FACING THAT WAY!!

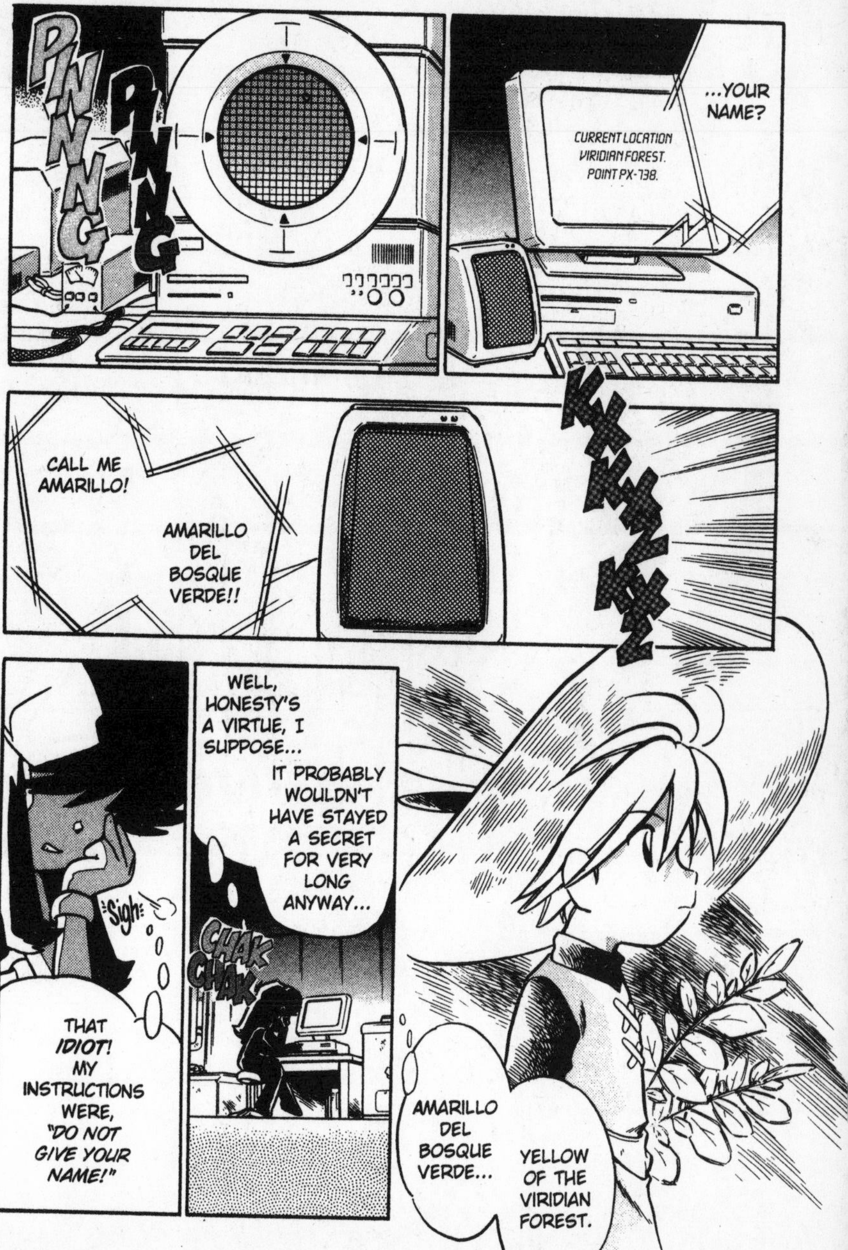
PINNNG
PINNNG
CURRENT LOCATION
VIRIDIAN FOREST.
POINT PX-738.
...YOUR NAME?
CALL ME AMARILLO!
AMARILLO DEL BOSQUE VERDE!!
WELL, HONESTY'S A VIRTUE, I SUPPOSE...
IT PROBABLY WOULDN'T HAVE STAYED A SECRET FOR VERY LONG ANYWAY...
Sigh
THAT IDIOT! MY INSTRUCTIONS WERE, "DO NOT GIVE YOUR NAME!"
CHAK CHAK
AMARILLO DEL BOSQUE VERDE...
YELLOW OF THE VIRIDIAN FOREST.

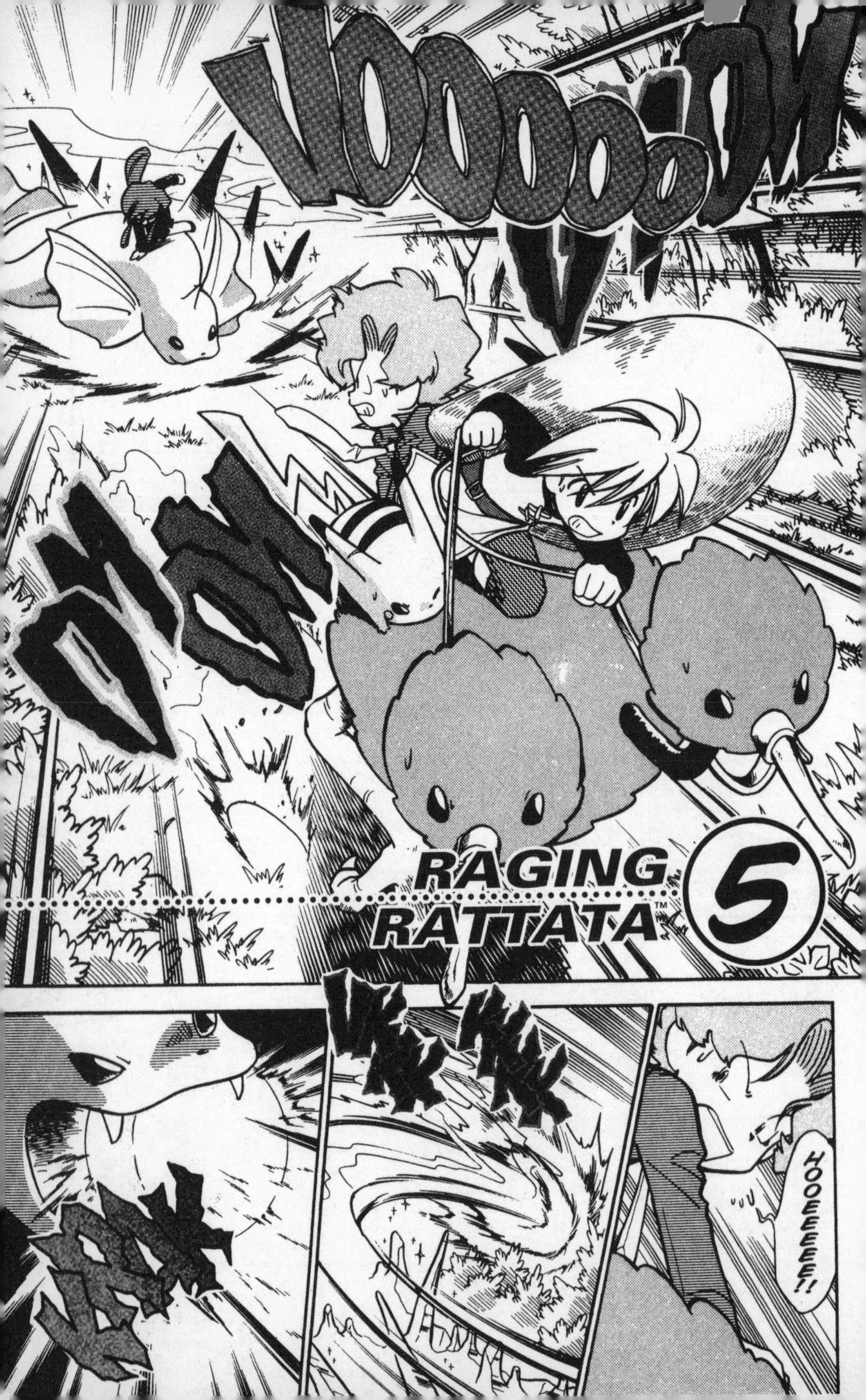
RAGING RATTATA™ 5
HOOEEEEE!!

THAT DEWGONG! IT'S CHASIN' US BY MAKIN' ITS OWN ICE-SKATIN' RINK!

DNDNDNDNDM

KRKKL KRKKL

I WAS SURE DODUO'D HAVE THE ADVANTAGE IN A LAND RACE, BUT... WELL... SO MUCH FOR ME!

HA HA HA...

DM DM DM

THEY'RE ALMOST ON TOP OF US!

HWOOOO

KREK

ICE BEAM!!

HOO

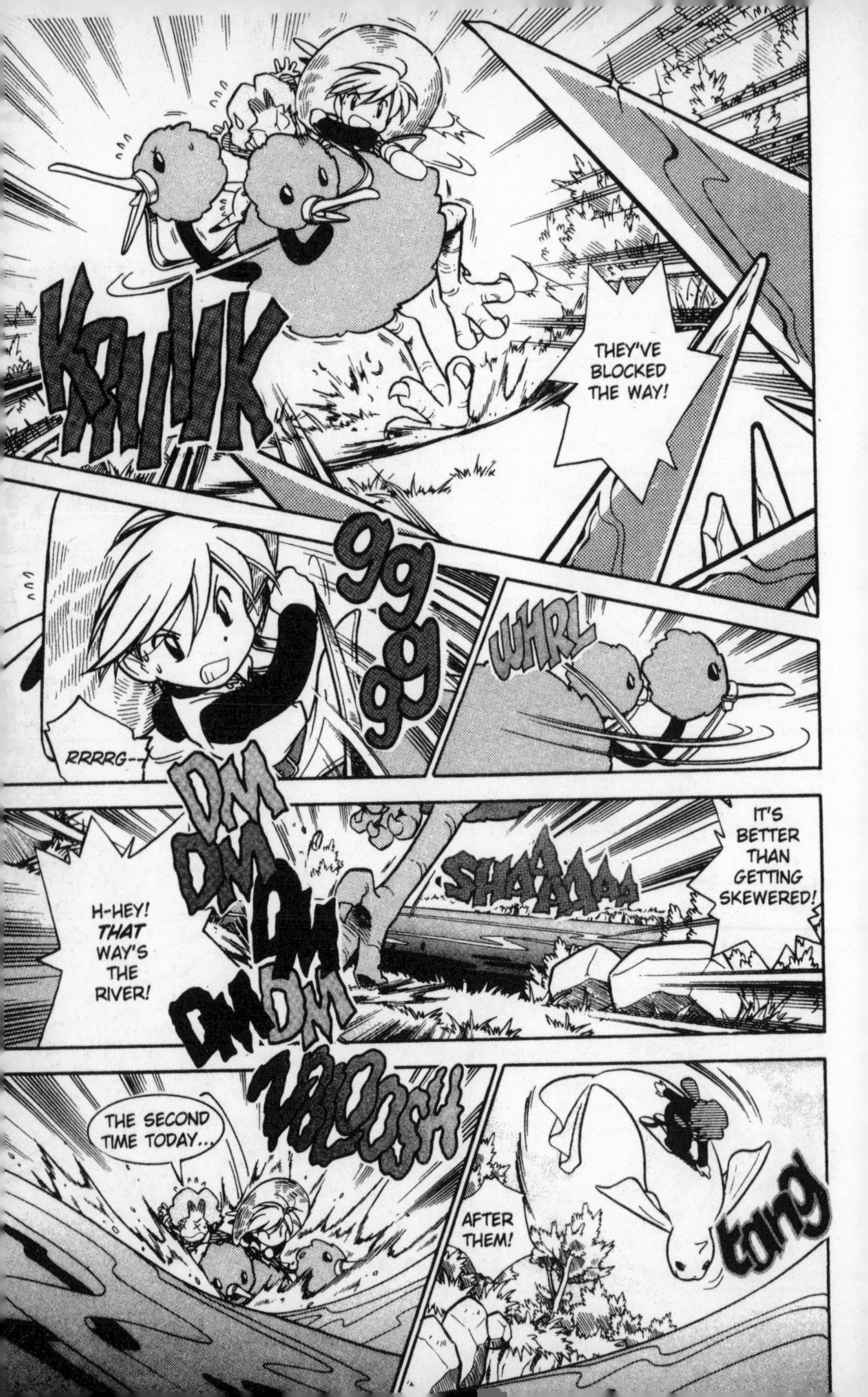
KRUNK
THEY'VE BLOCKED THE WAY!
RRRRG--
gg gg
WHRL
H-HEY! *THAT* WAY'S THE RIVER!
DM DM DM DM DM DM
SHAAAAA
IT'S BETTER THAN GETTING SKEWERED!
THE SECOND TIME TODAY...
VBLOOSH
AFTER THEM!
tang

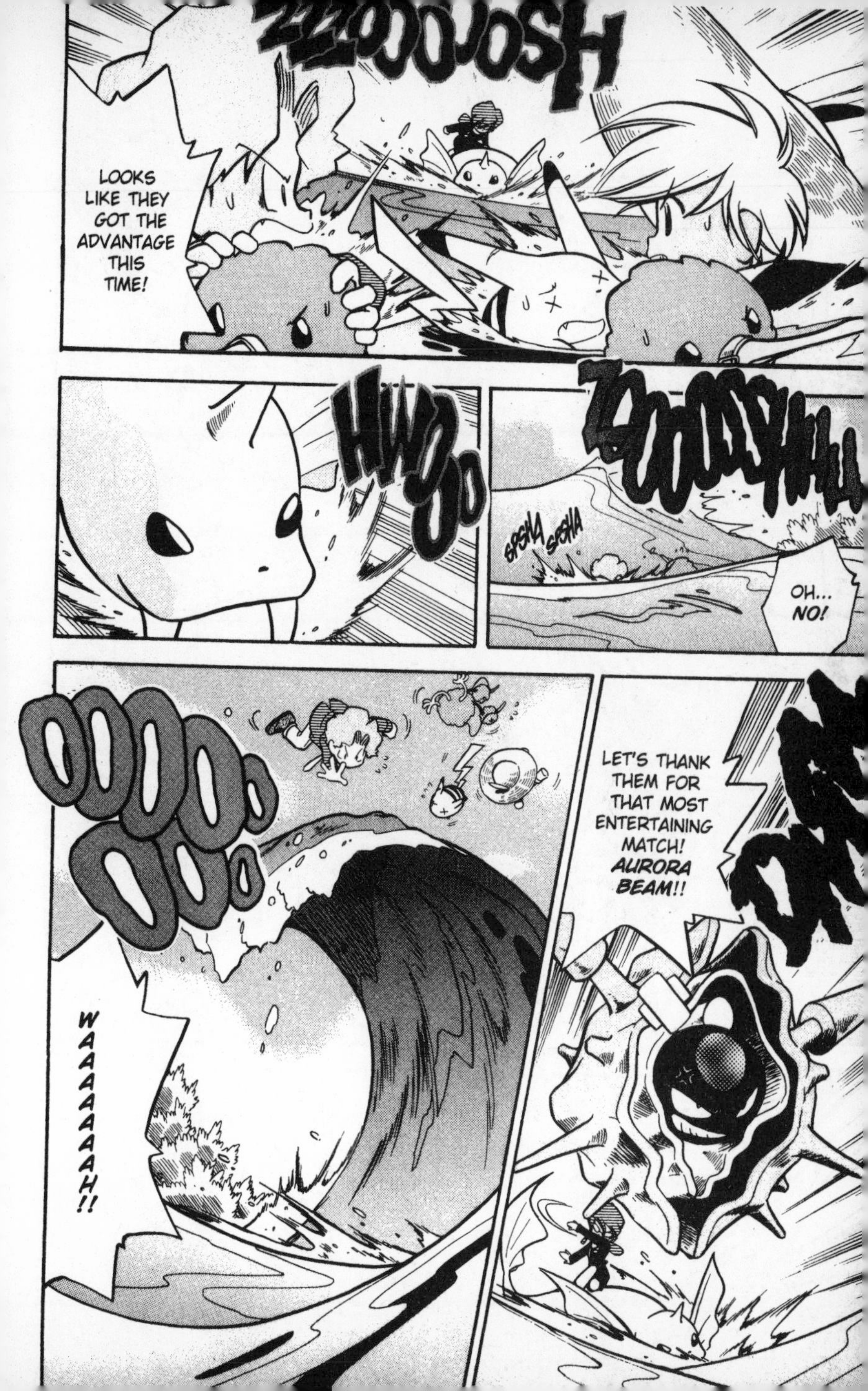
LOOKS LIKE THEY GOT THE ADVANTAGE THIS TIME!
OH... NO!
LET'S THANK THEM FOR THAT MOST ENTERTAINING MATCH! AURORA BEAM!!
WAAAAAAAAAH!!

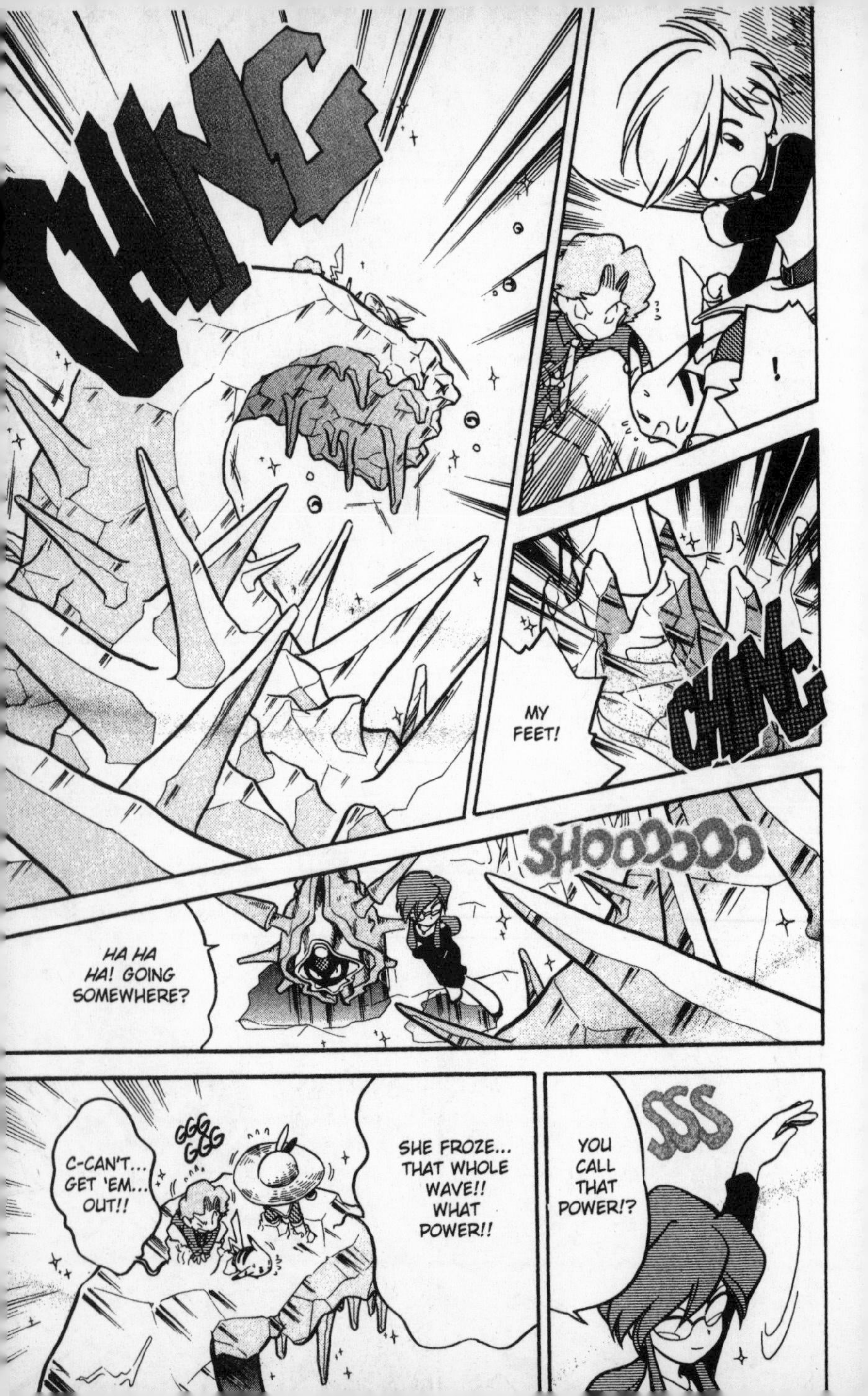
CHING
!
MY FEET!
CHING
SHOOOOOO
HA HA HA! GOING SOMEWHERE?
C-CAN'T... GET 'EM... OUT!!
GGG GGG
SHE FROZE... THAT WHOLE WAVE!! WHAT POWER!!
SSS
YOU CALL THAT POWER!?

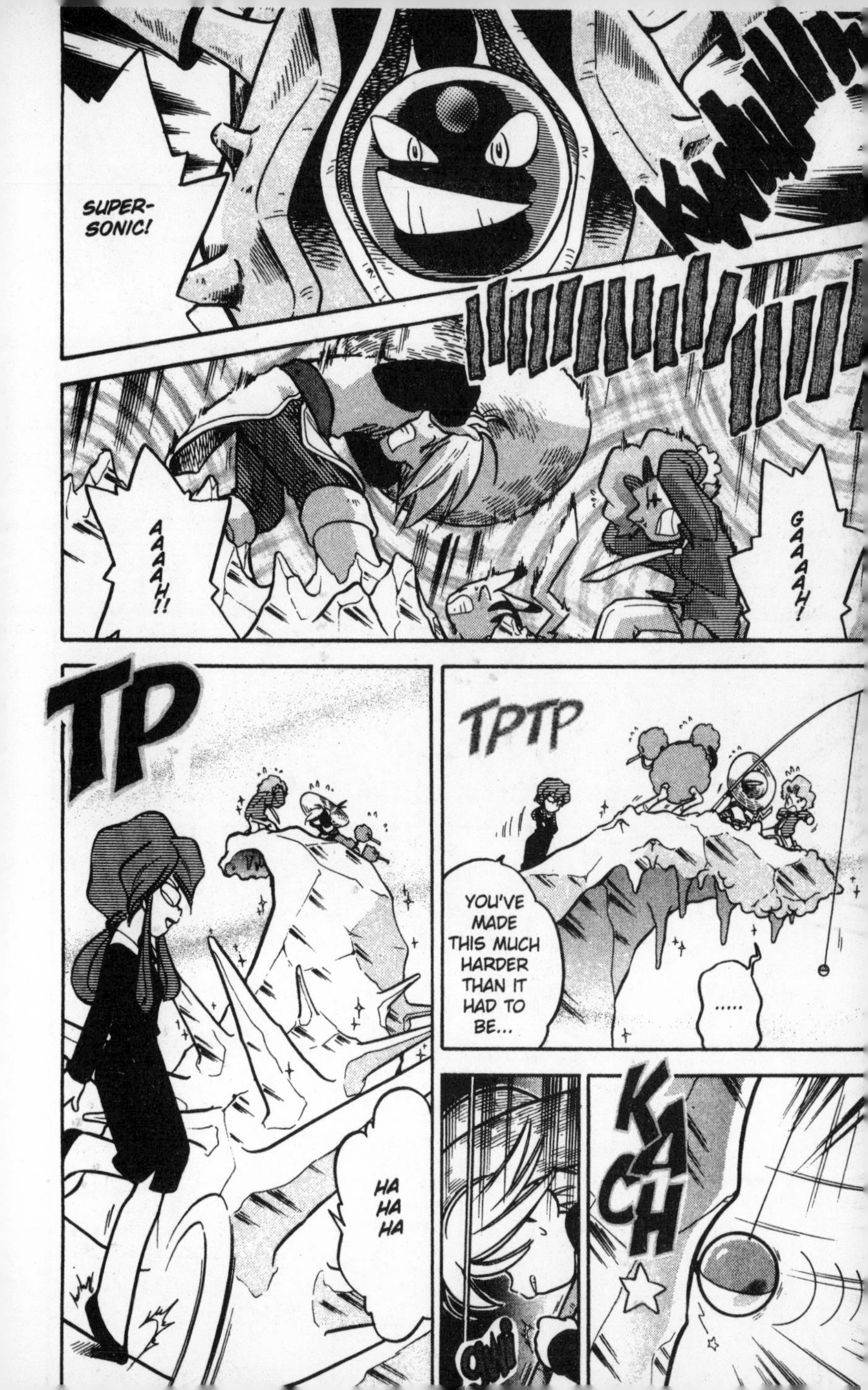
SUPER-SONIC!
GAAAAAH!
AAAAAH!!
TPTP
YOU'VE MADE THIS MUCH HARDER THAN IT HAD TO BE...
.....
TP
HA HA HA
KACH

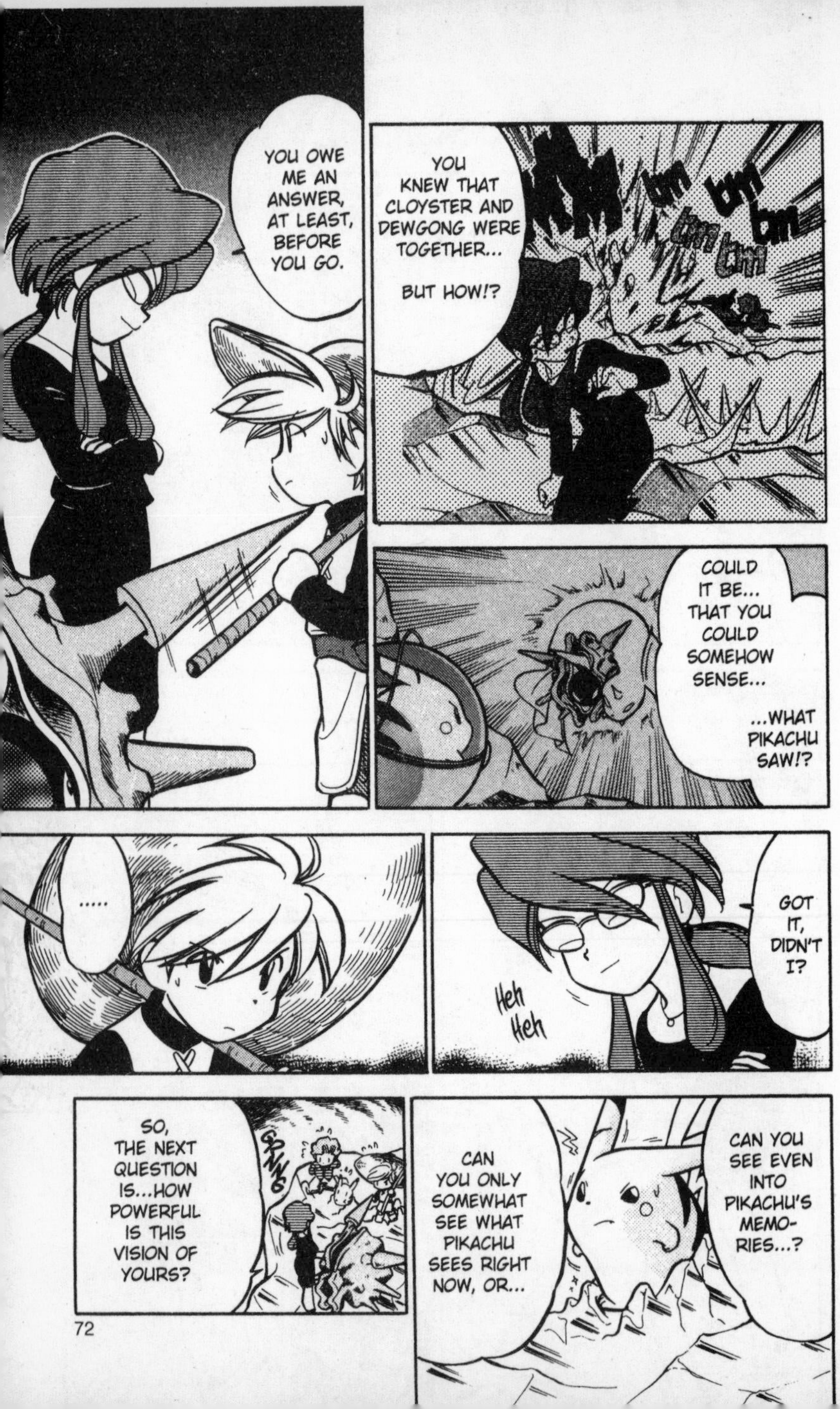

YOU OWE ME AN ANSWER, AT LEAST, BEFORE YOU GO.
YOU KNEW THAT CLOYSTER AND DEWGONG WERE TOGETHER...
BUT HOW!?
COULD IT BE... THAT YOU COULD SOMEHOW SENSE...
...WHAT PIKACHU SAW!?
.....
GOT IT, DIDN'T I?
Heh Heh
SO, THE NEXT QUESTION IS...HOW POWERFUL IS THIS VISION OF YOURS?
CAN YOU ONLY SOMEWHAT SEE WHAT PIKACHU SEES RIGHT NOW, OR...
CAN YOU SEE EVEN INTO PIKACHU'S MEMORIES...?

CAN I ASSUME, THEN, THAT YOU DON'T KNOW MUCH ABOUT THAT BATTLE?

THAT YOU COULDN'T SEE THE MEMORIES OF THE BATTLE IN PIKACHU'S MIND?

WHEN I FIRST TOLD YOU ABOUT THE BATTLE BETWEEN RED AND BRUNO...

YOU LOOKED AT ME AS IF YOU WERE TRYING TO FIGURE ME OUT.

I THINK NOT.

WELL!? AM I WRONG?

NO MATTER THOUGH, SINCE...

SCRAPE SCRAPE

EH?

SCRAAAPE

WHAT IS THAT?

??

TH-THIS SOUND... WHAT...?

SCRAAAAPE SCRAPE SCRAAA SCRAAA SCRAPE SCRAAA SCRAPE SCRAPE SCRAAAA

KSSSSSHHHHHHHH

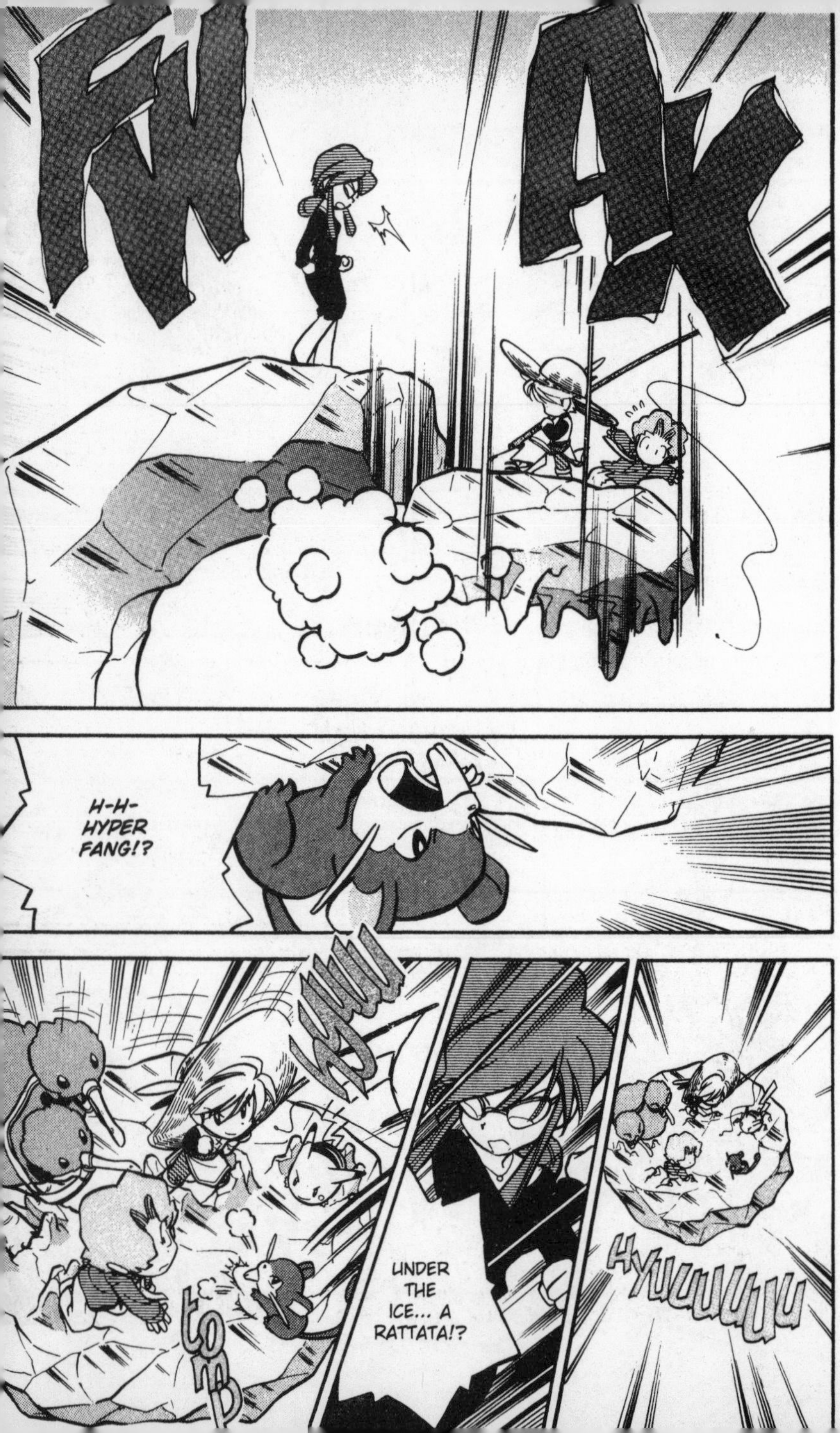
FWAK
H-H-HYPER FANG!?
HYUUUUUUU
UNDER THE ICE... A RATTATA!?
HYUUUU
tomp

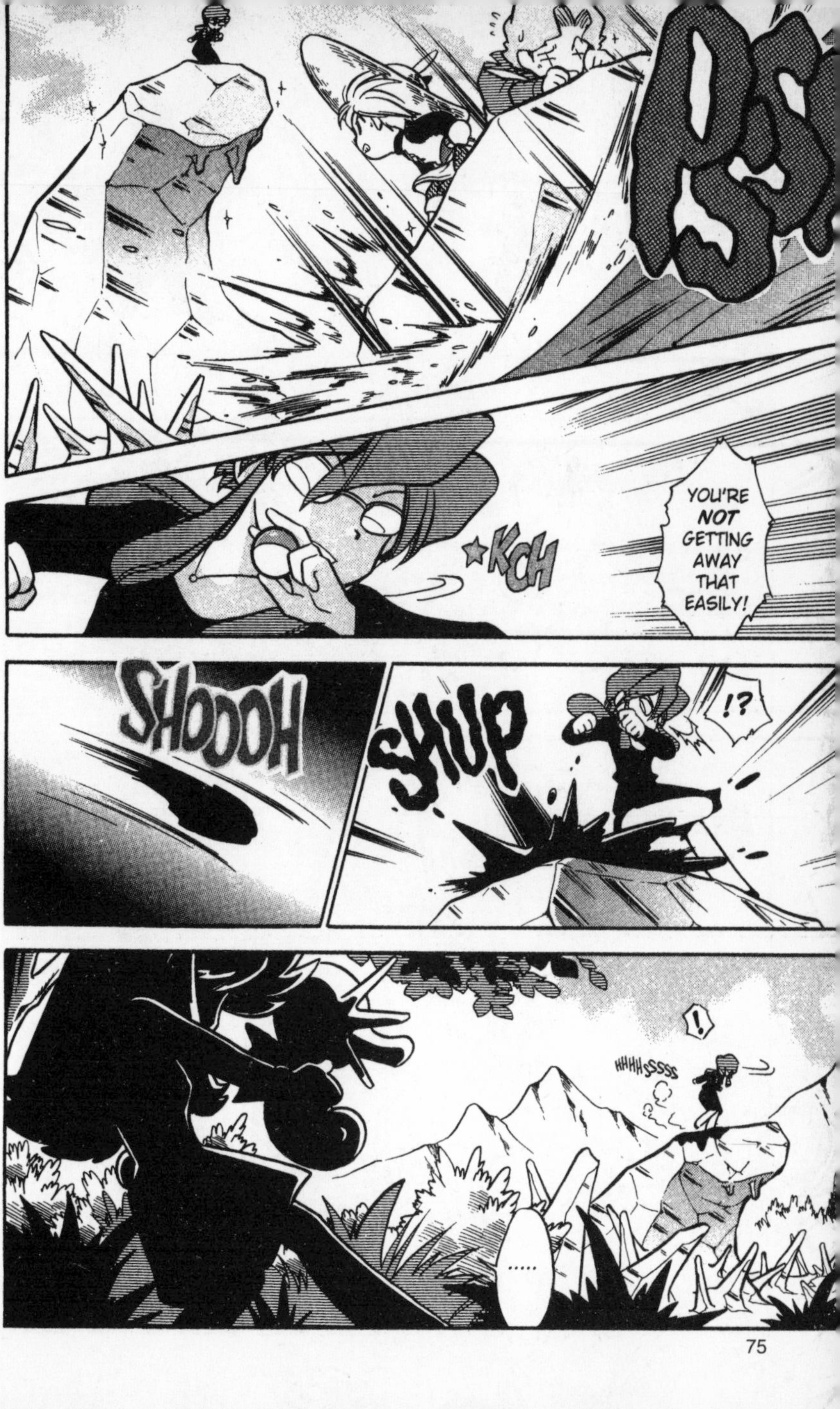

YOU'RE NOT GETTING AWAY THAT EASILY!
KCH
!?
SHUP
SHOOOH
!
HHHHSSSSS
.....

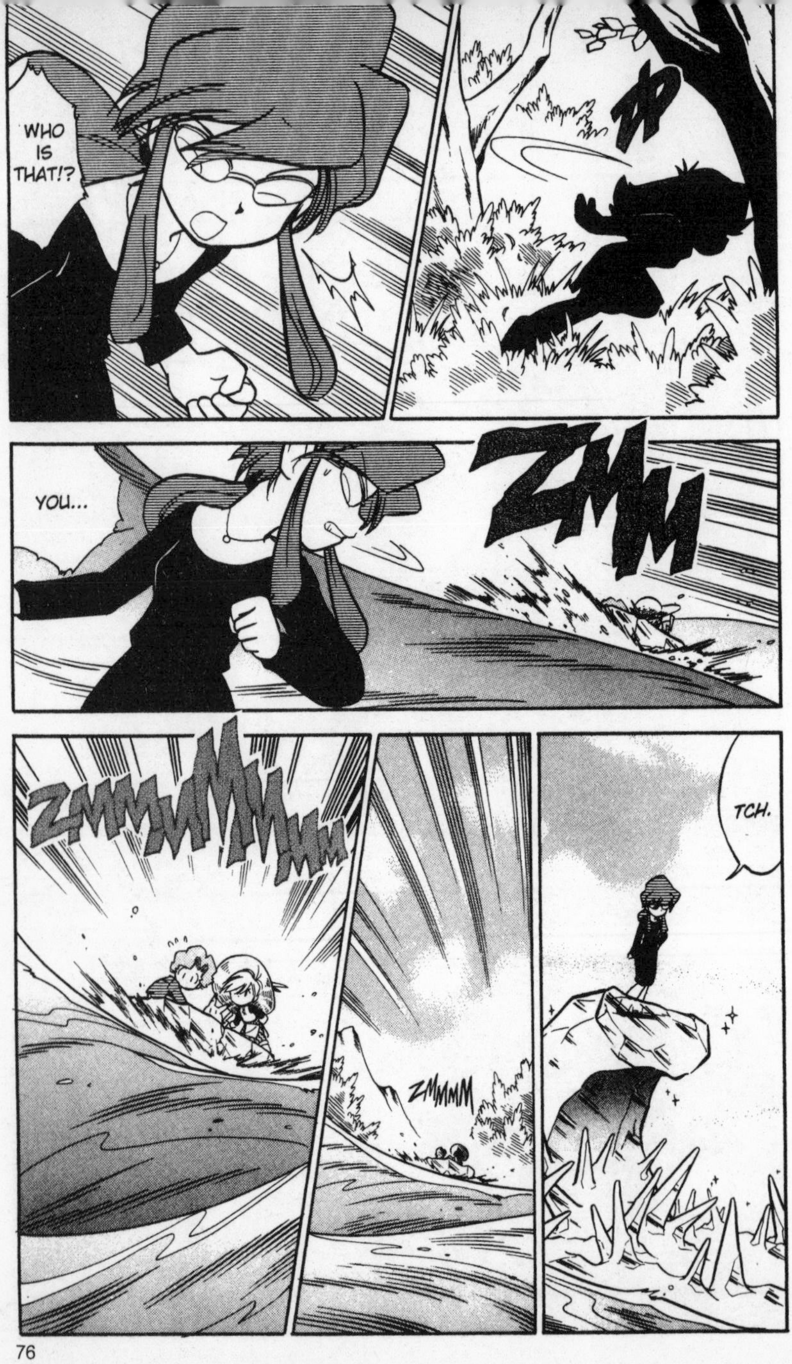
WHO IS THAT!?
ZIP
YOU...
ZMM
ZMMMMMMMM
ZMMMM
TCH.

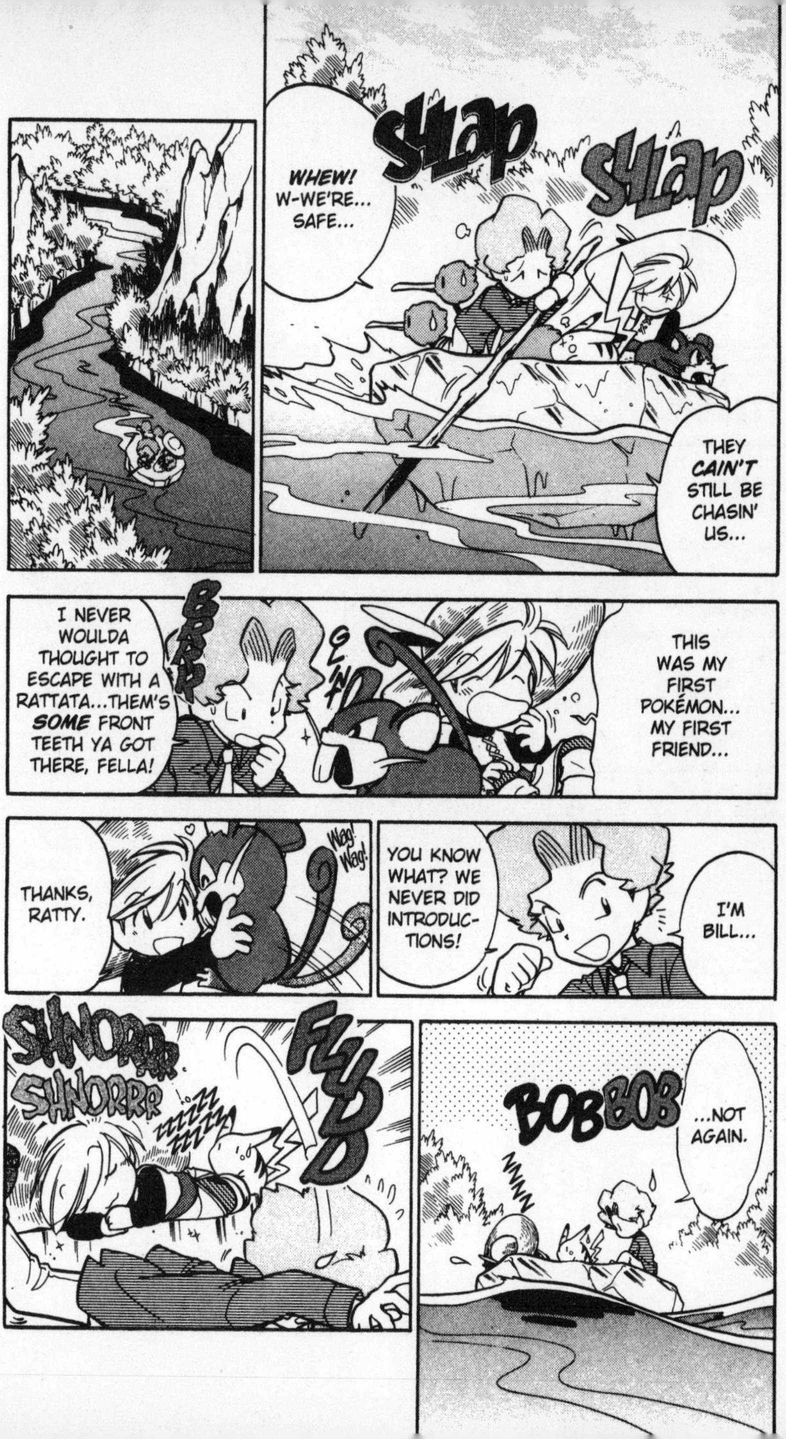

WHEW! W-WE'RE... SAFE...
THEY CAIN'T STILL BE CHASIN' US...
I NEVER WOULDA THOUGHT TO ESCAPE WITH A RATTATA...THEM'S SOME FRONT TEETH YA GOT THERE, FELLA!
THIS WAS MY FIRST POKÉMON... MY FIRST FRIEND...
THANKS, RATTY.
Wag! Wag!
YOU KNOW WHAT? WE NEVER DID INTRODUC-TIONS!
I'M BILL...
SHNORRR
SHNORRR
BOB BOB
...NOT AGAIN.

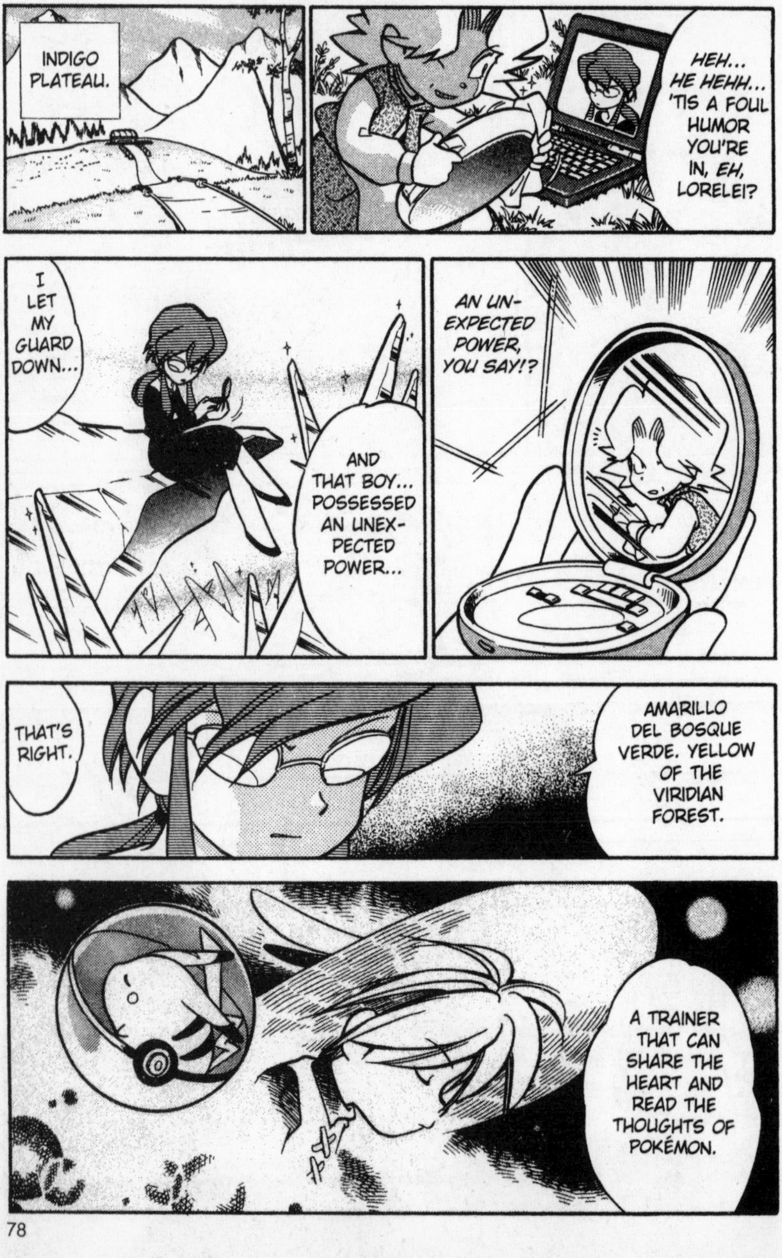
INDIGO PLATEAU.
HEH... HE HEHH... 'TIS A FOUL HUMOR YOU'RE IN, EH, LORELEI?
I LET MY GUARD DOWN...
AND THAT BOY... POSSESSED AN UNEXPECTED POWER...
AN UNEXPECTED POWER, YOU SAY!?
THAT'S RIGHT.
AMARILLO DEL BOSQUE VERDE. YELLOW OF THE VIRIDIAN FOREST.
A TRAINER THAT CAN SHARE THE HEART AND READ THE THOUGHTS OF POKÉMON.

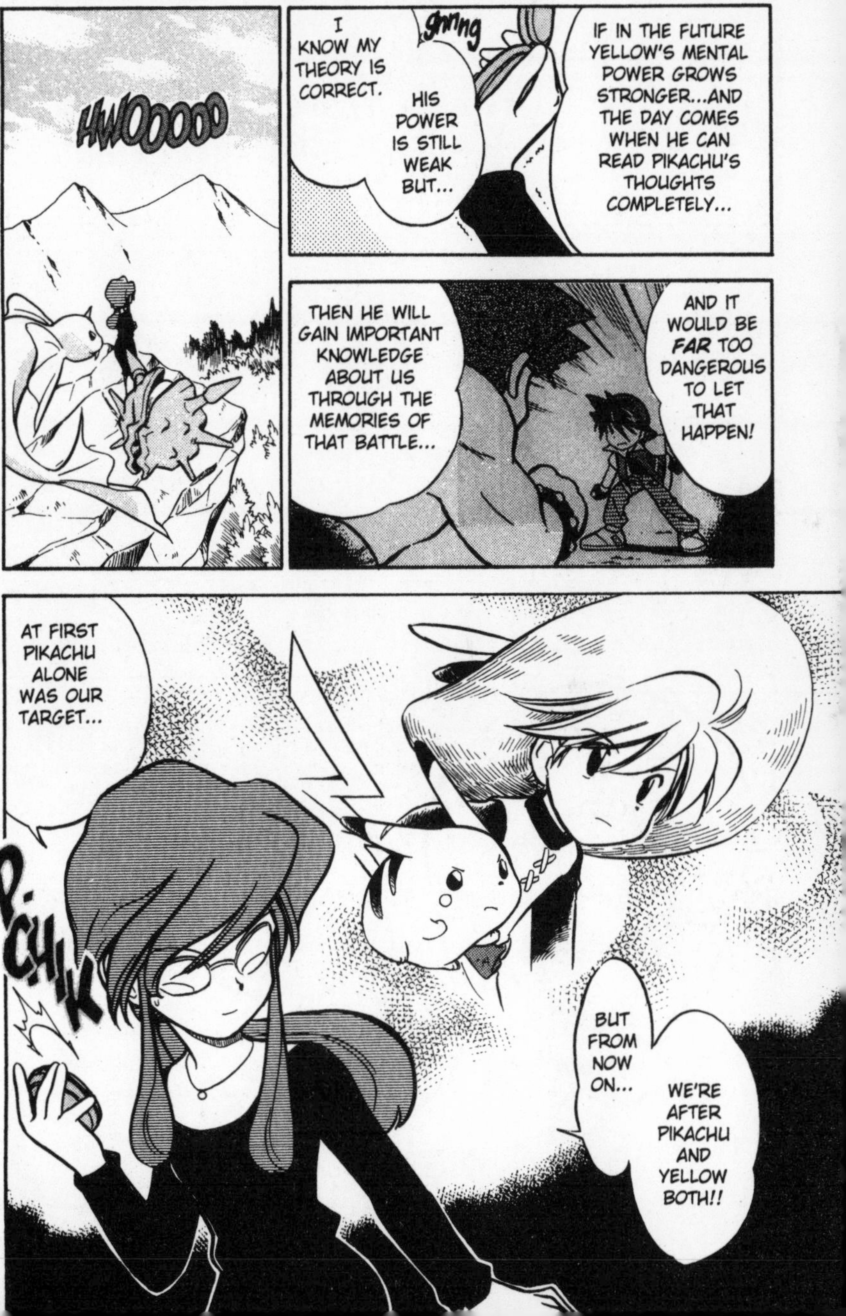
HWOOOOO
I KNOW MY THEORY IS CORRECT.
gnnng
HIS POWER IS STILL WEAK BUT...
IF IN THE FUTURE YELLOW'S MENTAL POWER GROWS STRONGER...AND THE DAY COMES WHEN HE CAN READ PIKACHU'S THOUGHTS COMPLETELY...
THEN HE WILL GAIN IMPORTANT KNOWLEDGE ABOUT US THROUGH THE MEMORIES OF THAT BATTLE...
AND IT WOULD BE **FAR** TOO DANGEROUS TO LET THAT HAPPEN!
AT FIRST PIKACHU ALONE WAS OUR TARGET...
P-CHIK
BUT FROM NOW ON...
WE'RE AFTER PIKACHU AND YELLOW BOTH!!

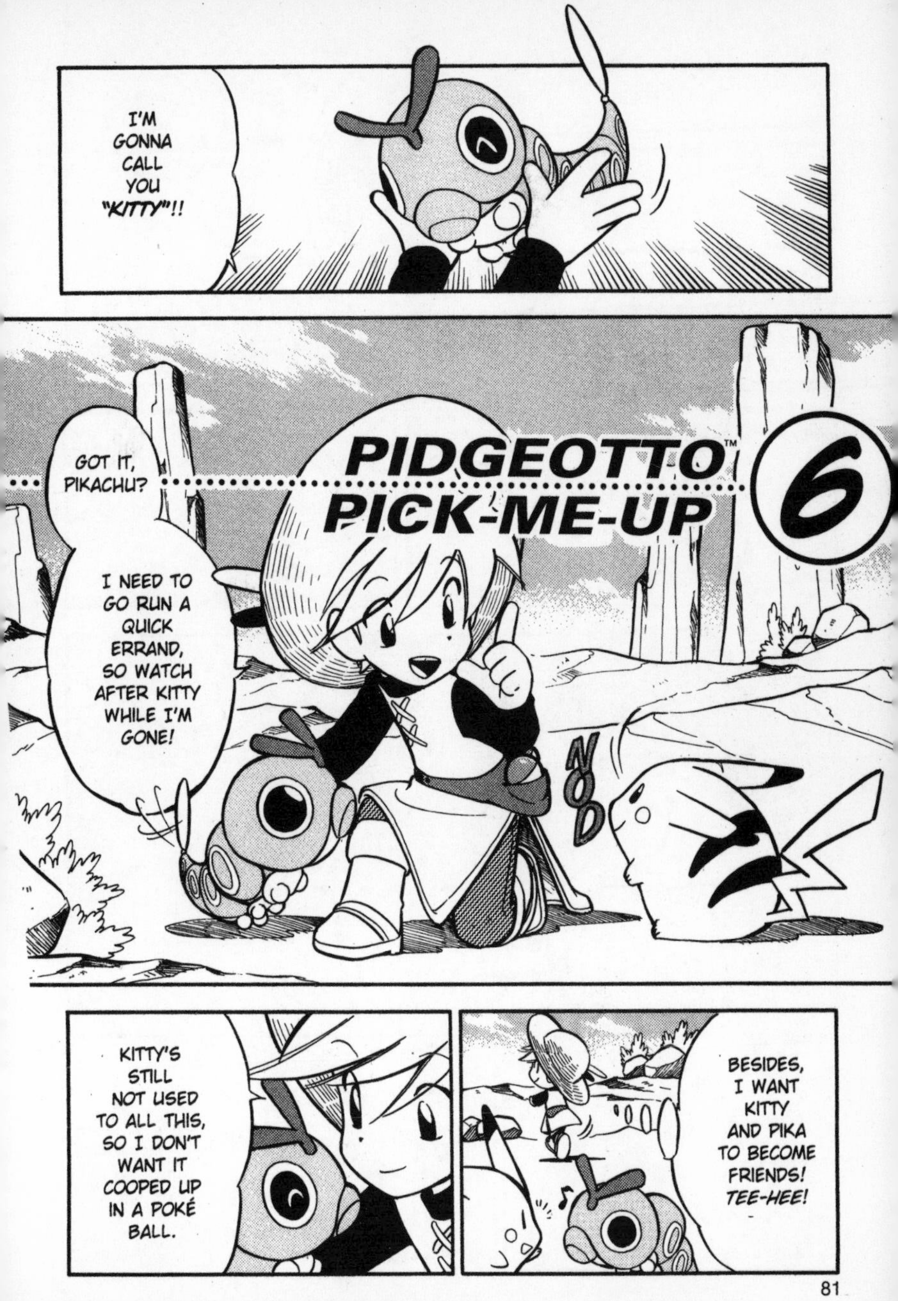

I'M GONNA CALL YOU "KITTY"!!
PIDGEOTTO PICK-ME-UP
6
GOT IT, PIKACHU?
I NEED TO GO RUN A QUICK ERRAND, SO WATCH AFTER KITTY WHILE I'M GONE!
NOD
KITTY'S STILL NOT USED TO ALL THIS, SO I DON'T WANT IT COOPED UP IN A POKÉ BALL.
BESIDES, I WANT KITTY AND PIKA TO BECOME FRIENDS! TEE-HEE!

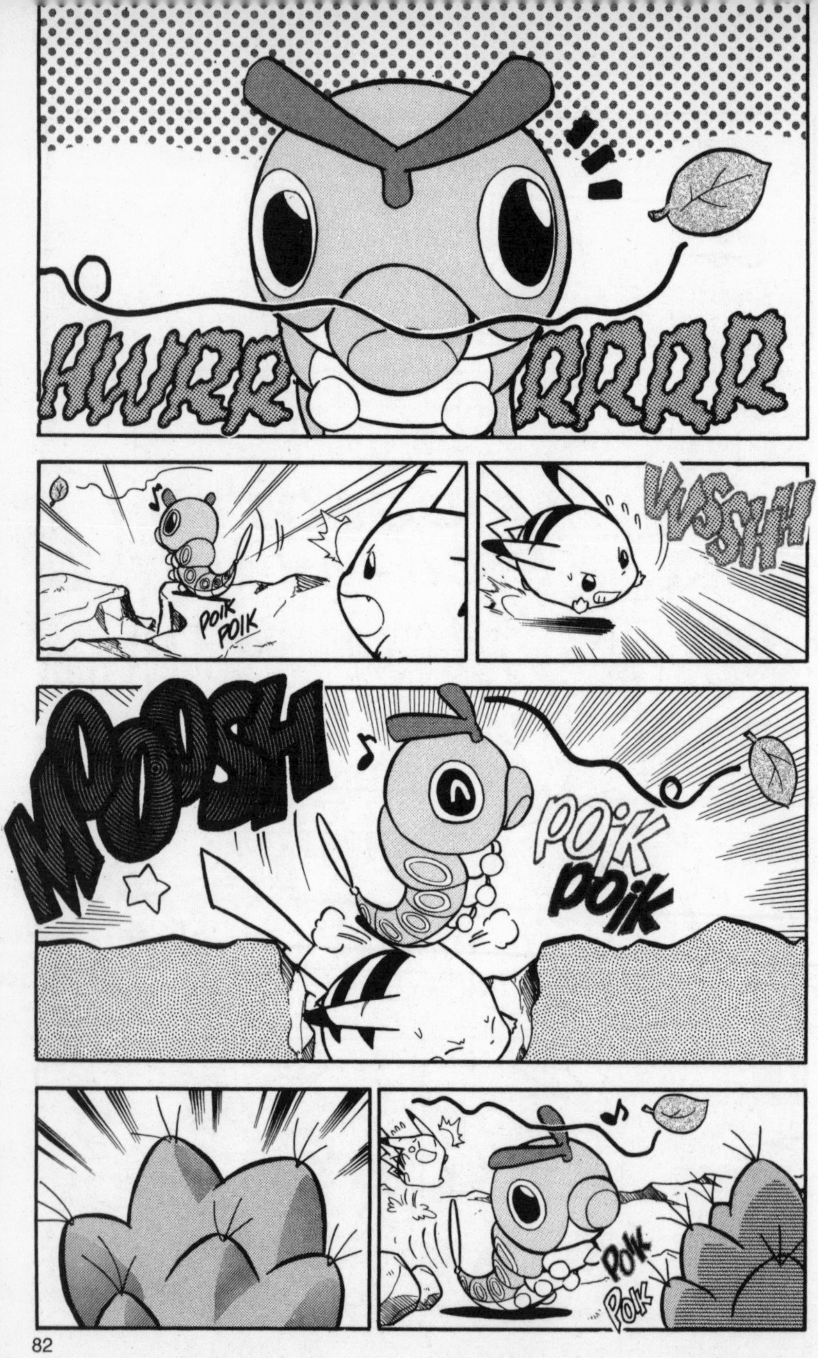
HWURR RRRR
POIK POIK
WSSH
WOOSH
POIK POIK
POIK POIK

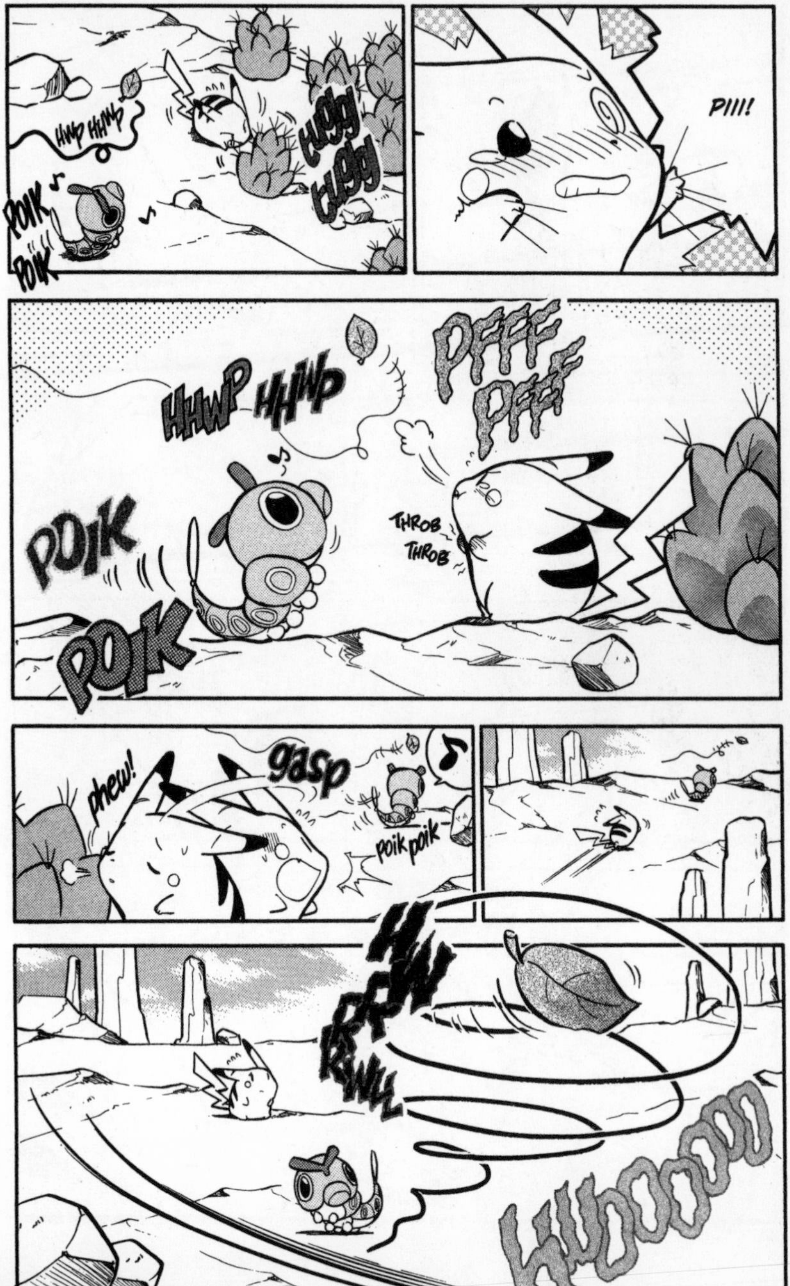
HHWP HHWP
POIK
POIK
tugg tugg
PIII!
HHWP HHWP
PFFF PFFF
POIK
POIK
THROB
THROB
phew!
gasp
poik poik
HWRRRWLL
HUOOOOO

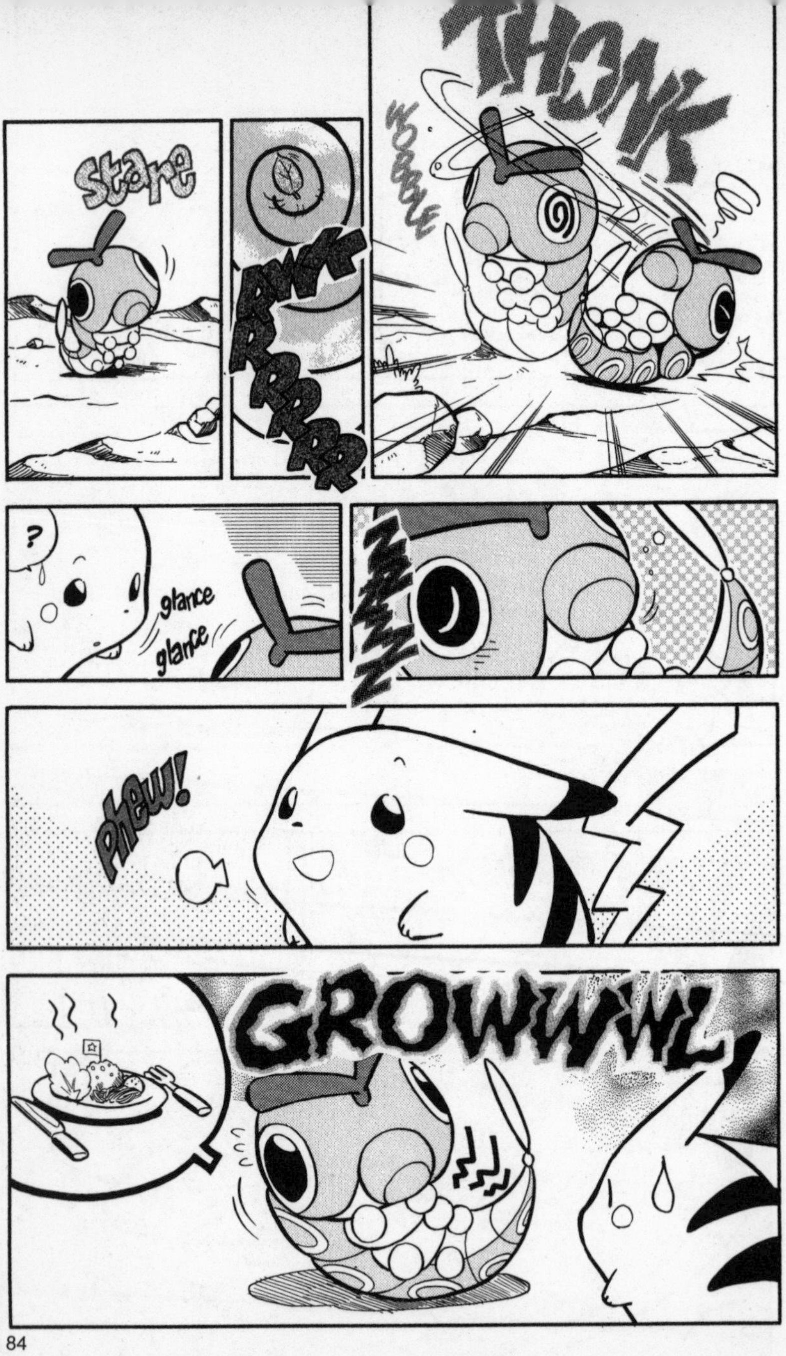

Stare
AWK
RRRRR
THONK
WOBBLE
?
glance
glance
NNNNN
phew!
GROWWWL

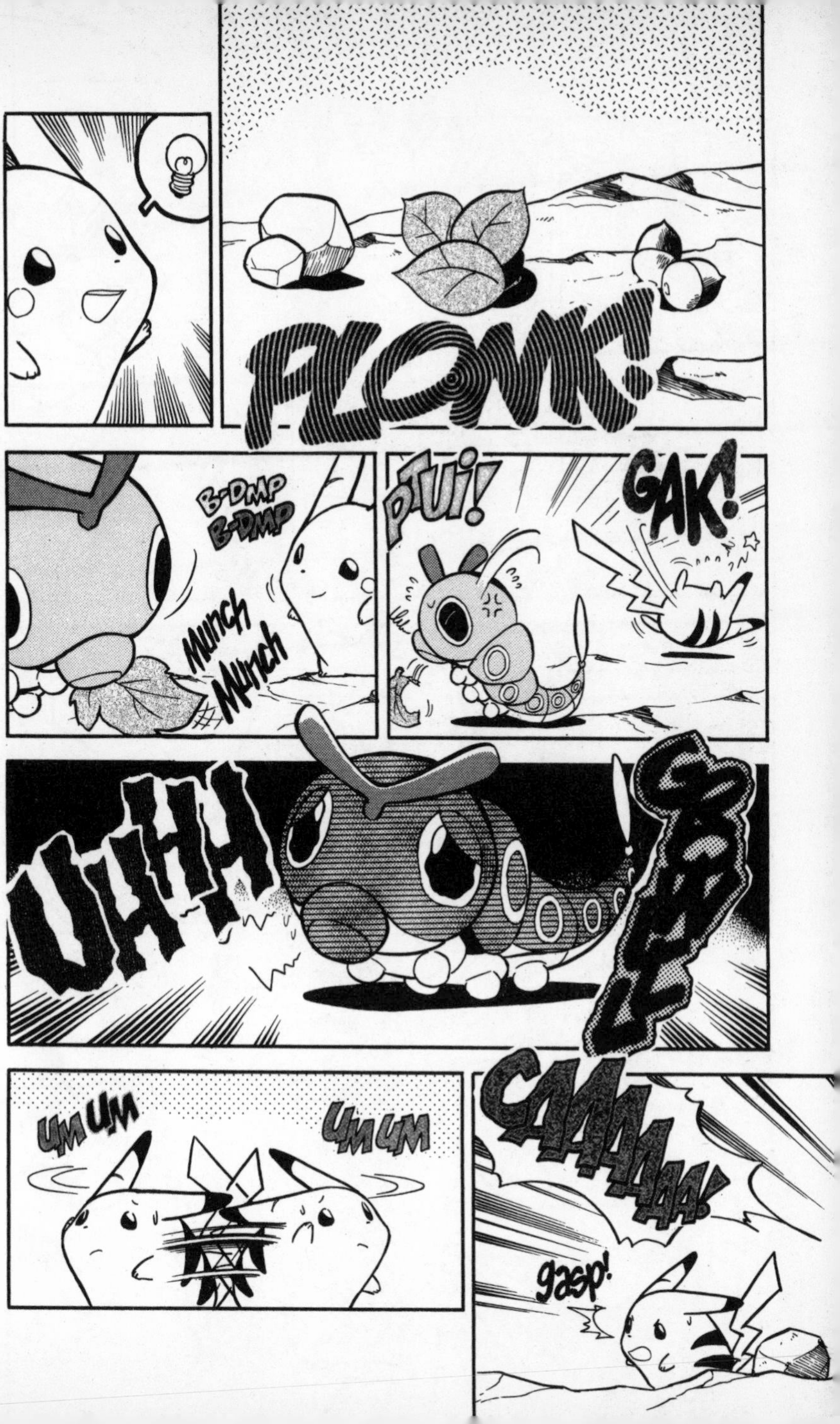
PLONK!
B-DMP
B-DMP
Munch
Munch
PTUI!
GAK!
UHH
UM UM
UM UM
CAAAAAA!
gasp!

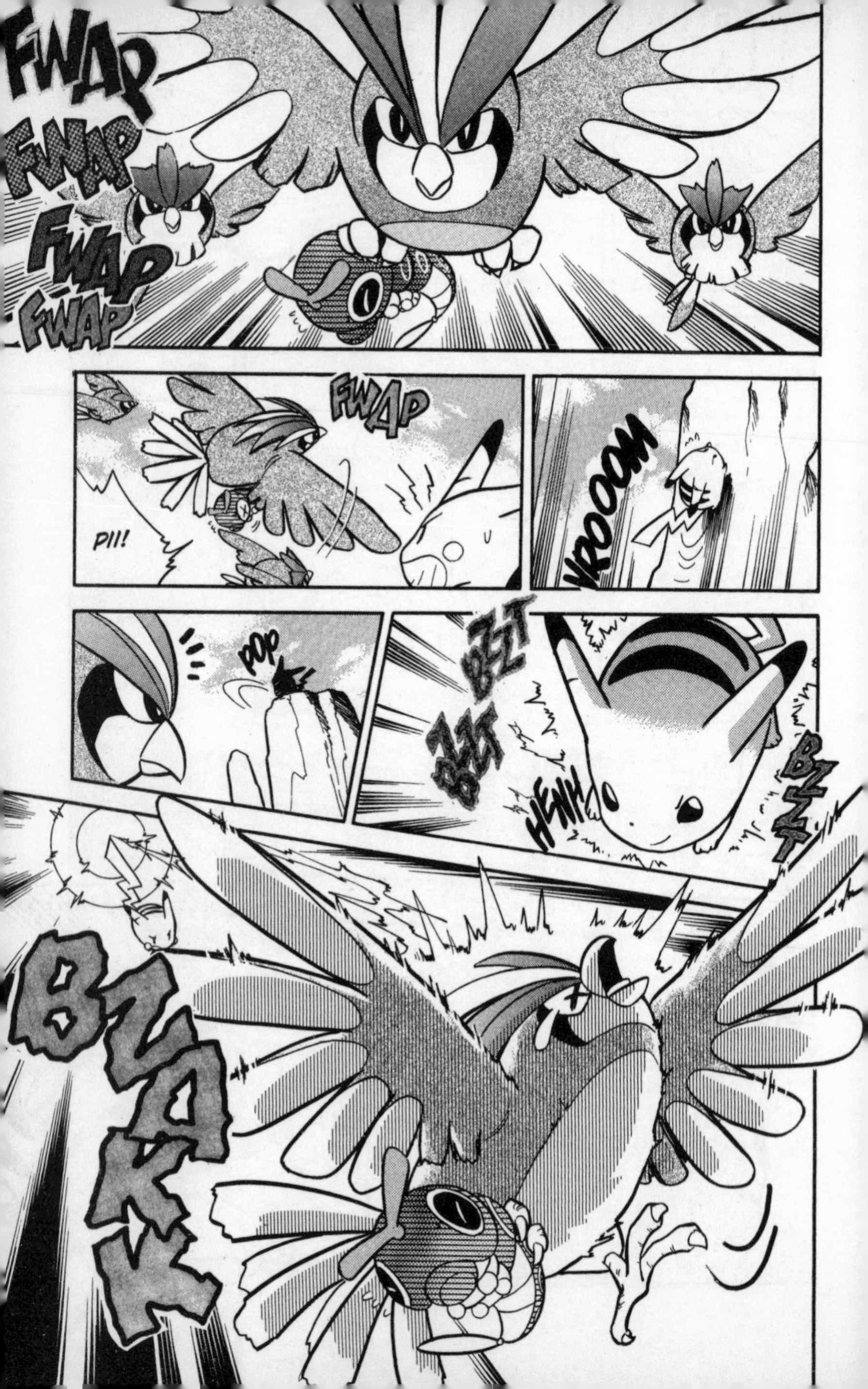
FWAP
FWAP
FWAP
FWAP
FWAP
PII!
VROOOOM
POP
BZZT
BZZT
HENH
BZZT
BZAKK

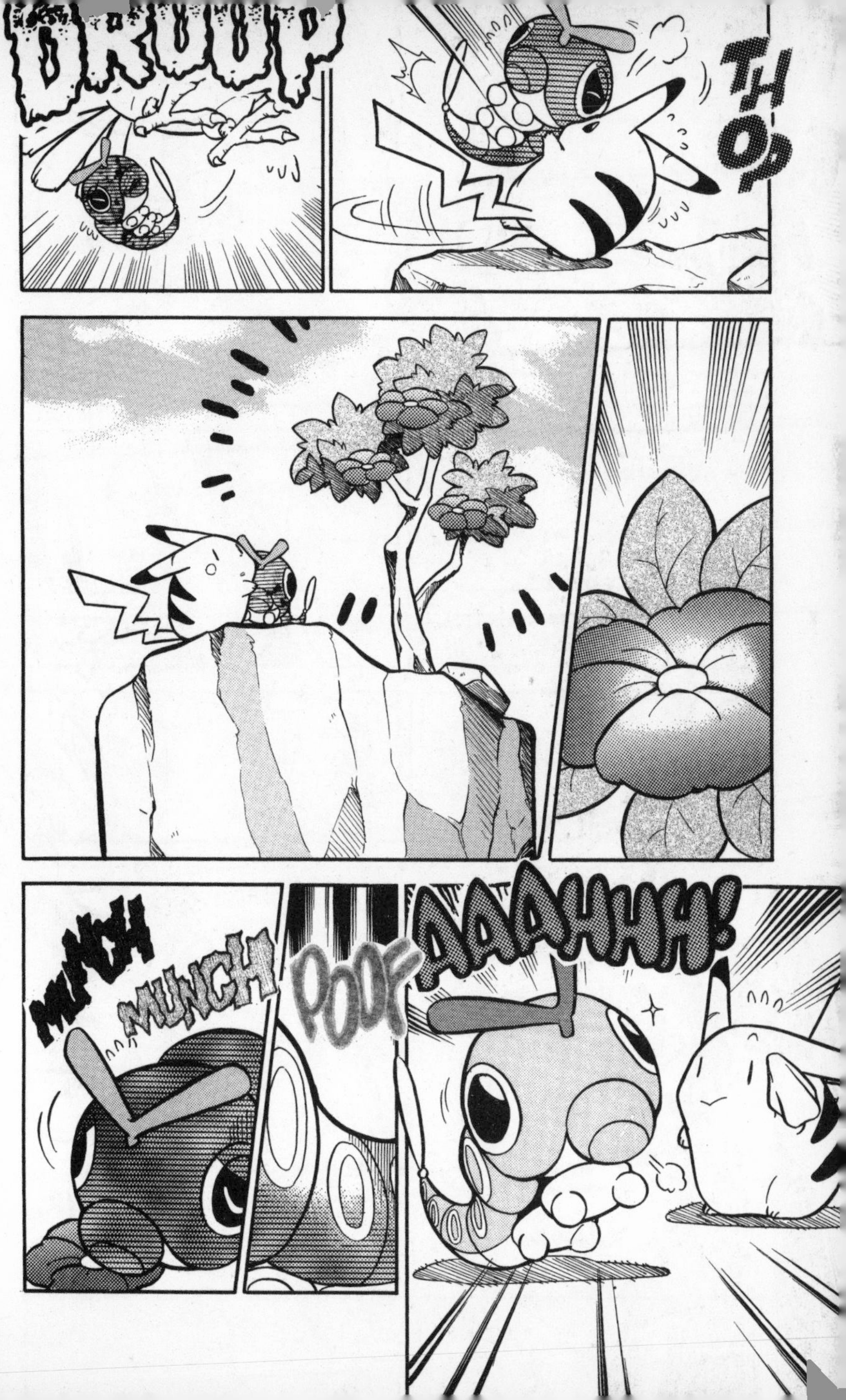
DROOP
THOP
MUNCH
MUNCH
POOF
AAAHHH!

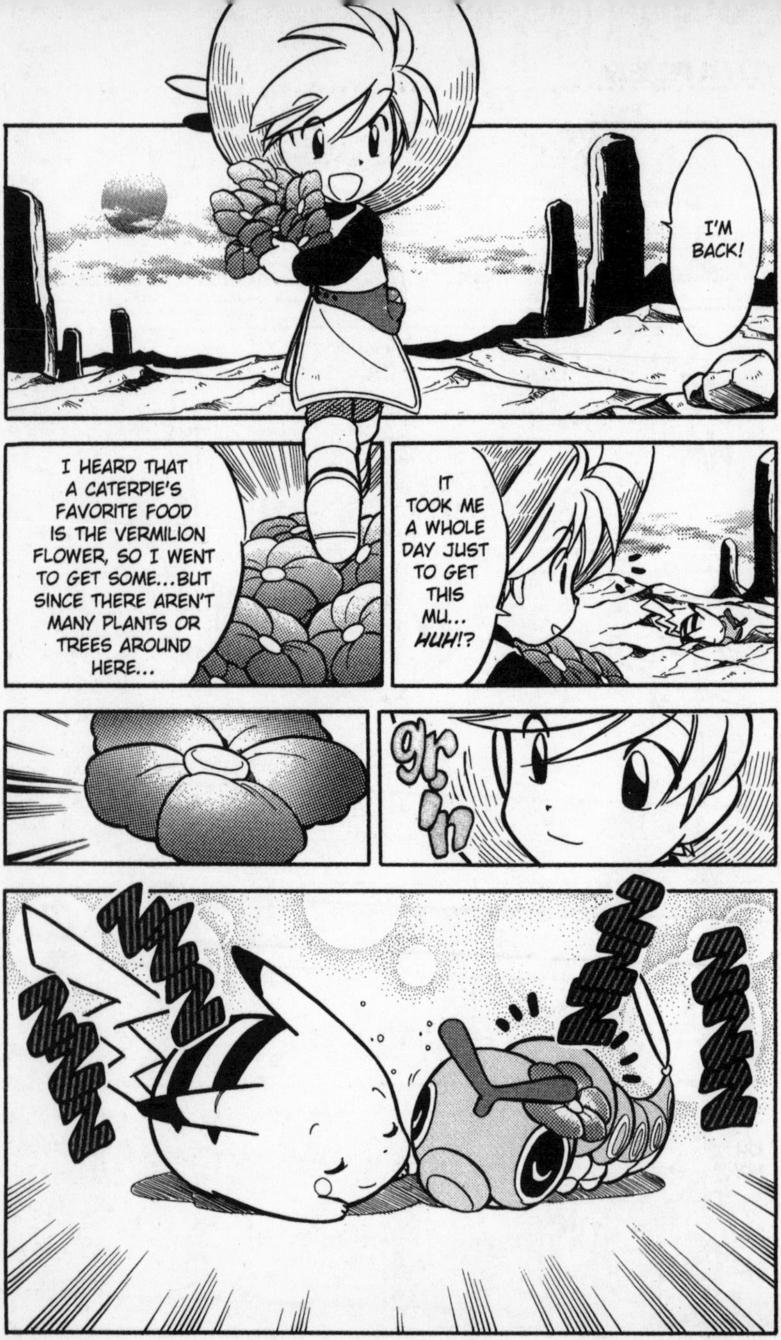
I'M BACK!
I HEARD THAT A CATERPIE'S FAVORITE FOOD IS THE VERMILION FLOWER, SO I WENT TO GET SOME...BUT SINCE THERE AREN'T MANY PLANTS OR TREES AROUND HERE...
IT TOOK ME A WHOLE DAY JUST TO GET THIS MU... HUH!?
grin

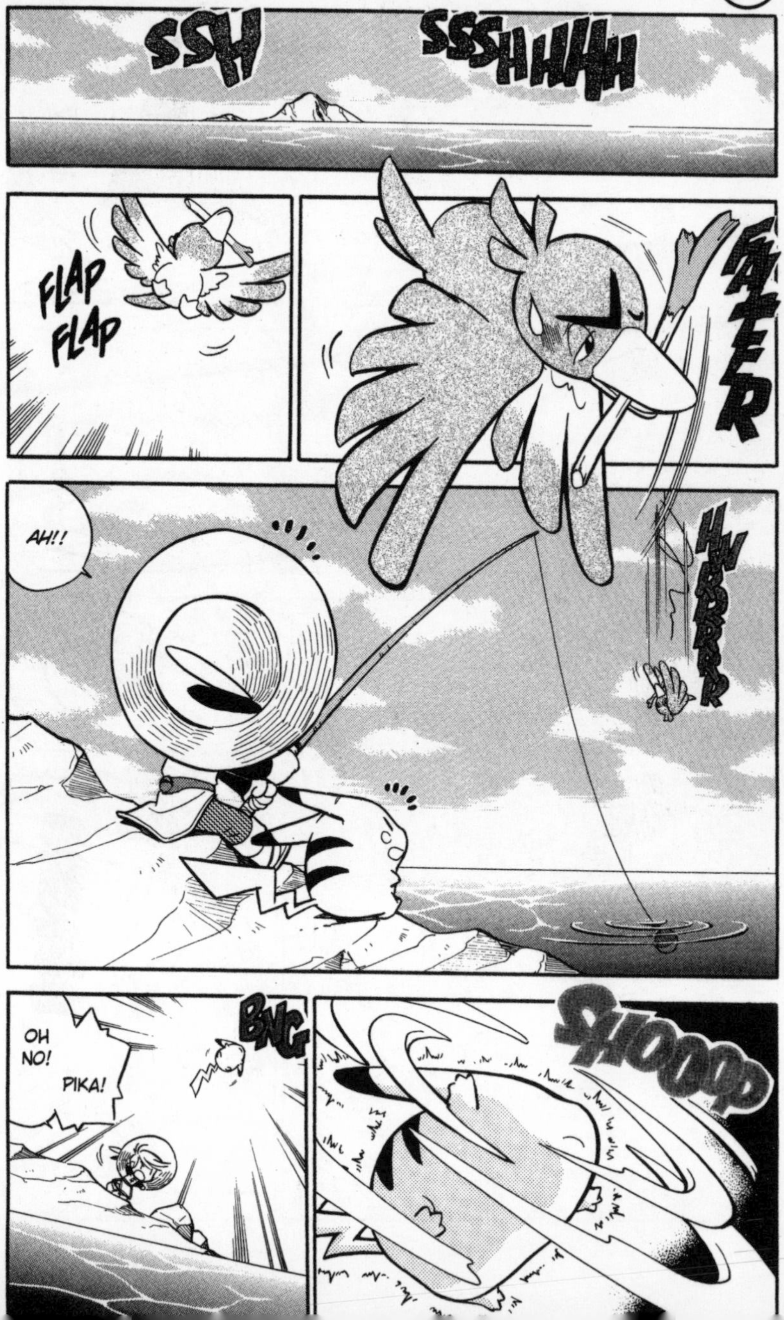
SSH
SSSHHHHH
FLAP
FLAP
FALTER
AH!!
HWRRRRR
BNG
OH NO!
PIKA!
SHOOOP

EXTRICATED FROM EXEGGUTOR™

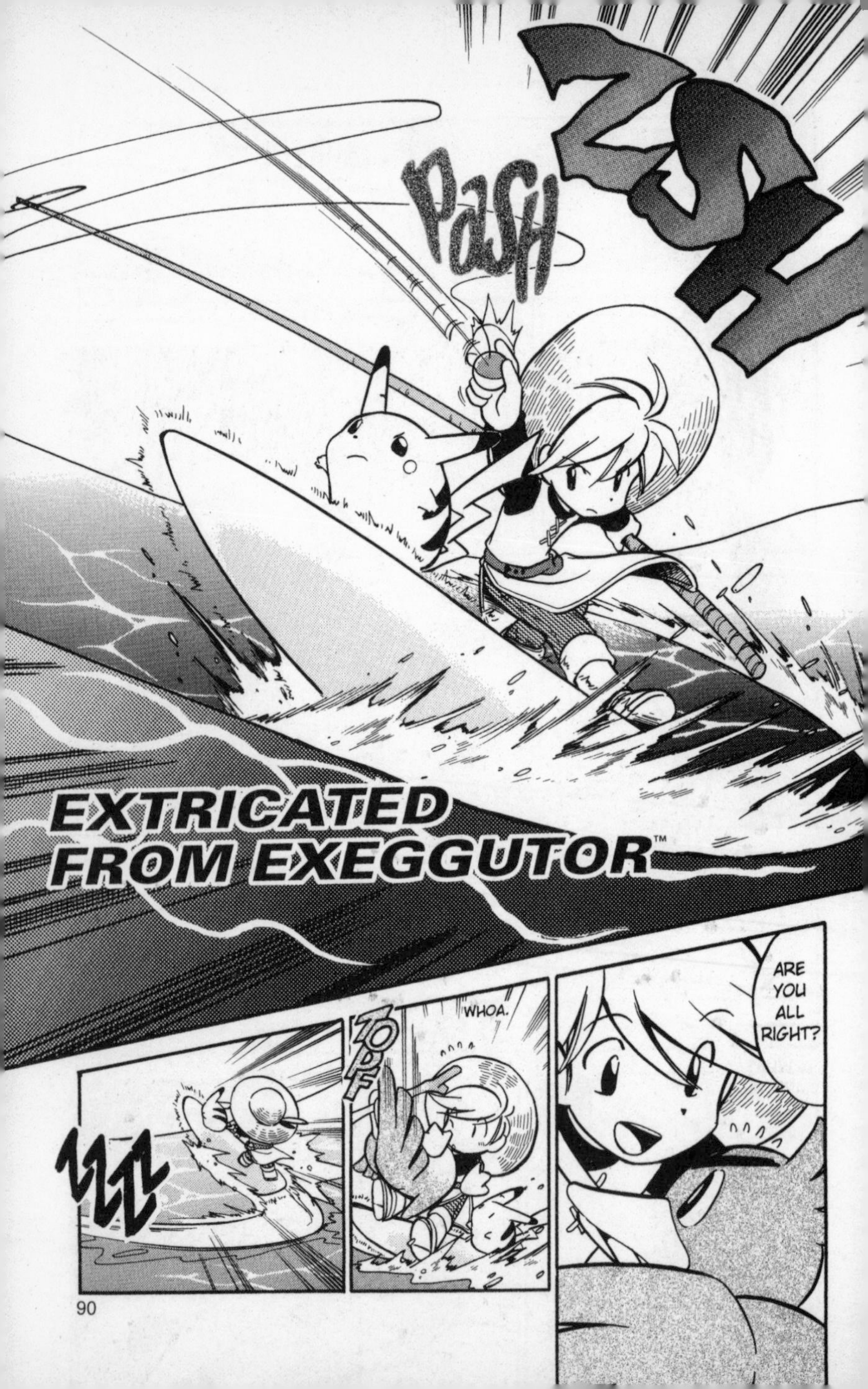
ZASH
PASH
WHOA.
ARE YOU ALL RIGHT?

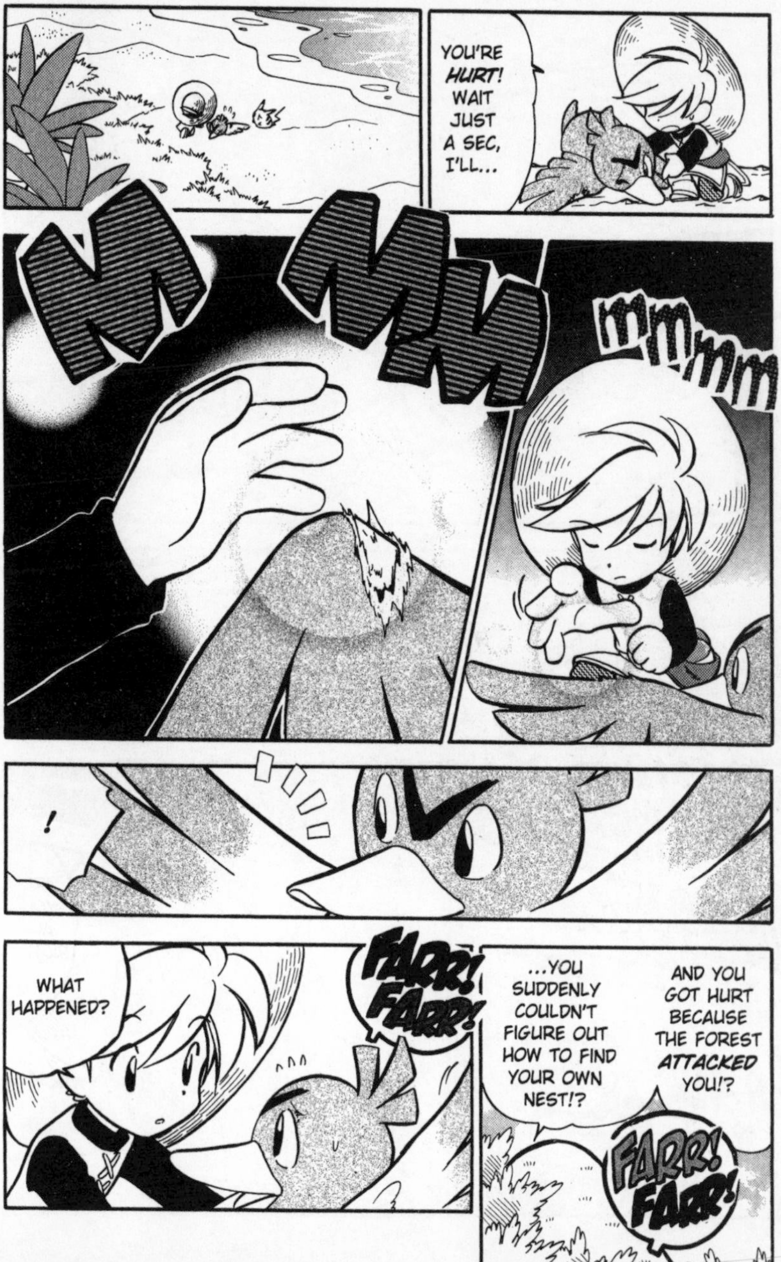
YOU'RE HURT! WAIT JUST A SEC, I'LL...
MMMM
mmmmm
!
WHAT HAPPENED?
FARR! FARR!
...YOU SUDDENLY COULDN'T FIGURE OUT HOW TO FIND YOUR OWN NEST!?
AND YOU GOT HURT BECAUSE THE FOREST ATTACKED YOU!?
FARR! FARR!

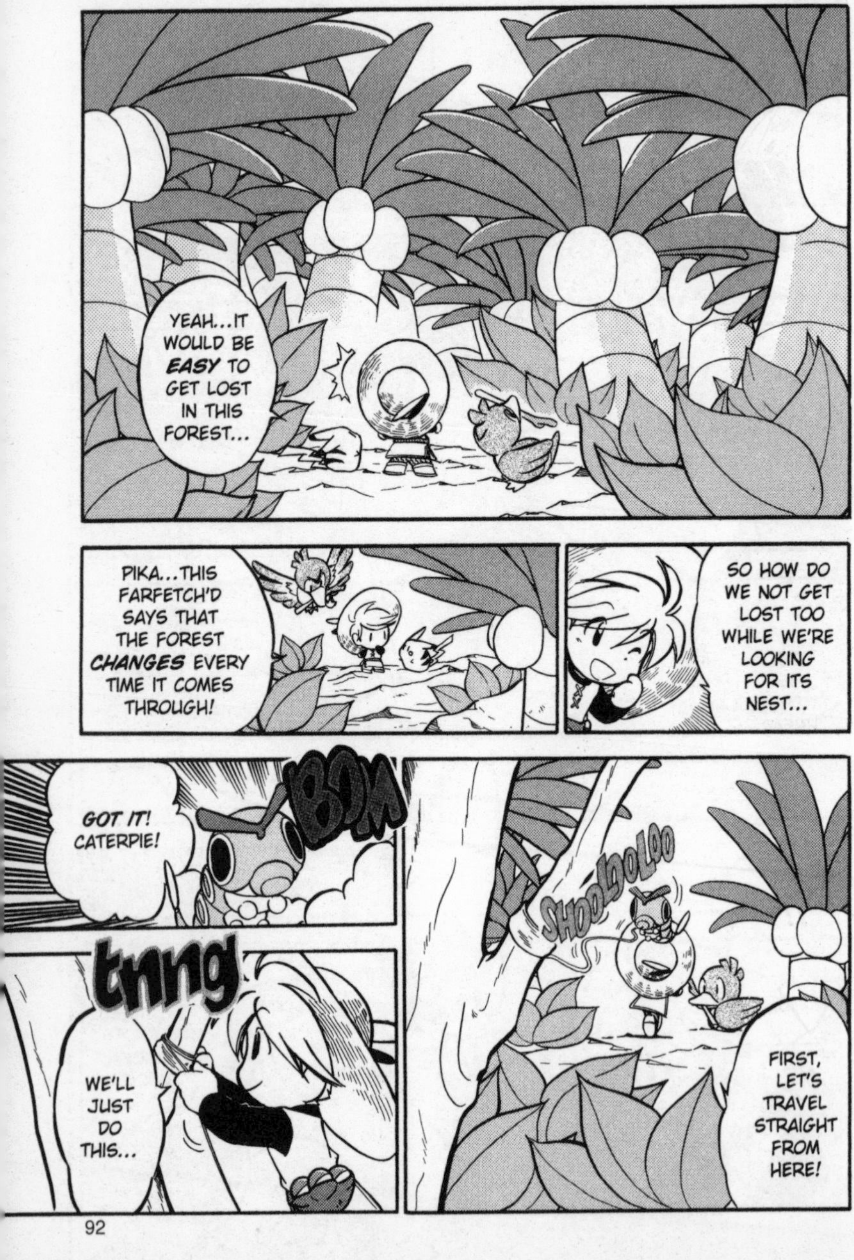
YEAH...IT WOULD BE *EASY* TO GET LOST IN THIS FOREST...
PIKA...THIS FARFETCH'D SAYS THAT THE FOREST *CHANGES* EVERY TIME IT COMES THROUGH!
SO HOW DO WE NOT GET LOST TOO WHILE WE'RE LOOKING FOR ITS NEST...
GOT IT! CATERPIE!
BOM
tnng
WE'LL JUST DO THIS...
SHOOLOOLOO
FIRST, LET'S TRAVEL STRAIGHT FROM HERE!

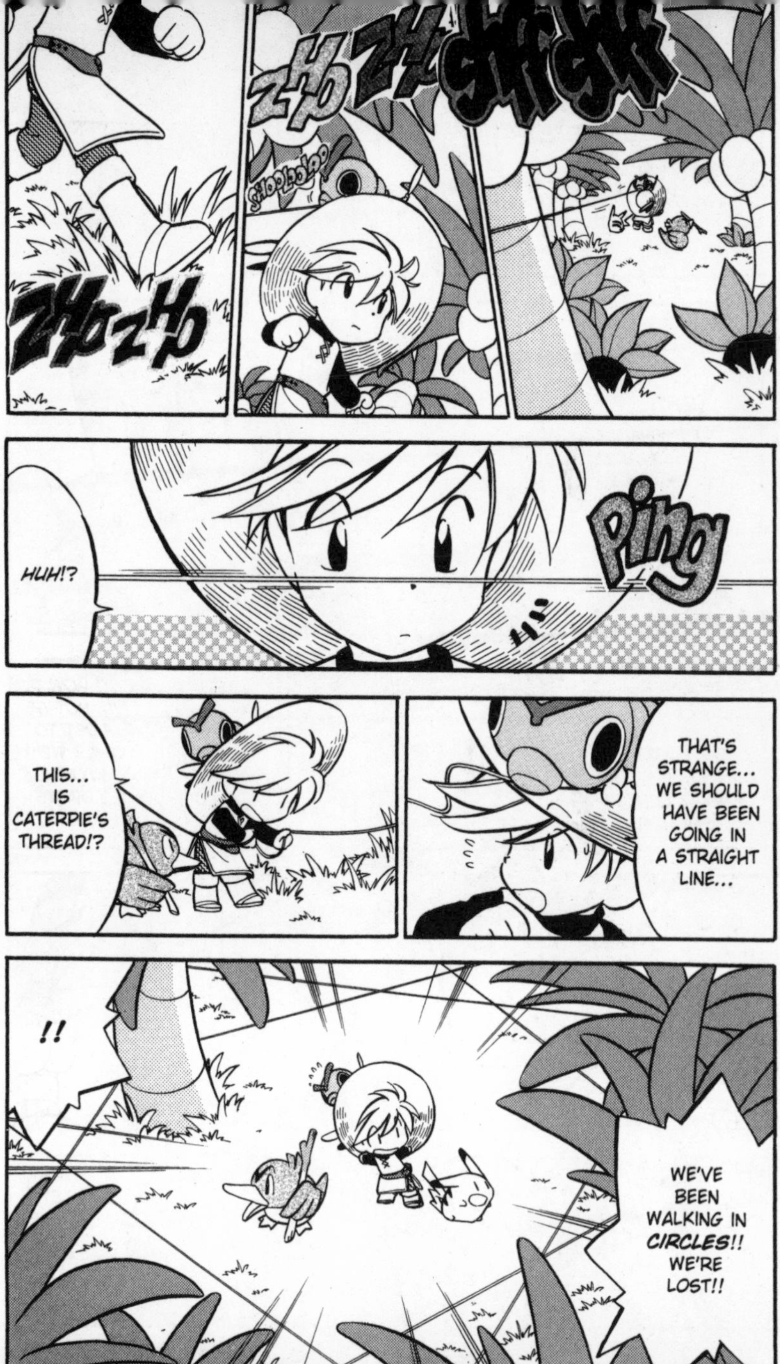
ZHO ZHO
ZHO ZHO
SHOOLOOLOO
ZHO ZHO
HUH!?
PING
THIS... IS CATERPIE'S THREAD!?
THAT'S STRANGE... WE SHOULD HAVE BEEN GOING IN A STRAIGHT LINE...
!!
WE'VE BEEN WALKING IN *CIRCLES*!! WE'RE LOST!!

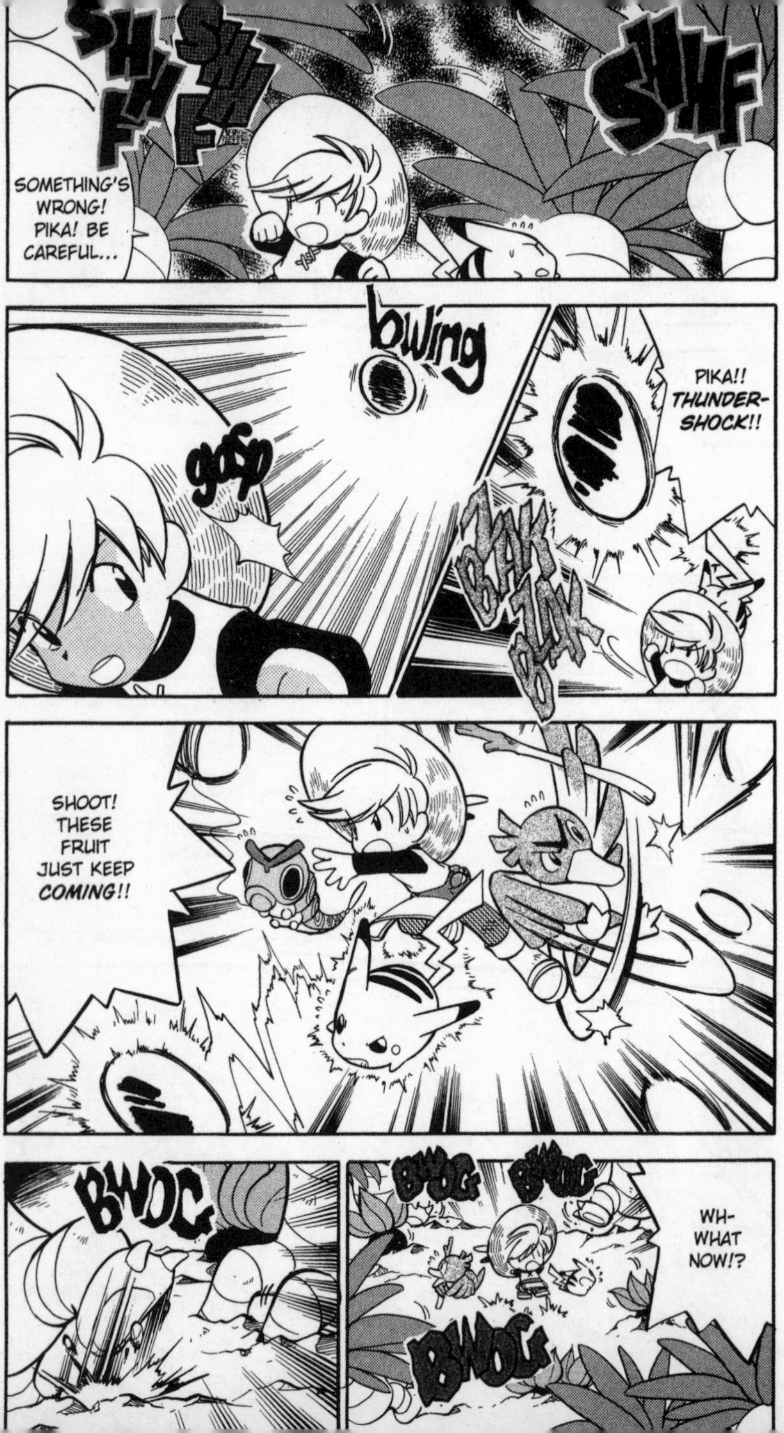
SOMETHING'S WRONG! PIKA! BE CAREFUL...
bwing
gasp
PIKA!! THUNDER-SHOCK!!
SHOOT! THESE FRUIT JUST KEEP COMING!!
BWOC
WH- WHAT NOW!?

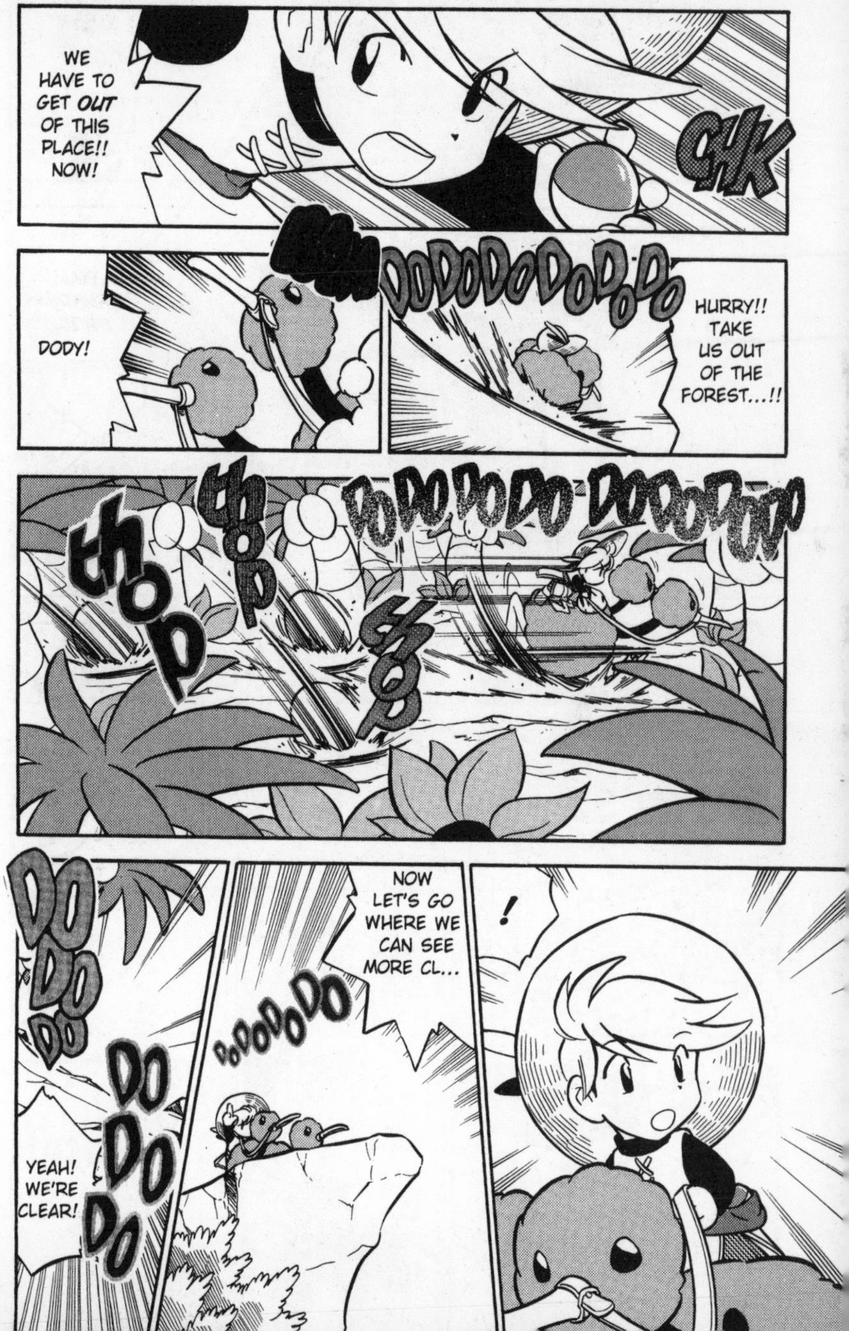
WE HAVE TO GET OUT OF THIS PLACE!! NOW!
CHK
DODY!
DODODODODODODO
HURRY!! TAKE US OUT OF THE FOREST...!!
thop
thop
DODODODODO DODODODO
thop
DODODODO
DODODODO
YEAH! WE'RE CLEAR!
DODODODO
DODODODODO
NOW LET'S GO WHERE WE CAN SEE MORE CL...
!

ZZZH ZZZH ZZZH ZZZH

!!

THE... THE FOREST... IT'S *MOVING!!*

NO... THAT'S NOT IT!!

P!P

WHAT WE THOUGHT WAS A FOREST...IS REALLY A MASS OF.....

DODODODODO

EXEG-GUTOR...

AND ODDISH!!

.....

SSSSHHHH

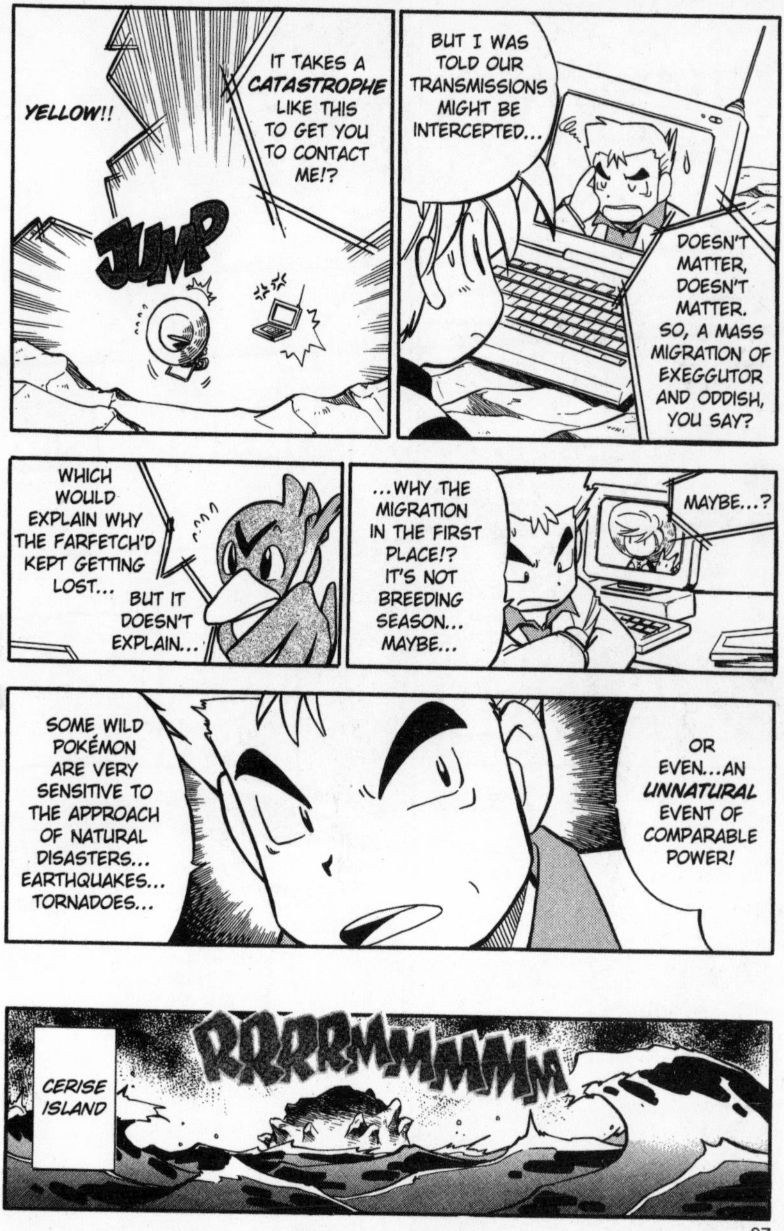

YELLOW!!
IT TAKES A CATASTROPHE LIKE THIS TO GET YOU TO CONTACT ME!?
JUMP
BUT I WAS TOLD OUR TRANSMISSIONS MIGHT BE INTERCEPTED...
DOESN'T MATTER, DOESN'T MATTER. SO, A MASS MIGRATION OF EXEGGUTOR AND ODDISH, YOU SAY?
WHICH WOULD EXPLAIN WHY THE FARFETCH'D KEPT GETTING LOST...
BUT IT DOESN'T EXPLAIN...
...WHY THE MIGRATION IN THE FIRST PLACE!? IT'S NOT BREEDING SEASON... MAYBE...
MAYBE...?
SOME WILD POKÉMON ARE VERY SENSITIVE TO THE APPROACH OF NATURAL DISASTERS... EARTHQUAKES... TORNADOES...
OR EVEN...AN UNNATURAL EVENT OF COMPARABLE POWER!
CERISE ISLAND
RRRRMMMMMM

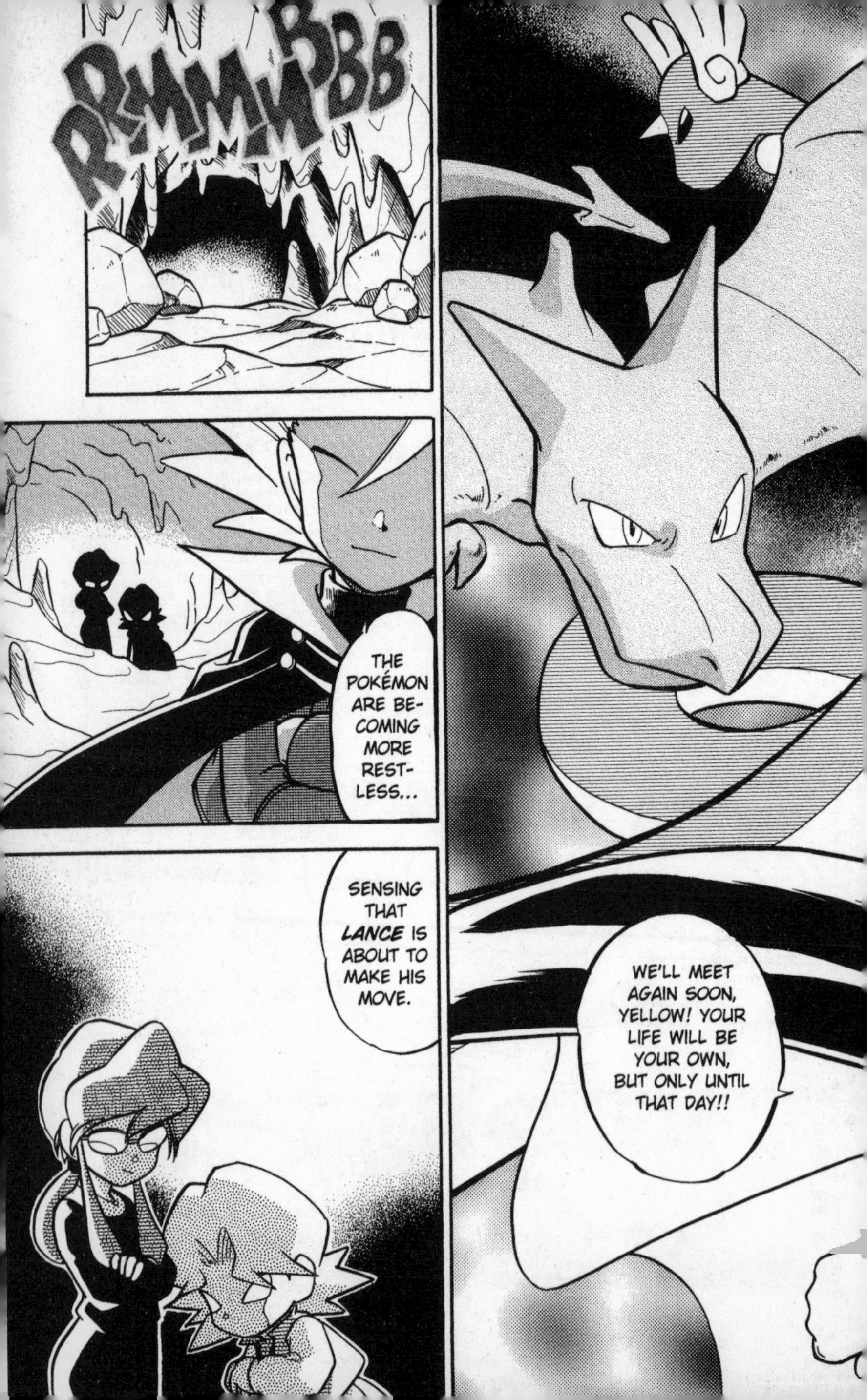
WE'LL MEET AGAIN SOON, YELLOW! YOUR LIFE WILL BE YOUR OWN, BUT ONLY UNTIL THAT DAY!!
THE POKÉMON ARE BE-COMING MORE REST-LESS...
SENSING THAT LANCE IS ABOUT TO MAKE HIS MOVE.

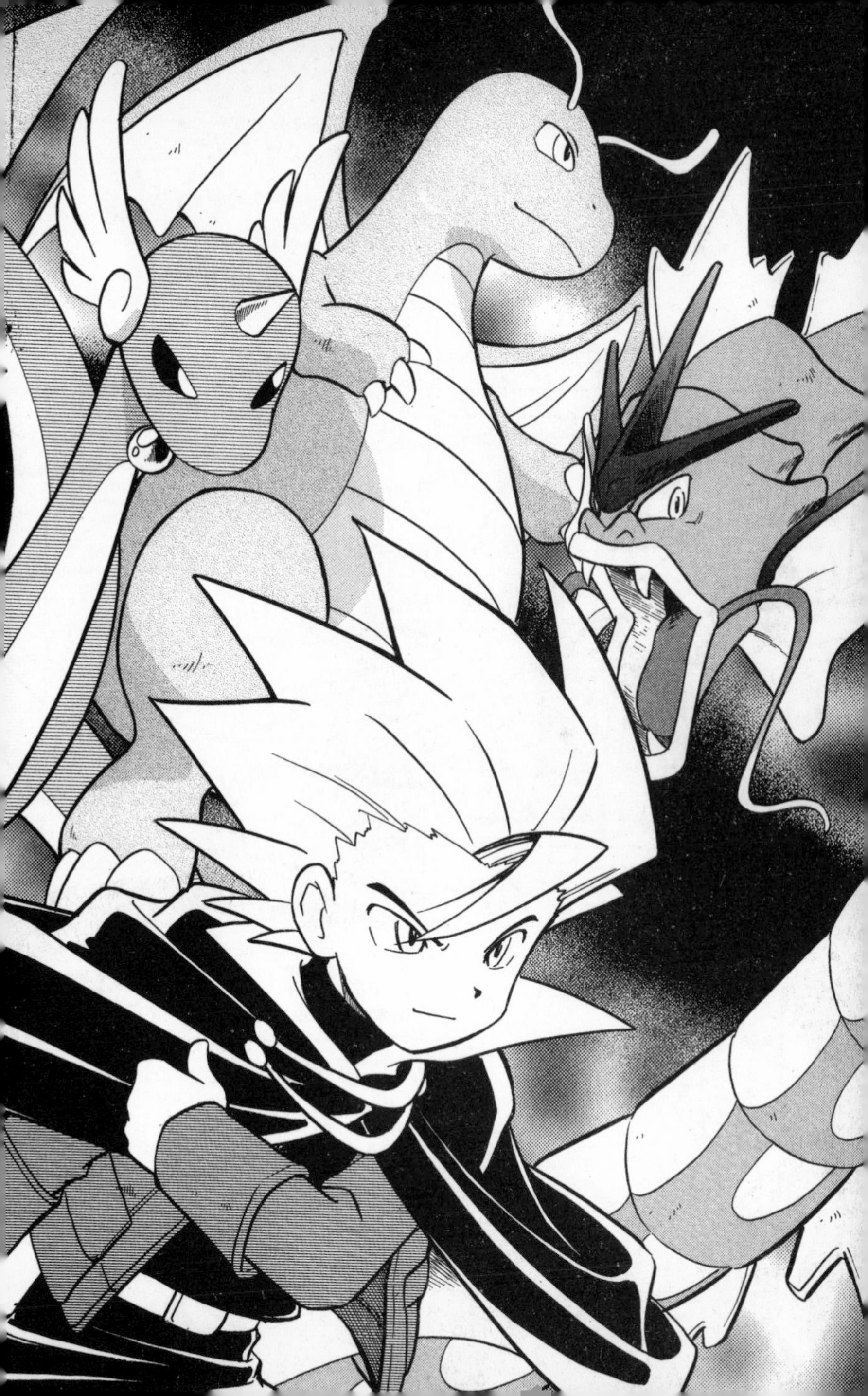

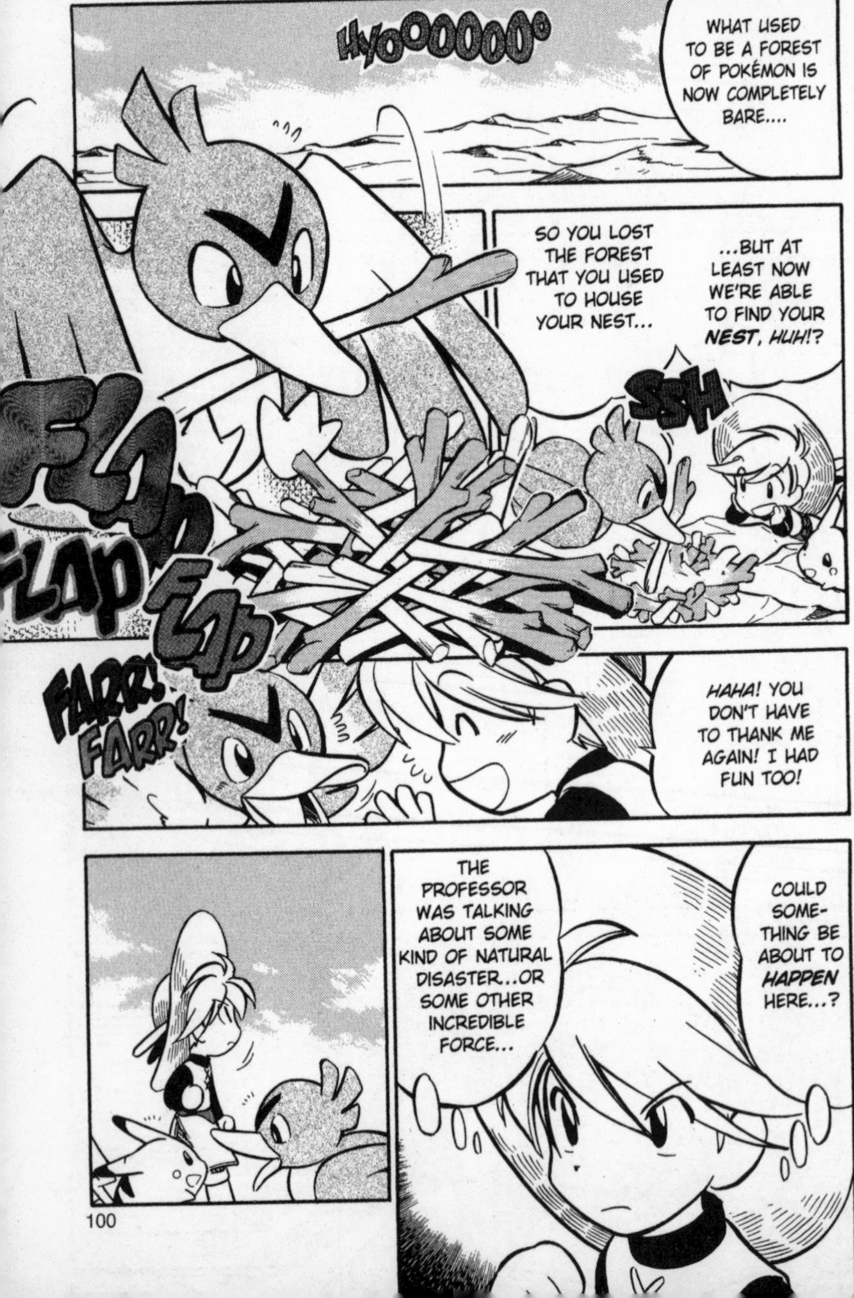
WHAT USED TO BE A FOREST OF POKÉMON IS NOW COMPLETELY BARE....
HYOOOOOOO
SO YOU LOST THE FOREST THAT YOU USED TO HOUSE YOUR NEST...
...BUT AT LEAST NOW WE'RE ABLE TO FIND YOUR NEST, HUH!?
SSH
FLAP FLAP FLAP
FARR! FARR!
HAHA! YOU DON'T HAVE TO THANK ME AGAIN! I HAD FUN TOO!
COULD SOMETHING BE ABOUT TO HAPPEN HERE...?
THE PROFESSOR WAS TALKING ABOUT SOME KIND OF NATURAL DISASTER...OR SOME OTHER INCREDIBLE FORCE...

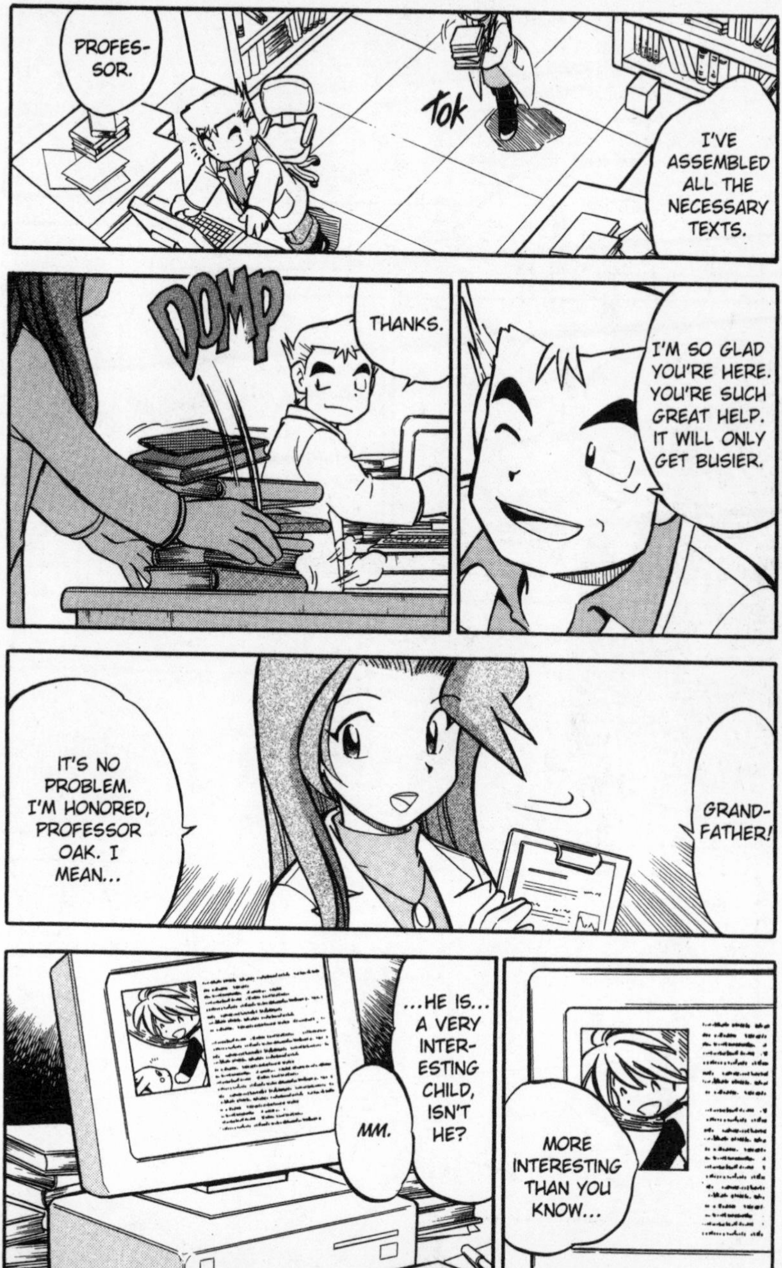
PROFES-SOR.
TOK
I'VE ASSEMBLED ALL THE NECESSARY TEXTS.
DOMP
THANKS.
I'M SO GLAD YOU'RE HERE. YOU'RE SUCH GREAT HELP. IT WILL ONLY GET BUSIER.
IT'S NO PROBLEM. I'M HONORED, PROFESSOR OAK. I MEAN...
GRAND-FATHER!
...HE IS... A VERY INTER-ESTING CHILD, ISN'T HE?
MM.
MORE INTERESTING THAN YOU KNOW...

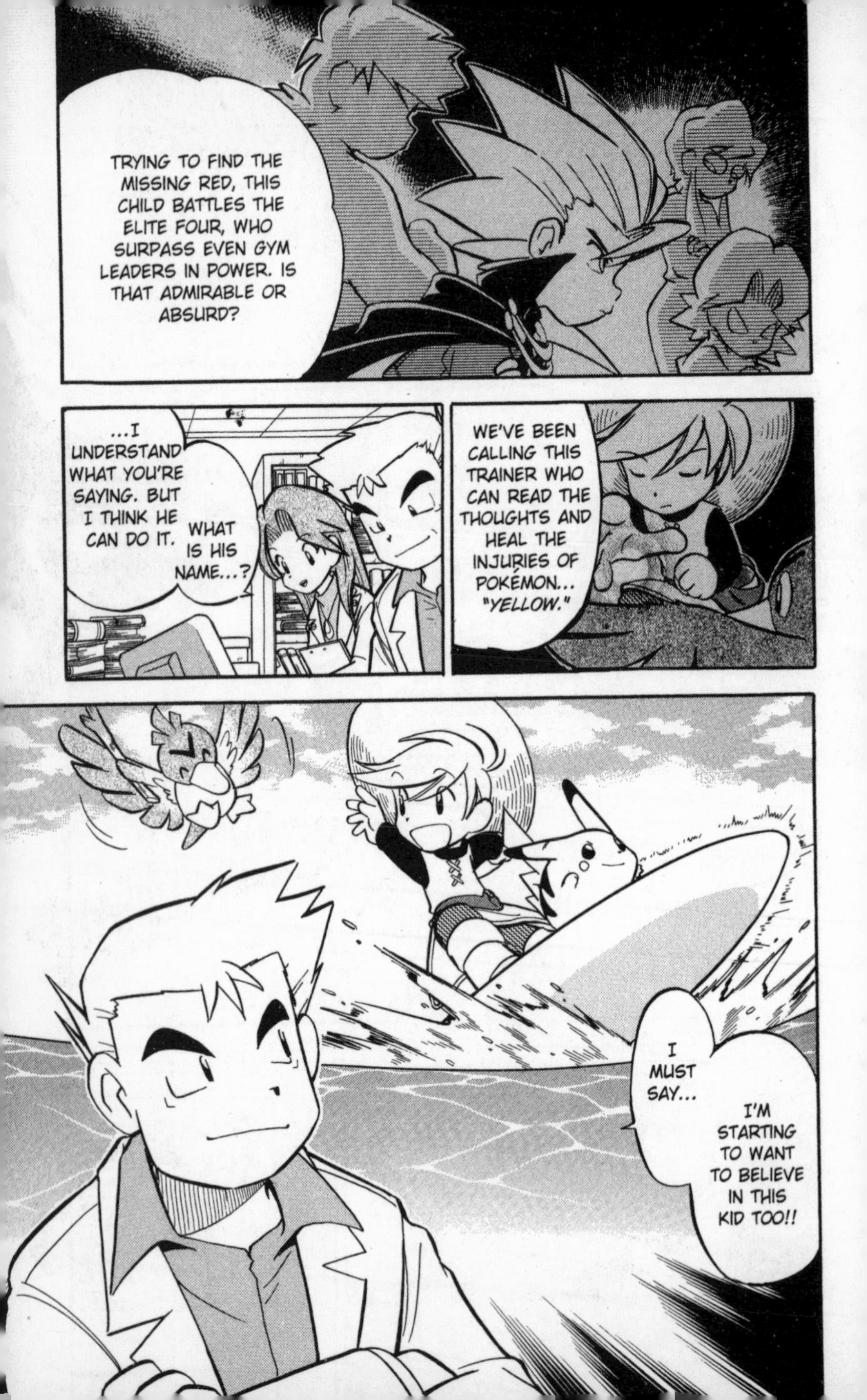
TRYING TO FIND THE MISSING RED, THIS CHILD BATTLES THE ELITE FOUR, WHO SURPASS EVEN GYM LEADERS IN POWER. IS THAT ADMIRABLE OR ABSURD?
...I UNDERSTAND WHAT YOU'RE SAYING. BUT I THINK HE CAN DO IT.
WHAT IS HIS NAME...?
WE'VE BEEN CALLING THIS TRAINER WHO CAN READ THE THOUGHTS AND HEAL THE INJURIES OF POKÉMON... "YELLOW."
I MUST SAY...
I'M STARTING TO WANT TO BELIEVE IN THIS KID TOO!!

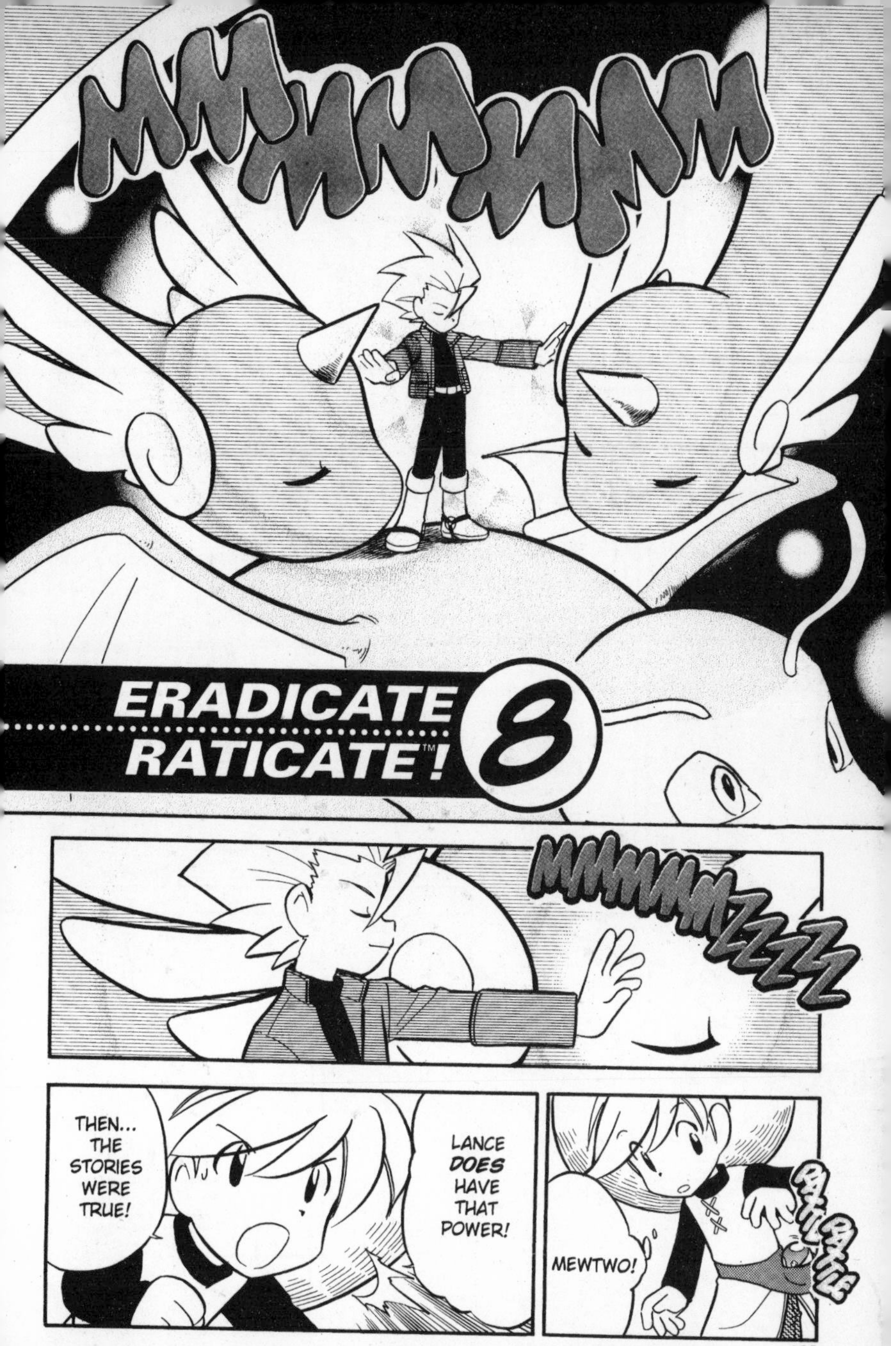
ERADICATE
RATICATE!™
8
THEN... THE STORIES WERE TRUE!
LANCE *DOES* HAVE THAT POWER!
MEWTWO!

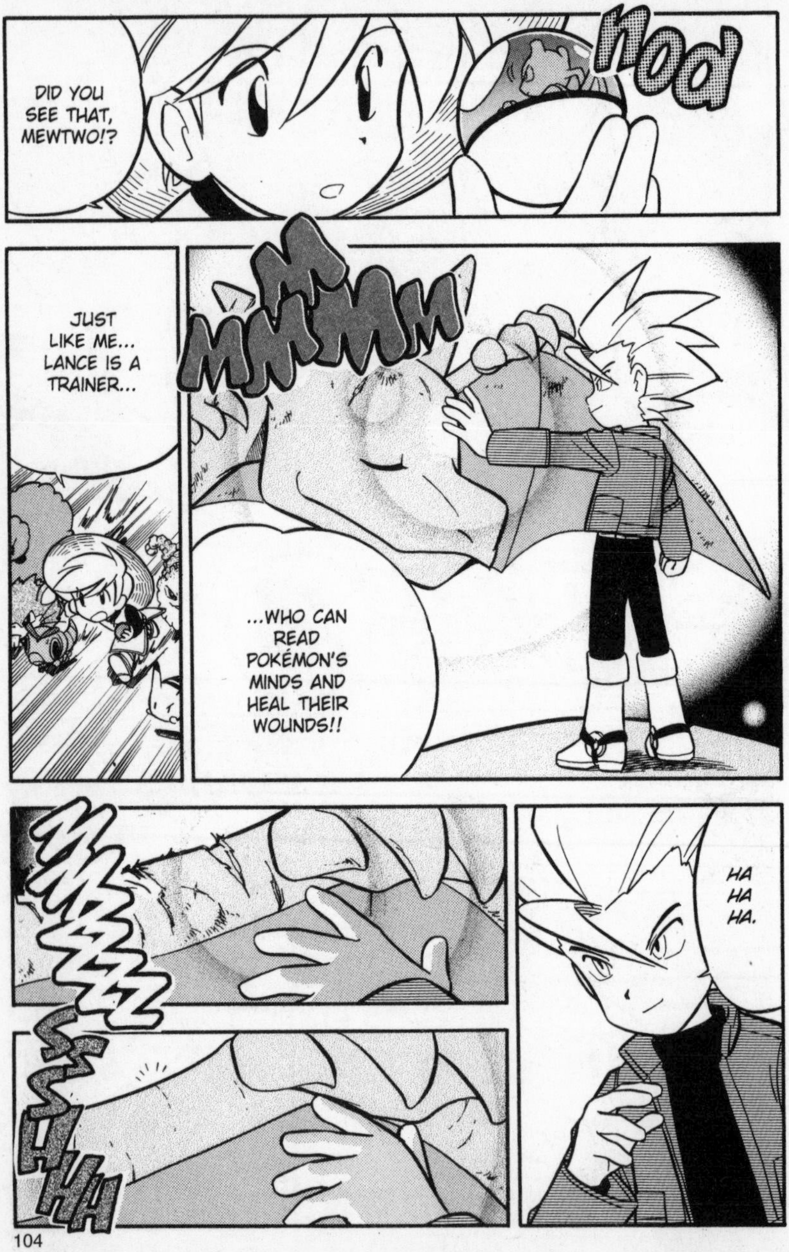
nod
DID YOU SEE THAT, MEWTWO!?
MMMMMM
JUST LIKE ME... LANCE IS A TRAINER...
...WHO CAN READ POKÉMON'S MINDS AND HEAL THEIR WOUNDS!!
HA HA HA.
MMMMMMSSSHHHA

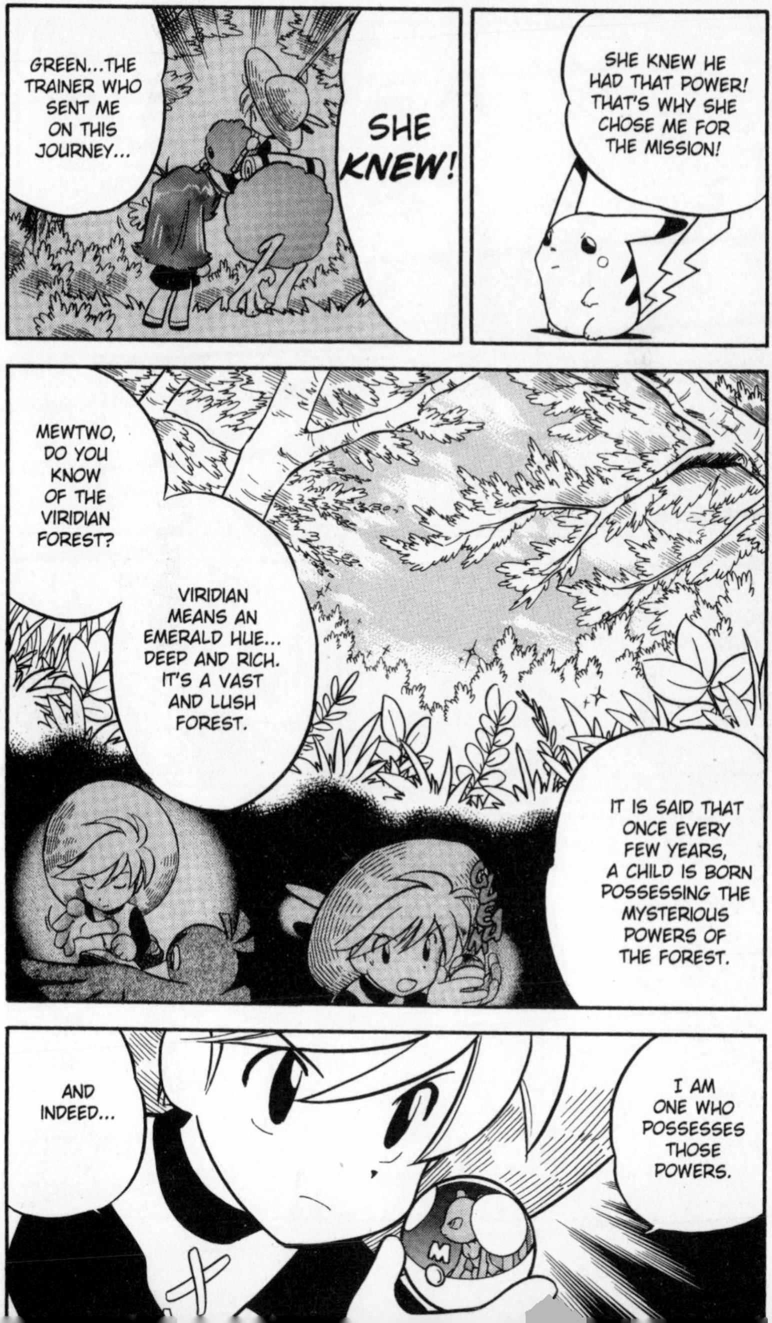
GREEN...THE TRAINER WHO SENT ME ON THIS JOURNEY...
SHE KNEW!
SHE KNEW HE HAD THAT POWER! THAT'S WHY SHE CHOSE ME FOR THE MISSION!
MEWTWO, DO YOU KNOW OF THE VIRIDIAN FOREST?
VIRIDIAN MEANS AN EMERALD HUE... DEEP AND RICH. IT'S A VAST AND LUSH FOREST.
IT IS SAID THAT ONCE EVERY FEW YEARS, A CHILD IS BORN POSSESSING THE MYSTERIOUS POWERS OF THE FOREST.
AND INDEED...
I AM ONE WHO POSSESSES THOSE POWERS.

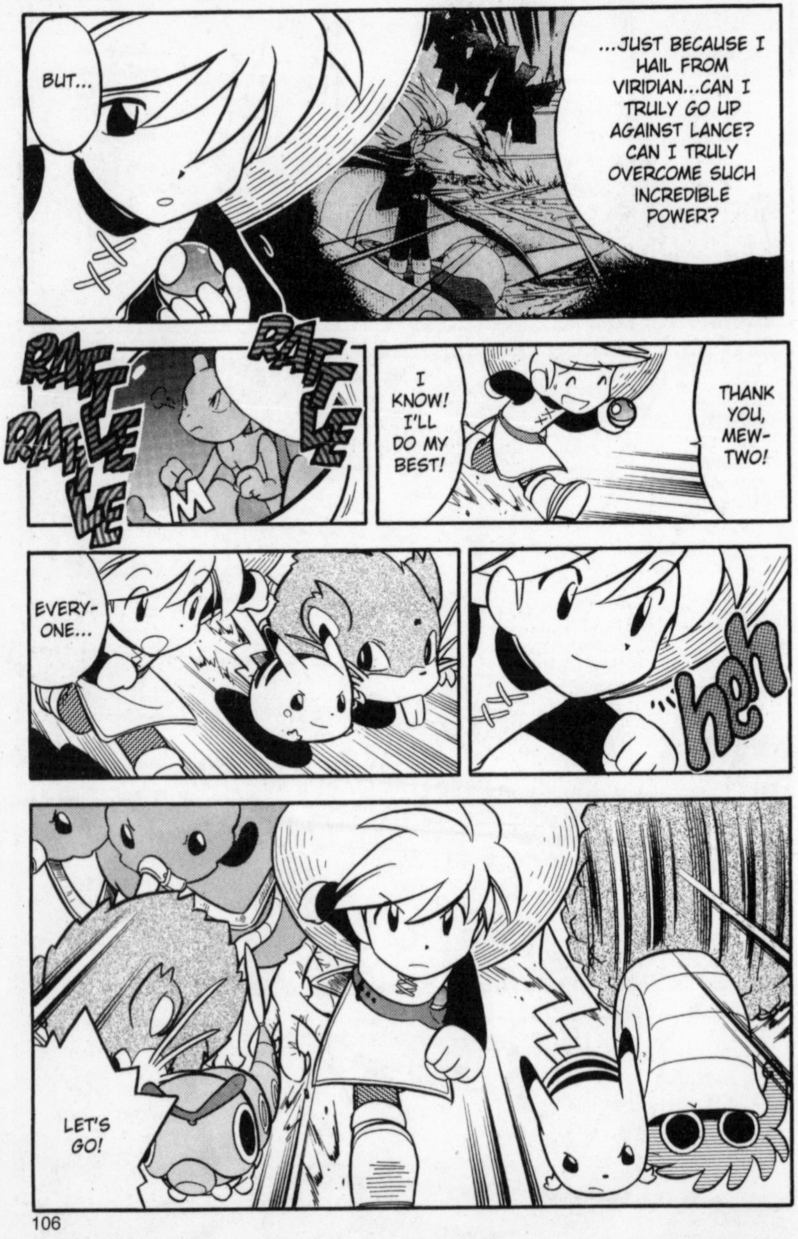
...JUST BECAUSE I HAIL FROM VIRIDIAN...CAN I TRULY GO UP AGAINST LANCE? CAN I TRULY OVERCOME SUCH INCREDIBLE POWER?
BUT...
THANK YOU, MEW-TWO!
I KNOW! I'LL DO MY BEST!
RATTLE
RATTLE
RATTLE
heh
EVERY-ONE...
LET'S GO!

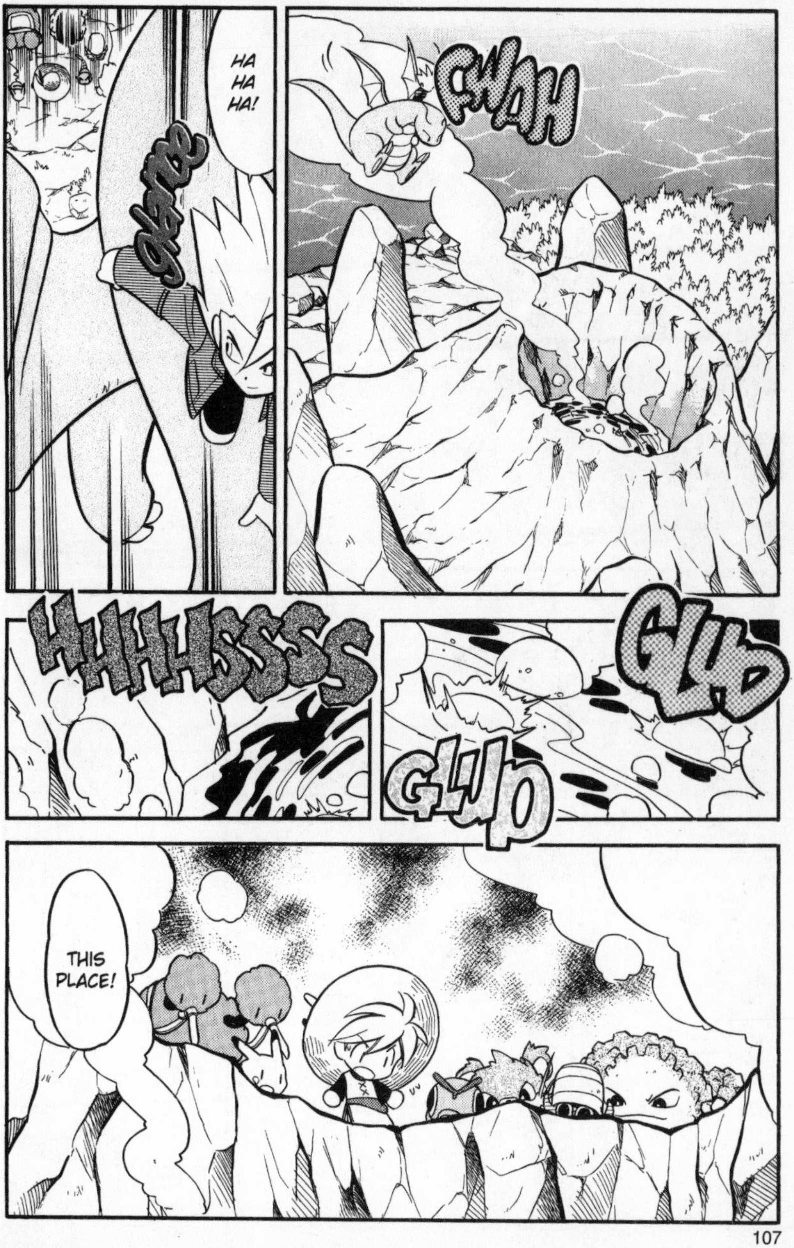

HA HA HA!
glare
GWAH
HHHHSSSS
GLUB
GLUB
THIS PLACE!

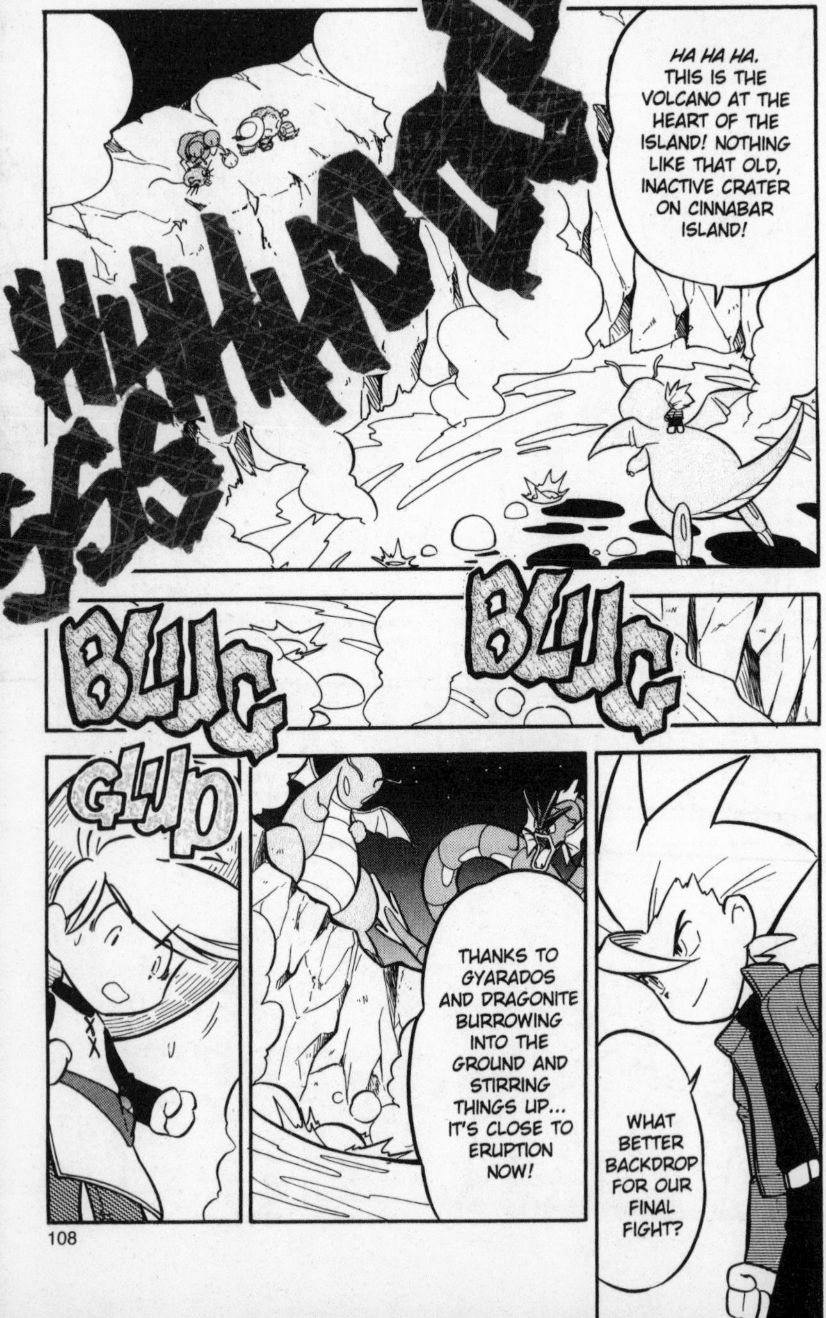
HA HA HA. THIS IS THE VOLCANO AT THE HEART OF THE ISLAND! NOTHING LIKE THAT OLD, INACTIVE CRATER ON CINNABAR ISLAND!
BLUG
BLUG
GLUP
THANKS TO GYARADOS AND DRAGONITE BURROWING INTO THE GROUND AND STIRRING THINGS UP... IT'S CLOSE TO ERUPTION NOW!
WHAT BETTER BACKDROP FOR OUR FINAL FIGHT?

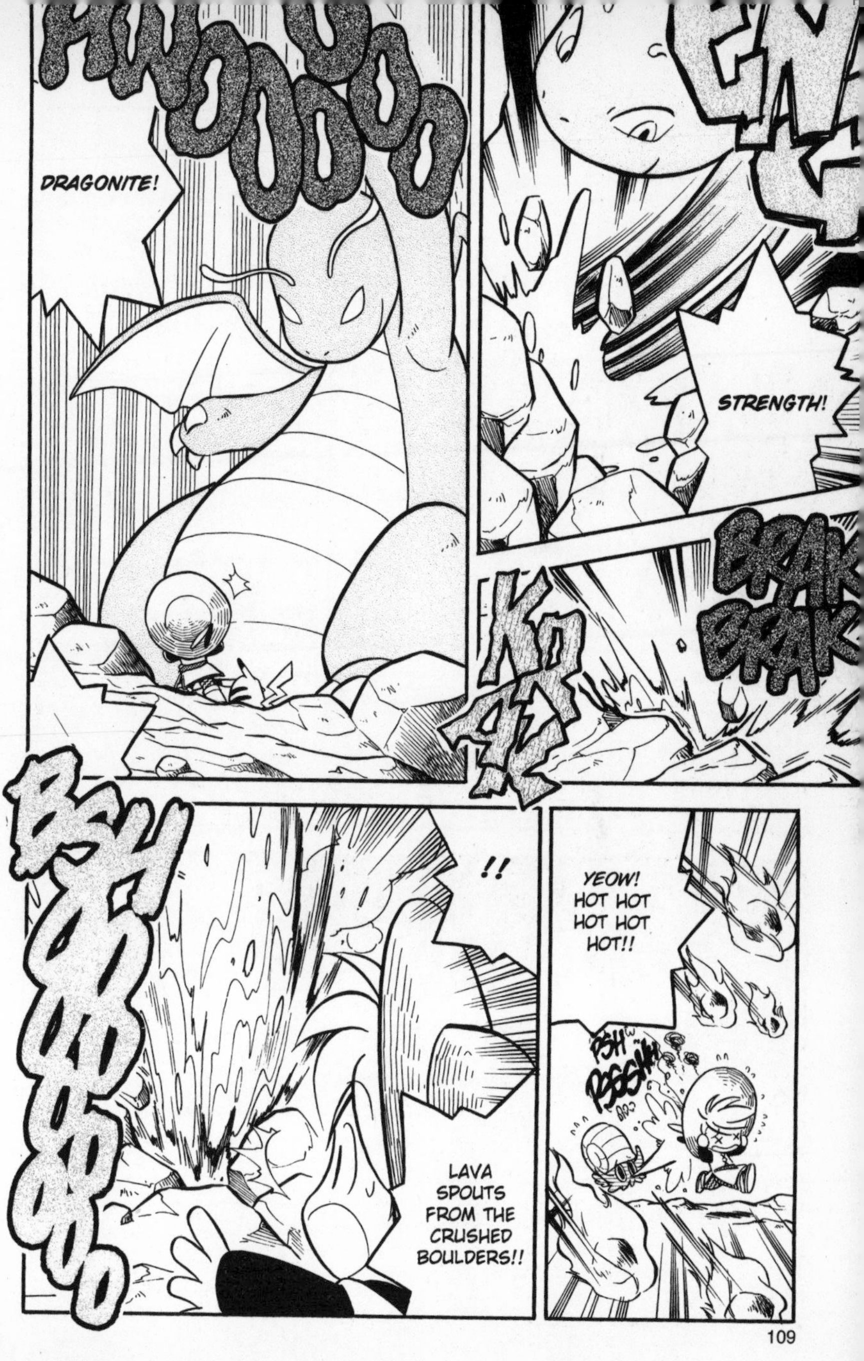
STRENGTH!
DRAGONITE!
!!
YEOW! HOT HOT HOT HOT HOT!!
LAVA SPOUTS FROM THE CRUSHED BOULDERS!!

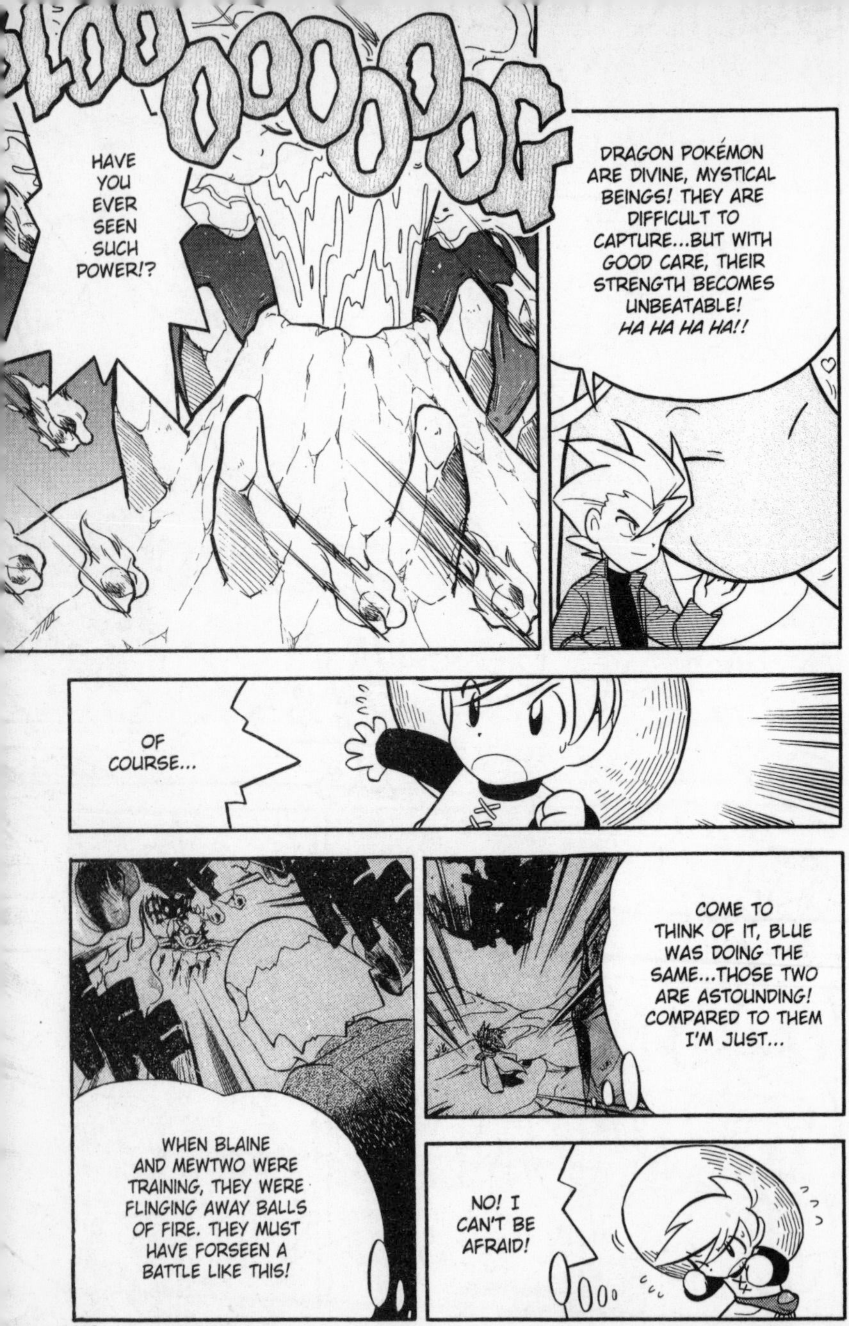
HAVE YOU EVER SEEN SUCH POWER!?
DRAGON POKÉMON ARE DIVINE, MYSTICAL BEINGS! THEY ARE DIFFICULT TO CAPTURE...BUT WITH GOOD CARE, THEIR STRENGTH BECOMES UNBEATABLE! *HA HA HA HA!!*
OF COURSE...
WHEN BLAINE AND MEWTWO WERE TRAINING, THEY WERE FLINGING AWAY BALLS OF FIRE. THEY MUST HAVE FORSEEN A BATTLE LIKE THIS!
COME TO THINK OF IT, BLUE WAS DOING THE SAME...THOSE TWO ARE ASTOUNDING! COMPARED TO THEM I'M JUST...
NO! I CAN'T BE AFRAID!

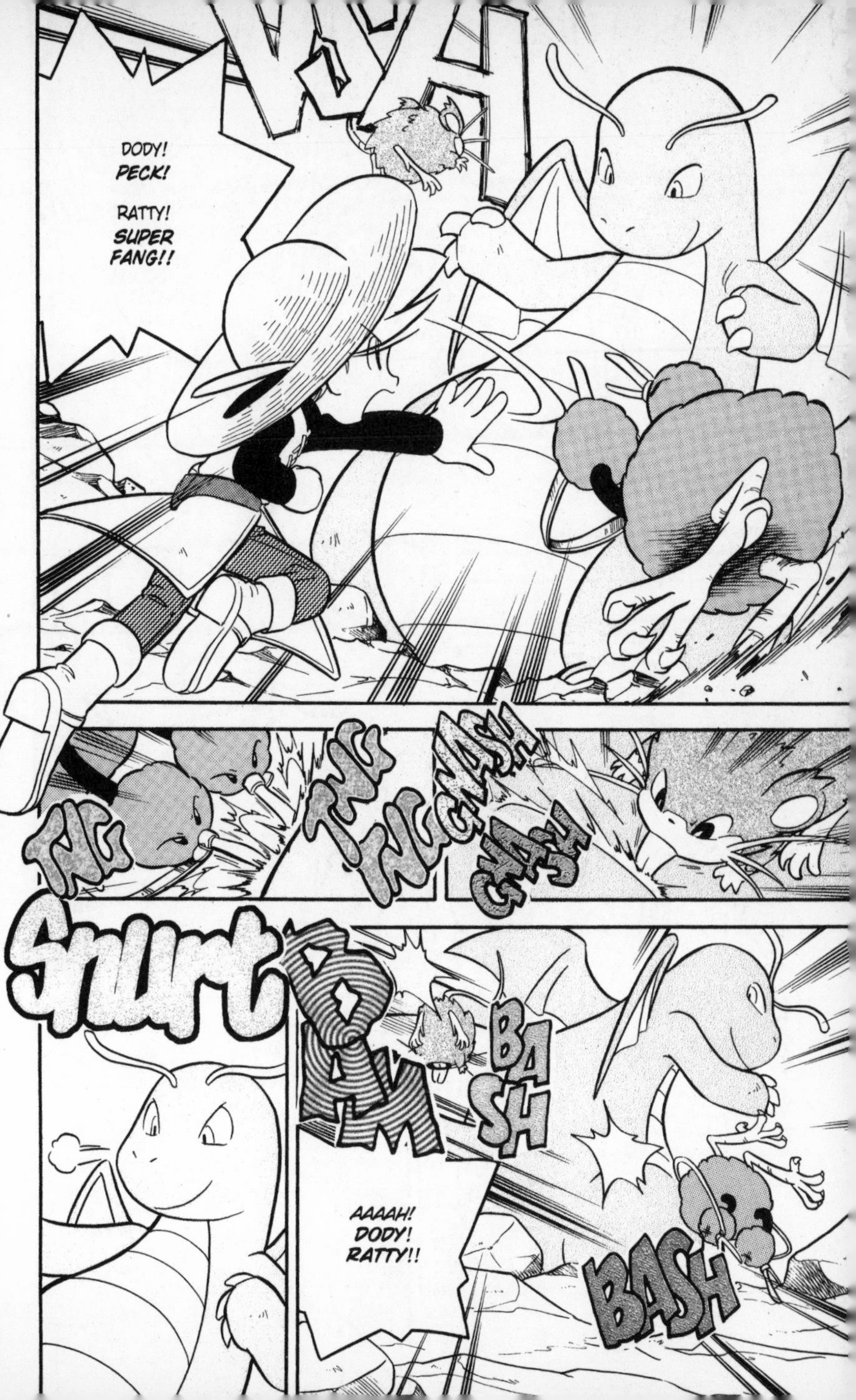
DODY!
PECK!
RATTY!
SUPER FANG!!
BASH
AAAAH! DODY! RATTY!!
BASH

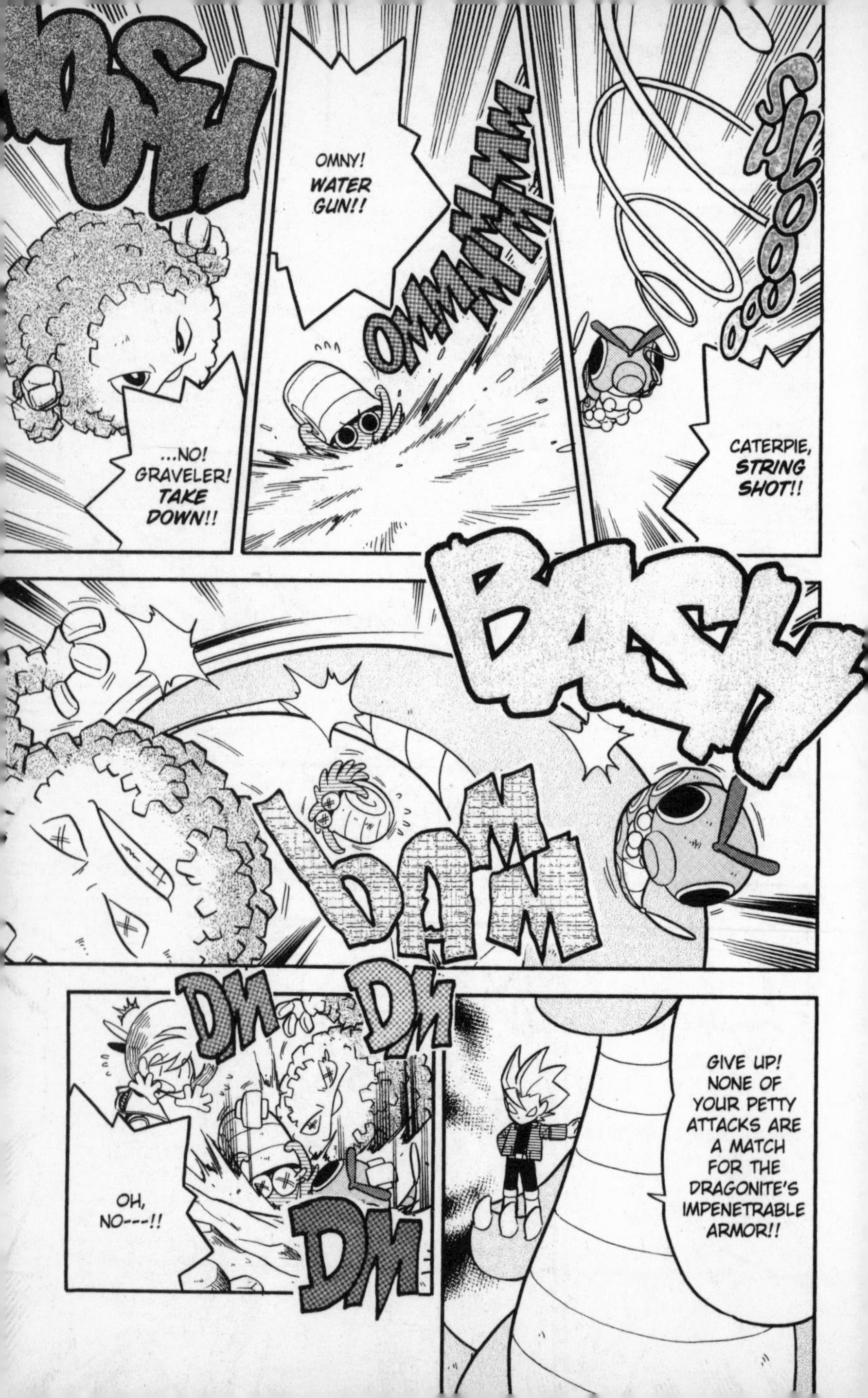

...NO! GRAVELER! TAKE DOWN!!
OMNY! WATER GUN!!
CATERPIE, STRING SHOT!!
BASH
DAM
DM
DM
DM
OH, NO---!!
GIVE UP! NONE OF YOUR PETTY ATTACKS ARE A MATCH FOR THE DRAGONITE'S IMPENETRABLE ARMOR!!

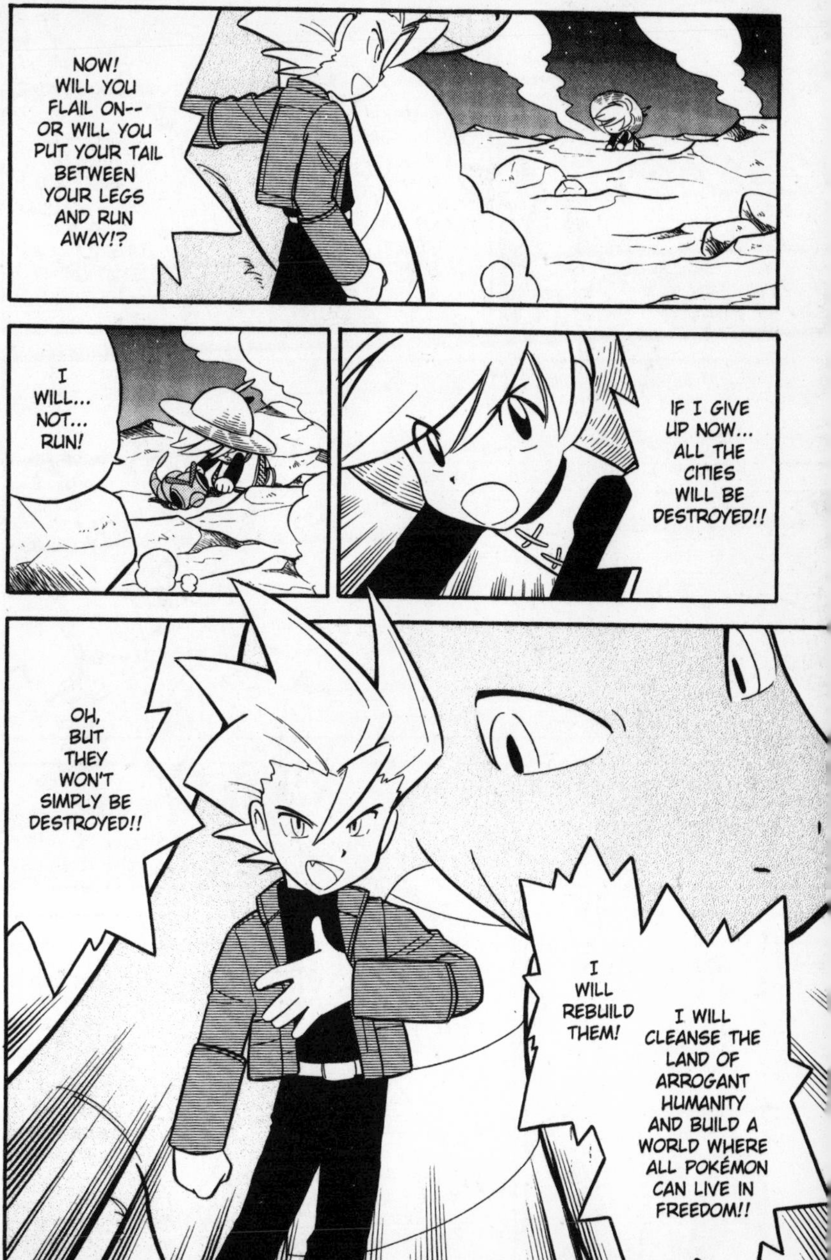
NOW! WILL YOU FLAIL ON-- OR WILL YOU PUT YOUR TAIL BETWEEN YOUR LEGS AND RUN AWAY!?
I WILL... NOT... RUN!
IF I GIVE UP NOW... ALL THE CITIES WILL BE DESTROYED!!
OH, BUT THEY WON'T SIMPLY BE DESTROYED!!
I WILL REBUILD THEM!
I WILL CLEANSE THE LAND OF ARROGANT HUMANITY AND BUILD A WORLD WHERE ALL POKÉMON CAN LIVE IN FREEDOM!!

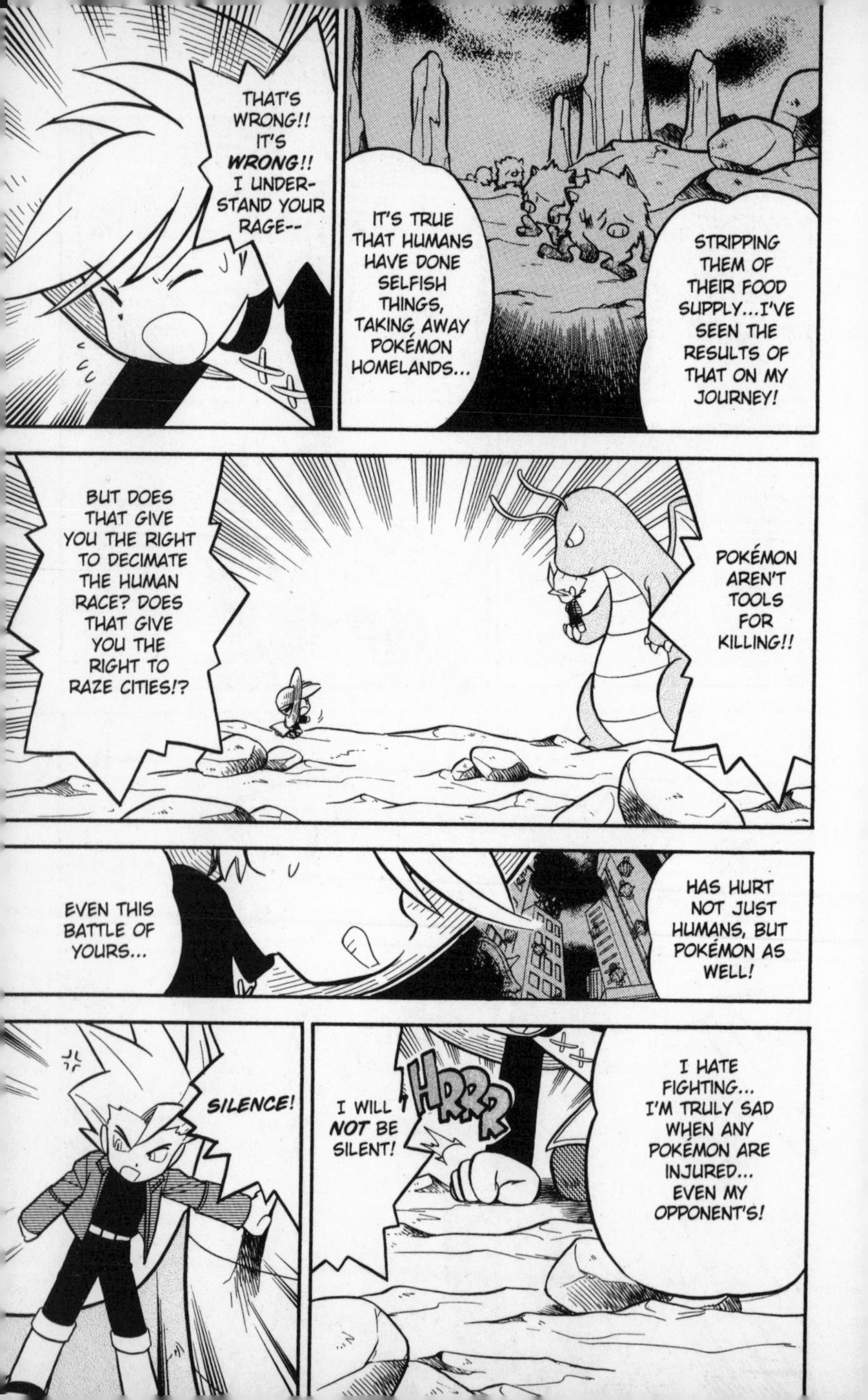
THAT'S WRONG!! IT'S WRONG!! I UNDERSTAND YOUR RAGE--
IT'S TRUE THAT HUMANS HAVE DONE SELFISH THINGS, TAKING AWAY POKÉMON HOMELANDS...
STRIPPING THEM OF THEIR FOOD SUPPLY...I'VE SEEN THE RESULTS OF THAT ON MY JOURNEY!
BUT DOES THAT GIVE YOU THE RIGHT TO DECIMATE THE HUMAN RACE? DOES THAT GIVE YOU THE RIGHT TO RAZE CITIES!?
POKÉMON AREN'T TOOLS FOR KILLING!!
EVEN THIS BATTLE OF YOURS...
HAS HURT NOT JUST HUMANS, BUT POKÉMON AS WELL!
SILENCE!
I WILL NOT BE SILENT!
HRRR
I HATE FIGHTING... I'M TRULY SAD WHEN ANY POKÉMON ARE INJURED... EVEN MY OPPONENT'S!

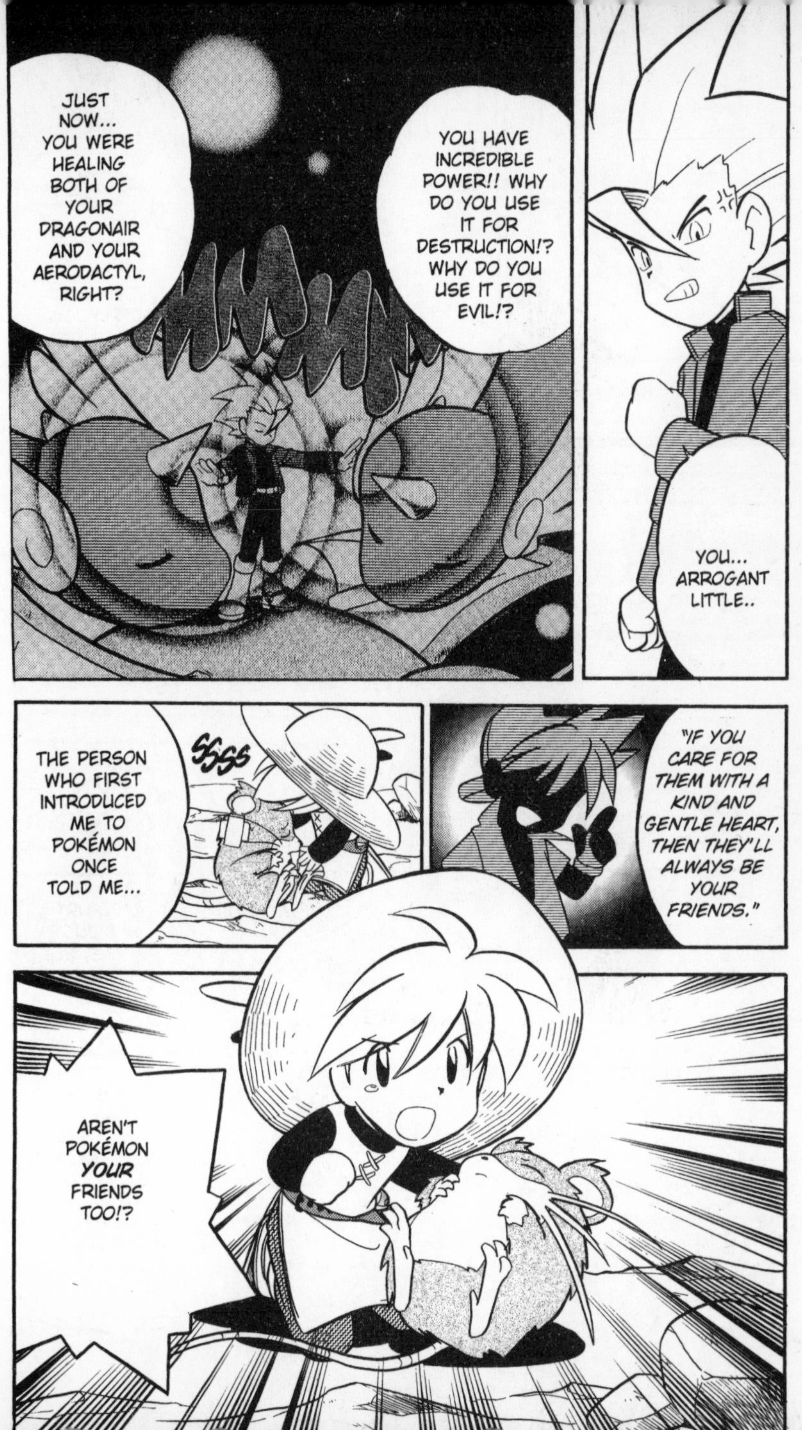
JUST NOW... YOU WERE HEALING BOTH OF YOUR DRAGONAIR AND YOUR AERODACTYL, RIGHT?
YOU HAVE INCREDIBLE POWER!! WHY DO YOU USE IT FOR DESTRUCTION!? WHY DO YOU USE IT FOR EVIL!?
YOU... ARROGANT LITTLE..
THE PERSON WHO FIRST INTRODUCED ME TO POKÉMON ONCE TOLD ME...
SSSS
"IF YOU CARE FOR THEM WITH A KIND AND GENTLE HEART, THEN THEY'LL ALWAYS BE YOUR FRIENDS."
AREN'T POKÉMON *YOUR* FRIENDS TOO!?

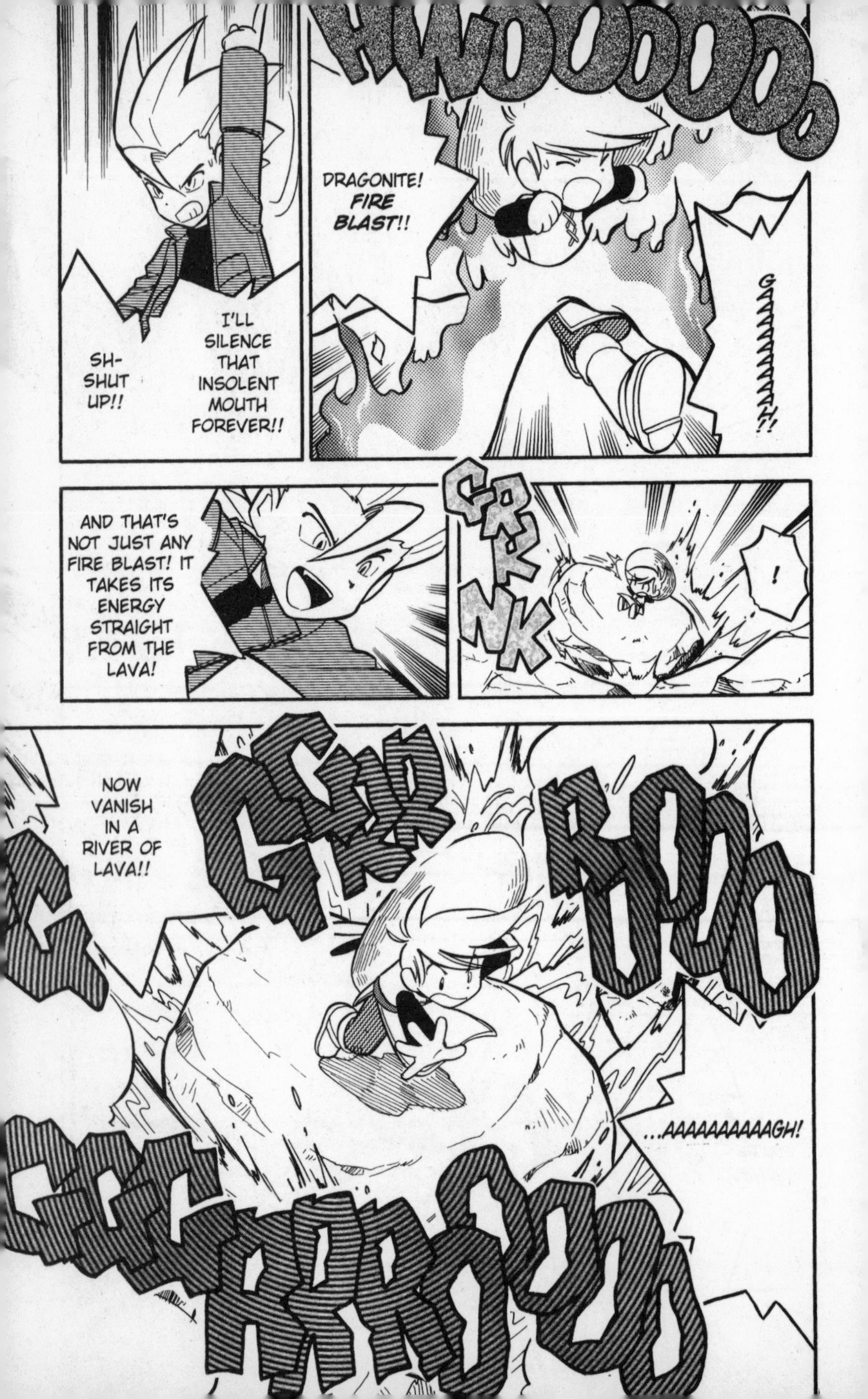
SH-SHUT UP!!
I'LL SILENCE THAT INSOLENT MOUTH FOREVER!!
DRAGONITE! FIRE BLAST!!
AND THAT'S NOT JUST ANY FIRE BLAST! IT TAKES ITS ENERGY STRAIGHT FROM THE LAVA!
!
NOW VANISH IN A RIVER OF LAVA!!
...AAAAAAAAAAGH!

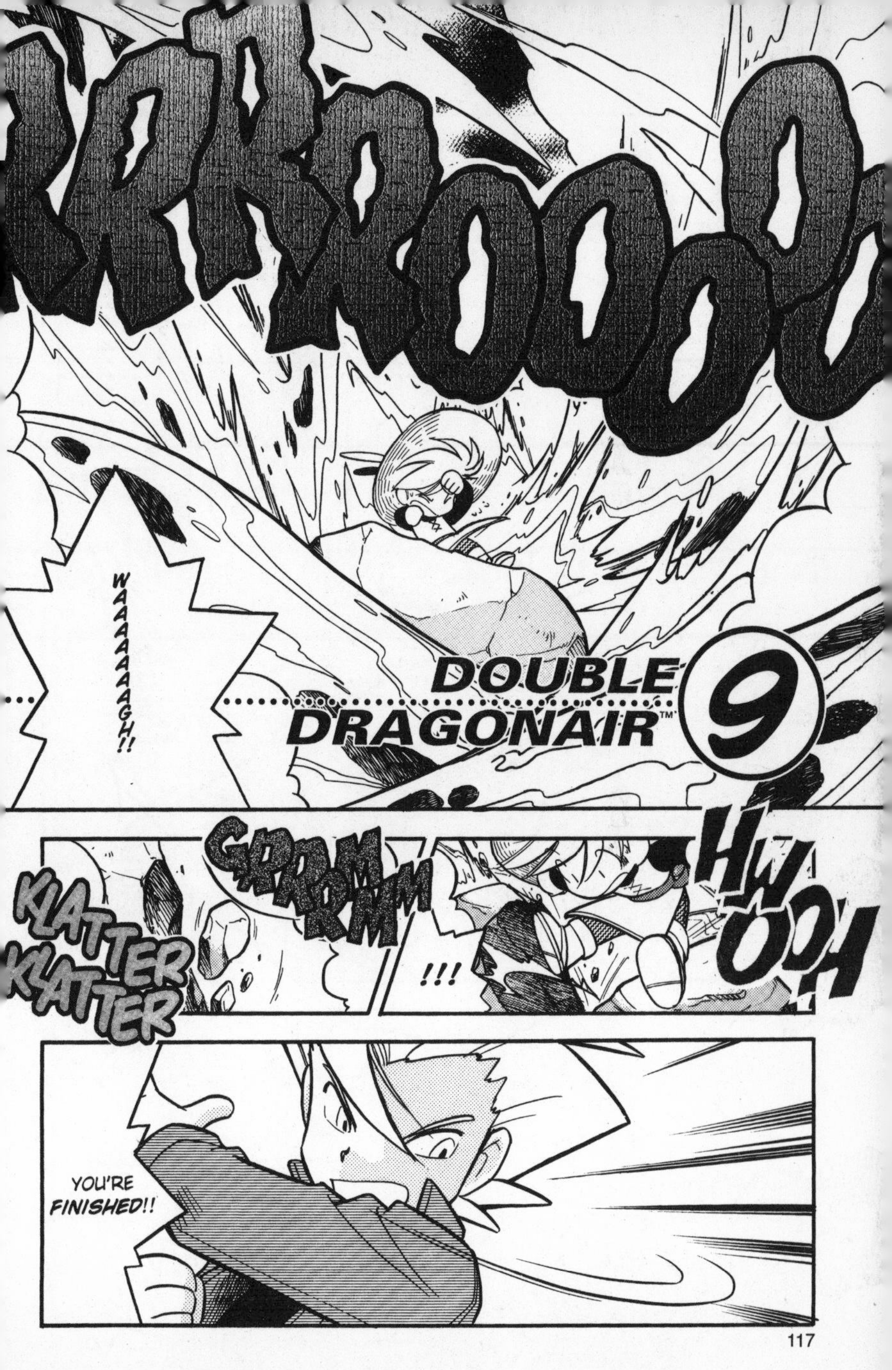
KRAKOOOOOOM
WAAAAAAAAAGH!!
DOUBLE DRAGONAIR™
9
HWOOH
GRRRUMMM
KLATTER KLATTER
!!!
YOU'RE FINISHED!!

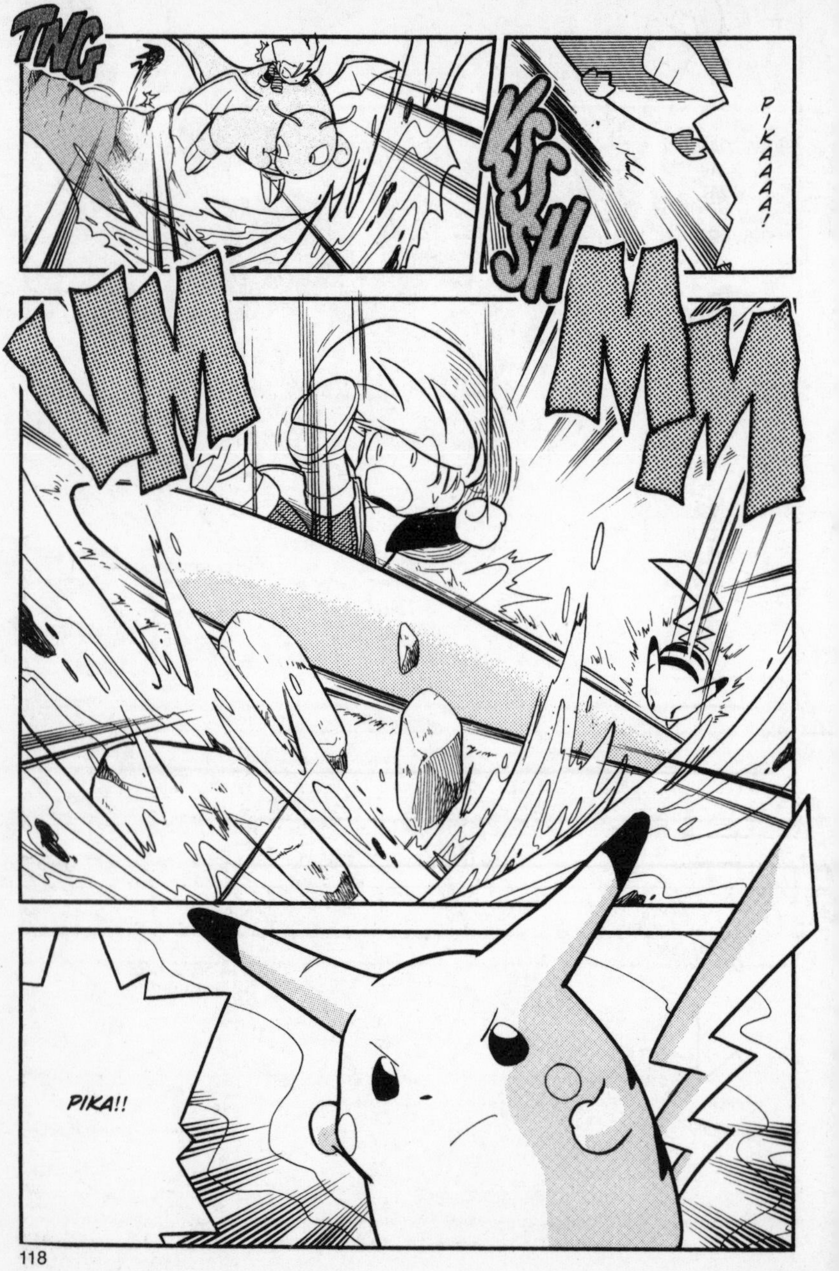
PIKAAAAA!
TNG
VSSH
VIM
MM
PIKA!!

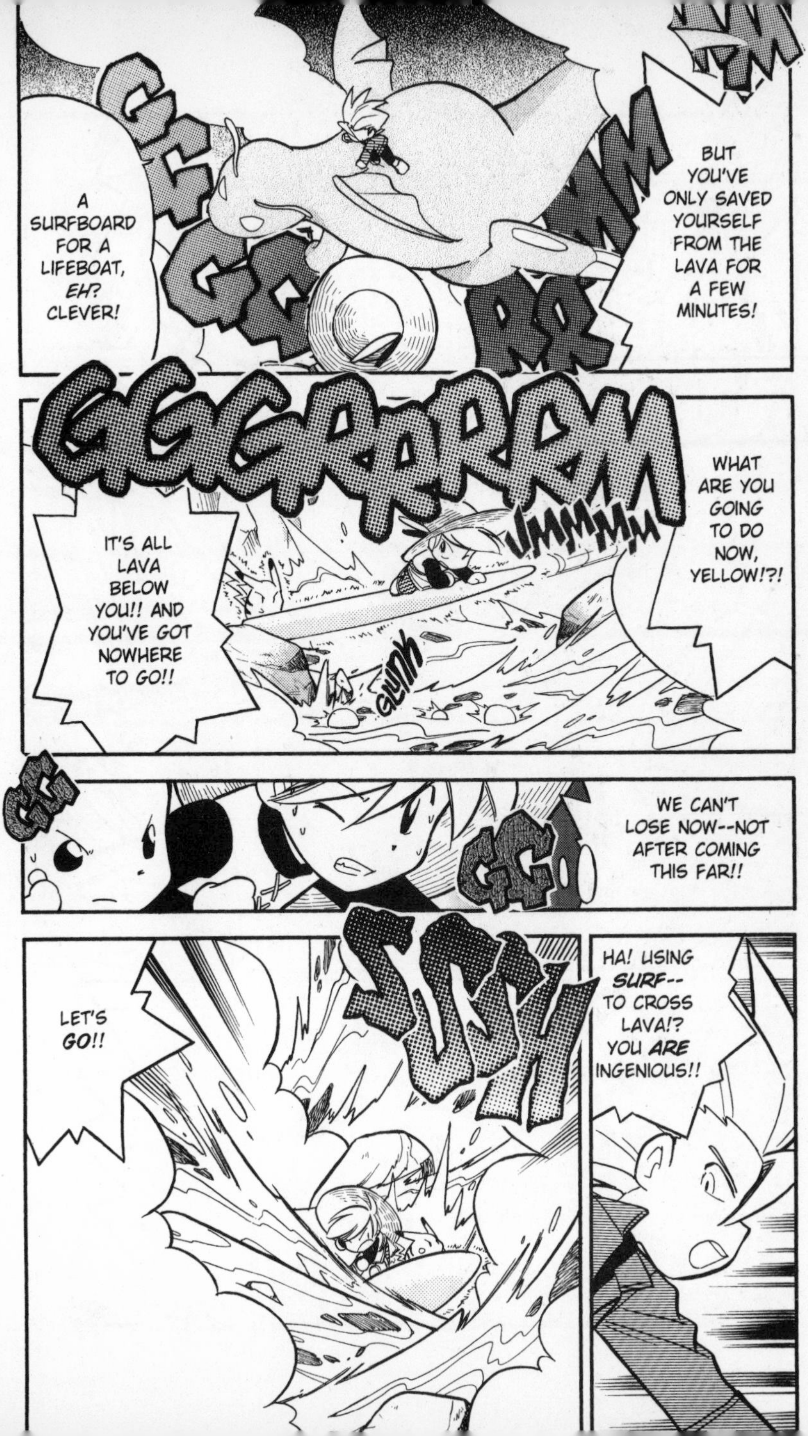
GG
GGOO
RR
MM
A SURFBOARD FOR A LIFEBOAT, EH? CLEVER!
BUT YOU'VE ONLY SAVED YOURSELF FROM THE LAVA FOR A FEW MINUTES!
GGGRRRRM
JMMMM
GLUNK
IT'S ALL LAVA BELOW YOU!! AND YOU'VE GOT NOWHERE TO GO!!
WHAT ARE YOU GOING TO DO NOW, YELLOW!?!
GG
GG
WE CAN'T LOSE NOW--NOT AFTER COMING THIS FAR!!
SSSH
LET'S GO!!
HA! USING SURF-- TO CROSS LAVA!? YOU ARE INGENIOUS!!

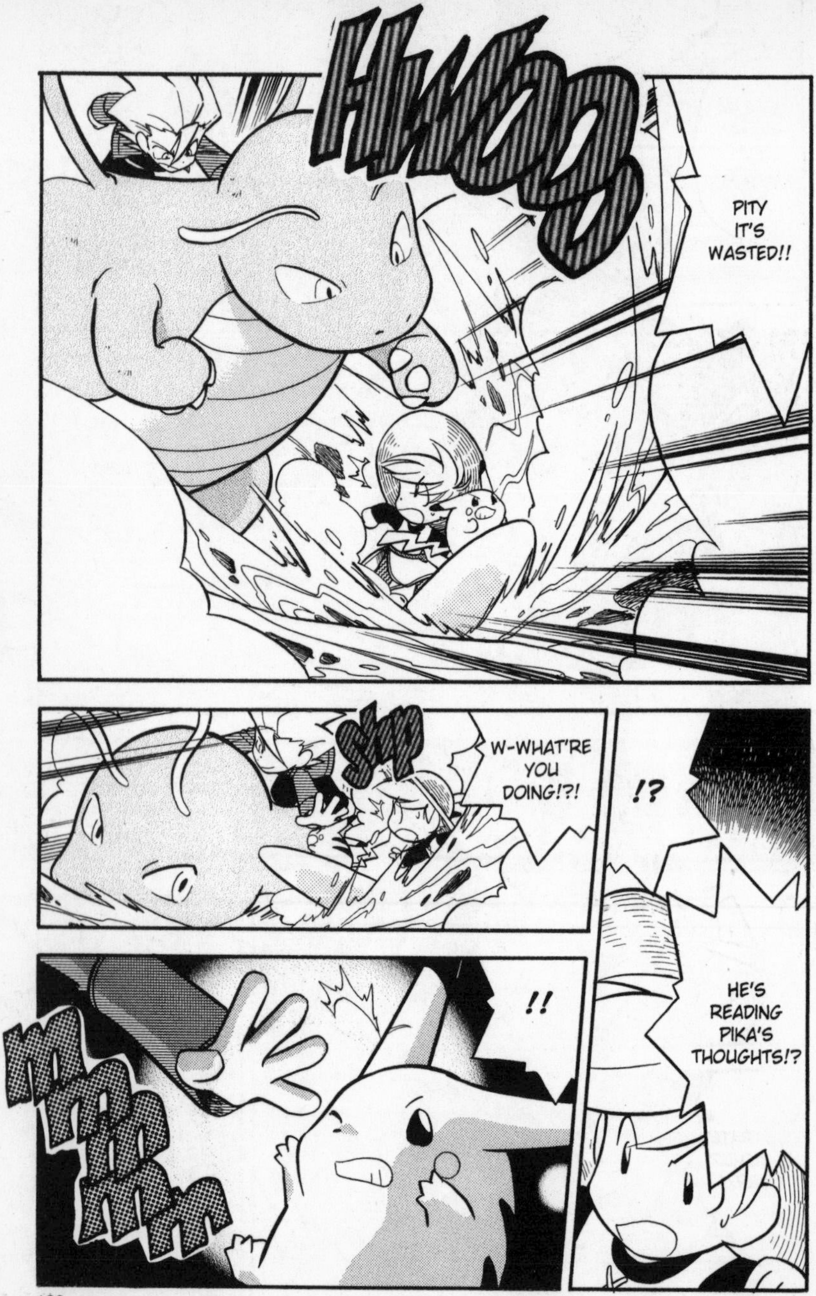
PITY IT'S WASTED!!
W-WHAT'RE YOU DOING!?!
!?
!!
HE'S READING PIKA'S THOUGHTS!?

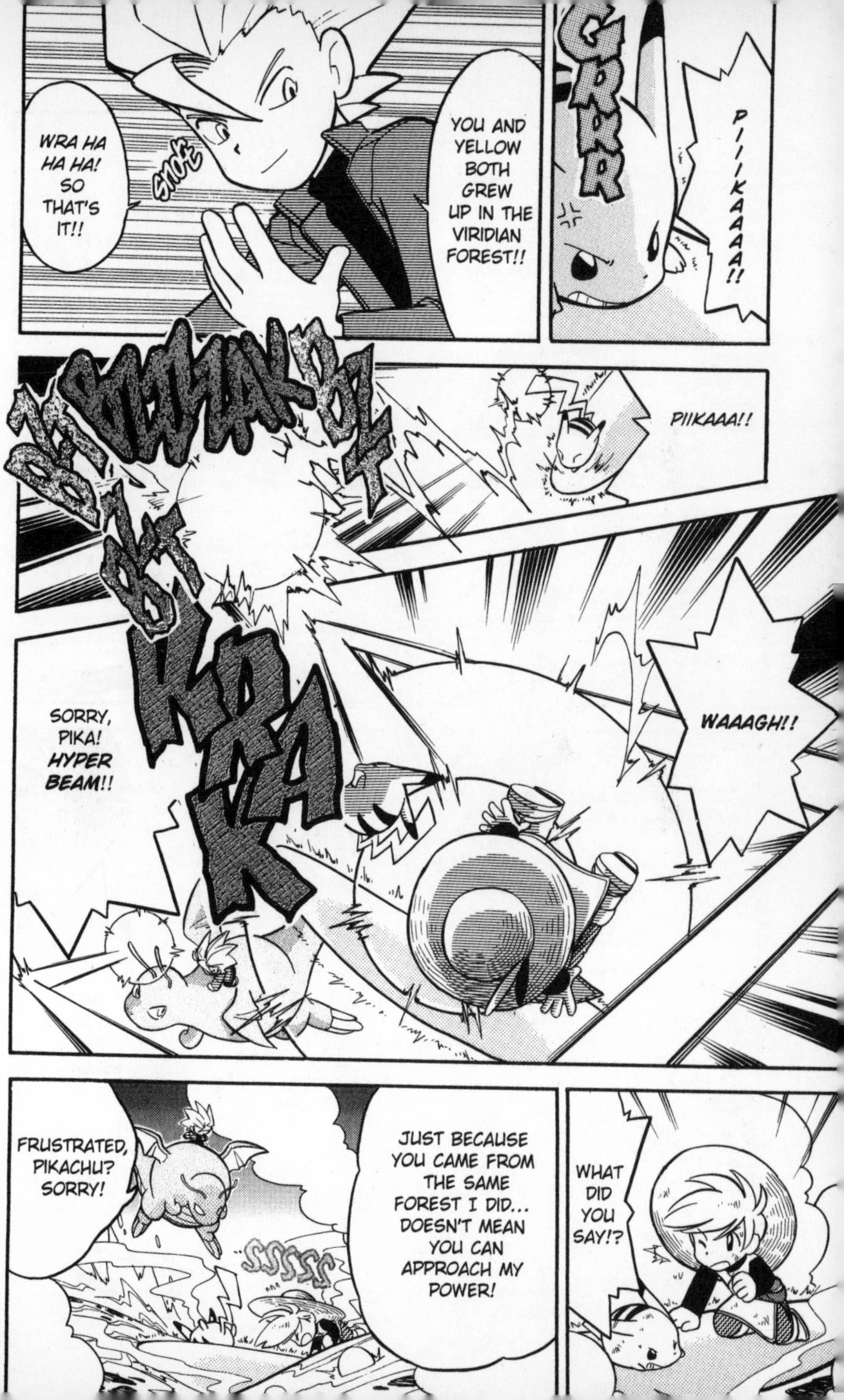
WRA HA HA HA! SO THAT'S IT!!
snort
YOU AND YELLOW BOTH GREW UP IN THE VIRIDIAN FOREST!!
GRRR
PIIIKAAAA!!
PIIKAAA!!
KRAK
SORRY, PIKA! *HYPER BEAM*!!
WAAAGH!!
FRUSTRATED, PIKACHU? SORRY!
JUST BECAUSE YOU CAME FROM THE SAME FOREST I DID... DOESN'T MEAN YOU CAN APPROACH MY POWER!
WHAT DID YOU SAY!?

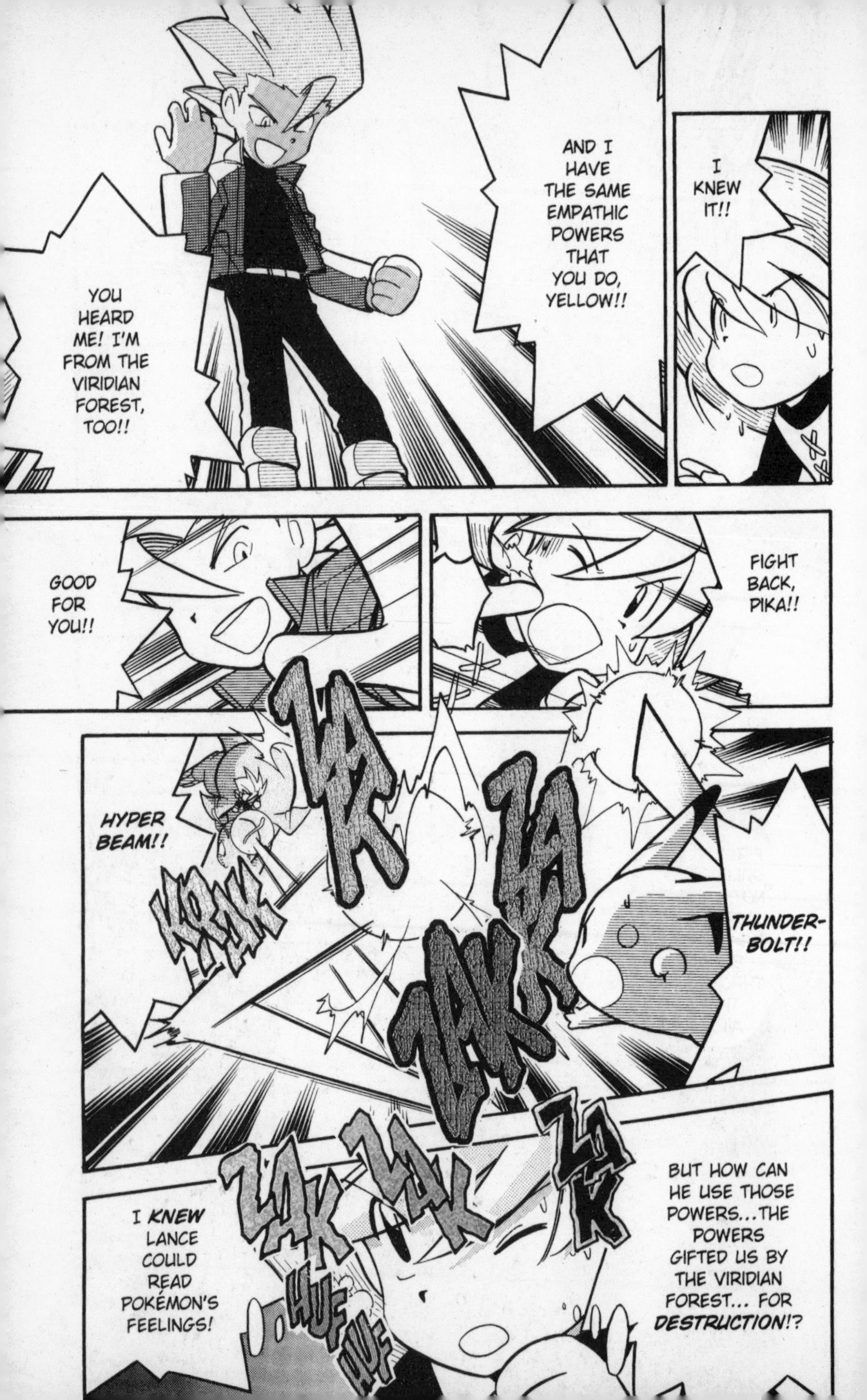
YOU HEARD ME! I'M FROM THE VIRIDIAN FOREST, TOO!!
AND I HAVE THE SAME EMPATHIC POWERS THAT YOU DO, YELLOW!!
I KNEW IT!!
GOOD FOR YOU!!
FIGHT BACK, PIKA!!
HYPER BEAM!!
THUNDER-BOLT!!
I *KNEW* LANCE COULD READ POKÉMON'S FEELINGS!
BUT HOW CAN HE USE THOSE POWERS...THE POWERS GIFTED US BY THE VIRIDIAN FOREST... FOR *DESTRUCTION*!?

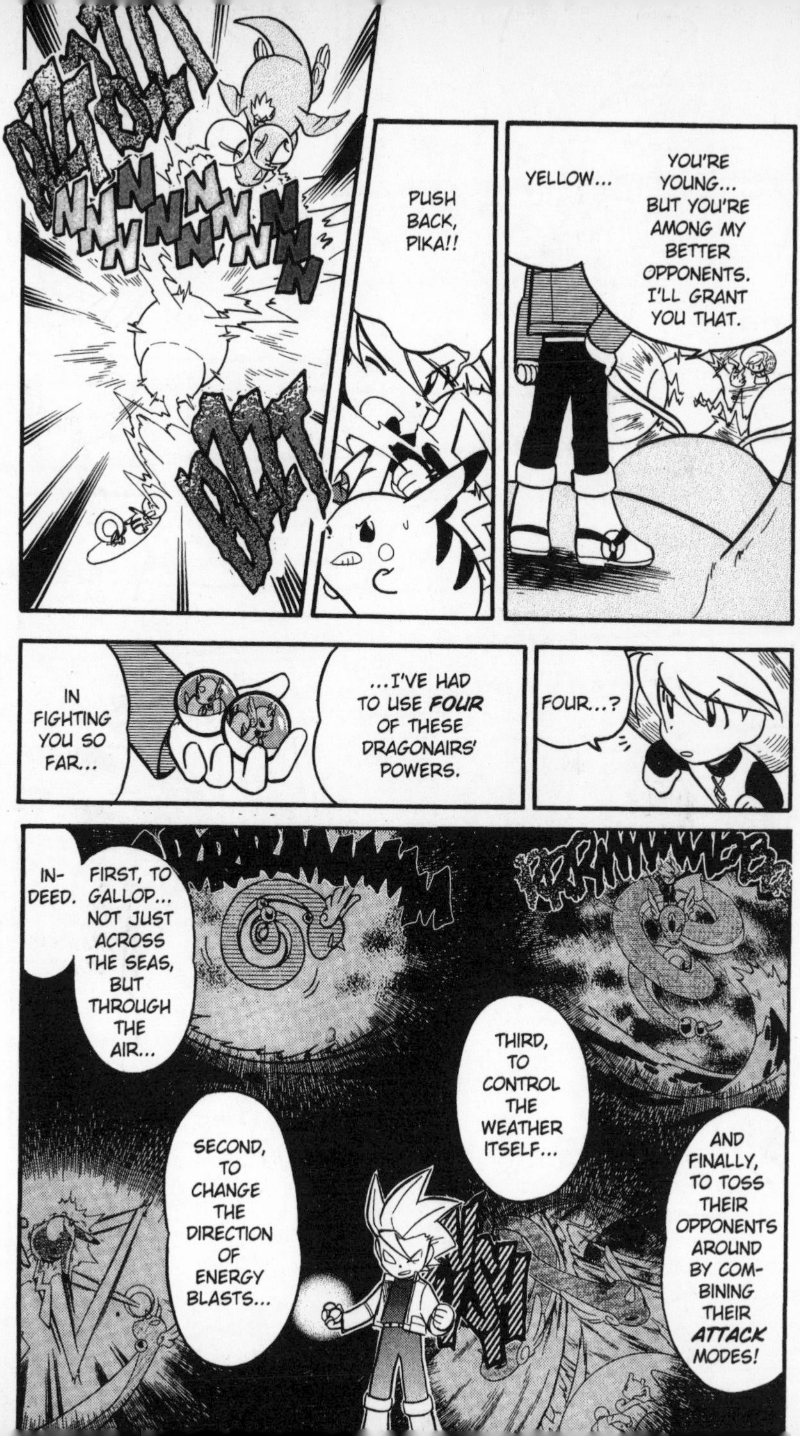

PUSH BACK, PIKA!!
YELLOW...
YOU'RE YOUNG... BUT YOU'RE AMONG MY BETTER OPPONENTS. I'LL GRANT YOU THAT.
IN FIGHTING YOU SO FAR...
...I'VE HAD TO USE FOUR OF THESE DRAGONAIRS' POWERS.
FOUR...?
IN-DEED.
FIRST, TO GALLOP... NOT JUST ACROSS THE SEAS, BUT THROUGH THE AIR...
SECOND, TO CHANGE THE DIRECTION OF ENERGY BLASTS...
THIRD, TO CONTROL THE WEATHER ITSELF...
AND FINALLY, TO TOSS THEIR OPPONENTS AROUND BY COM-BINING THEIR ATTACK MODES!

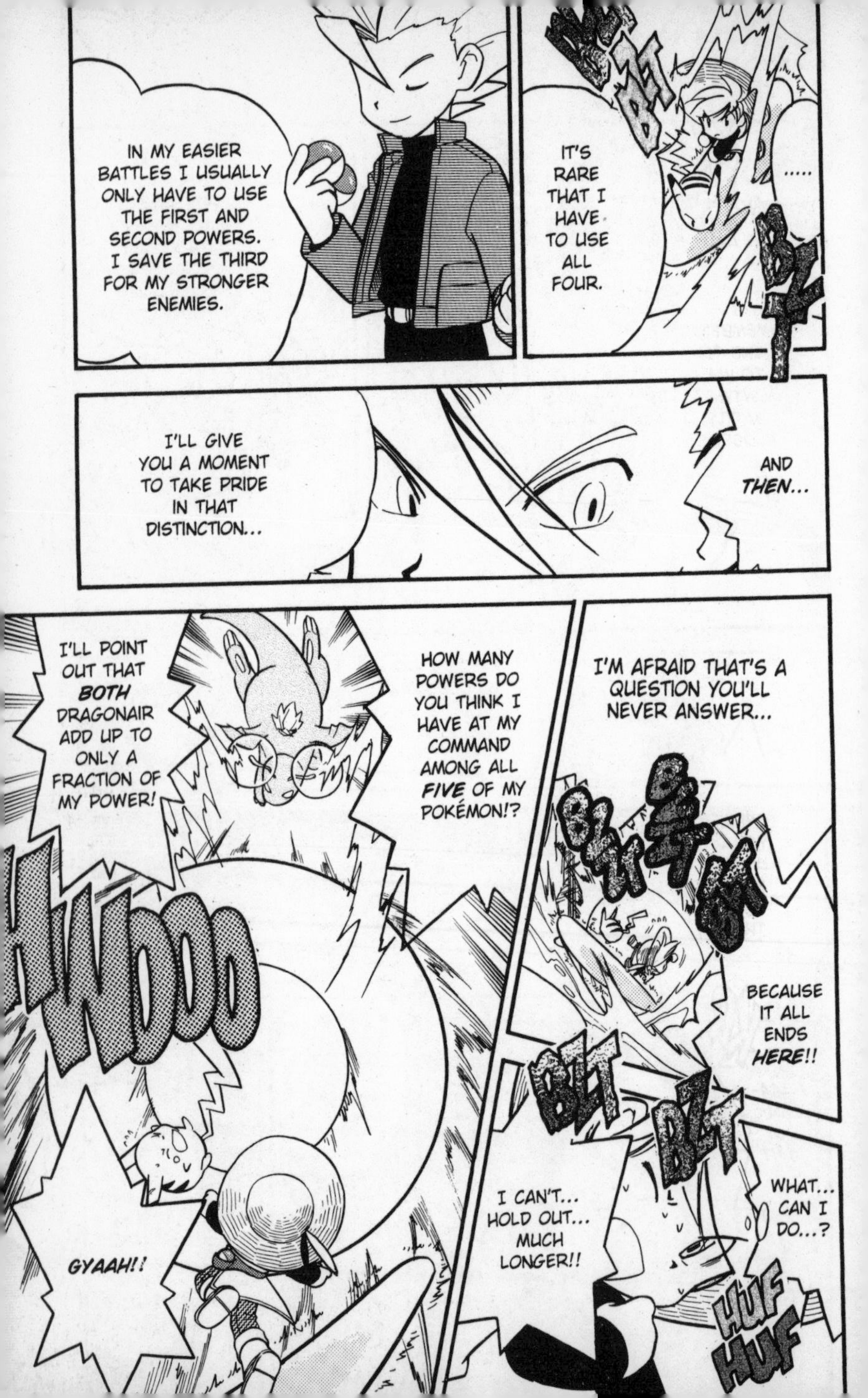
IN MY EASIER BATTLES I USUALLY ONLY HAVE TO USE THE FIRST AND SECOND POWERS. I SAVE THE THIRD FOR MY STRONGER ENEMIES.
BZT
BZT
IT'S RARE THAT I HAVE TO USE ALL FOUR.
.....
BZT
I'LL GIVE YOU A MOMENT TO TAKE PRIDE IN THAT DISTINCTION...
AND *THEN*...
I'LL POINT OUT THAT *BOTH* DRAGONAIR ADD UP TO ONLY A FRACTION OF MY POWER!
HOW MANY POWERS DO YOU THINK I HAVE AT MY COMMAND AMONG ALL *FIVE* OF MY POKÉMON!?
HWOOO
GYAAH!!
I'M AFRAID THAT'S A QUESTION YOU'LL NEVER ANSWER...
BECAUSE IT ALL ENDS *HERE*!!
BZT
BZT
I CAN'T... HOLD OUT... MUCH LONGER!!
WHAT... CAN I DO...?
HUF HUF

...MEW-TWO...

I REMEMBER... BLAINE TOLD ME TO WATCH MEWTWO'S BATTLE CLOSELY!

RATTLE RATTLE

NGH!!

RRH!!

ba-ba-BAMM

GLE.M YES

I CAN'T COMMAND MEWTWO... I'M NOT ITS TRAINER...BUT... IF I CAN IMITATE ITS FIGHTING STYLE...

WHAT ARE YOU DOING? RUNNING AWAY FROM ME... AND INTO THE LAVA!?

HAAA-HA HA HA!!

KRAK

KRAK

RRRK

PIKA! YOU CAN DO IT!

!?

MWURB

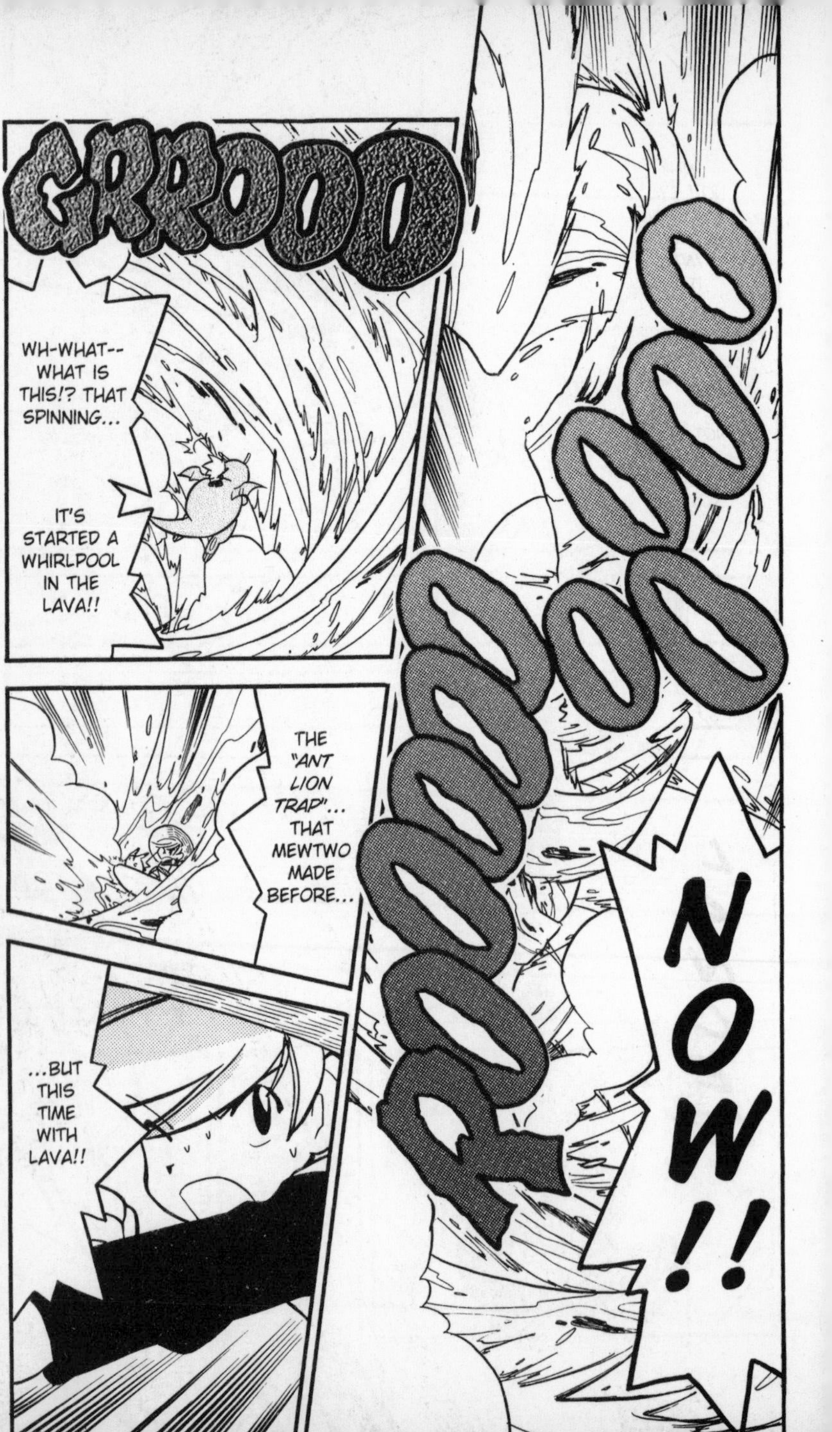
GRROOOO
WH-WHAT-- WHAT IS THIS!? THAT SPINNING...
IT'S STARTED A WHIRLPOOL IN THE LAVA!!
ROOOOOOOOOO
THE "ANT LION TRAP"... THAT MEWTWO MADE BEFORE...
...BUT THIS TIME WITH LAVA!!
NOW!!

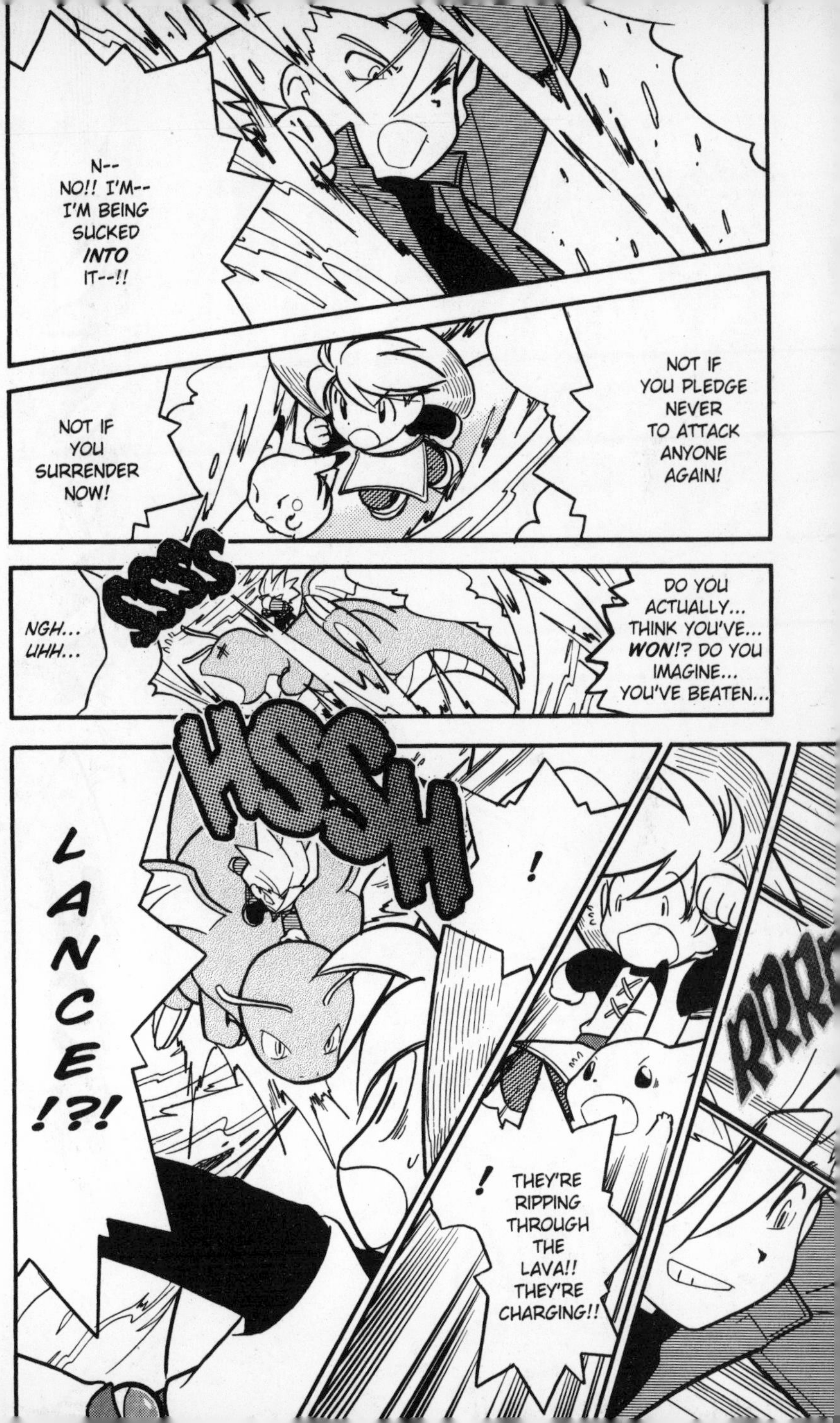
N-- NO!! I'M-- I'M BEING SUCKED *INTO* IT--!!
NOT IF YOU PLEDGE NEVER TO ATTACK ANYONE AGAIN!
NOT IF YOU SURRENDER NOW!
SSS
DO YOU ACTUALLY... THINK YOU'VE... *WON*!? DO YOU IMAGINE... YOU'VE BEATEN...
NGH... UHH...
HSSH
!
LANCE!?!
THEY'RE RIPPING THROUGH THE LAVA!! THEY'RE CHARGING!!
!

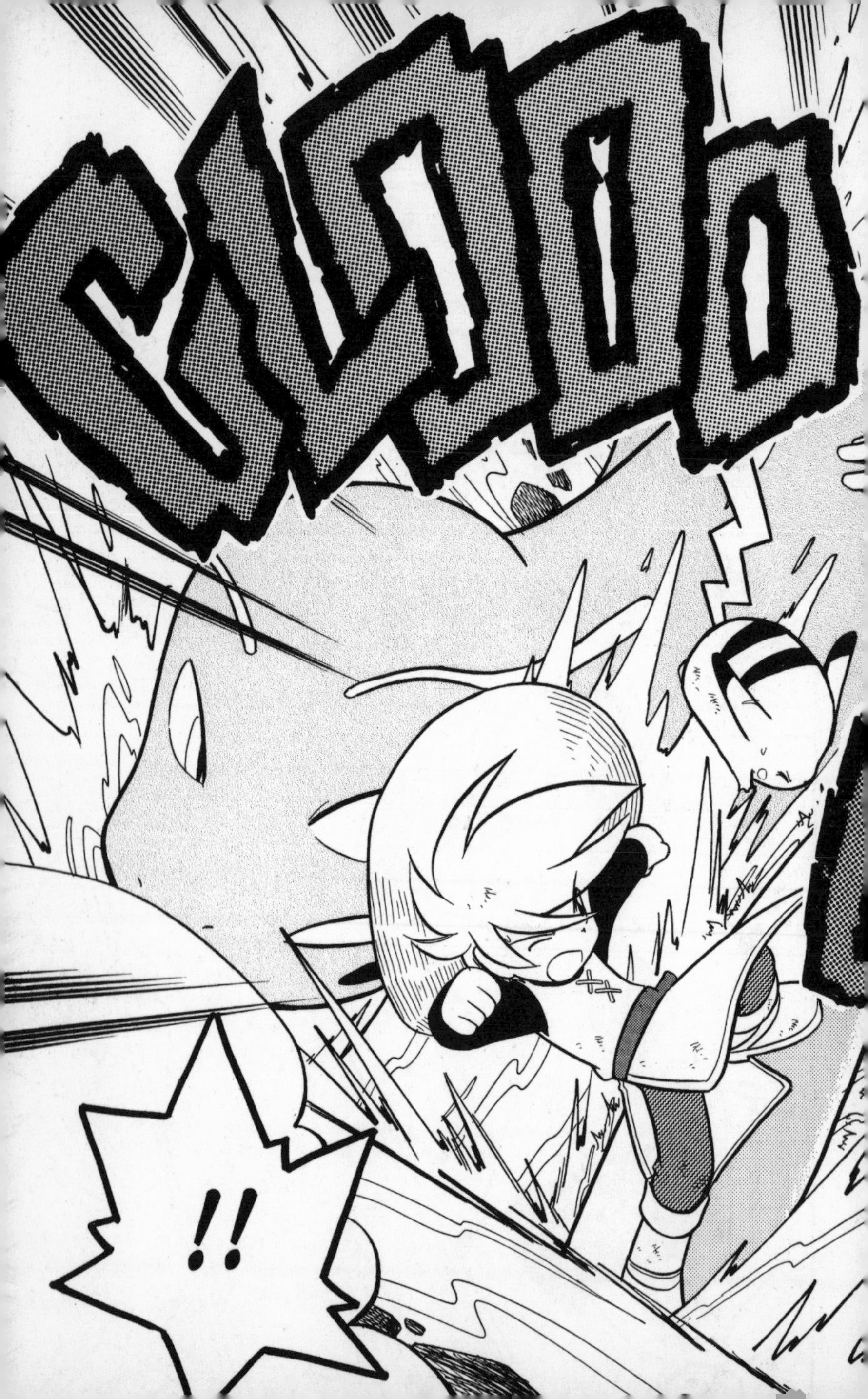
!!

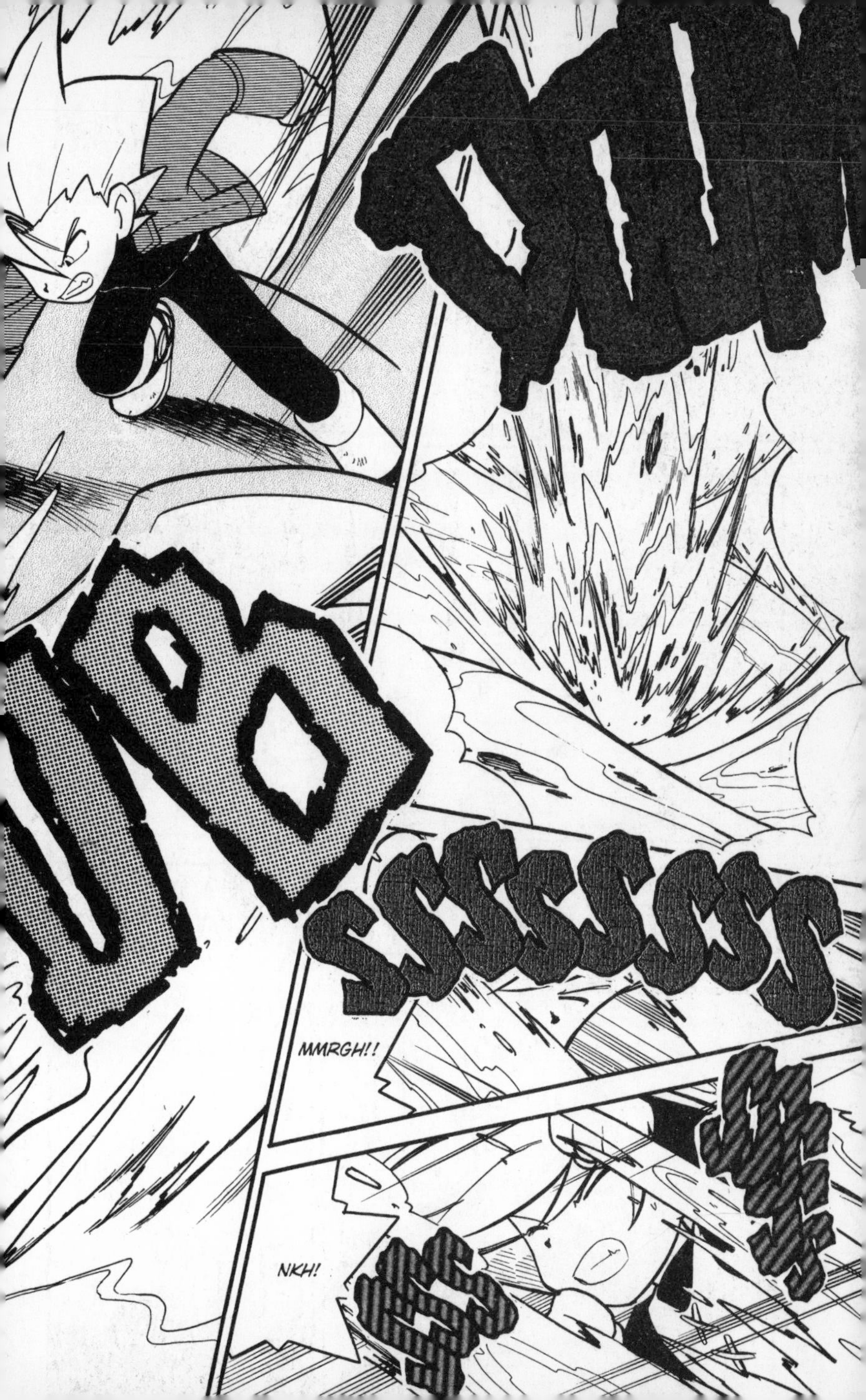
MMRGH!!
NKH!

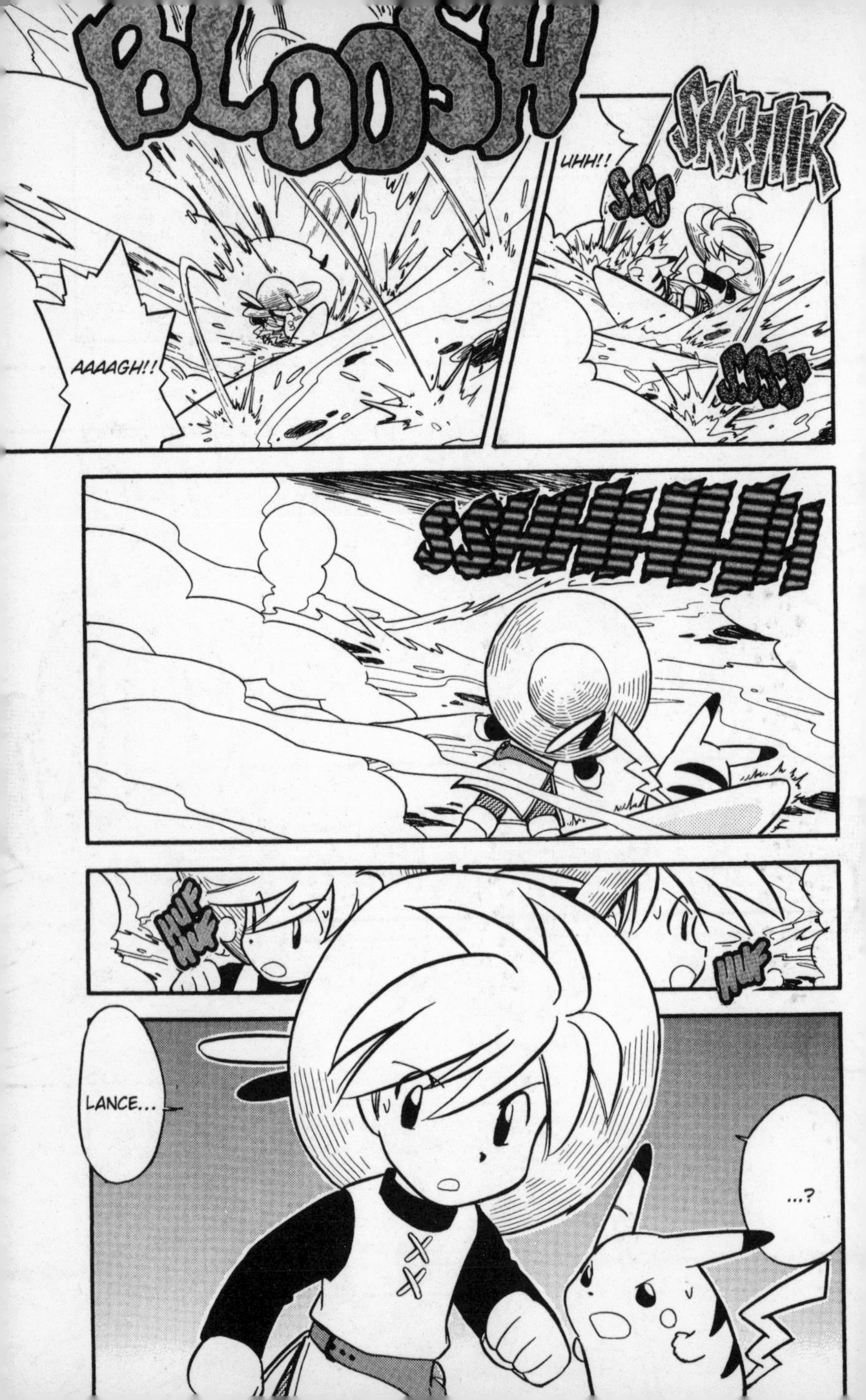
BLOOSH
AAAAGH!!
SKRIIIK
UHH!!
SSS
SSSS
SSHHHHHHH
HUF HUF
HUF
LANCE...
...?

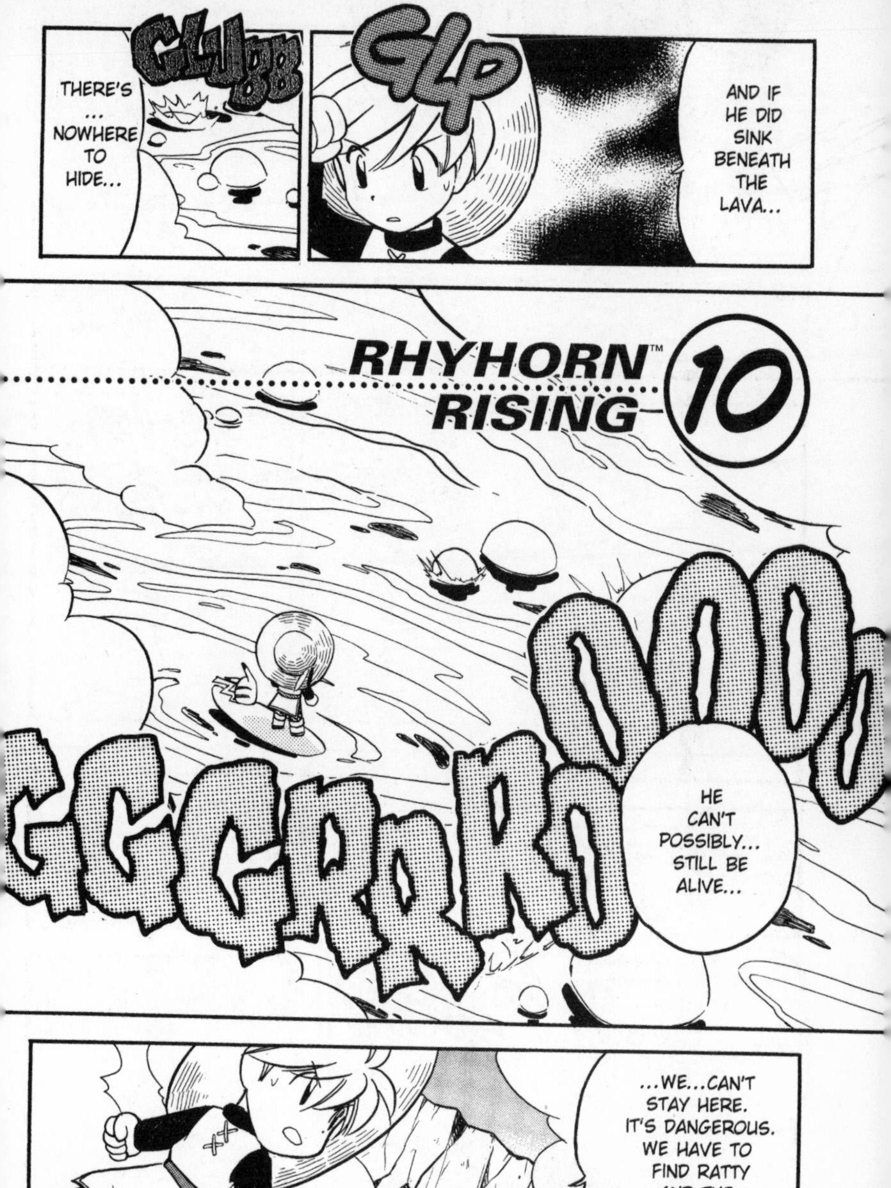
GLUBB
THERE'S ... NOWHERE TO HIDE...
GLP
AND IF HE DID SINK BENEATH THE LAVA...
RHYHORN™ RISING
10
GGGRRROOOO
HE CAN'T POSSIBLY... STILL BE ALIVE...
...WE...CAN'T STAY HERE. IT'S DANGEROUS. WE HAVE TO FIND RATTY AND THE OTHERS...

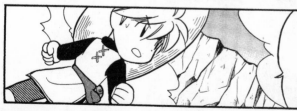

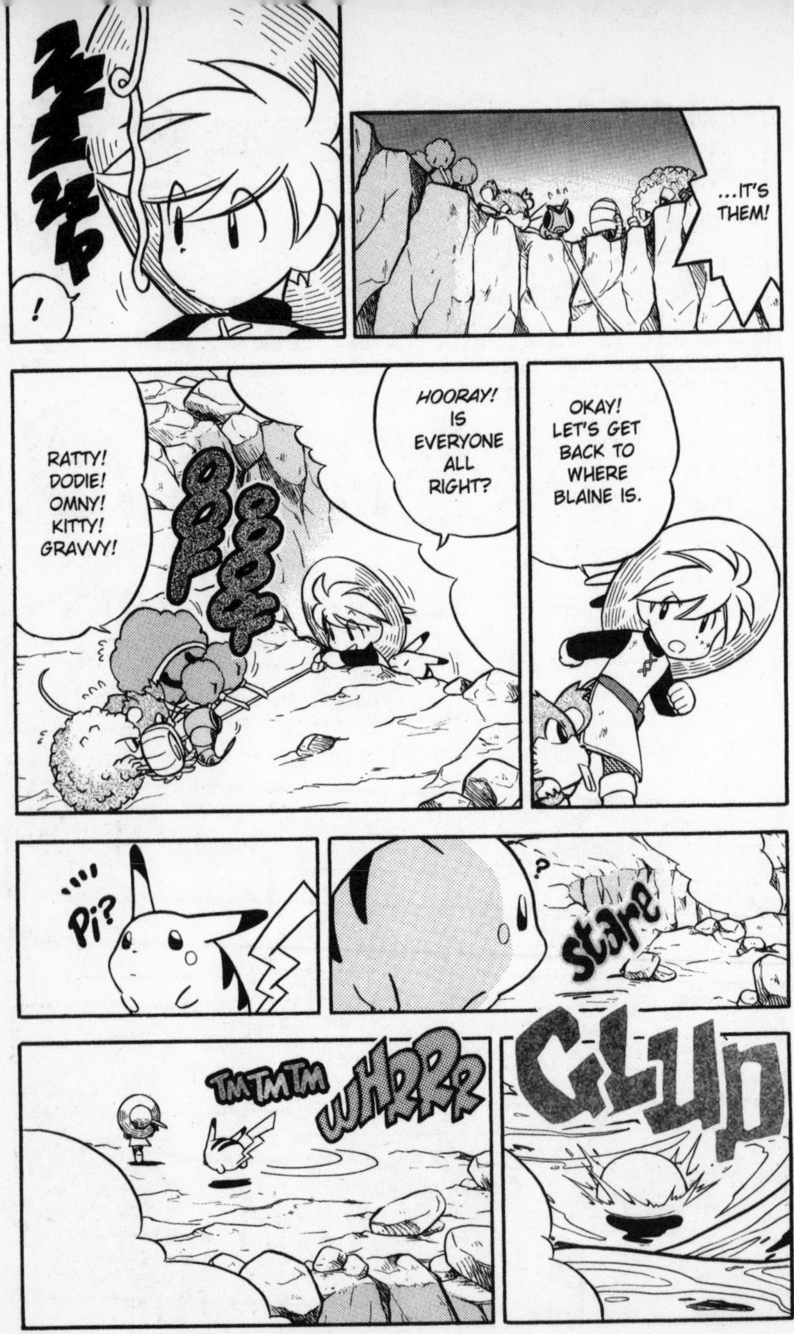
!
...IT'S THEM!
RATTY! DODIE! OMNY! KITTY! GRAVVY!
HOORAY! IS EVERYONE ALL RIGHT?
OKAY! LET'S GET BACK TO WHERE BLAINE IS.
...Pi?
?
stare
TMTMTM
GLUP

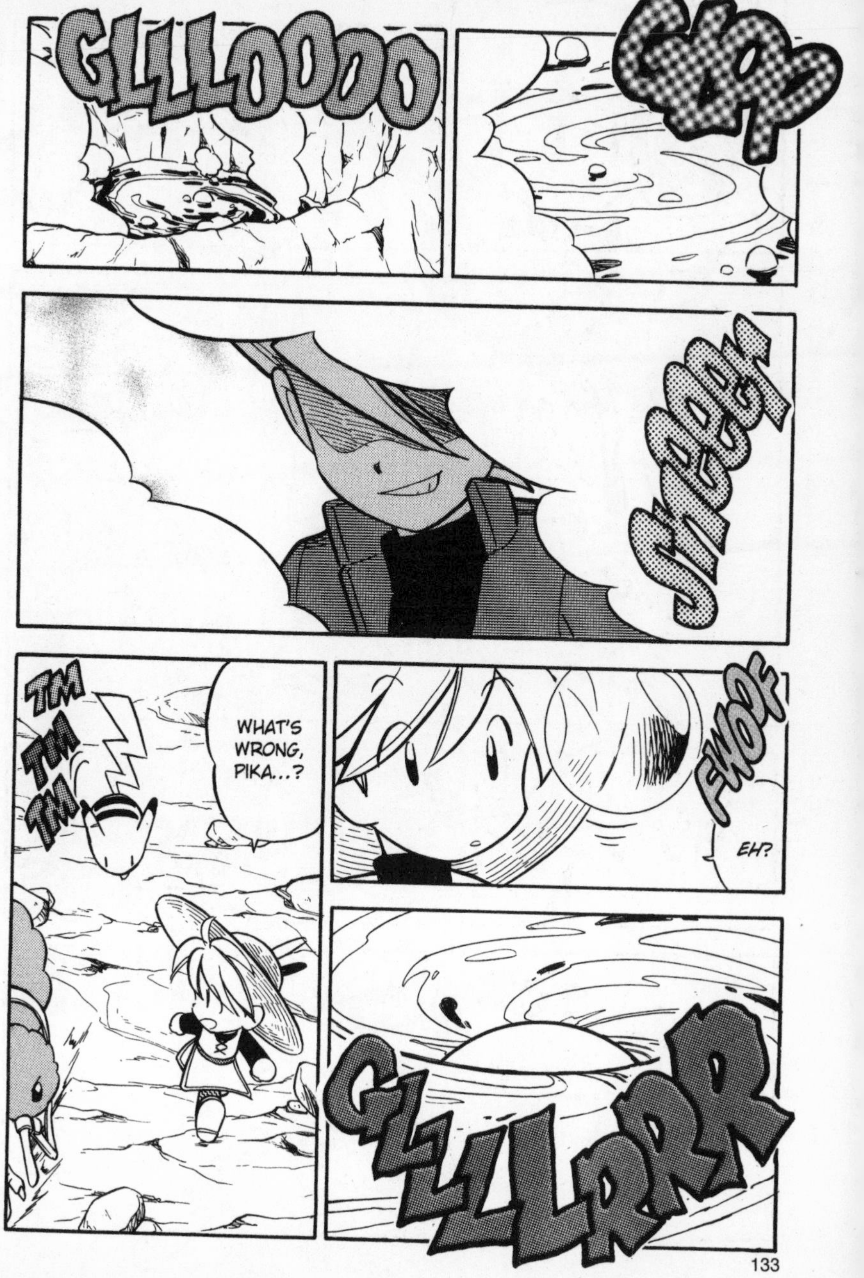
GLLLOOOO
GLOP
TM
TM
TM
WHAT'S WRONG, PIKA...?
FWOOF
EH?
GLLLRRR

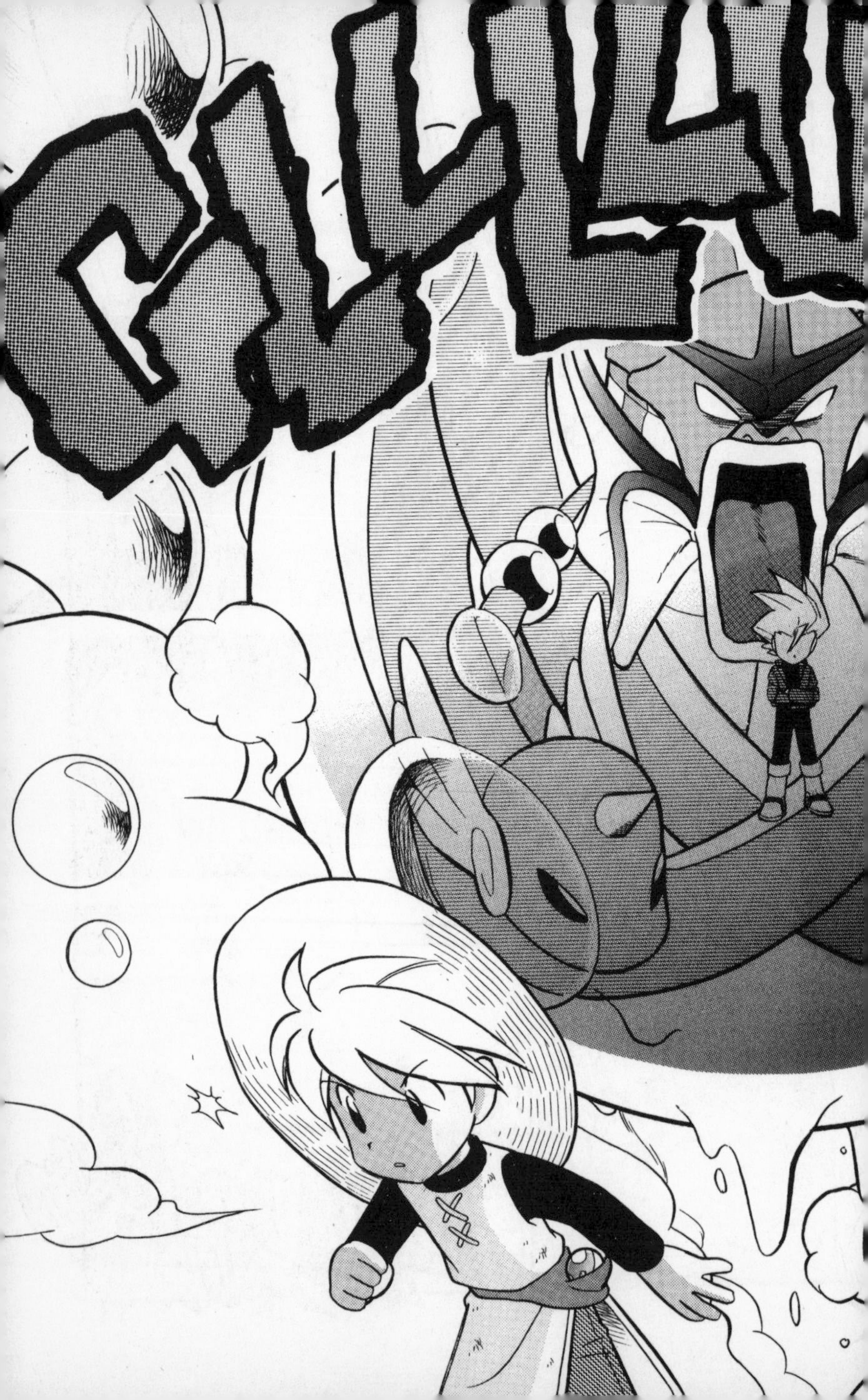

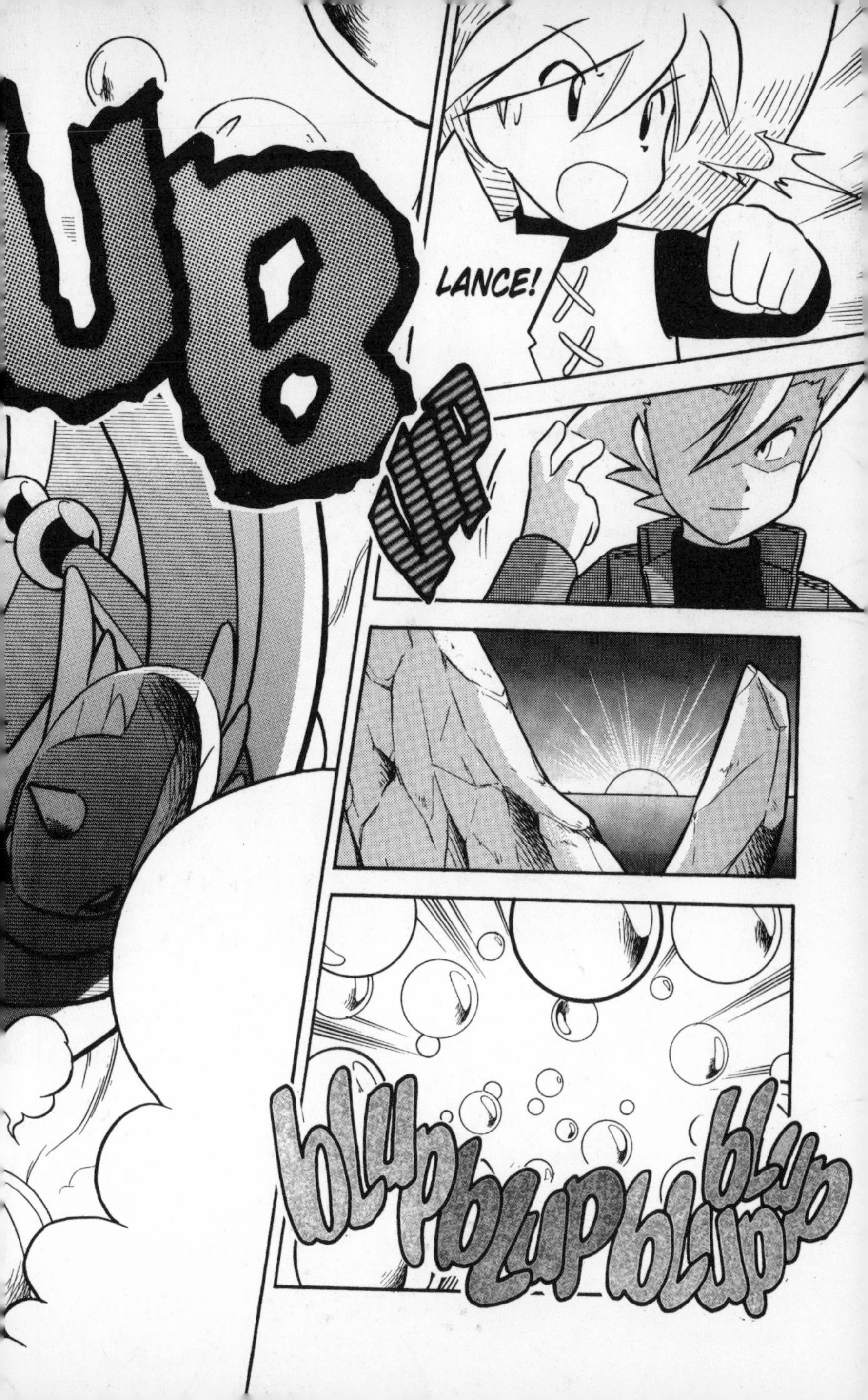
LANCE!
blup blup blup blup

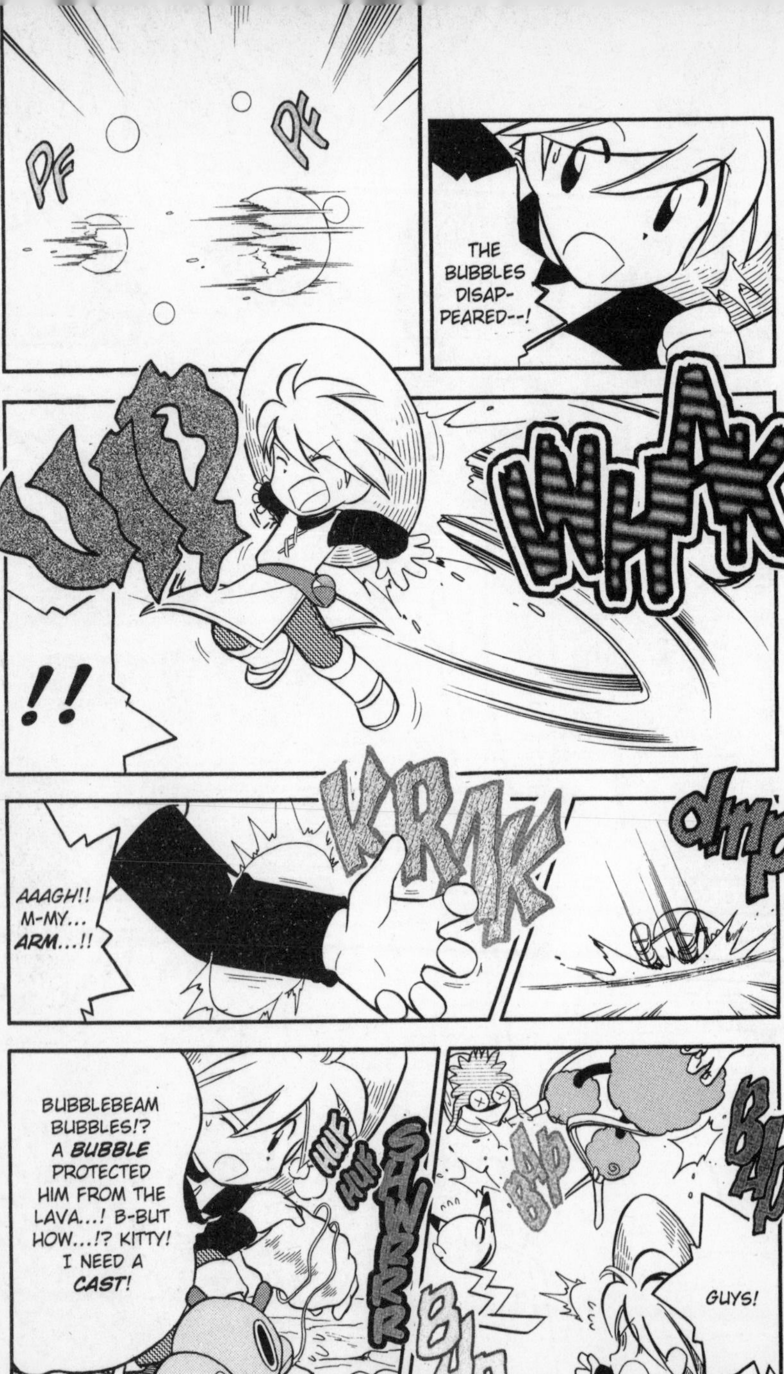
PF
PF
THE BUBBLES DISAPPEARED--!
WHAK
!!
drip
KRAK
AAAGH!! M-MY... ***ARM***...!!
BAP
BAP
GUYS!
BAP
SHWRRR
HUF HUF
BUBBLEBEAM BUBBLES!? A ***BUBBLE*** PROTECTED HIM FROM THE LAVA...! B-BUT HOW...!? KITTY! I NEED A ***CAST***!

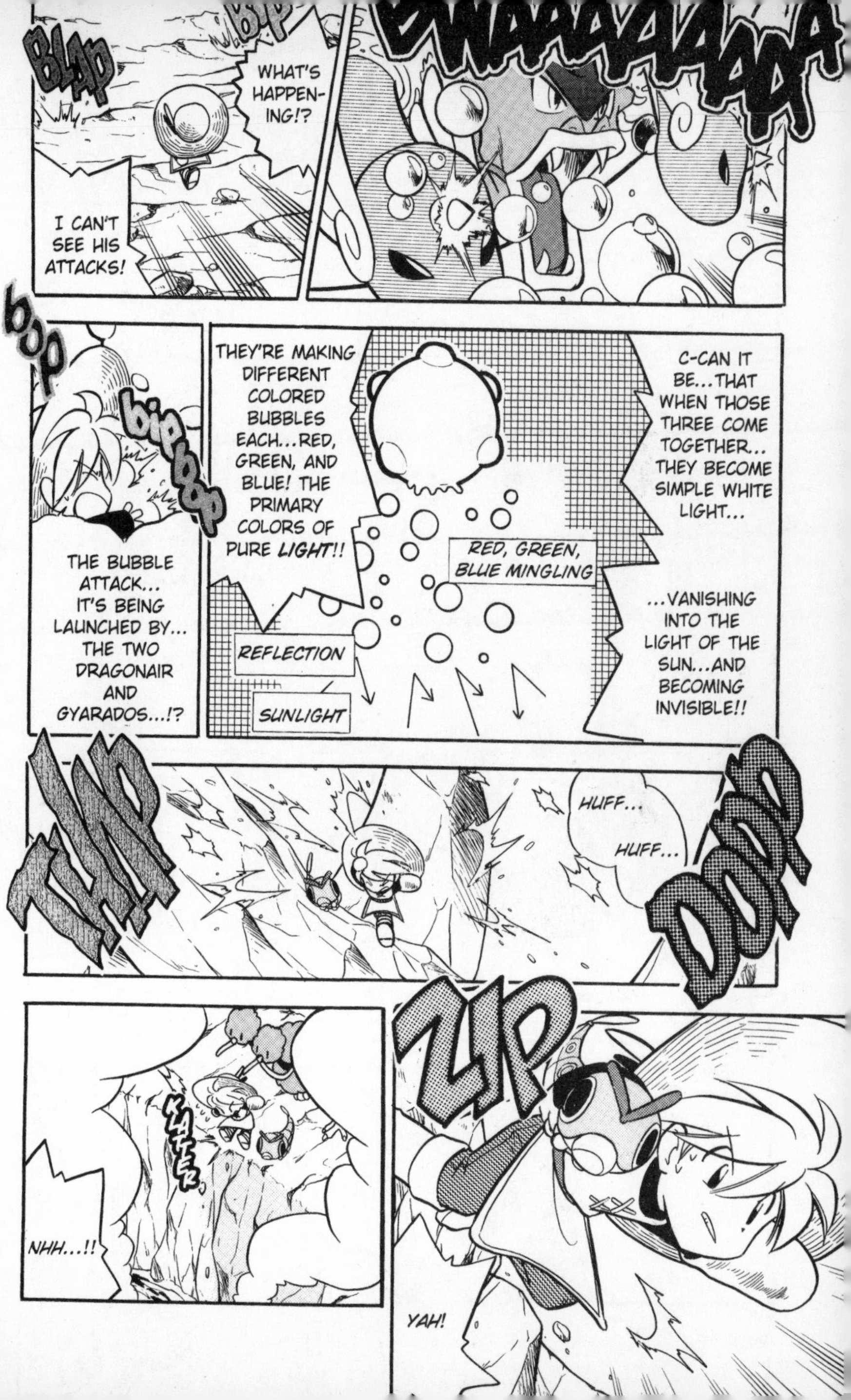
BLAP
BIP
WHAT'S HAPPEN-ING!?
I CAN'T SEE HIS ATTACKS!
BOOP
BIP BOOP
THE BUBBLE ATTACK... IT'S BEING LAUNCHED BY... THE TWO DRAGONAIR AND GYARADOS...!?
THEY'RE MAKING DIFFERENT COLORED BUBBLES EACH...RED, GREEN, AND BLUE! THE PRIMARY COLORS OF PURE LIGHT!!
REFLECTION
SUNLIGHT
RED, GREEN, BLUE MINGLING
C-CAN IT BE...THAT WHEN THOSE THREE COME TOGETHER... THEY BECOME SIMPLE WHITE LIGHT...
...VANISHING INTO THE LIGHT OF THE SUN...AND BECOMING INVISIBLE!!
HUFF...
HUFF...
ZIP
NHH...!!
YAH!

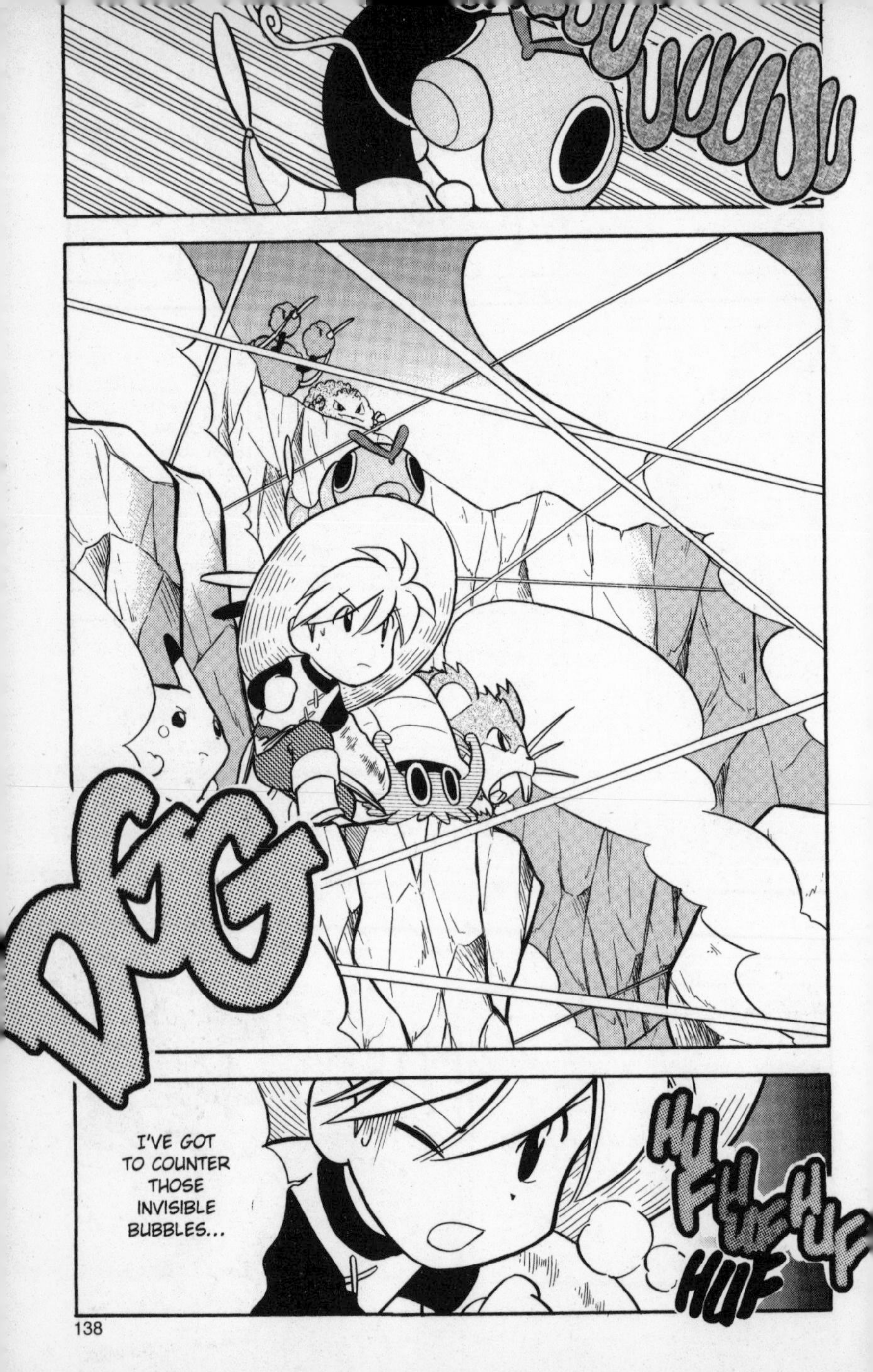
DIG
I'VE GOT TO COUNTER THOSE INVISIBLE BUBBLES...
HUF HUF HUF HUF

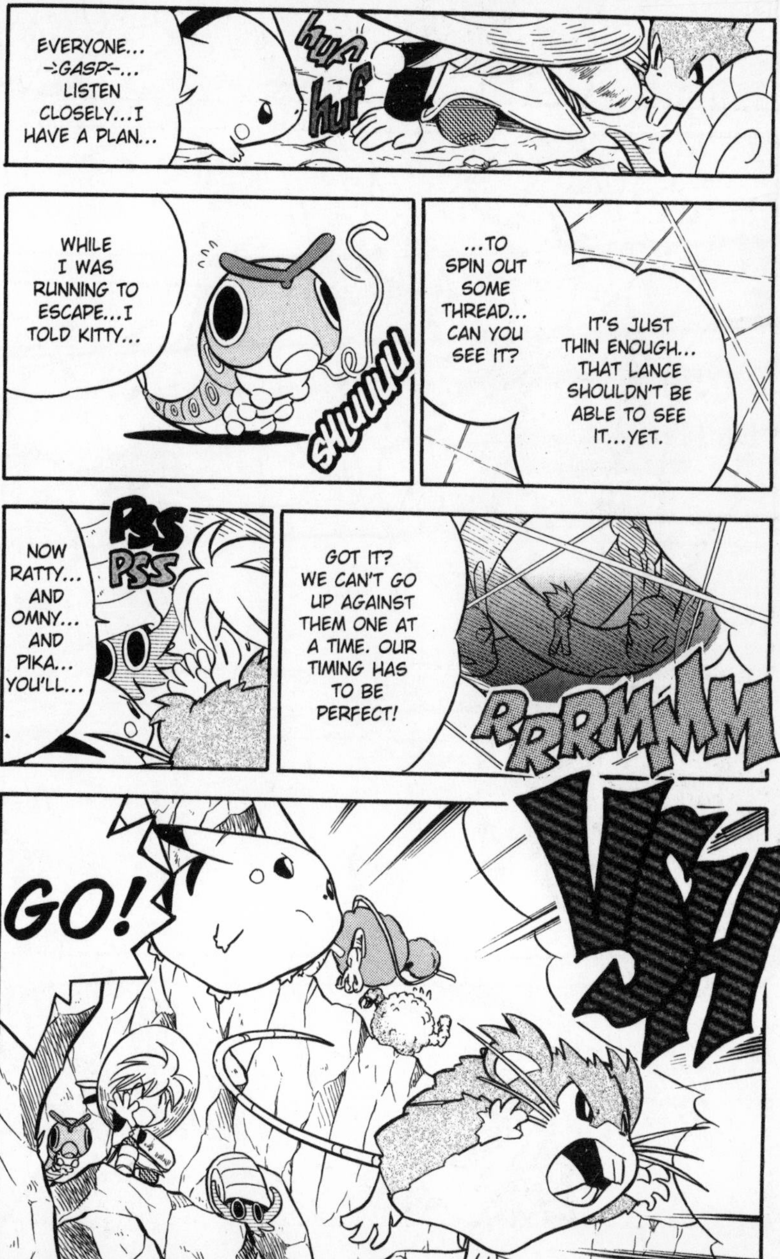
EVERYONE... -GASP-... LISTEN CLOSELY...I HAVE A PLAN...
huf huf
WHILE I WAS RUNNING TO ESCAPE...I TOLD KITTY...
SHUUUU
...TO SPIN OUT SOME THREAD... CAN YOU SEE IT?
IT'S JUST THIN ENOUGH... THAT LANCE SHOULDN'T BE ABLE TO SEE IT...YET.
NOW RATTY... AND OMNY... AND PIKA... YOU'LL...
PSS PSS
GOT IT? WE CAN'T GO UP AGAINST THEM ONE AT A TIME. OUR TIMING HAS TO BE PERFECT!
RRRMMM
GO!

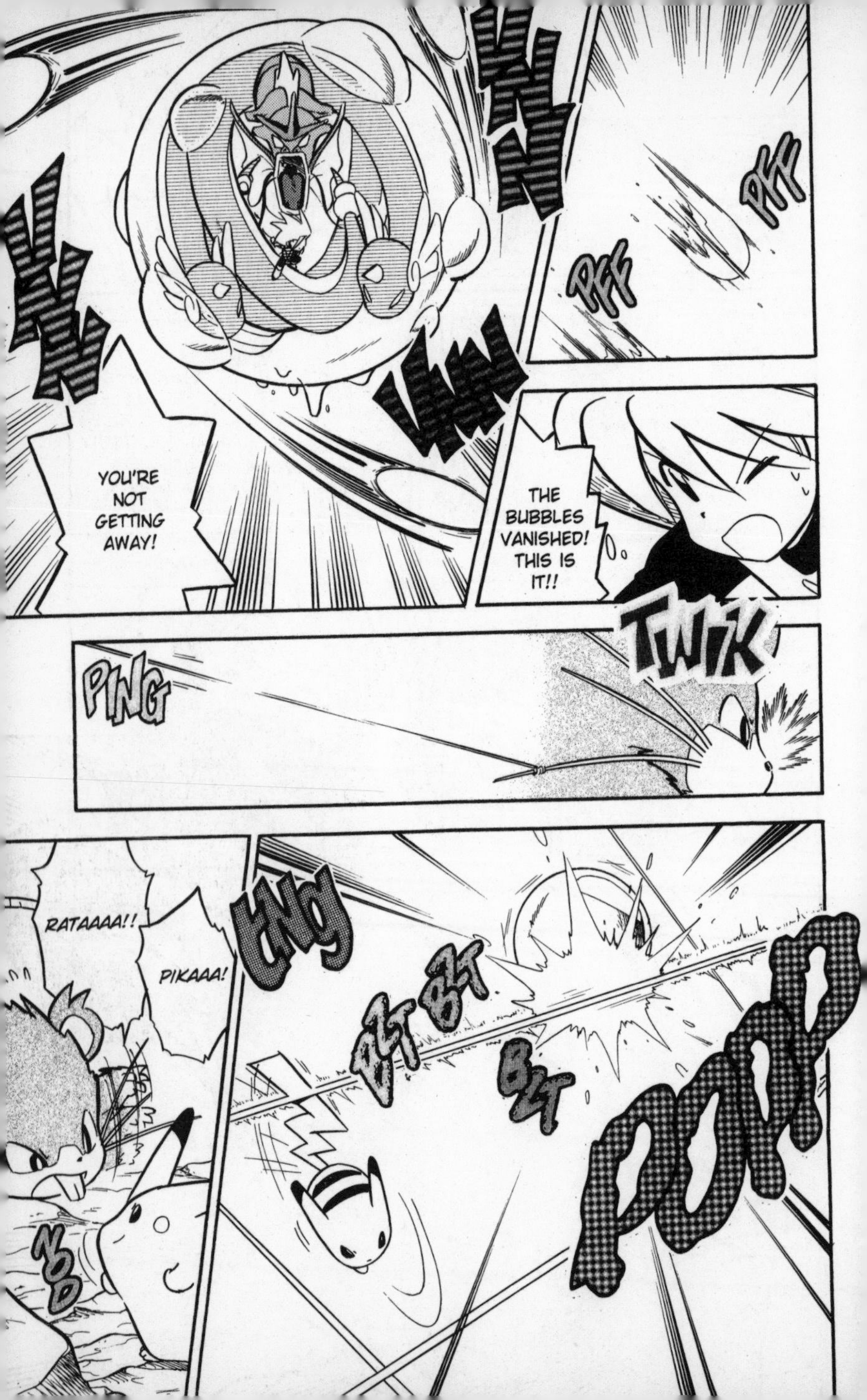
KWN
PFF
PFF
KWN
WN
YOU'RE NOT GETTING AWAY!
THE BUBBLES VANISHED! THIS IS IT!!
TWIK
PING
TNG
RATAAAA!!
PIKAAA!
BZT BZT
BZT
POP
ZG

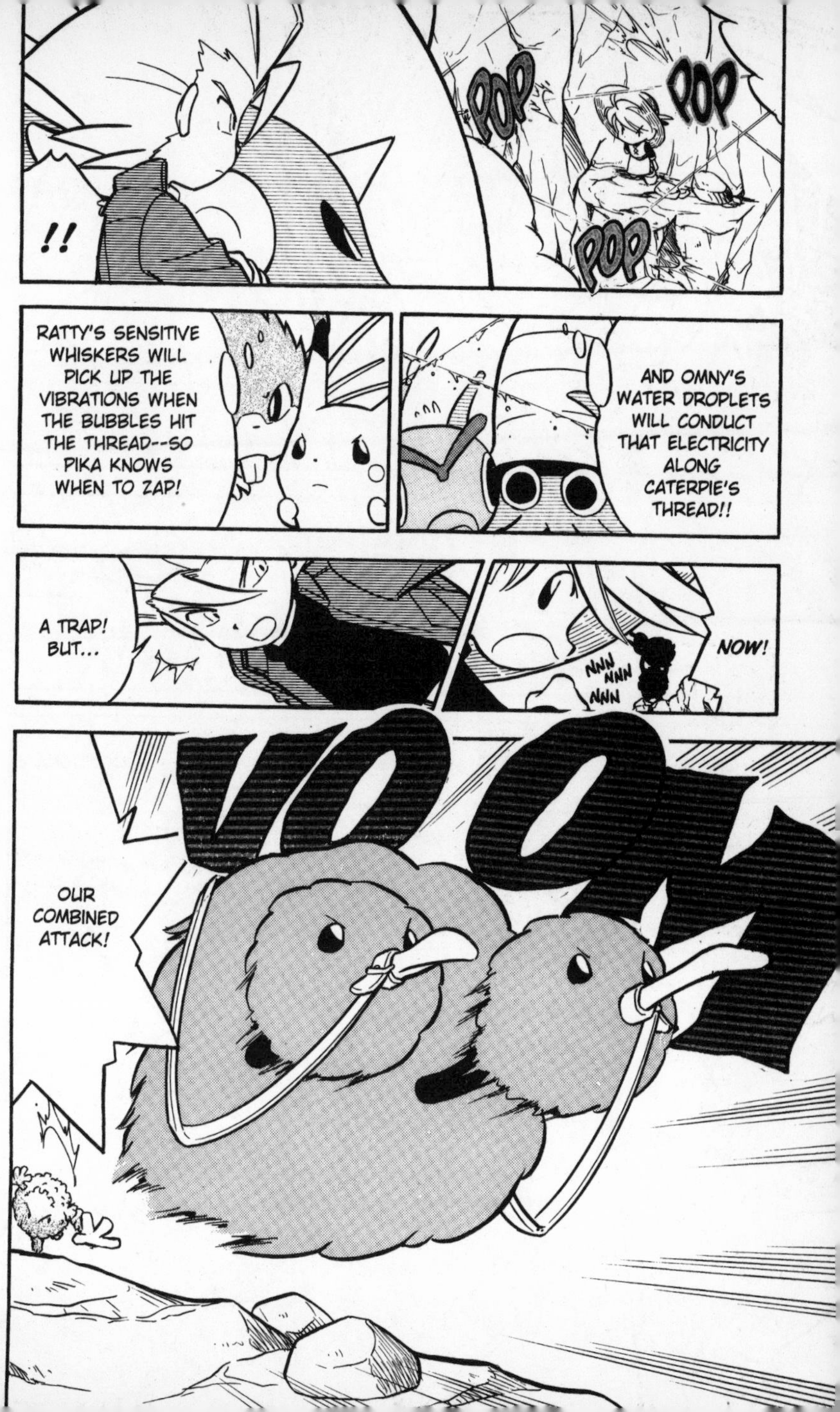
!!
POP
POP
POP
RATTY'S SENSITIVE WHISKERS WILL PICK UP THE VIBRATIONS WHEN THE BUBBLES HIT THE THREAD--SO PIKA KNOWS WHEN TO ZAP!
AND OMNY'S WATER DROPLETS WILL CONDUCT THAT ELECTRICITY ALONG CATERPIE'S THREAD!!
A TRAP! BUT...
NNN NNN NNN
NOW!
VOOM
OUR COMBINED ATTACK!

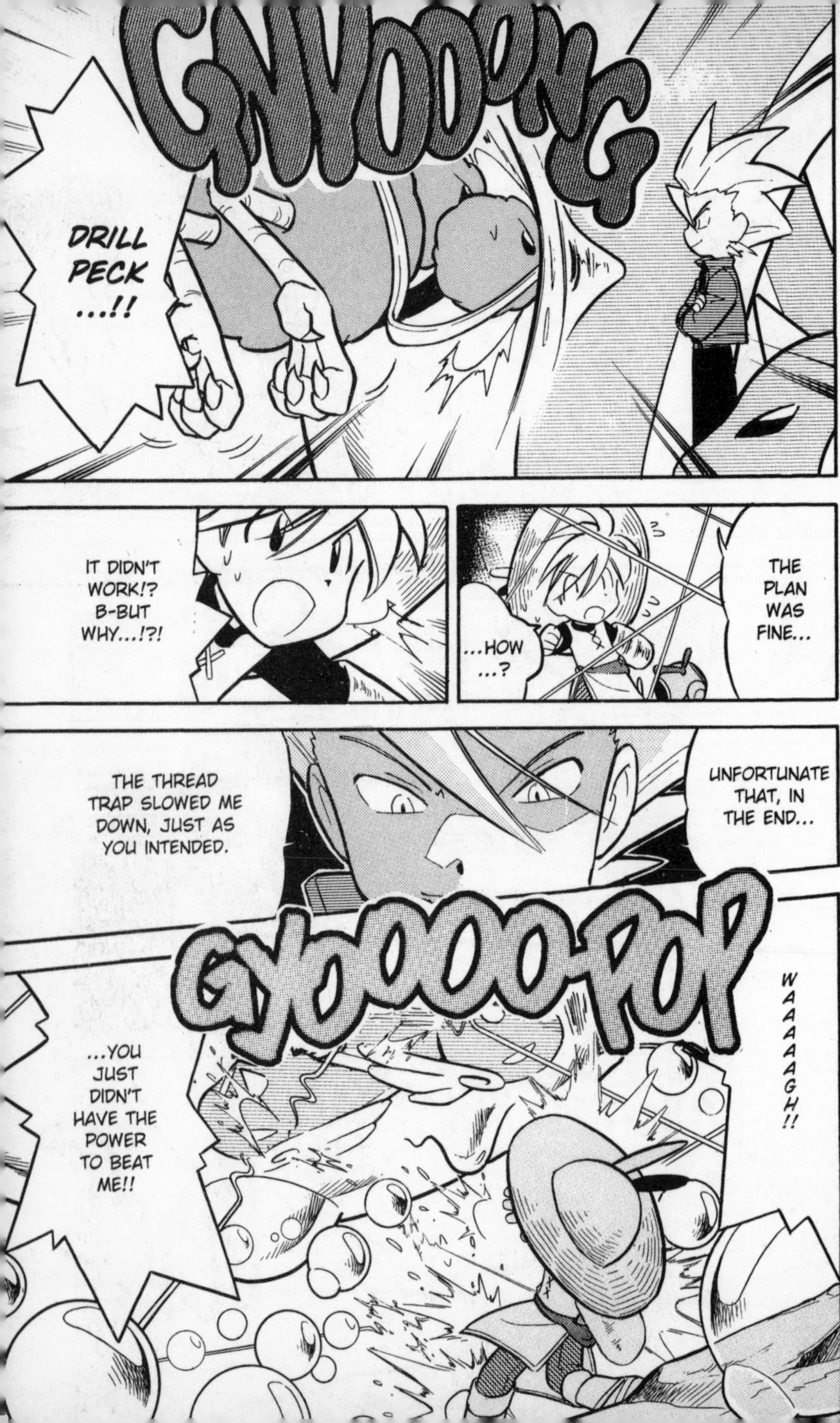
GNYOOONG
DRILL PECK ...!!
IT DIDN'T WORK!? B-BUT WHY...!?!
...HOW ...?
THE PLAN WAS FINE...
THE THREAD TRAP SLOWED ME DOWN, JUST AS YOU INTENDED.
UNFORTUNATE THAT, IN THE END...
GYOOOO-POP
...YOU JUST DIDN'T HAVE THE POWER TO BEAT ME!!
WAAAAAAGH!!

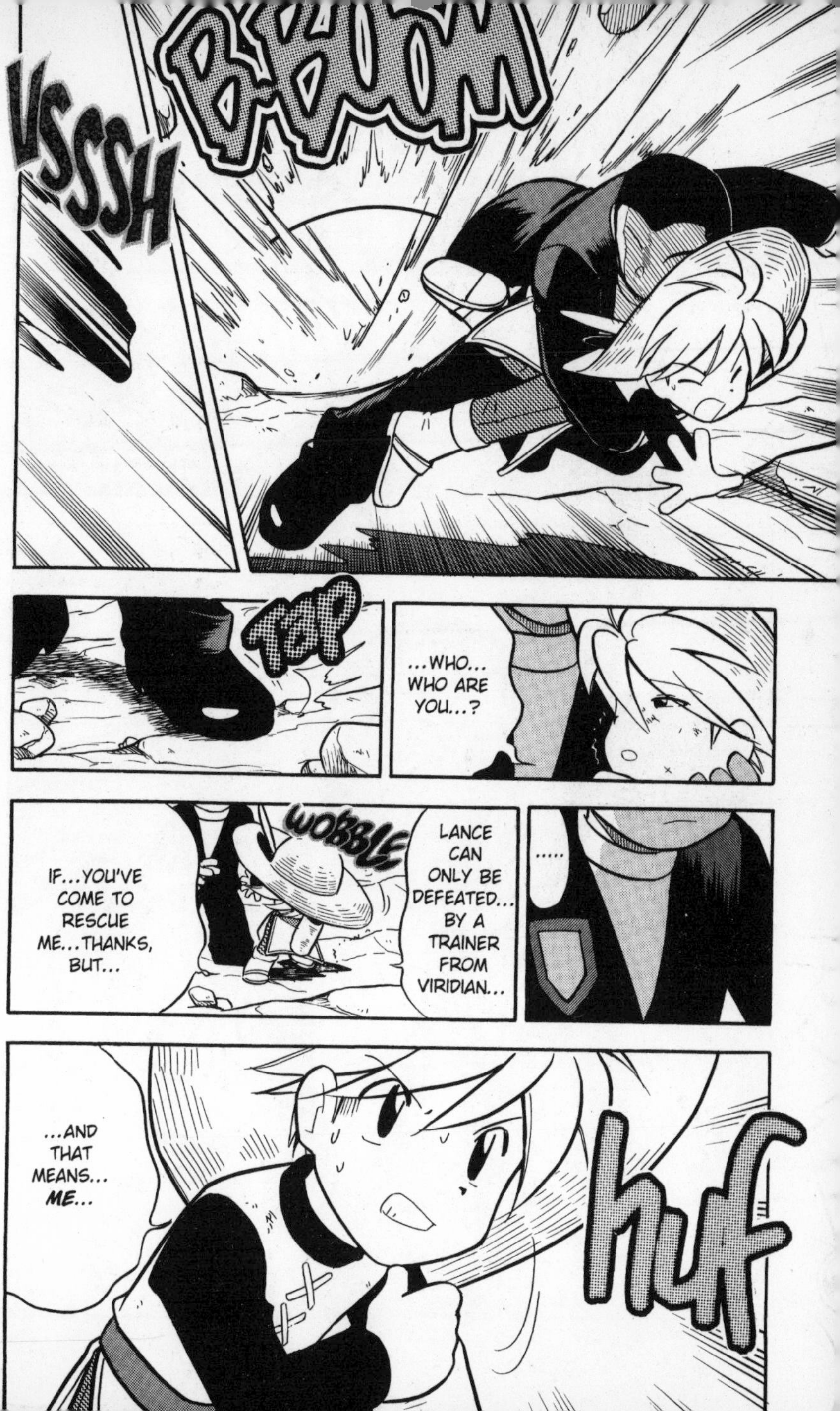
VSSSH
BBOOM
TAP
...WHO... WHO ARE YOU...?
WOBBLE
IF...YOU'VE COME TO RESCUE ME...THANKS, BUT...
LANCE CAN ONLY BE DEFEATED... BY A TRAINER FROM VIRIDIAN...
.....
...AND THAT MEANS... *ME*...
HUF

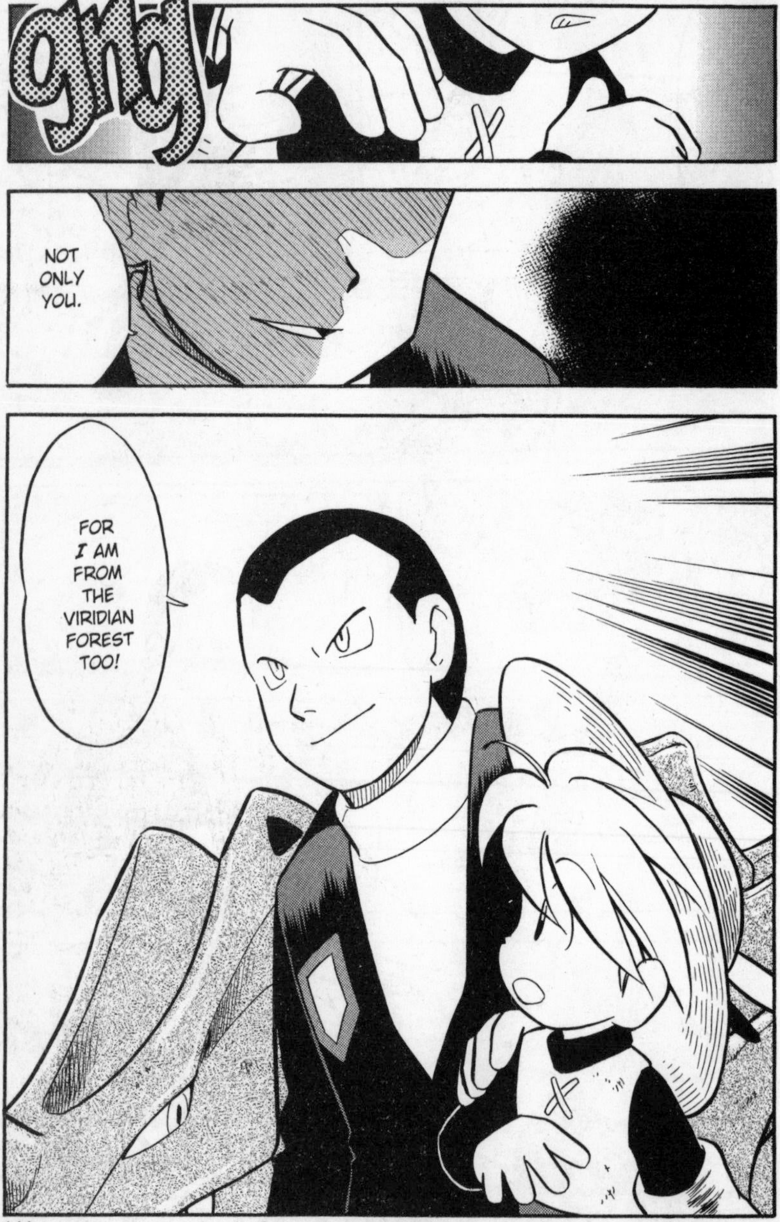
gng
NOT ONLY YOU.
FOR *I* AM FROM THE VIRIDIAN FOREST TOO!

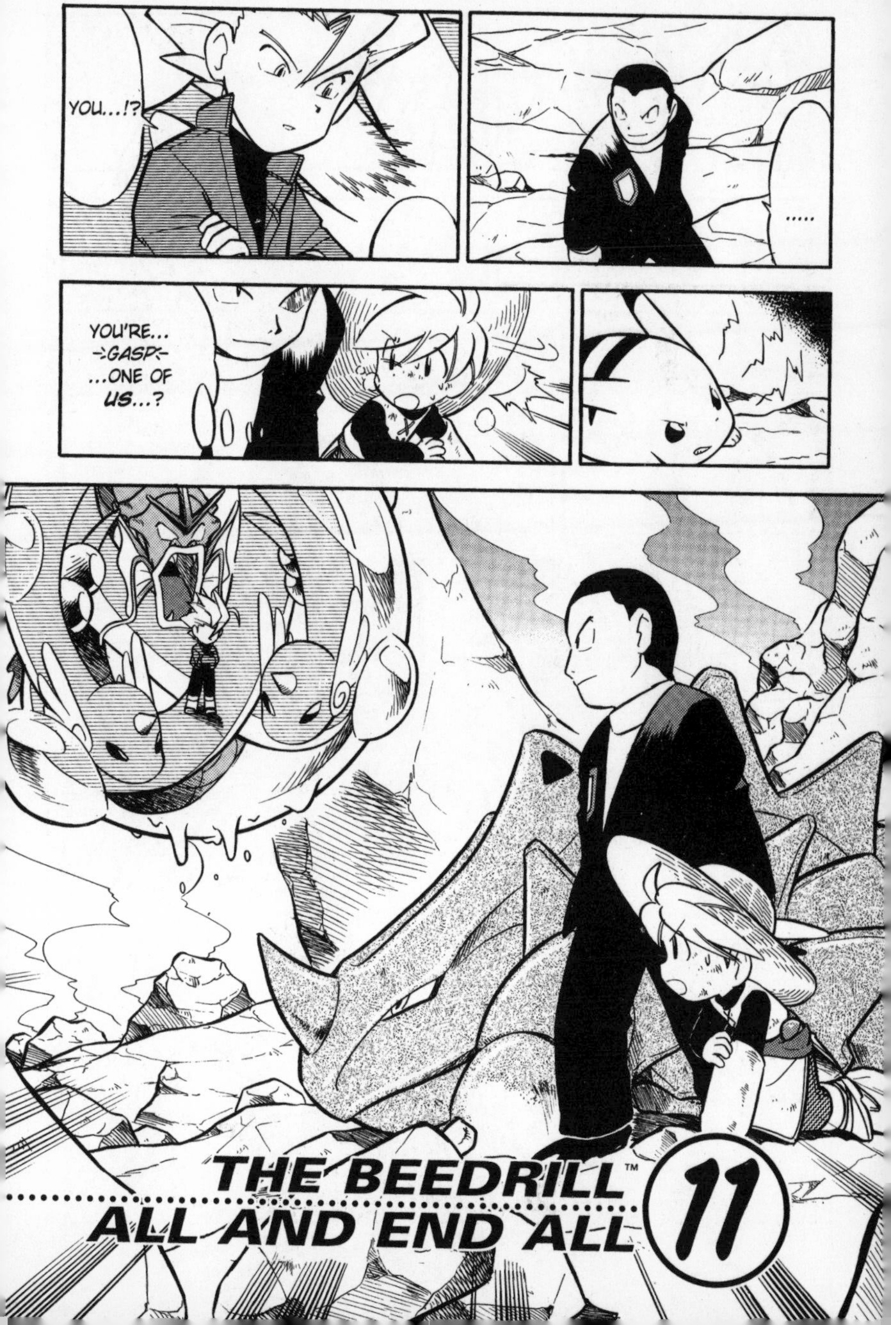

.....
YOU...!?
YOU'RE...
-GASP-
...ONE OF
US...?
THE BEEDRILL™
ALL AND END ALL
11

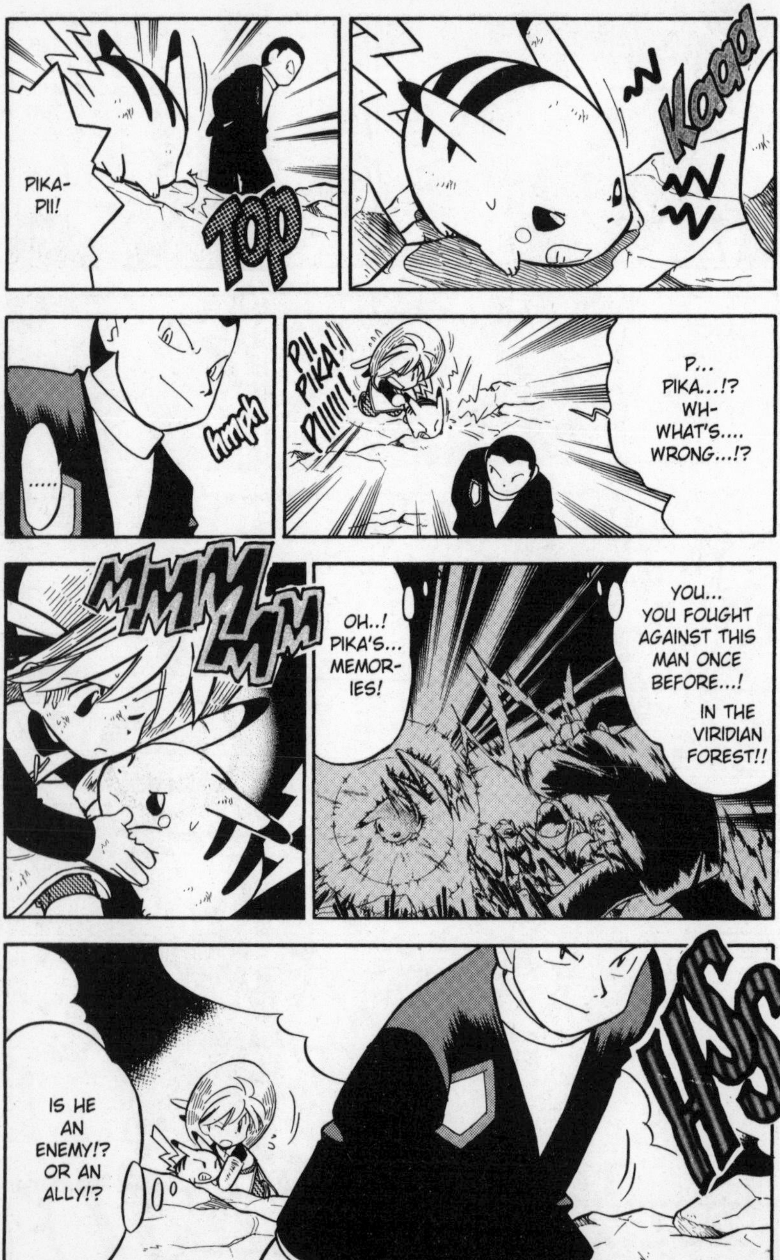
PIKA-PII!
TOP
Kaaa
hmph
......
PI! PIKA!! PI!!!!!!
P... PIKA...!? WH-WHAT'S.... WRONG...!?
MMMMMM
OH..! PIKA'S... MEMORIES!
YOU... YOU FOUGHT AGAINST THIS MAN ONCE BEFORE...!
IN THE VIRIDIAN FOREST!!
IS HE AN ENEMY!? OR AN ALLY!?
HISS

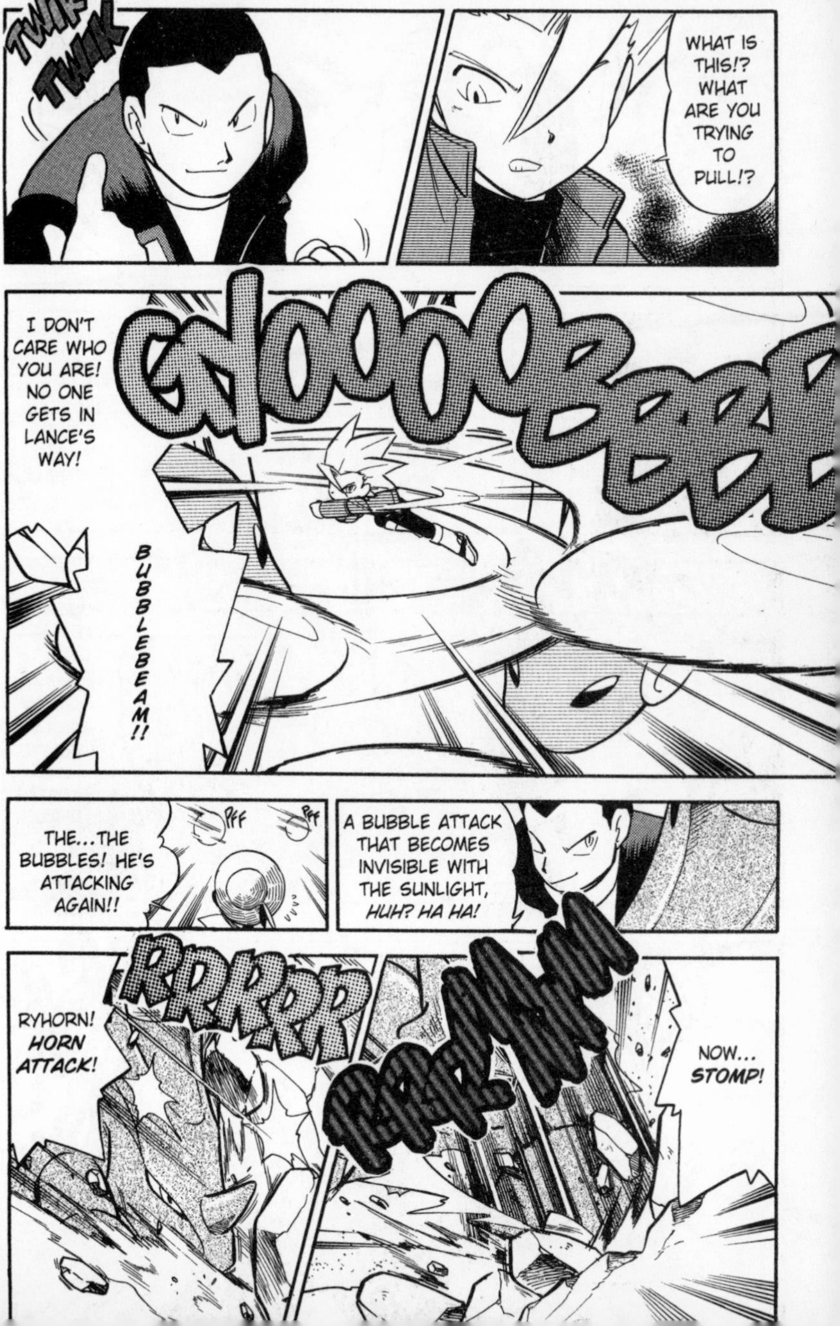
TWIK TWIK
WHAT IS THIS!? WHAT ARE YOU TRYING TO PULL!?
I DON'T CARE WHO YOU ARE! NO ONE GETS IN LANCE'S WAY!
BUBBLEBEAM!!
PFF
PFF
THE...THE BUBBLES! HE'S ATTACKING AGAIN!!
A BUBBLE ATTACK THAT BECOMES INVISIBLE WITH THE SUNLIGHT, *HUH? HA HA!*
RYHORN! *HORN ATTACK!*
NOW... *STOMP!*

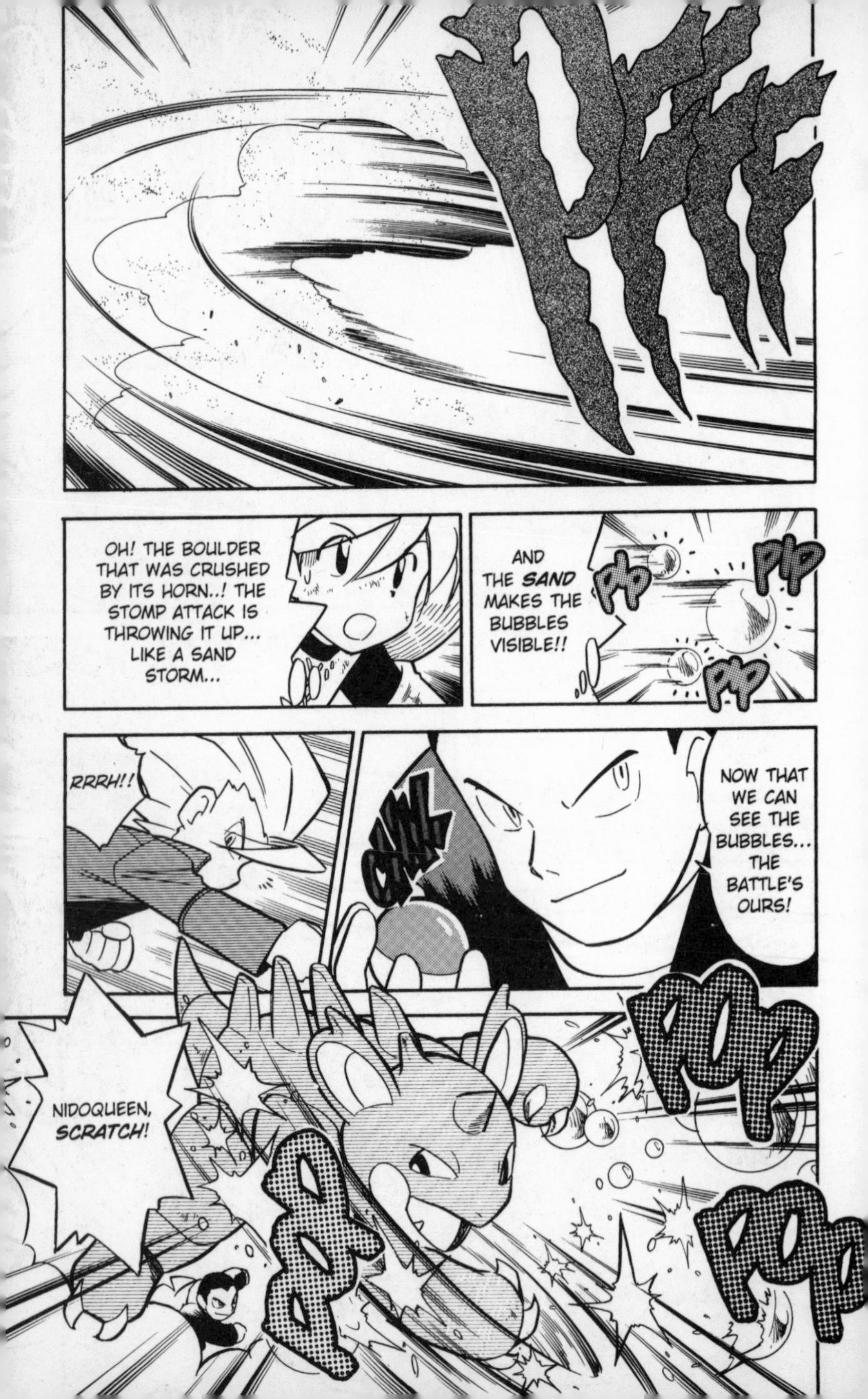
OH! THE BOULDER THAT WAS CRUSHED BY ITS HORN..! THE STOMP ATTACK IS THROWING IT UP... LIKE A SAND STORM...
AND THE SAND MAKES THE BUBBLES VISIBLE!!
PIP
PIP
PIP
RRRH!!
NOW THAT WE CAN SEE THE BUBBLES... THE BATTLE'S OURS!
NIDOQUEEN, SCRATCH!
POP
POP
POP

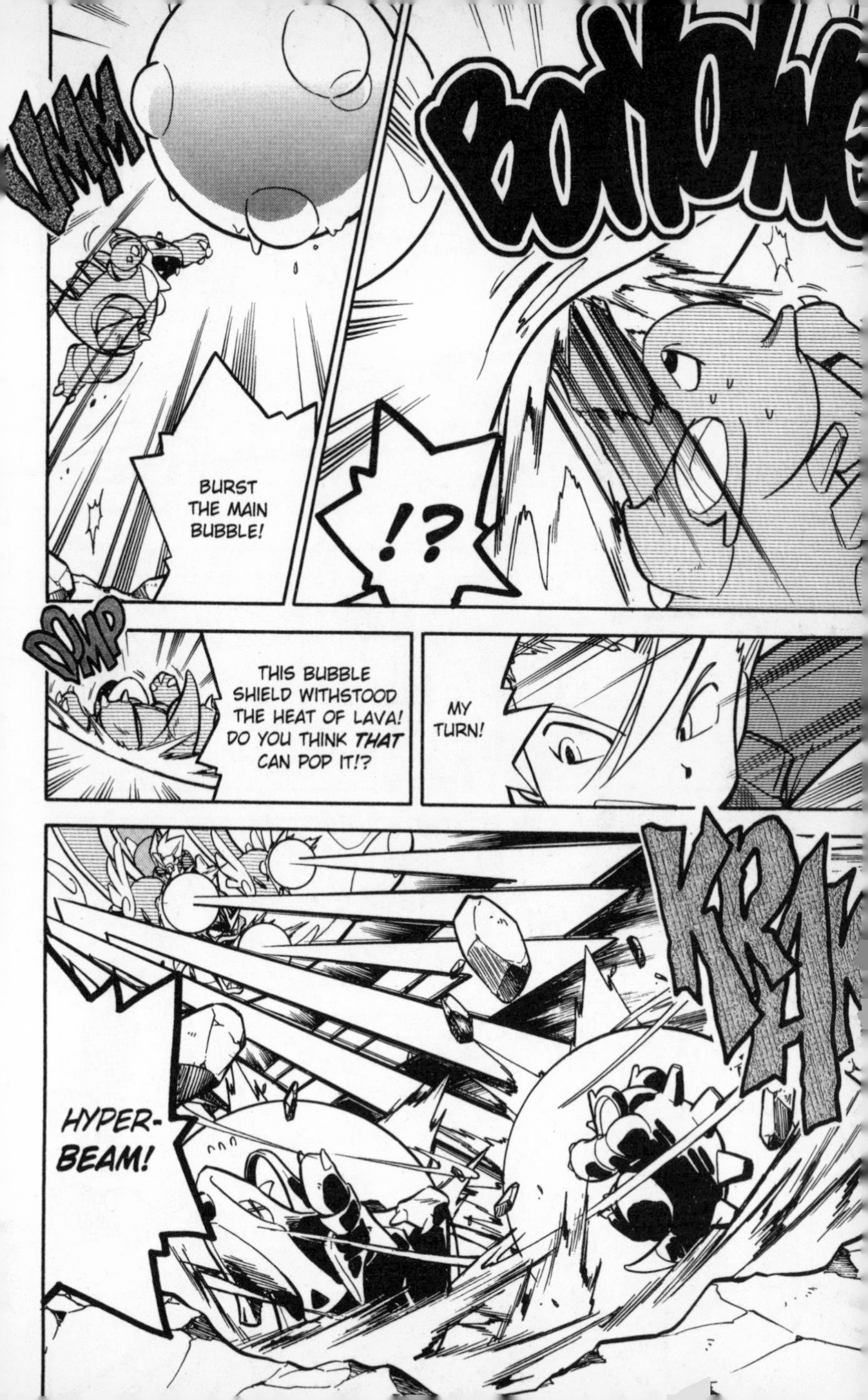
!?
BURST THE MAIN BUBBLE!
MY TURN!
THIS BUBBLE SHIELD WITHSTOOD THE HEAT OF LAVA! DO YOU THINK *THAT* CAN POP IT!?
HYPER-BEAM!

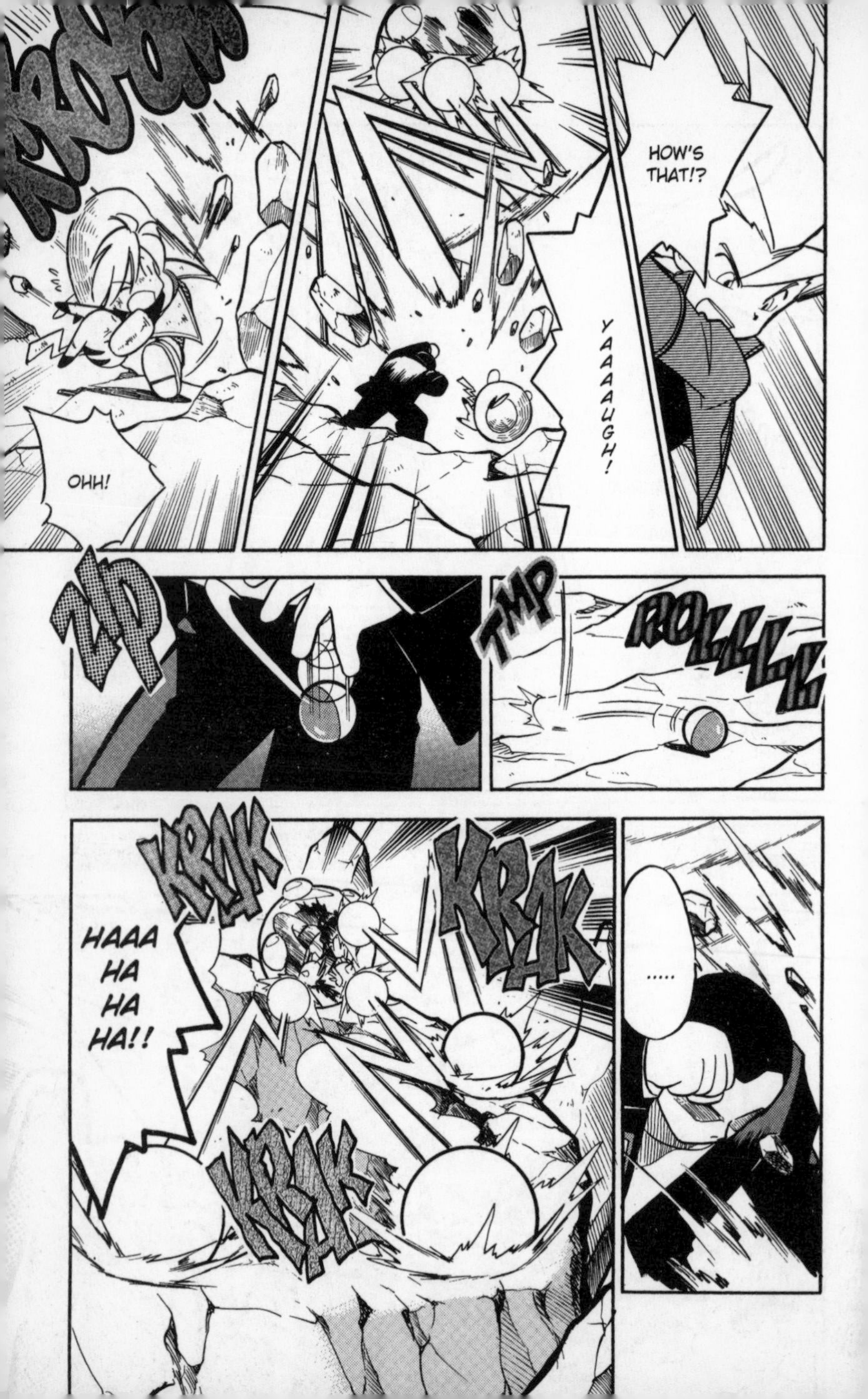
OHH!
YAAAAAUGH!
HOW'S THAT!?
ZIP
TMP
ROLLLL
KRAK
HAAA HA HA HA!!
KRAK
KRAK
.....

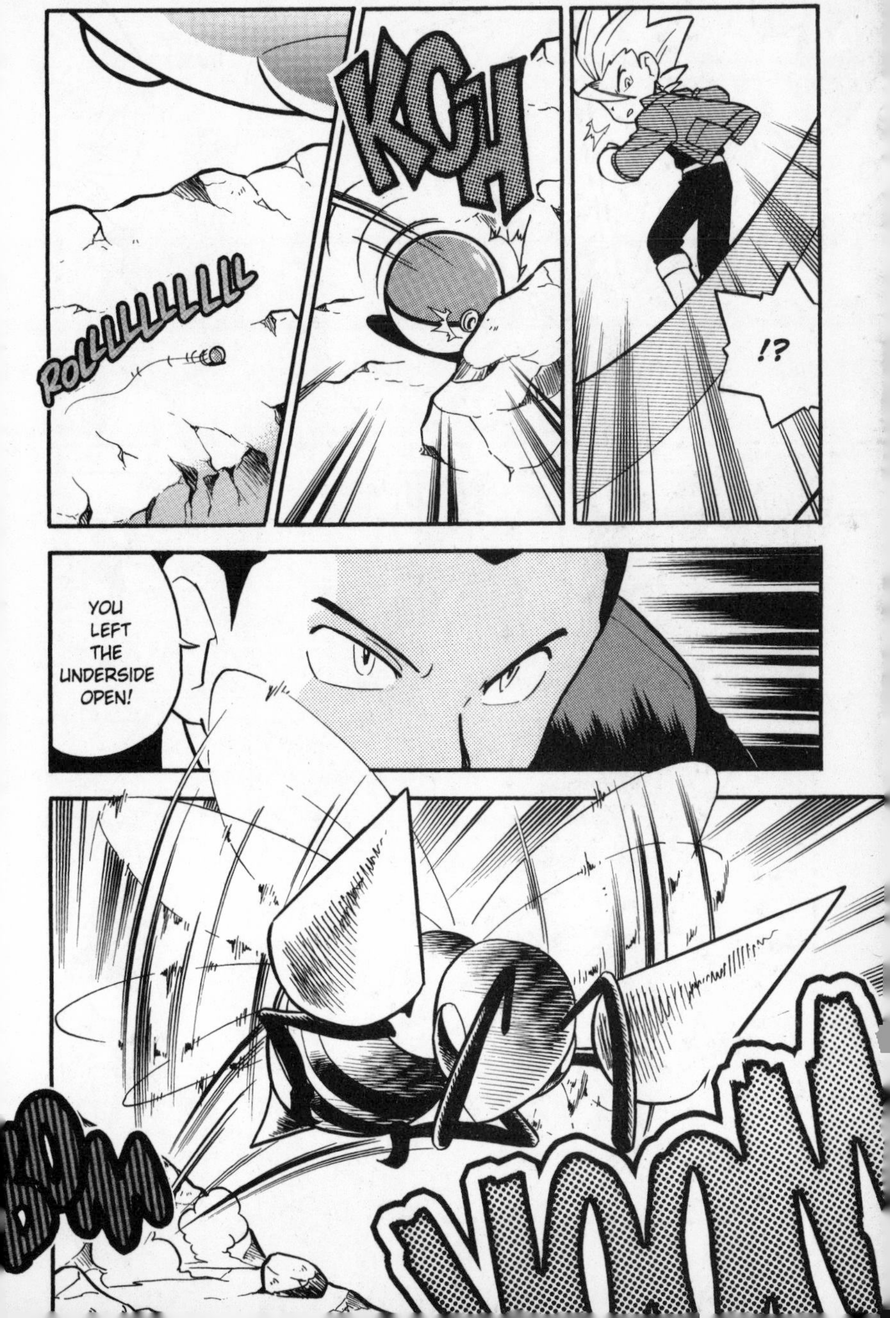
ROLLLLLLLLL
KGH
!?
YOU LEFT THE UNDERSIDE OPEN!

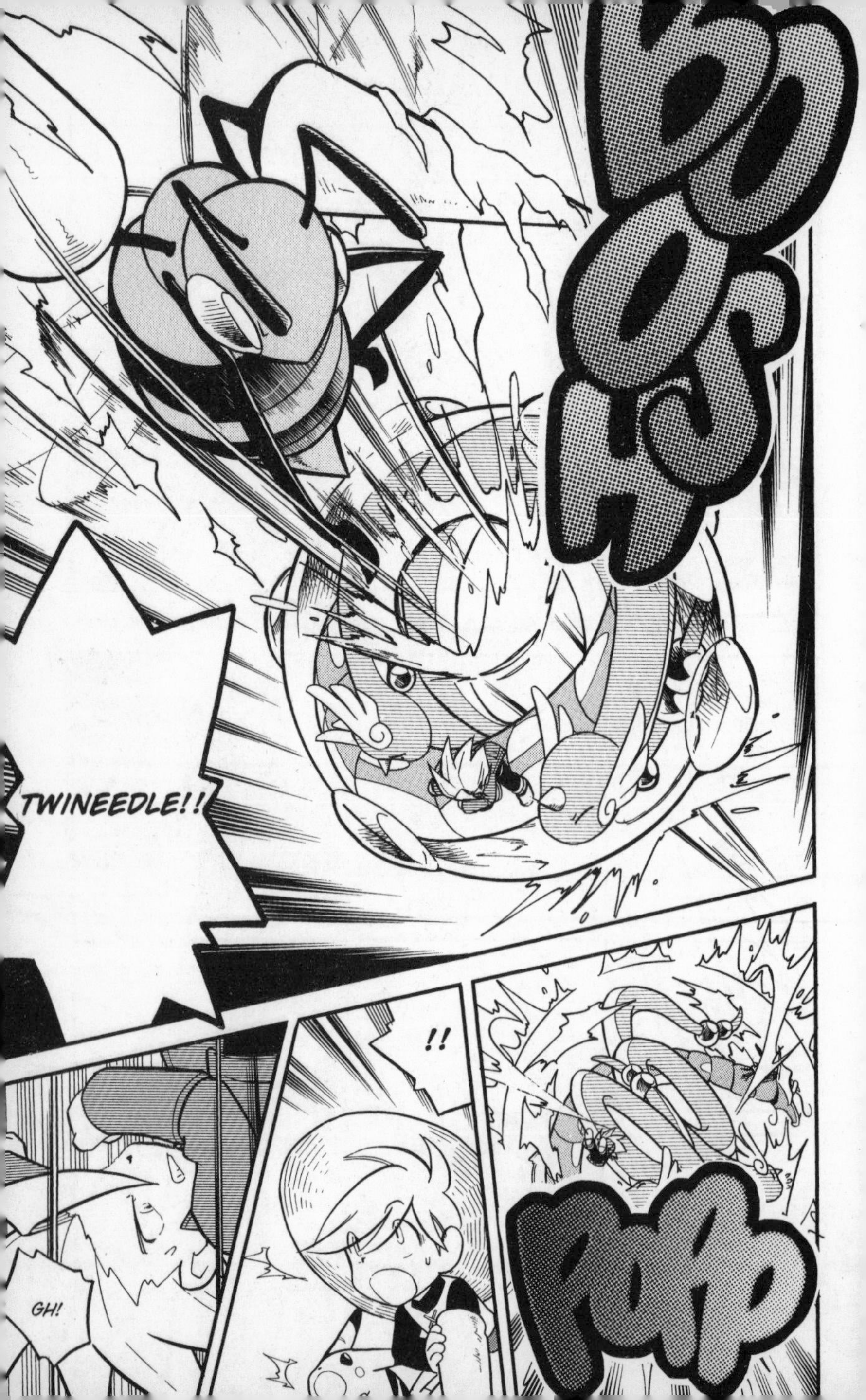
TWINEEDLE!!
!!
GH!

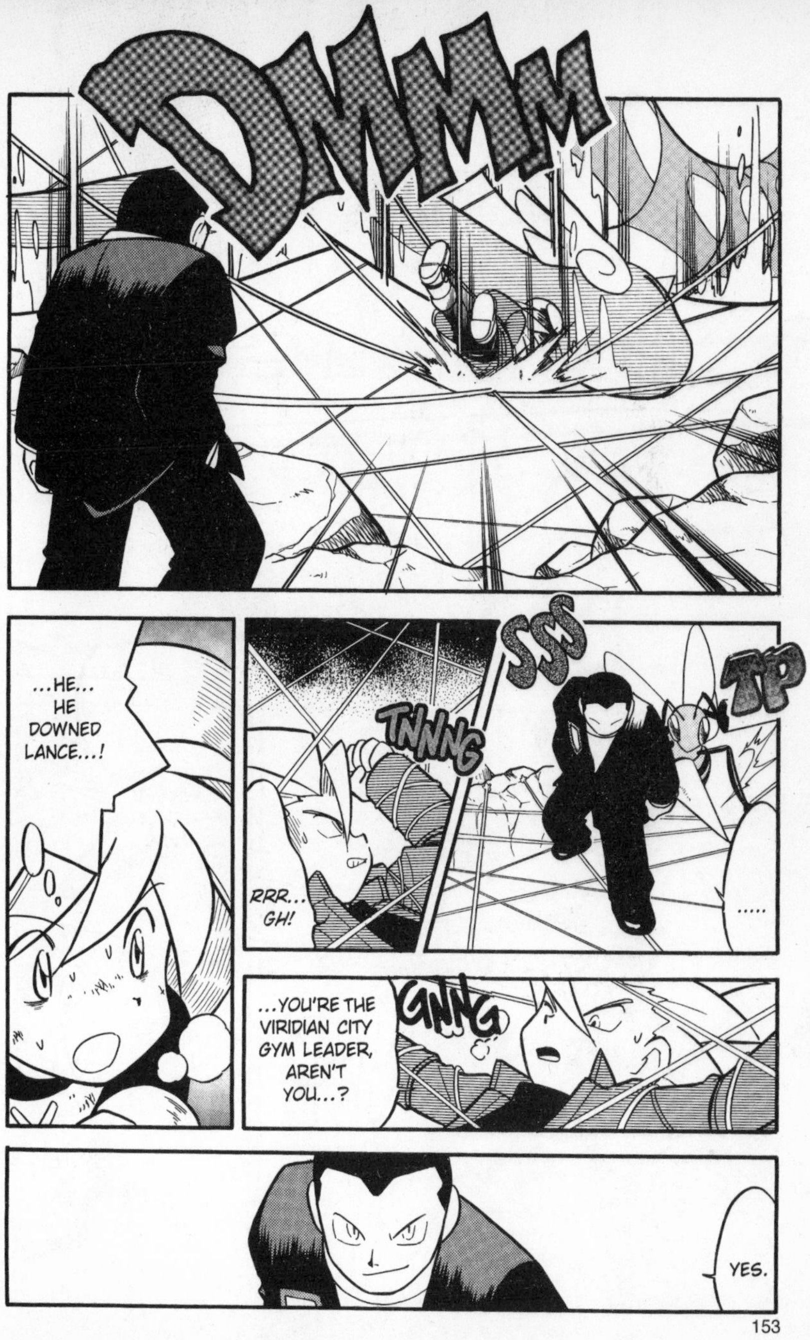
DMMMM
...HE...
HE
DOWNED
LANCE...!
TNNNG
SSS
TP
RRR...
GH!
.....
...YOU'RE THE
VIRIDIAN CITY
GYM LEADER,
AREN'T
YOU...?
GNNG
YES.

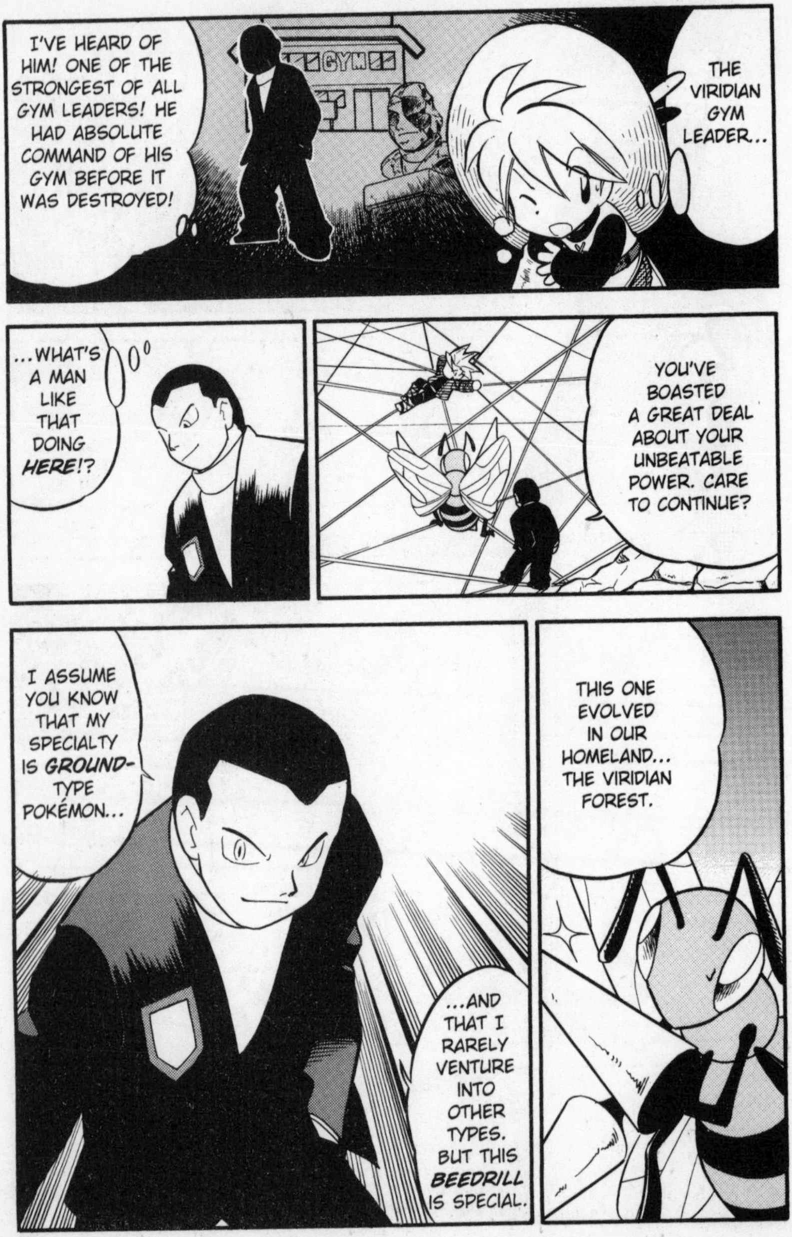
THE VIRIDIAN GYM LEADER...
I'VE HEARD OF HIM! ONE OF THE STRONGEST OF ALL GYM LEADERS! HE HAD ABSOLUTE COMMAND OF HIS GYM BEFORE IT WAS DESTROYED!
GYM
...WHAT'S A MAN LIKE THAT DOING *HERE*!?
YOU'VE BOASTED A GREAT DEAL ABOUT YOUR UNBEATABLE POWER. CARE TO CONTINUE?
I ASSUME YOU KNOW THAT MY SPECIALTY IS *GROUND*-TYPE POKÉMON...
...AND THAT I RARELY VENTURE INTO OTHER TYPES. BUT THIS *BEEDRILL* IS SPECIAL.
THIS ONE EVOLVED IN OUR HOMELAND... THE VIRIDIAN FOREST.

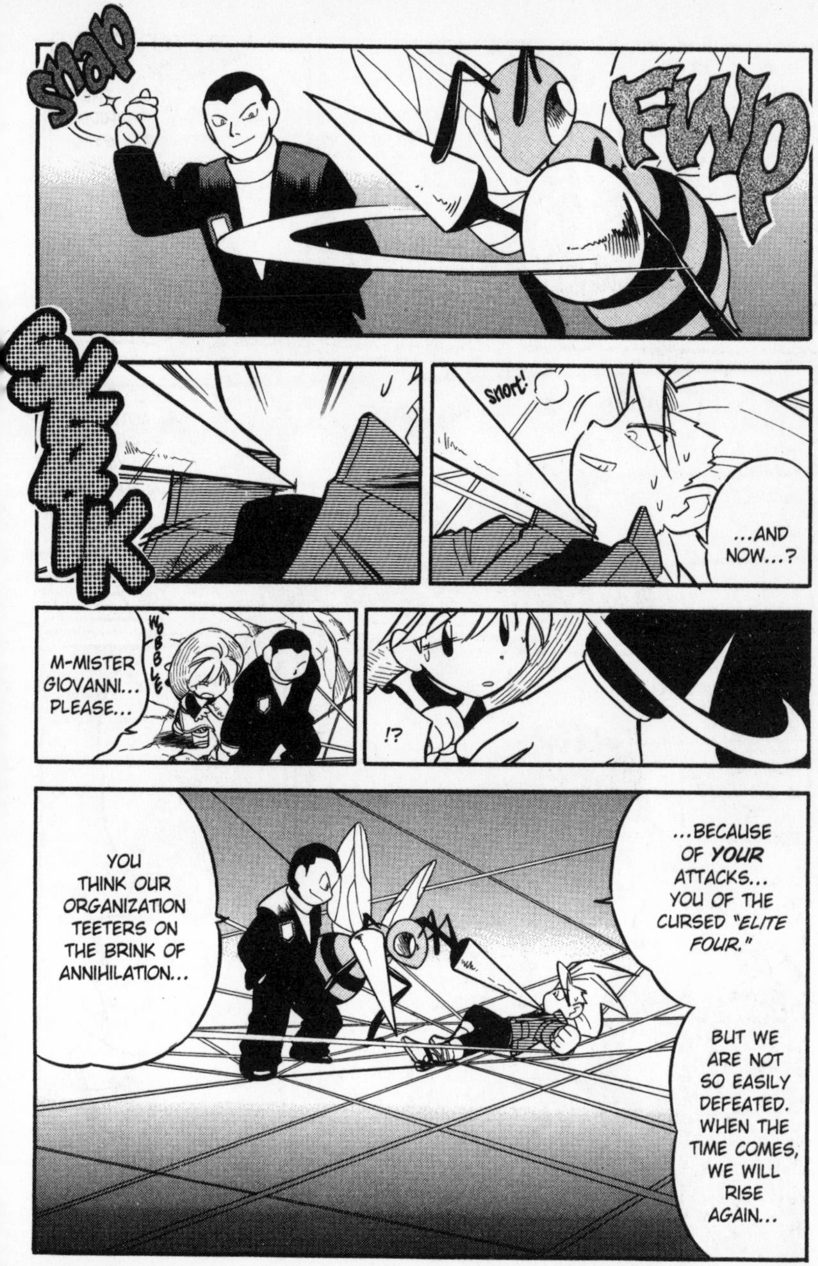
SNAP
FWP
snort!
...AND NOW...?
WOBBLE
M-MISTER GIOVANNI... PLEASE...
!?
YOU THINK OUR ORGANIZATION TEETERS ON THE BRINK OF ANNIHILATION...
...BECAUSE OF *YOUR* ATTACKS... YOU OF THE CURSED *"ELITE FOUR."*
BUT WE ARE NOT SO EASILY DEFEATED. WHEN THE TIME COMES, WE WILL RISE AGAIN...

AND *YOU* WILL FALL!!

"OUR ORGANIZATION"?

TNNG

NOW... I FIND MYSELF... HUFF... AGAINST A TRUE OPPONENT...

YOU ARE A REMARKABLE GYM LEADER.

OR.. SHOULD I SAY, RATHER...

...THAT YOU DESERVE YOUR ROLE...AS THE LEADER OF *TEAM ROCKET*!?

EH, *MASTER GIOVANNI*!?

!! ..... *TEAM ROCKET*!!

B-BUT THEY'RE EVIL... ONCE THEY USED POKÉMON TO CAUSE CHAOS AND DESTRUCTION ALL OVER THE MAINLAND...!

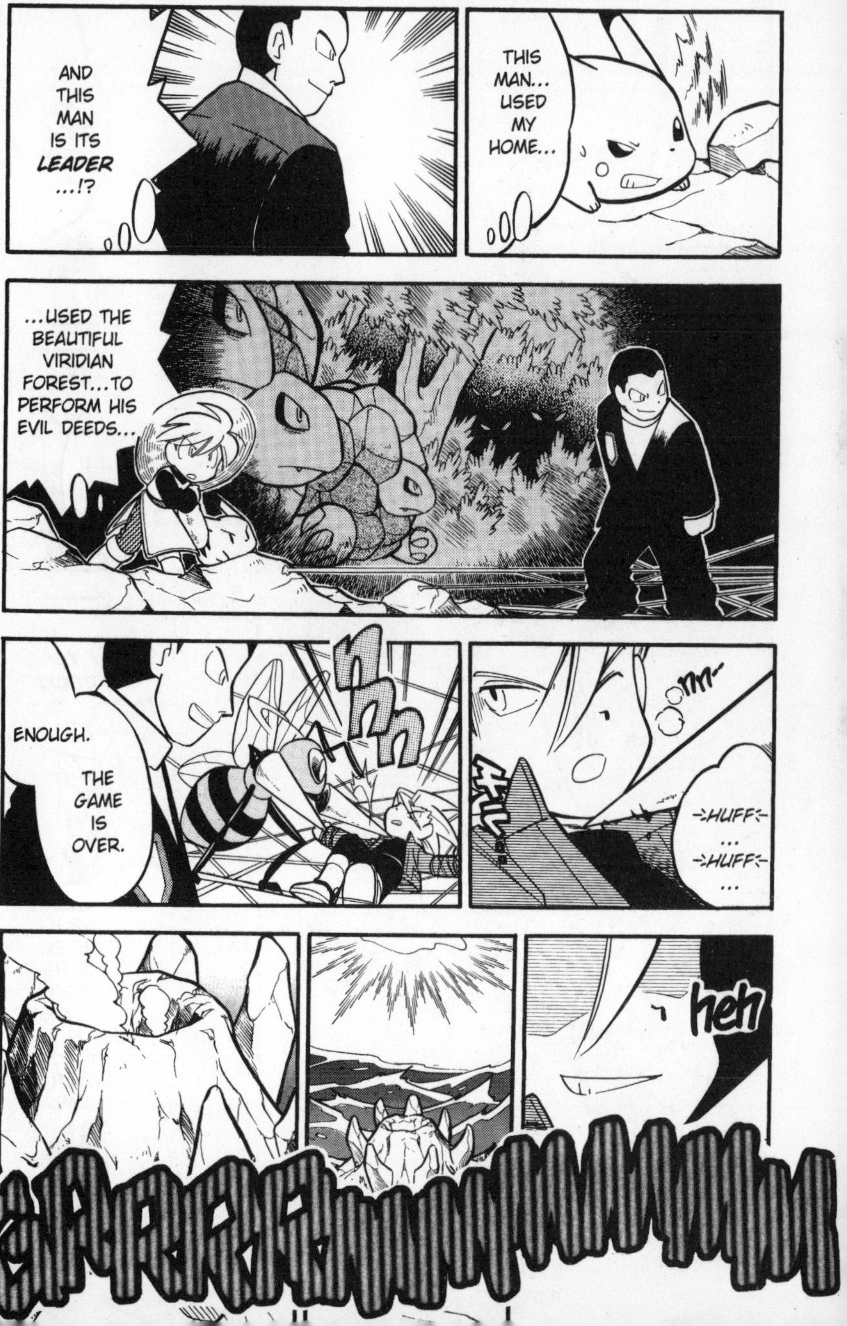
AND THIS MAN IS ITS LEADER ...!?
THIS MAN... USED MY HOME...
...USED THE BEAUTIFUL VIRIDIAN FOREST...TO PERFORM HIS EVIL DEEDS...
ENOUGH.
THE GAME IS OVER.
nn-
-HUFF- ... -HUFF- ...
heh

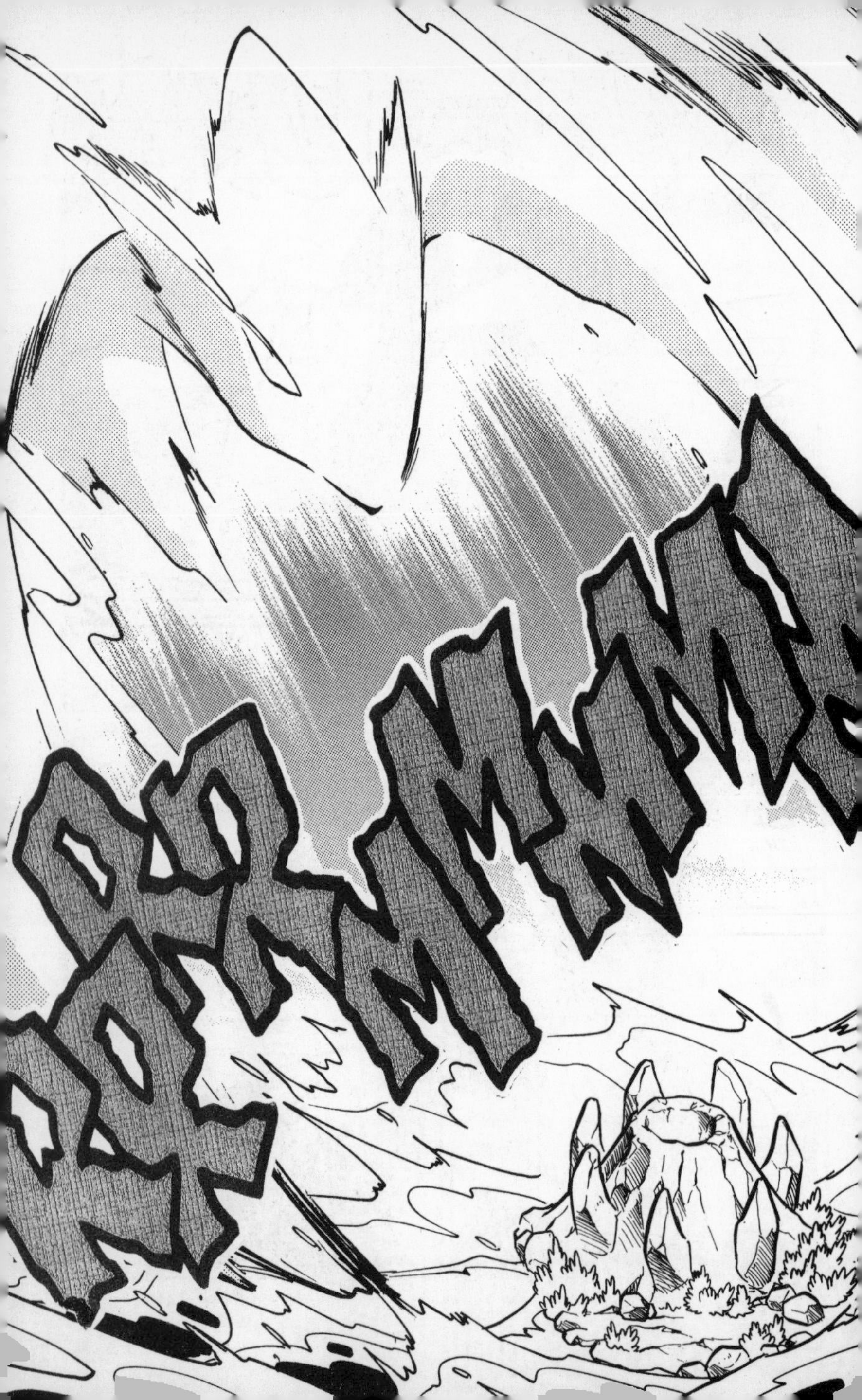
BRMMMM

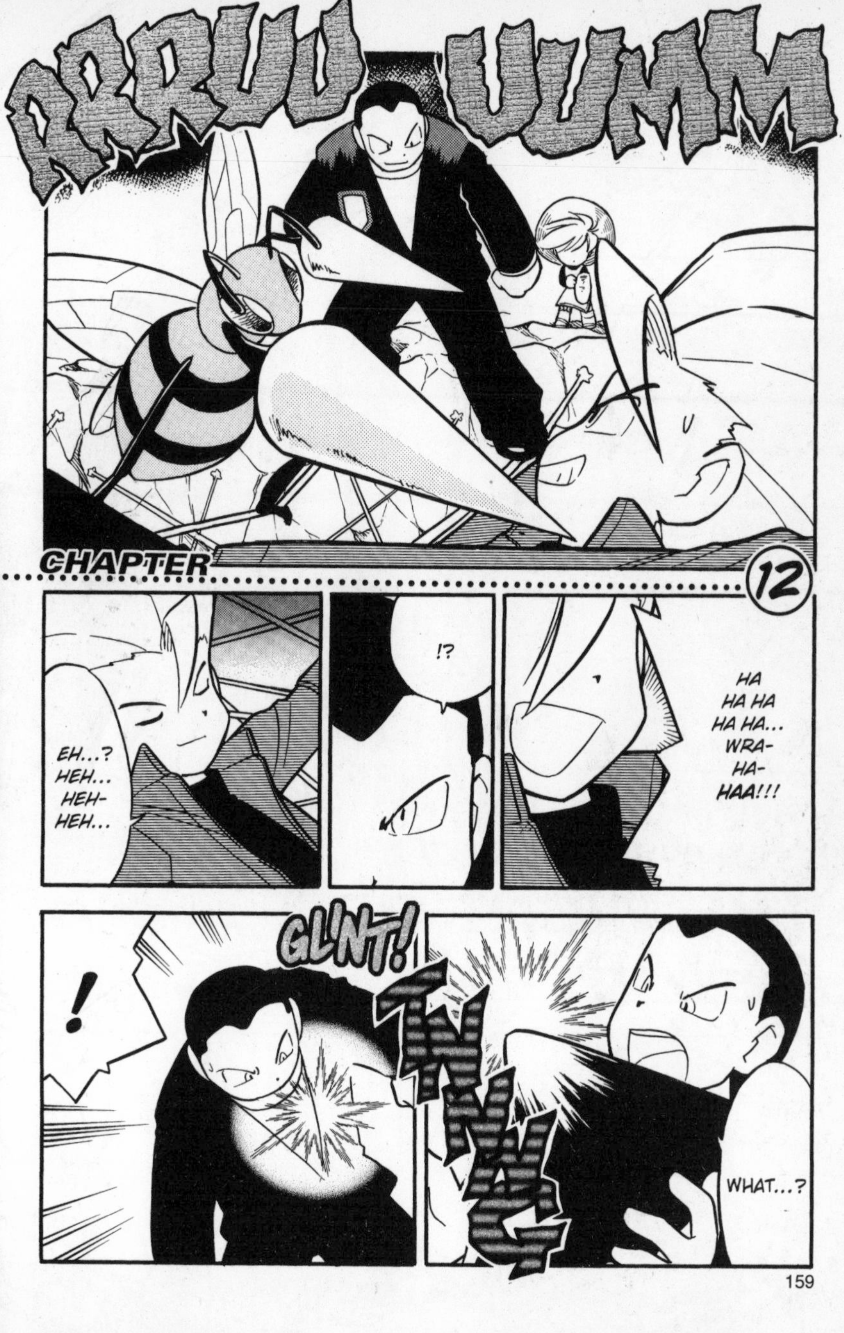
RRRUU UUMM
CHAPTER 12
EH...? HEH... HEH-HEH...
!?
HA HA HA HA HA... WRA-HA-HAA!!!
!
GLINT!
TING
WHAT...?

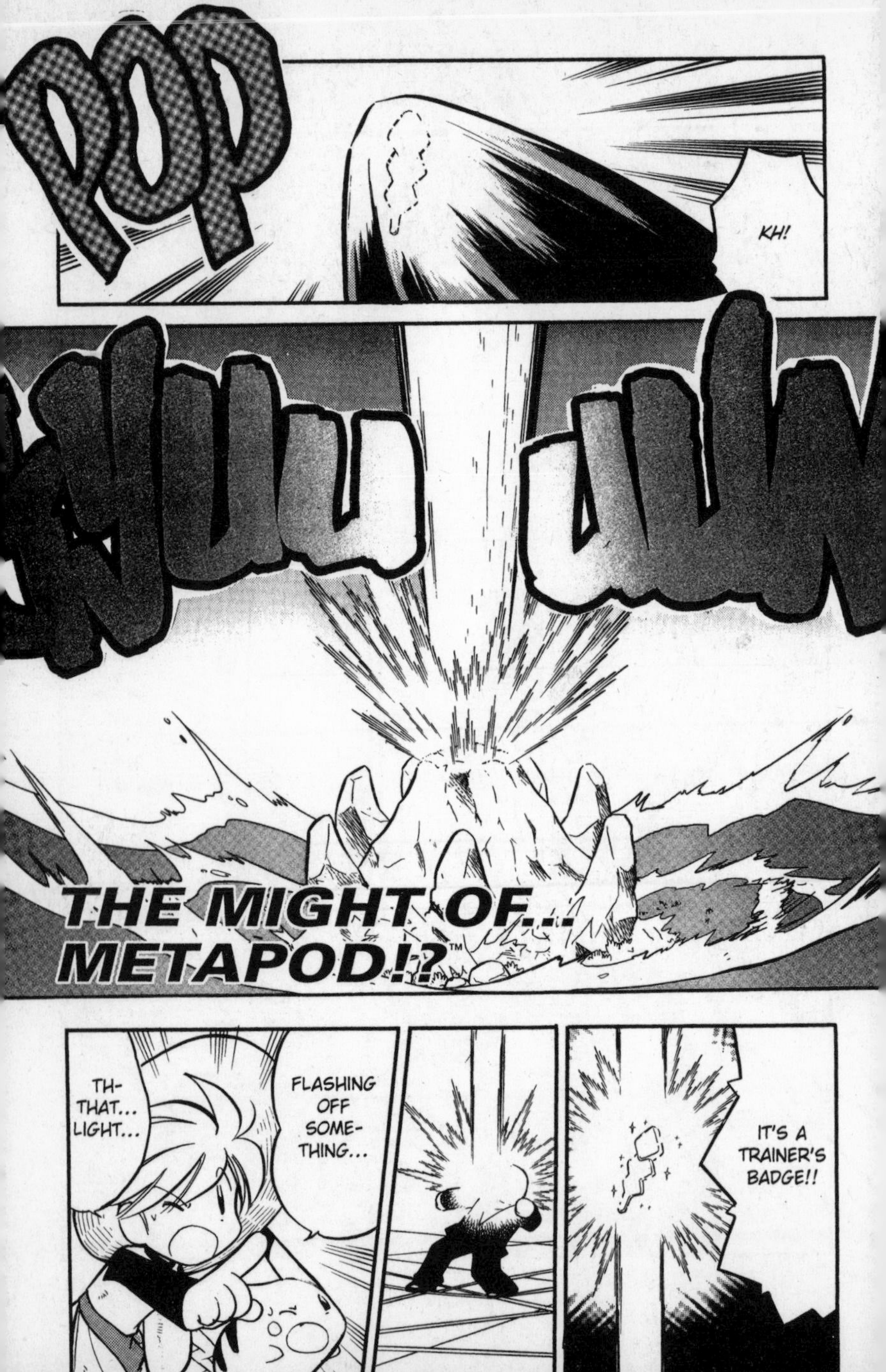
POP
KH!
THE MIGHT OF... METAPOD!?™
TH-THAT... LIGHT...
FLASHING OFF SOME-THING...
IT'S A TRAINER'S BADGE!!

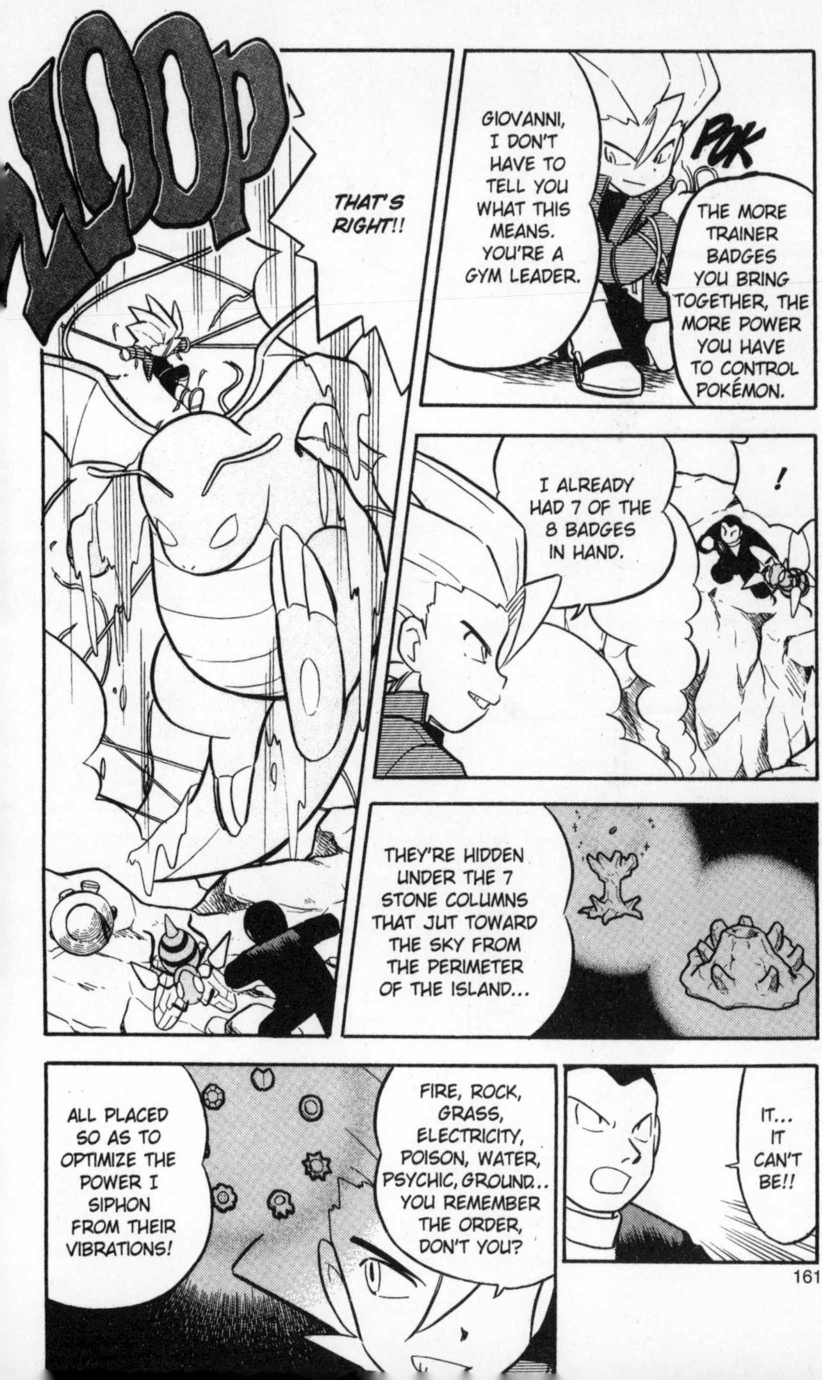

ZLOOP
THAT'S RIGHT!!
GIOVANNI, I DON'T HAVE TO TELL YOU WHAT THIS MEANS. YOU'RE A GYM LEADER.
PUK
THE MORE TRAINER BADGES YOU BRING TOGETHER, THE MORE POWER YOU HAVE TO CONTROL POKÉMON.
I ALREADY HAD 7 OF THE 8 BADGES IN HAND.
!
THEY'RE HIDDEN UNDER THE 7 STONE COLUMNS THAT JUT TOWARD THE SKY FROM THE PERIMETER OF THE ISLAND...
FIRE, ROCK, GRASS, ELECTRICITY, POISON, WATER, PSYCHIC, GROUND... YOU REMEMBER THE ORDER, DON'T YOU?
ALL PLACED SO AS TO OPTIMIZE THE POWER I SIPHON FROM THEIR VIBRATIONS!
IT... IT CAN'T BE!!

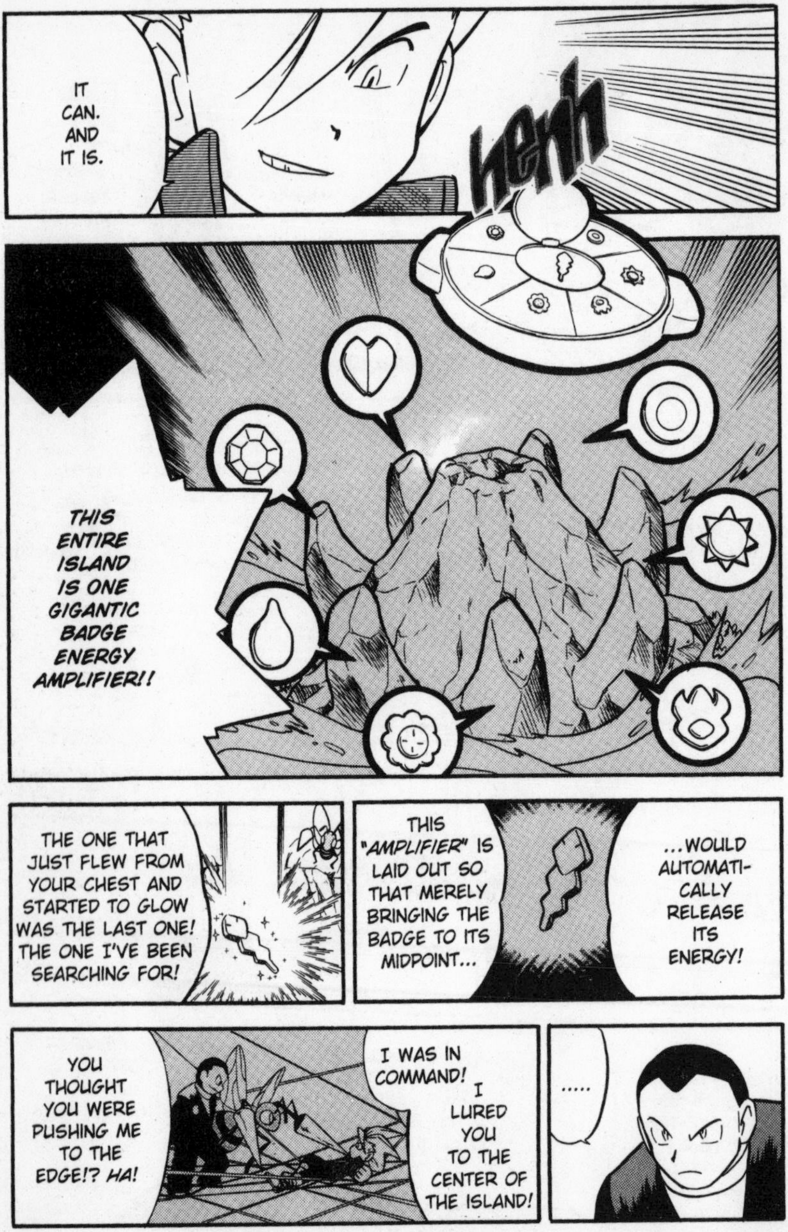
IT CAN. AND IT IS.
HENH
THIS ENTIRE ISLAND IS ONE GIGANTIC BADGE ENERGY AMPLIFIER!!
THE ONE THAT JUST FLEW FROM YOUR CHEST AND STARTED TO GLOW WAS THE LAST ONE! THE ONE I'VE BEEN SEARCHING FOR!
THIS "AMPLIFIER" IS LAID OUT SO THAT MERELY BRINGING THE BADGE TO ITS MIDPOINT...
...WOULD AUTOMATI-CALLY RELEASE ITS ENERGY!
YOU THOUGHT YOU WERE PUSHING ME TO THE EDGE!? HA!
I WAS IN COMMAND!
I LURED YOU TO THE CENTER OF THE ISLAND!
.....

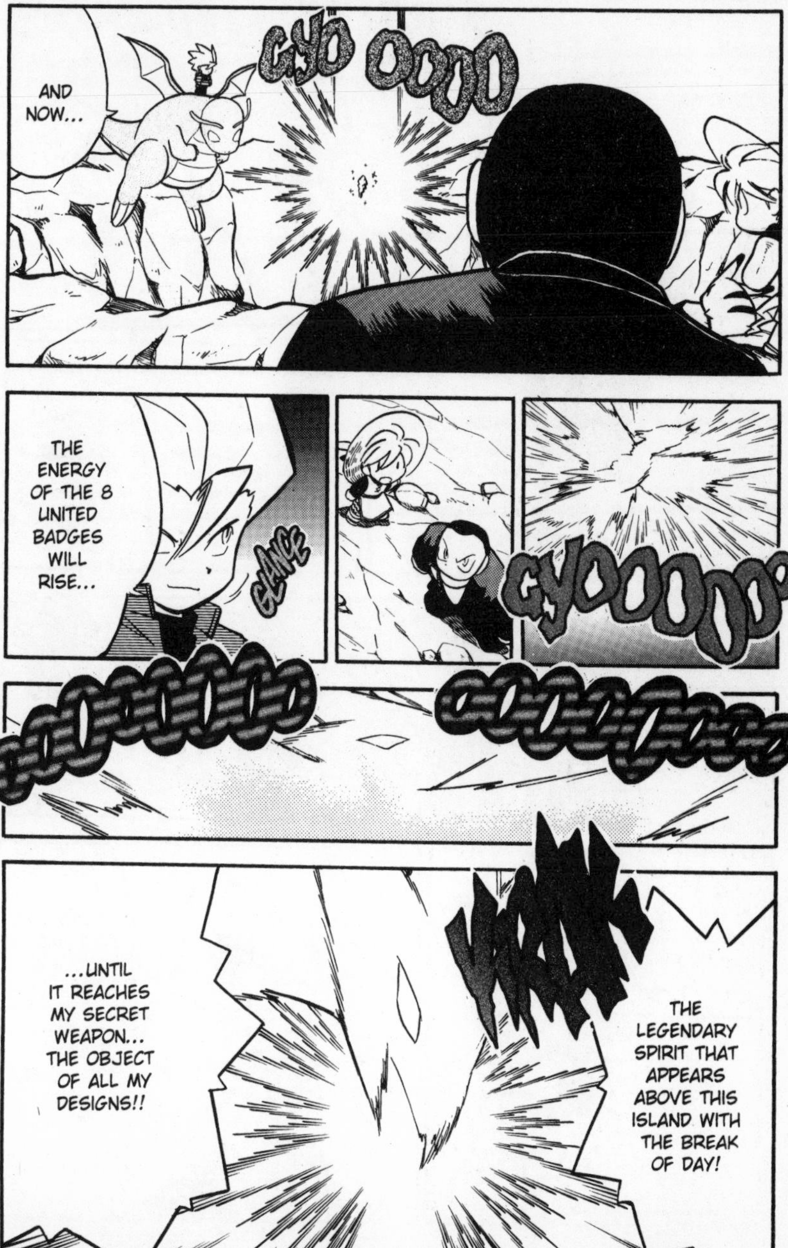
AND NOW...
GYO OOOO
THE ENERGY OF THE 8 UNITED BADGES WILL RISE...
GLANCE
...UNTIL IT REACHES MY SECRET WEAPON... THE OBJECT OF ALL MY DESIGNS!!
THE LEGENDARY SPIRIT THAT APPEARS ABOVE THIS ISLAND WITH THE BREAK OF DAY!

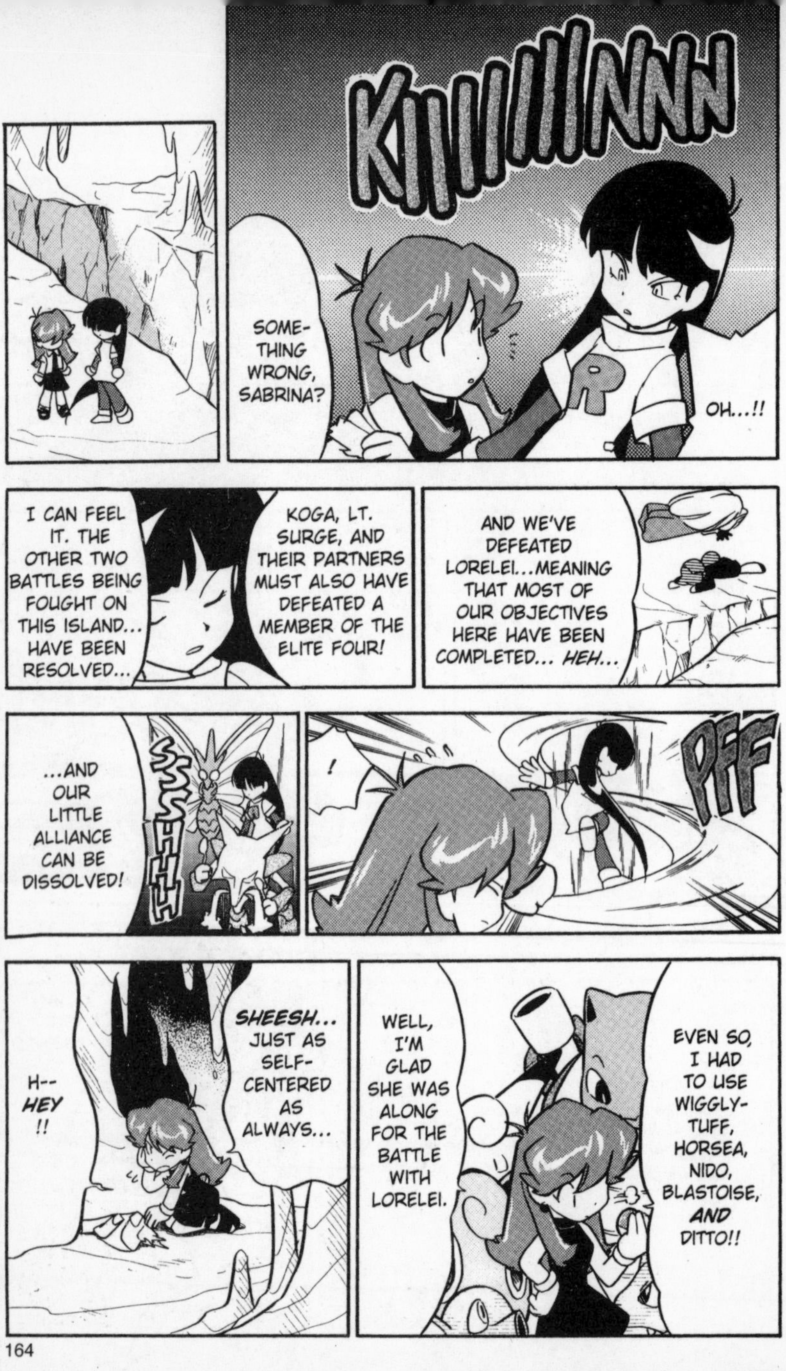

KIIIIIINNN
SOMETHING WRONG, SABRINA?
OH...!!
I CAN FEEL IT. THE OTHER TWO BATTLES BEING FOUGHT ON THIS ISLAND... HAVE BEEN RESOLVED...
KOGA, LT. SURGE, AND THEIR PARTNERS MUST ALSO HAVE DEFEATED A MEMBER OF THE ELITE FOUR!
AND WE'VE DEFEATED LORELEI...MEANING THAT MOST OF OUR OBJECTIVES HERE HAVE BEEN COMPLETED... *HEH*...
...AND OUR LITTLE ALLIANCE CAN BE DISSOLVED!
SSSHHHH
!
PFF
H-- *HEY* !!
SHEESH... JUST AS SELF-CENTERED AS ALWAYS...
WELL, I'M GLAD SHE WAS ALONG FOR THE BATTLE WITH LORELEI.
EVEN SO, I HAD TO USE WIGGLYTUFF, HORSEA, NIDO, BLASTOISE, *AND* DITTO!!

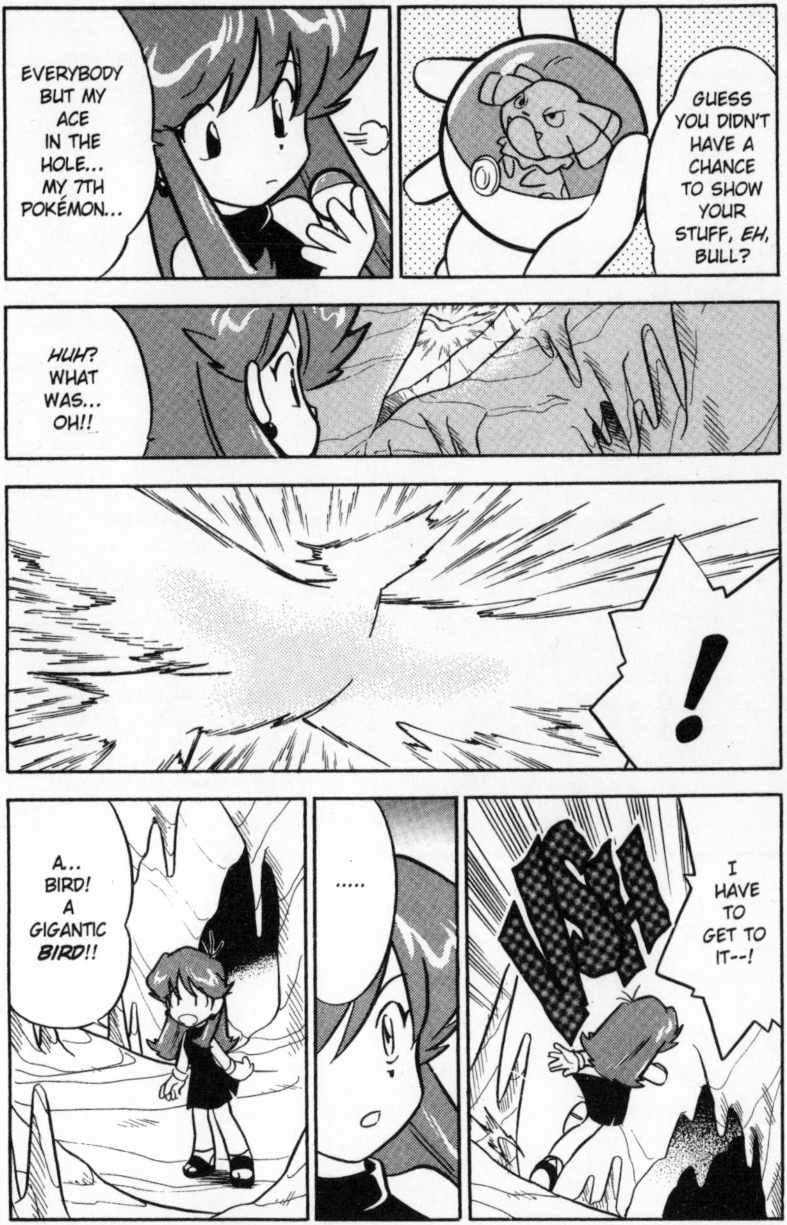
EVERYBODY BUT MY ACE IN THE HOLE... MY 7TH POKÉMON...
GUESS YOU DIDN'T HAVE A CHANCE TO SHOW YOUR STUFF, *EH*, BULL?
HUH? WHAT WAS... OH!!
!
A... BIRD! A GIGANTIC *BIRD*!!
.....
I HAVE TO GET TO IT--!

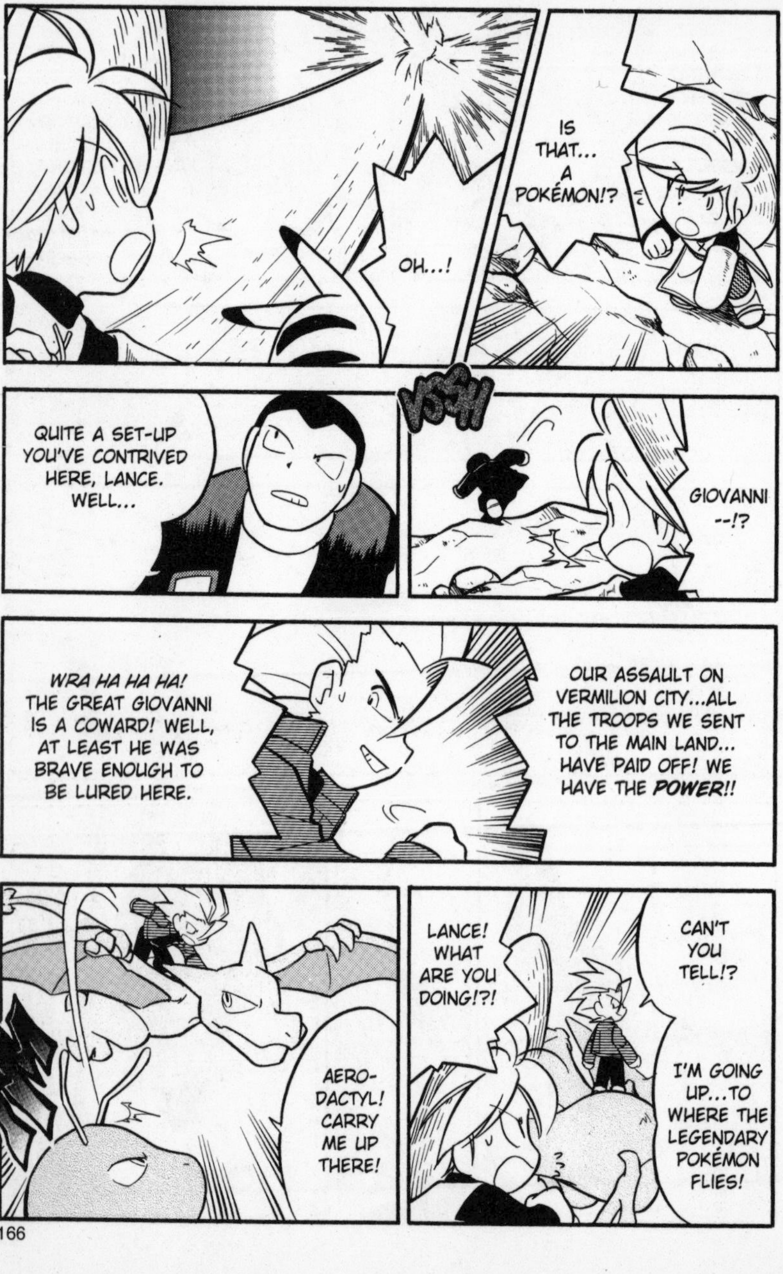
OH...!
IS THAT... A POKÉMON!?
QUITE A SET-UP YOU'VE CONTRIVED HERE, LANCE. WELL...
VSSH
GIOVANNI --!?
WRA HA HA HA! THE GREAT GIOVANNI IS A COWARD! WELL, AT LEAST HE WAS BRAVE ENOUGH TO BE LURED HERE.
OUR ASSAULT ON VERMILION CITY...ALL THE TROOPS WE SENT TO THE MAIN LAND... HAVE PAID OFF! WE HAVE THE ***POWER***!!
AERO-DACTYL! CARRY ME UP THERE!
LANCE! WHAT ARE YOU DOING!?!
CAN'T YOU TELL!?
I'M GOING UP...TO WHERE THE LEGENDARY POKÉMON FLIES!

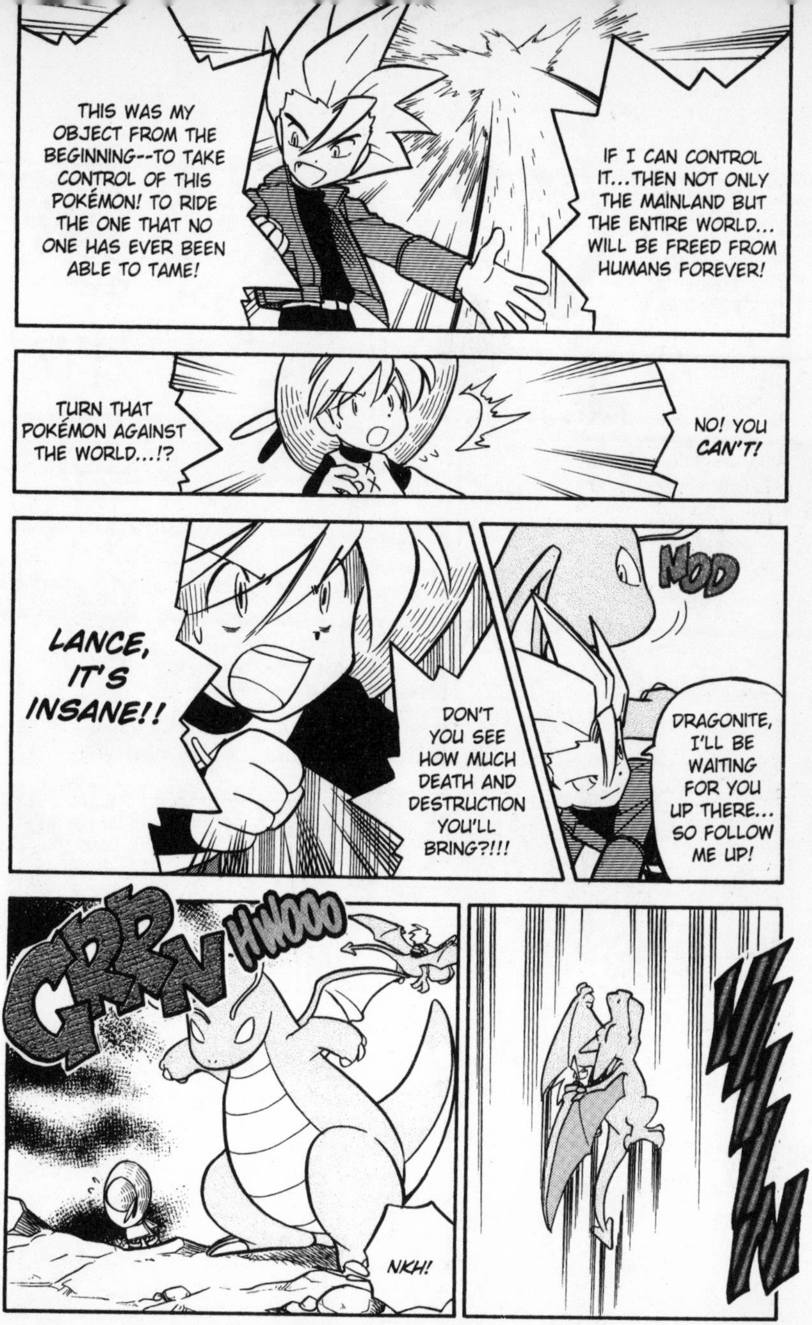
THIS WAS MY OBJECT FROM THE BEGINNING--TO TAKE CONTROL OF THIS POKÉMON! TO RIDE THE ONE THAT NO ONE HAS EVER BEEN ABLE TO TAME!
IF I CAN CONTROL IT...THEN NOT ONLY THE MAINLAND BUT THE ENTIRE WORLD... WILL BE FREED FROM HUMANS FOREVER!
TURN THAT POKÉMON AGAINST THE WORLD...!?
NO! YOU CAN'T!
LANCE, IT'S INSANE!!
DON'T YOU SEE HOW MUCH DEATH AND DESTRUCTION YOU'LL BRING?!!!
NOD
DRAGONITE, I'LL BE WAITING FOR YOU UP THERE... SO FOLLOW ME UP!
GRRN
HWOOO
NKH!

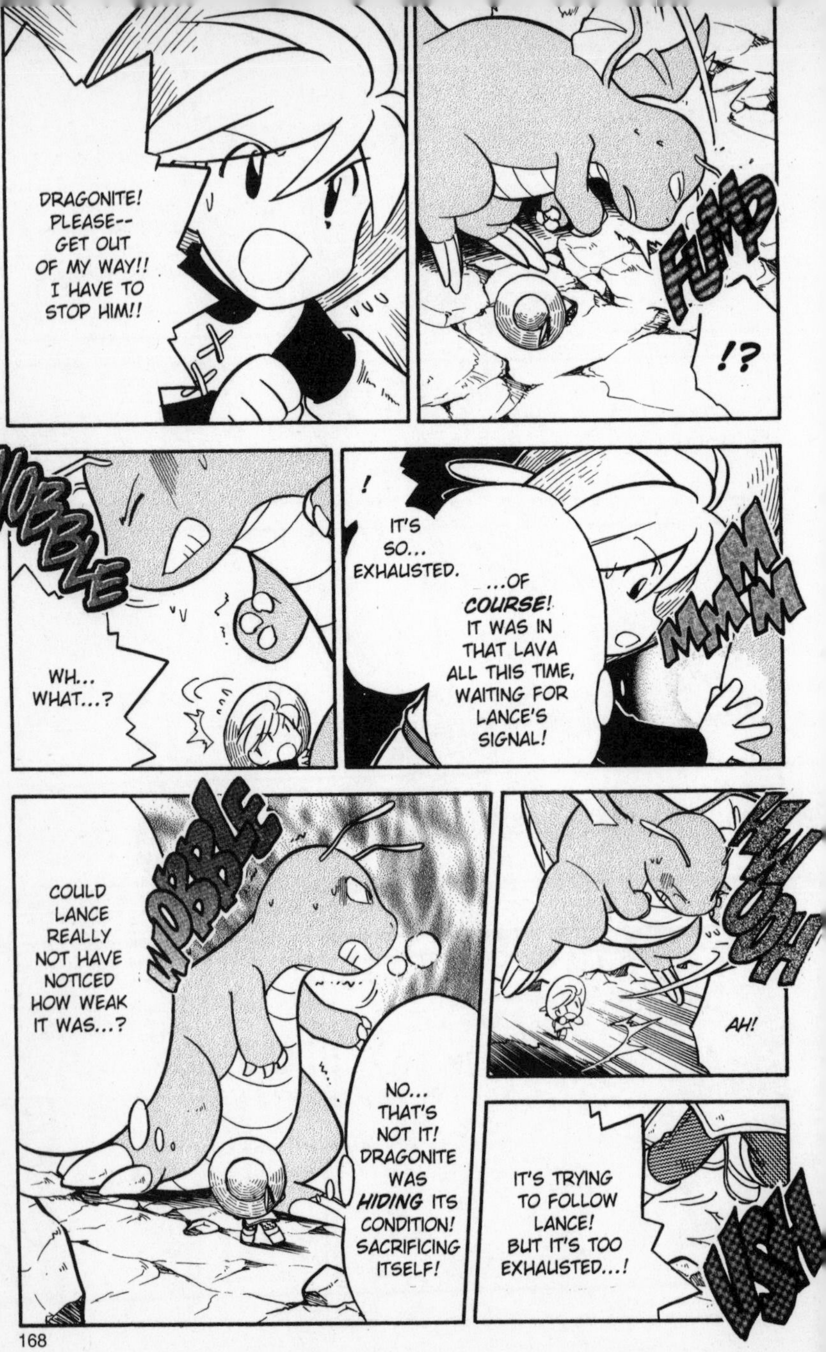
DRAGONITE! PLEASE-- GET OUT OF MY WAY!! I HAVE TO STOP HIM!!
FUMP
!?
WOBBLE
WH... WHAT...?
!
IT'S SO... EXHAUSTED.
...OF *COURSE*! IT WAS IN THAT LAVA ALL THIS TIME, WAITING FOR LANCE'S SIGNAL!
WOBBLE
COULD LANCE REALLY NOT HAVE NOTICED HOW WEAK IT WAS...?
NO... THAT'S NOT IT! DRAGONITE WAS *HIDING* ITS CONDITION! SACRIFICING ITSELF!
WHOOSH
AH!
IT'S TRYING TO FOLLOW LANCE! BUT IT'S TOO EXHAUSTED...!

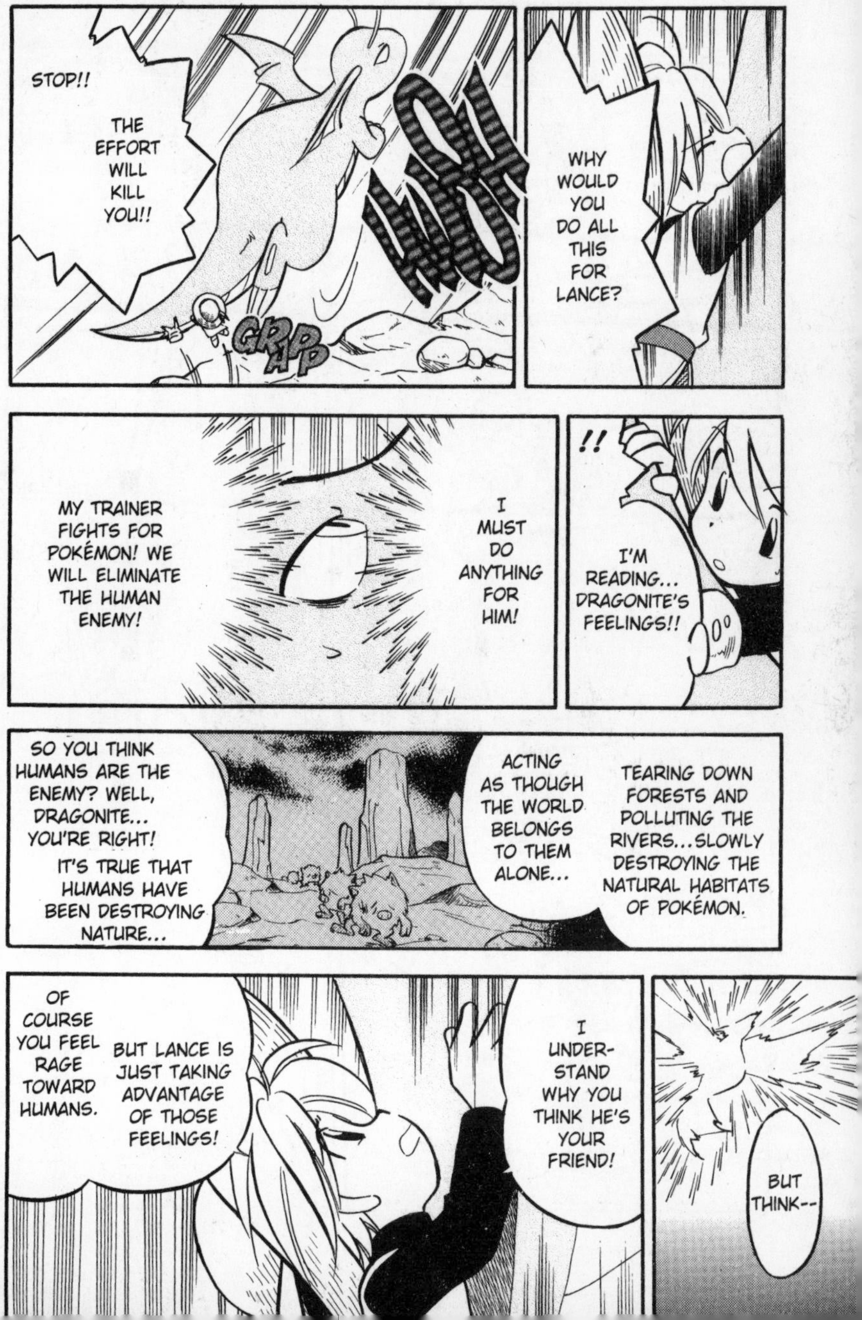
STOP!!
THE EFFORT WILL KILL YOU!!
WHY WOULD YOU DO ALL THIS FOR LANCE?
MY TRAINER FIGHTS FOR POKÉMON! WE WILL ELIMINATE THE HUMAN ENEMY!
I MUST DO ANYTHING FOR HIM!
!!
I'M READING... DRAGONITE'S FEELINGS!!
SO YOU THINK HUMANS ARE THE ENEMY? WELL, DRAGONITE... YOU'RE RIGHT!
IT'S TRUE THAT HUMANS HAVE BEEN DESTROYING NATURE...
ACTING AS THOUGH THE WORLD BELONGS TO THEM ALONE...
TEARING DOWN FORESTS AND POLLUTING THE RIVERS...SLOWLY DESTROYING THE NATURAL HABITATS OF POKÉMON.
OF COURSE YOU FEEL RAGE TOWARD HUMANS.
BUT LANCE IS JUST TAKING ADVANTAGE OF THOSE FEELINGS!
I UNDER-STAND WHY YOU THINK HE'S YOUR FRIEND!
BUT THINK--

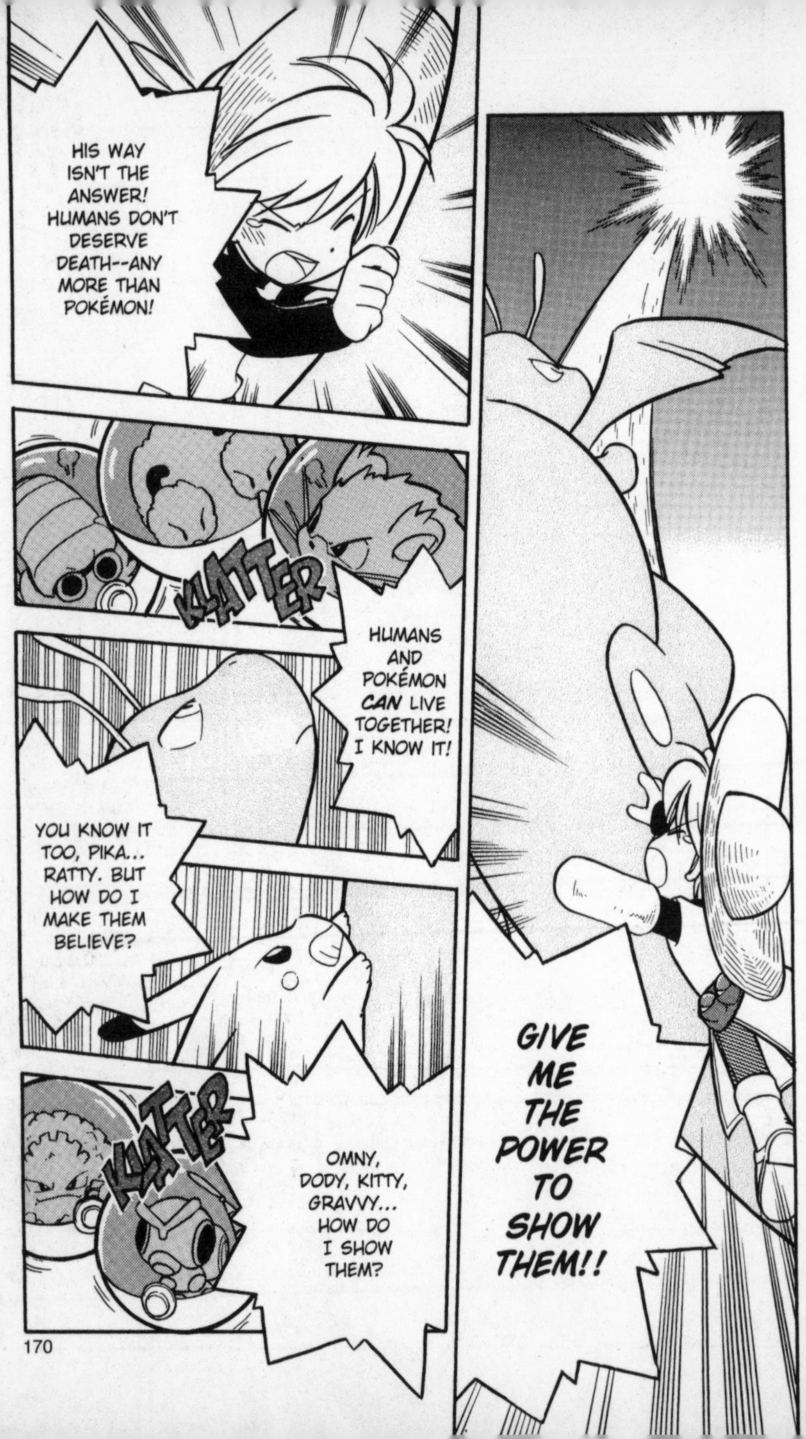
HIS WAY ISN'T THE ANSWER! HUMANS DON'T DESERVE DEATH--ANY MORE THAN POKÉMON!
KLATTER
HUMANS AND POKÉMON CAN LIVE TOGETHER! I KNOW IT!
YOU KNOW IT TOO, PIKA... RATTY. BUT HOW DO I MAKE THEM BELIEVE?
KLATTER
OMNY, DODY, KITTY, GRAVVY... HOW DO I SHOW THEM?
GIVE ME THE POWER TO SHOW THEM!!

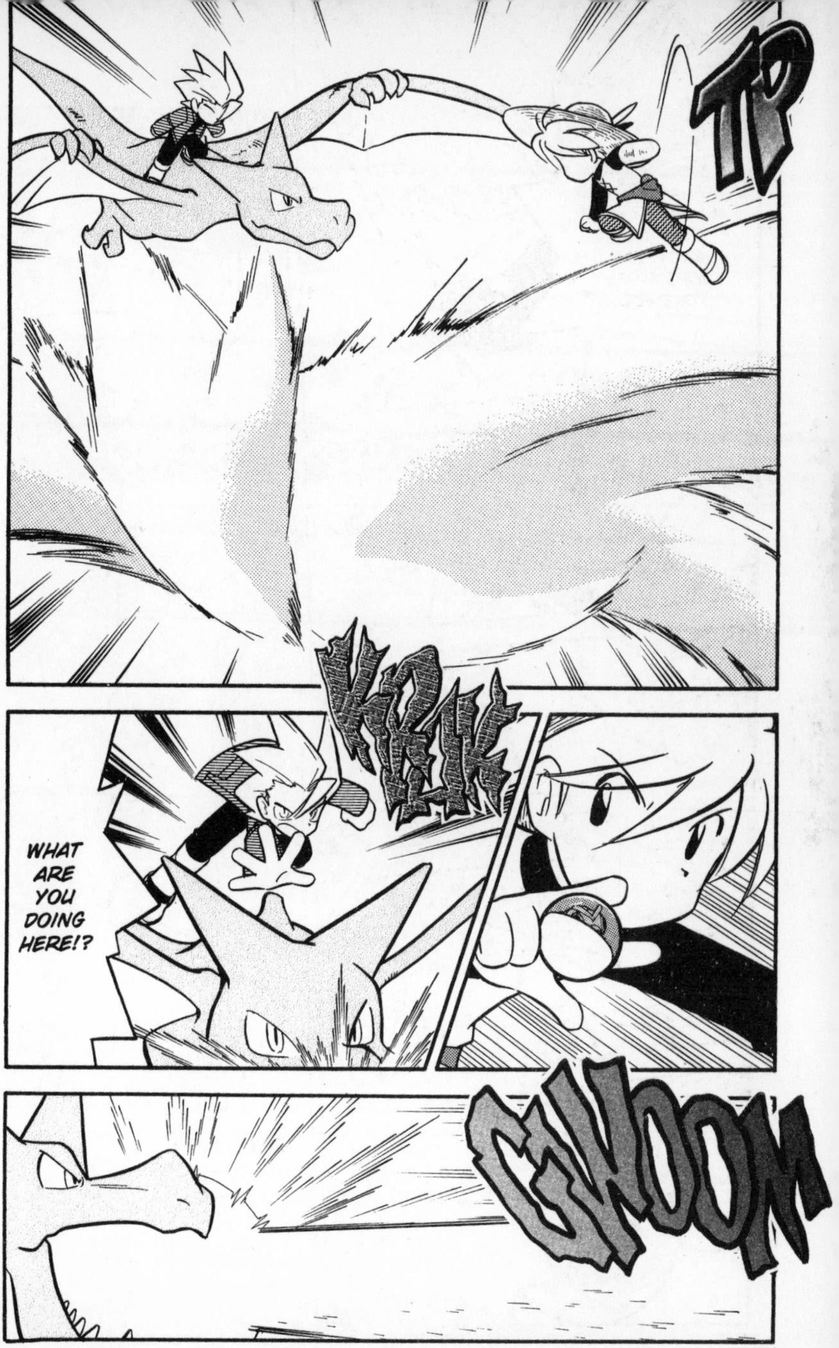
TP
KRAK
WHAT ARE YOU DOING HERE!?
CHOOM

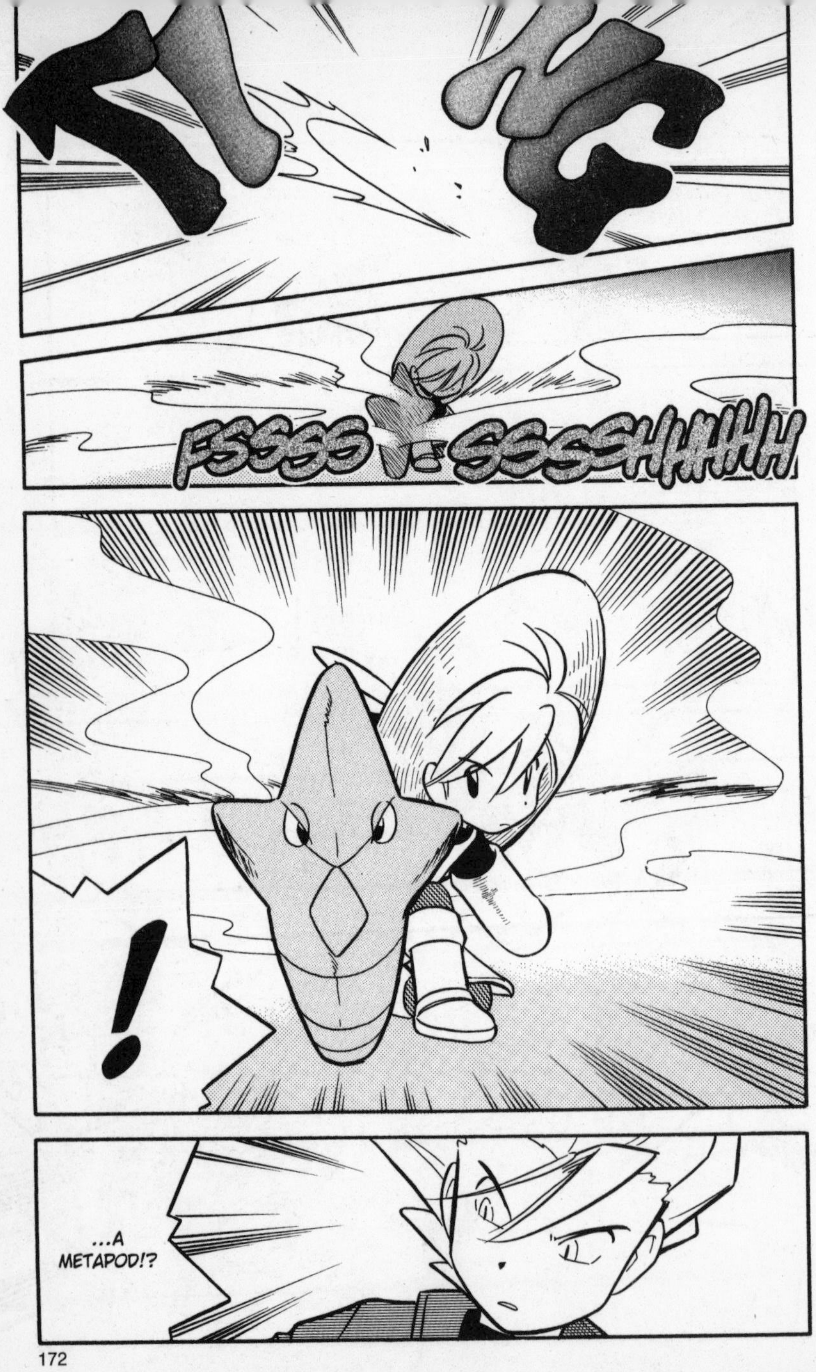
FSSSS
SSSSSHHHHH
!
...A METAPOD!?

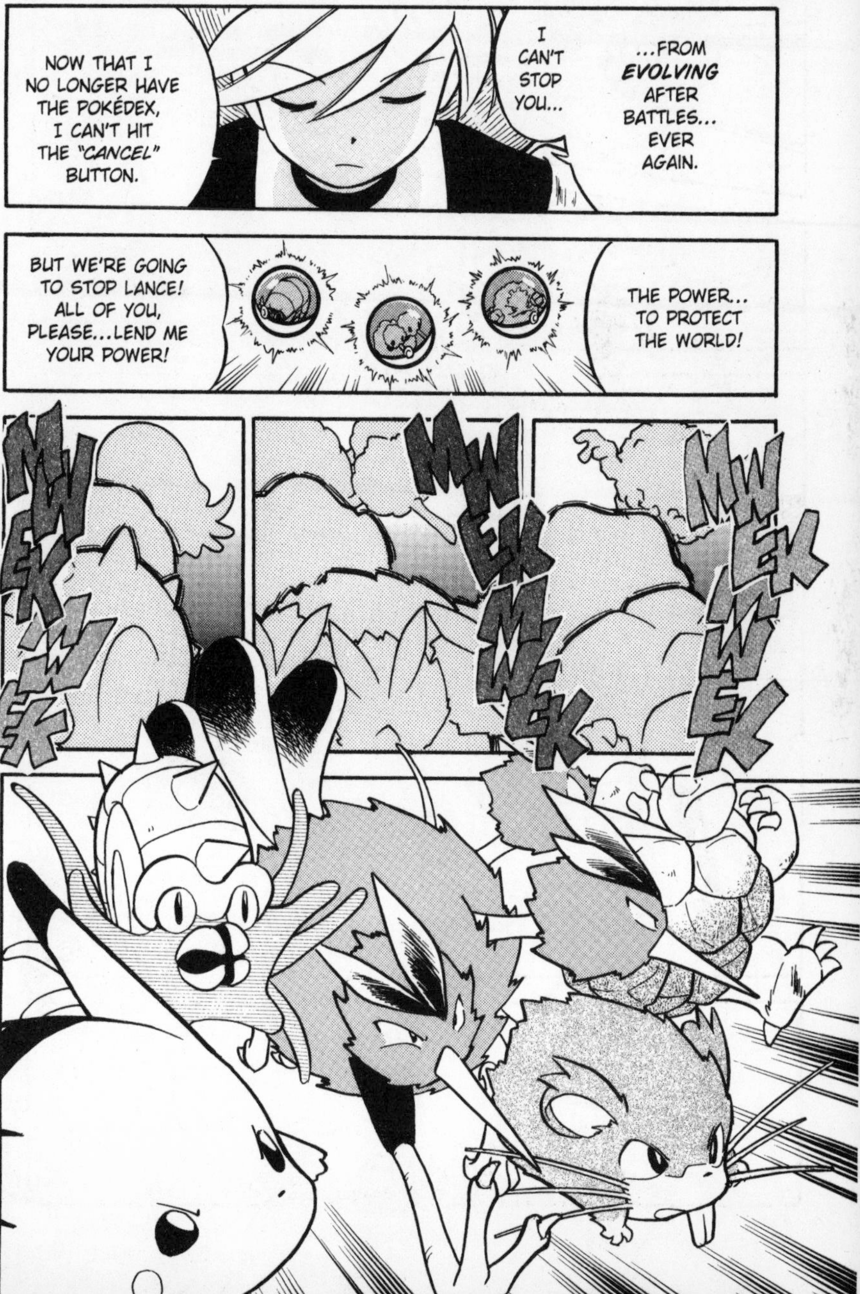
NOW THAT I NO LONGER HAVE THE POKÉDEX, I CAN'T HIT THE "CANCEL" BUTTON.
I CAN'T STOP YOU...
...FROM EVOLVING AFTER BATTLES... EVER AGAIN.
BUT WE'RE GOING TO STOP LANCE! ALL OF YOU, PLEASE...LEND ME YOUR POWER!
THE POWER... TO PROTECT THE WORLD!
MWEK MWEK

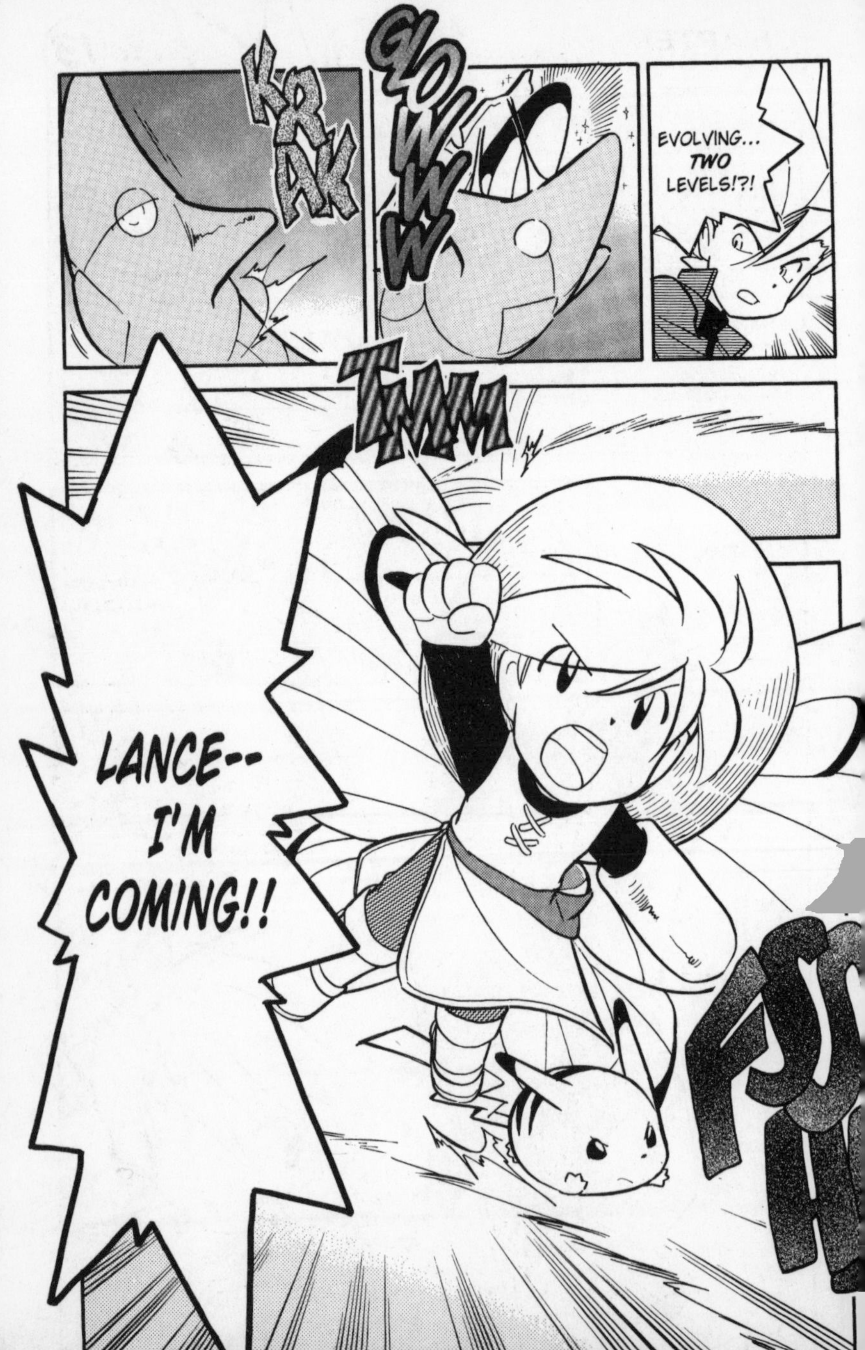
KRAK
GLOWWWW
EVOLVING... TWO LEVELS!?!
LANCE-- I'M COMING!!

CHAPTER 13

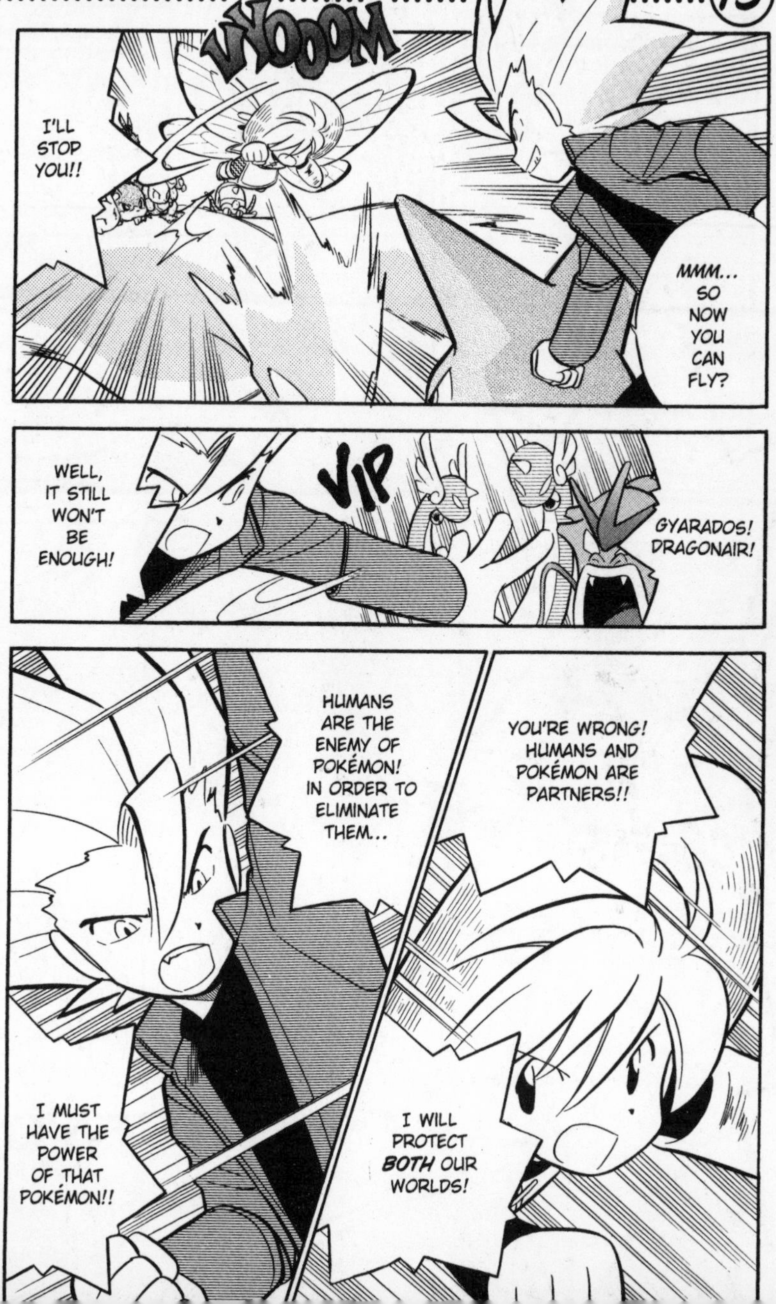
VYOOOM
I'LL STOP YOU!!
MMM... SO NOW YOU CAN FLY?
WELL, IT STILL WON'T BE ENOUGH!
VIP
GYARADOS! DRAGONAIR!
HUMANS ARE THE ENEMY OF POKÉMON! IN ORDER TO ELIMINATE THEM...
YOU'RE WRONG! HUMANS AND POKÉMON ARE PARTNERS!!
I MUST HAVE THE POWER OF THAT POKÉMON!!
I WILL PROTECT BOTH OUR WORLDS!

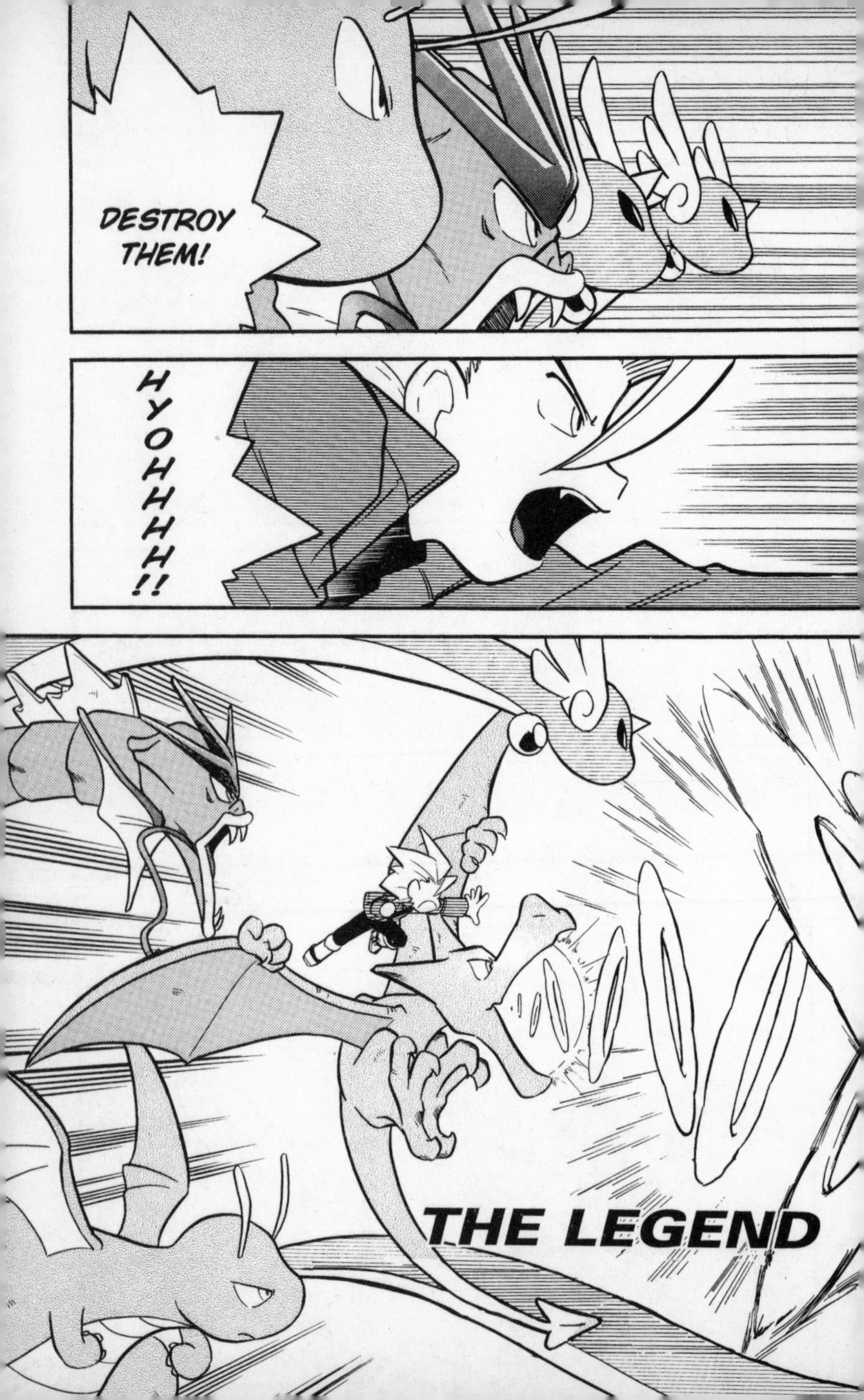
DESTROY THEM!
HYOHHHHH!!
THE LEGEND

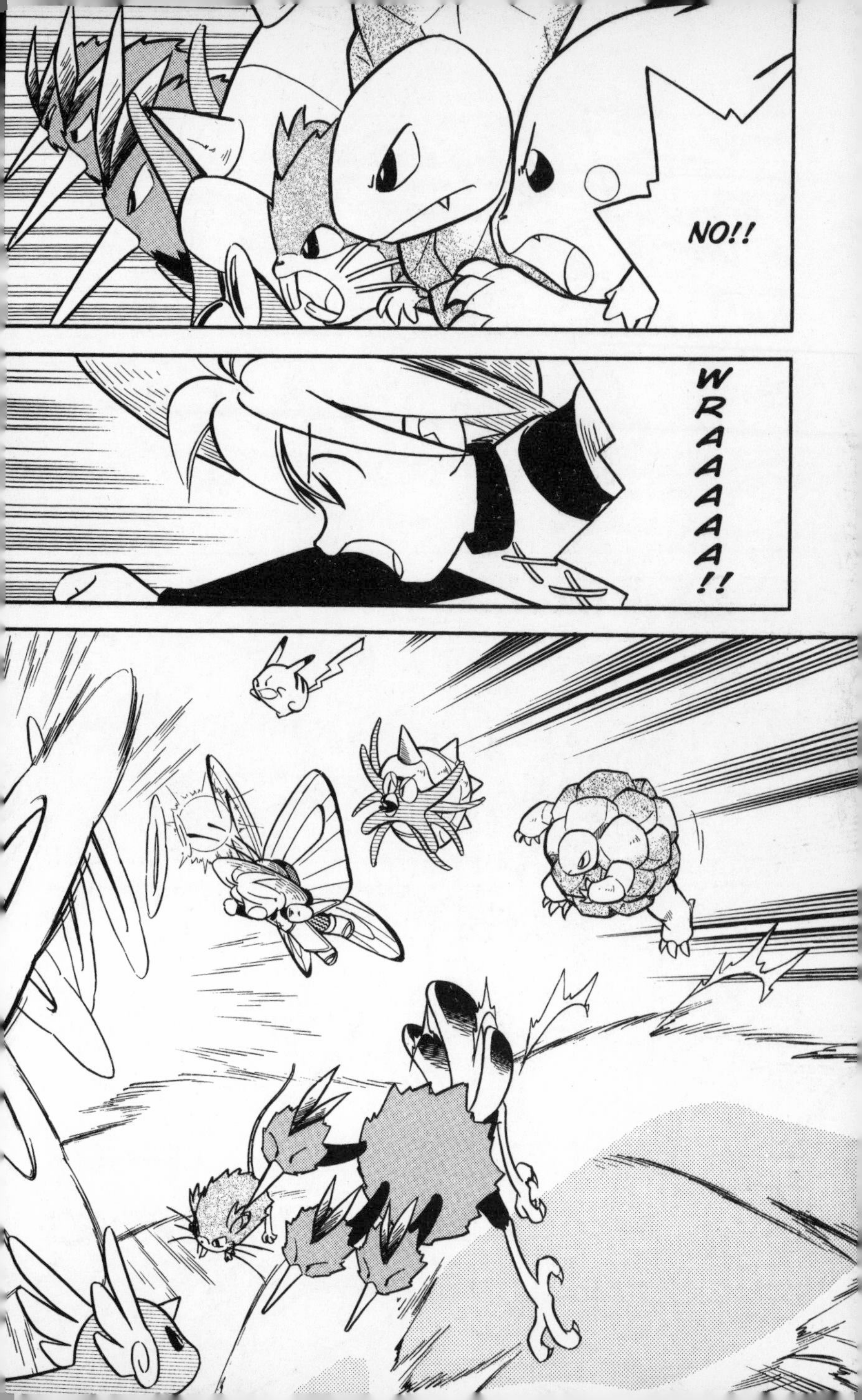
NO!!
WRAAAAAA!!

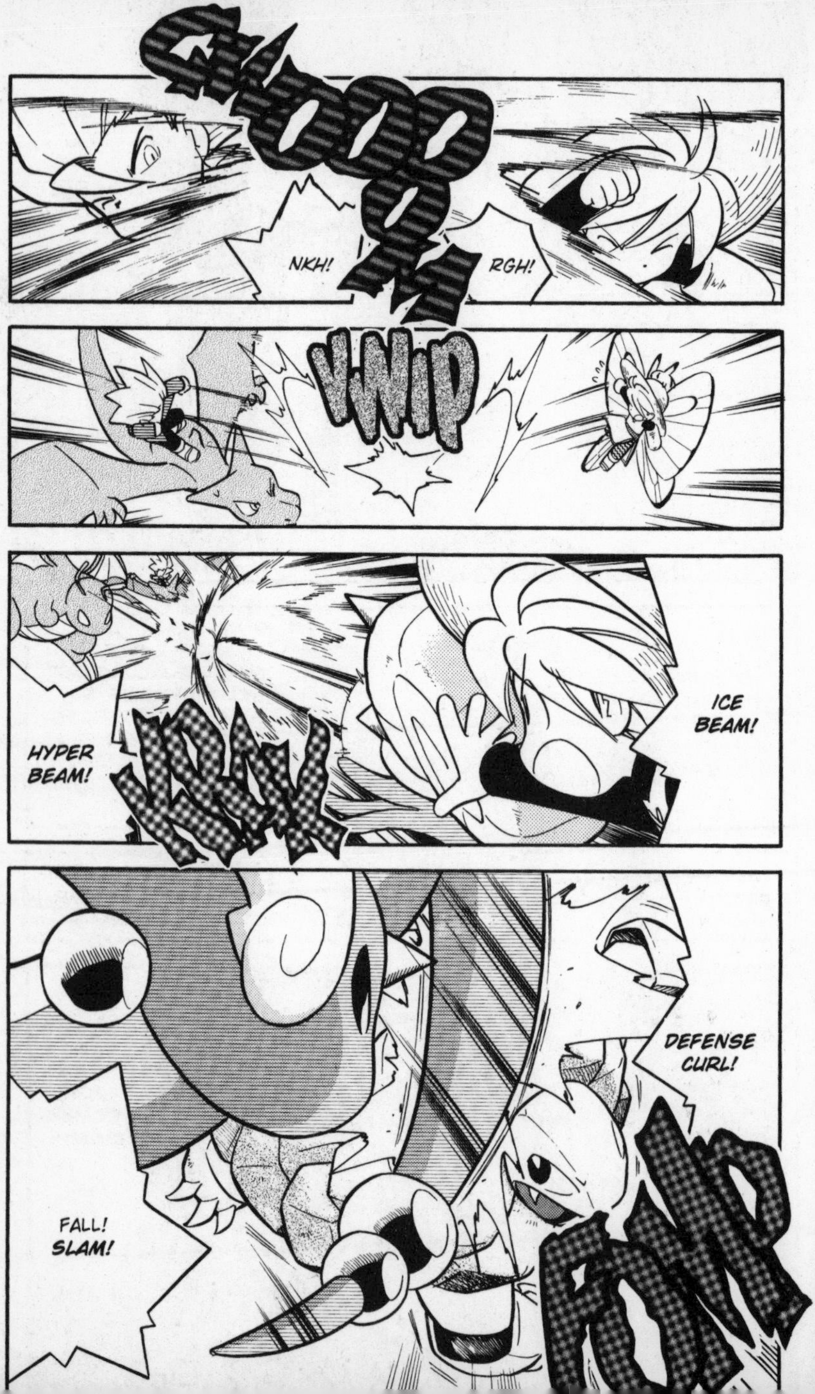
NKH!
RGH!
HYPER BEAM!
ICE BEAM!
DEFENSE CURL!
FALL! SLAM!

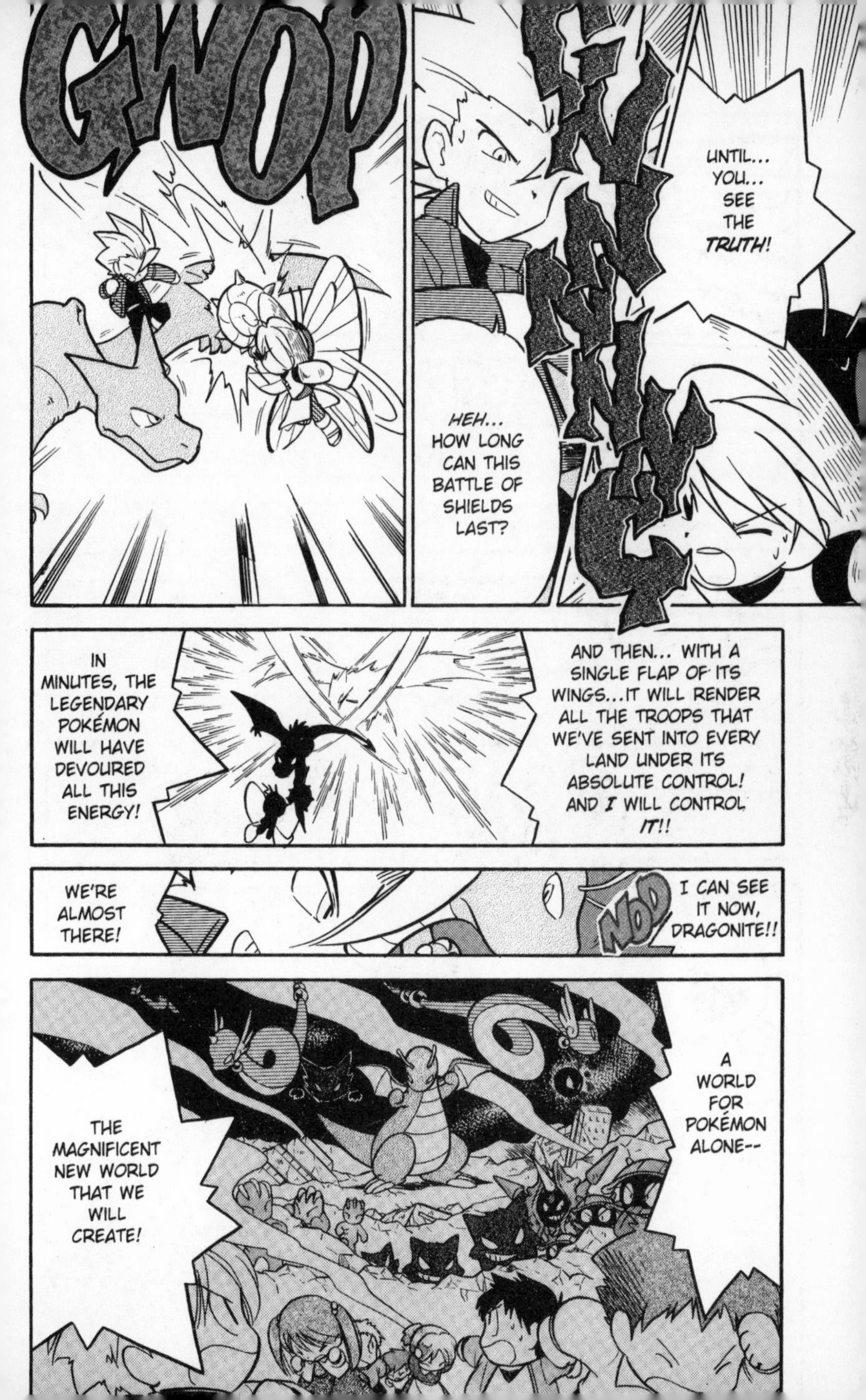
GWOP
HEH... HOW LONG CAN THIS BATTLE OF SHIELDS LAST?
UNTIL... YOU... SEE THE TRUTH!
IN MINUTES, THE LEGENDARY POKÉMON WILL HAVE DEVOURED ALL THIS ENERGY!
AND THEN... WITH A SINGLE FLAP OF ITS WINGS...IT WILL RENDER ALL THE TROOPS THAT WE'VE SENT INTO EVERY LAND UNDER ITS ABSOLUTE CONTROL! AND I WILL CONTROL IT!!
WE'RE ALMOST THERE!
NOD
I CAN SEE IT NOW, DRAGONITE!!
THE MAGNIFICENT NEW WORLD THAT WE WILL CREATE!
A WORLD FOR POKÉMON ALONE--

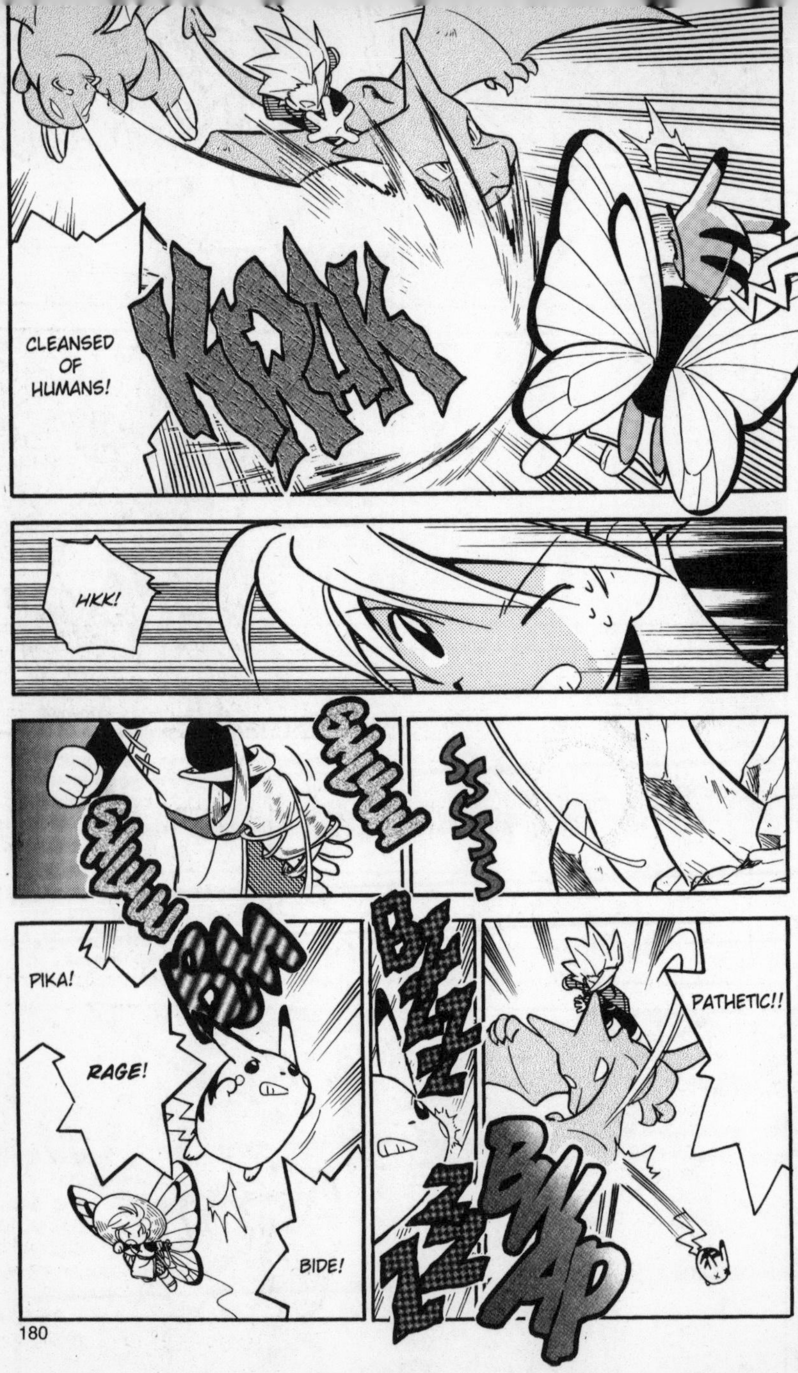
CLEANSED OF HUMANS!
HKK!
PIKA!
RAGE!
BIDE!
PATHETIC!!

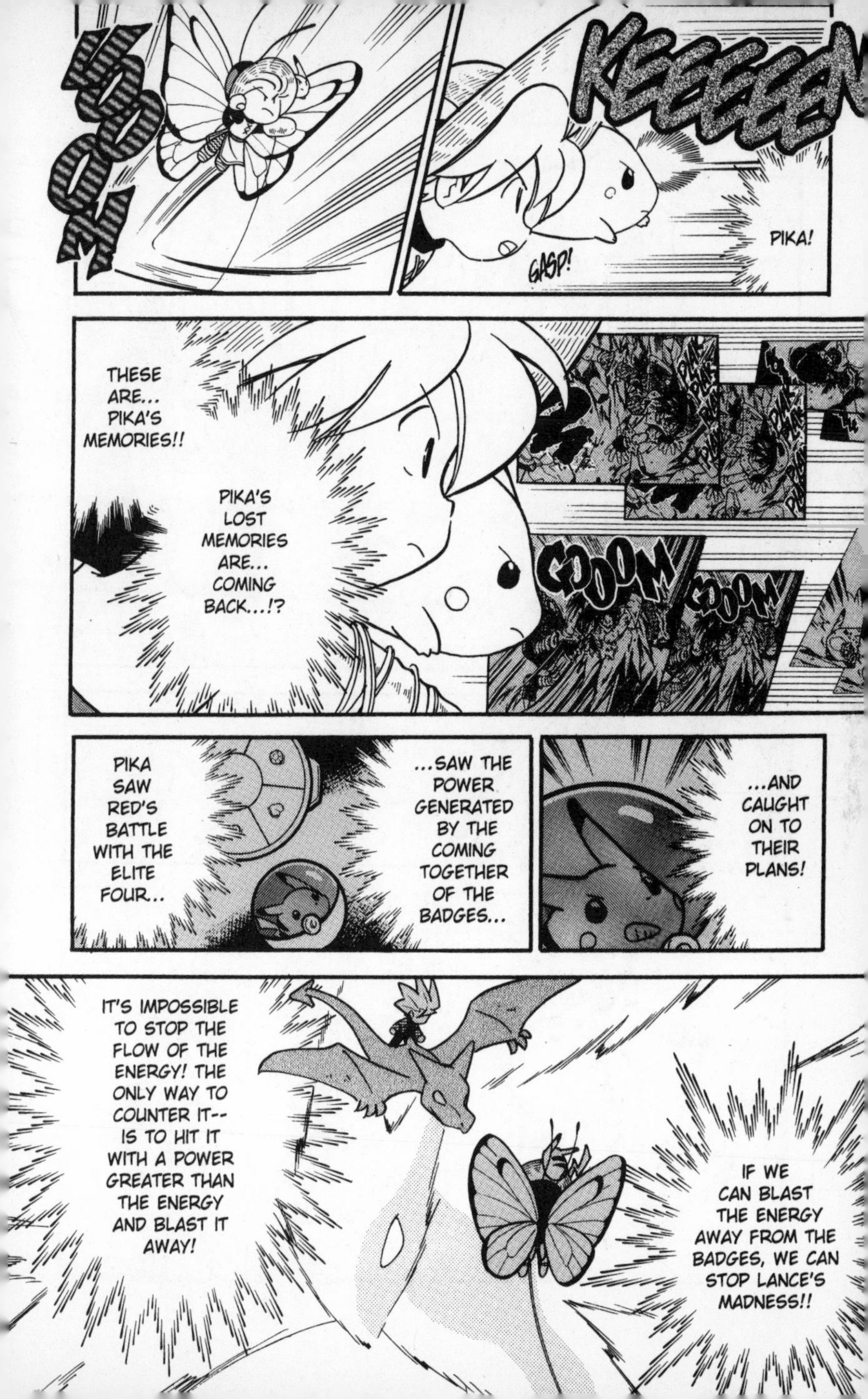
GASP!
PIKA!
THESE ARE... PIKA'S MEMORIES!!
PIKA'S LOST MEMORIES ARE... COMING BACK...!?
GOOOM
GOOOM
PIKA SAW RED'S BATTLE WITH THE ELITE FOUR...
...SAW THE POWER GENERATED BY THE COMING TOGETHER OF THE BADGES...
...AND CAUGHT ON TO THEIR PLANS!
IT'S IMPOSSIBLE TO STOP THE FLOW OF THE ENERGY! THE ONLY WAY TO COUNTER IT-- IS TO HIT IT WITH A POWER GREATER THAN THE ENERGY AND BLAST IT AWAY!
IF WE CAN BLAST THE ENERGY AWAY FROM THE BADGES, WE CAN STOP LANCE'S MADNESS!!

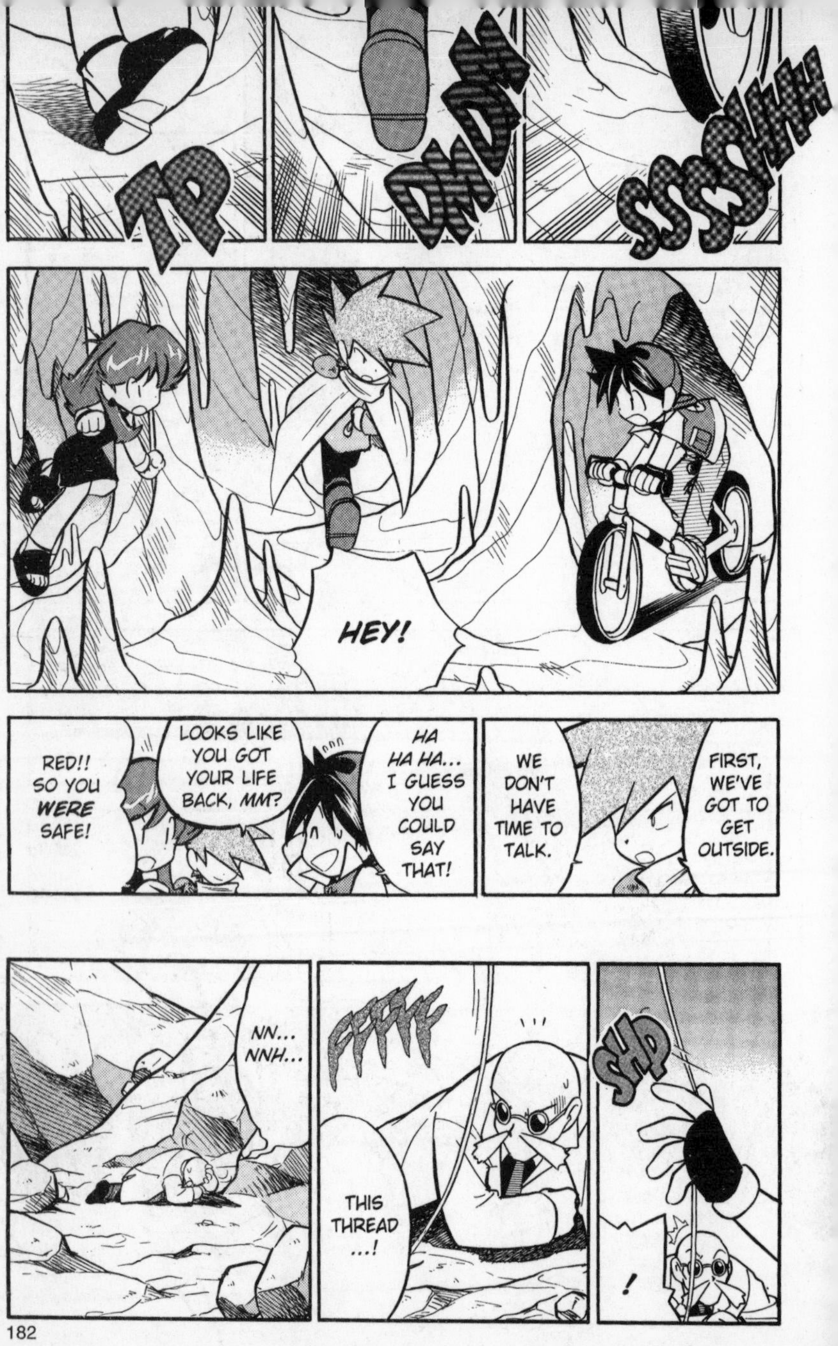
TP
DM DM
SSSSHHHH
HEY!
RED!! SO YOU WERE SAFE!
LOOKS LIKE YOU GOT YOUR LIFE BACK, MM?
HA HA HA... I GUESS YOU COULD SAY THAT!
WE DON'T HAVE TIME TO TALK.
FIRST, WE'VE GOT TO GET OUTSIDE.
NN... NNH...
THIS THREAD ...!
SHP
!

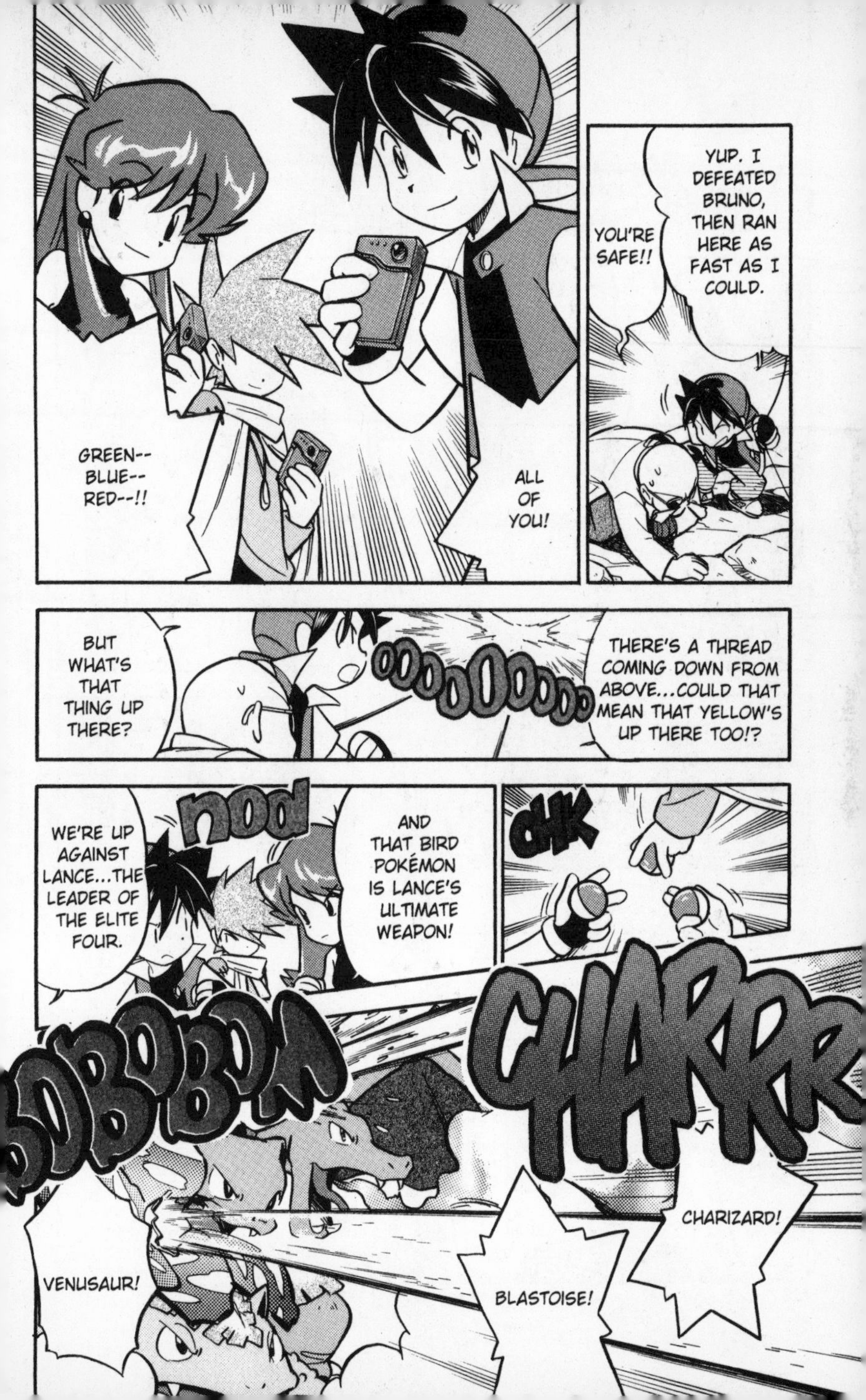
GREEN--
BLUE--
RED--!!
ALL OF YOU!
YOU'RE SAFE!!
YUP. I DEFEATED BRUNO, THEN RAN HERE AS FAST AS I COULD.
BUT WHAT'S THAT THING UP THERE?
THERE'S A THREAD COMING DOWN FROM ABOVE...COULD THAT MEAN THAT YELLOW'S UP THERE TOO!?
WE'RE UP AGAINST LANCE...THE LEADER OF THE ELITE FOUR.
nod
AND THAT BIRD POKÉMON IS LANCE'S ULTIMATE WEAPON!
CHK
CHARRR
VENUSAUR!
BLASTOISE!
CHARIZARD!

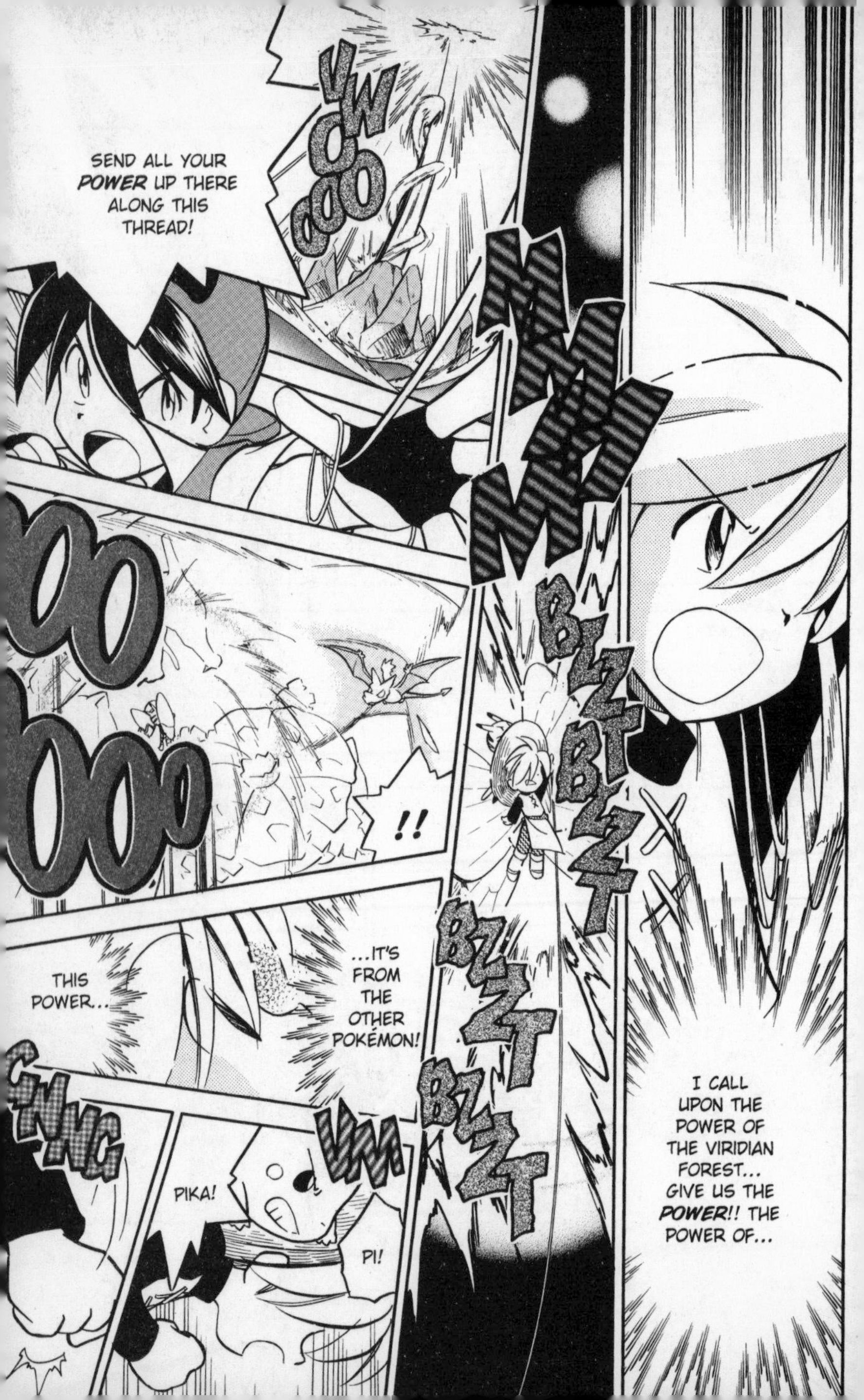
I CALL UPON THE POWER OF THE VIRIDIAN FOREST... GIVE US THE POWER!! THE POWER OF...
SEND ALL YOUR POWER UP THERE ALONG THIS THREAD!
BZZT
BZZT
BZZT
BZZT
!!
...IT'S FROM THE OTHER POKÉMON!
THIS POWER...
PIKA!
PI!

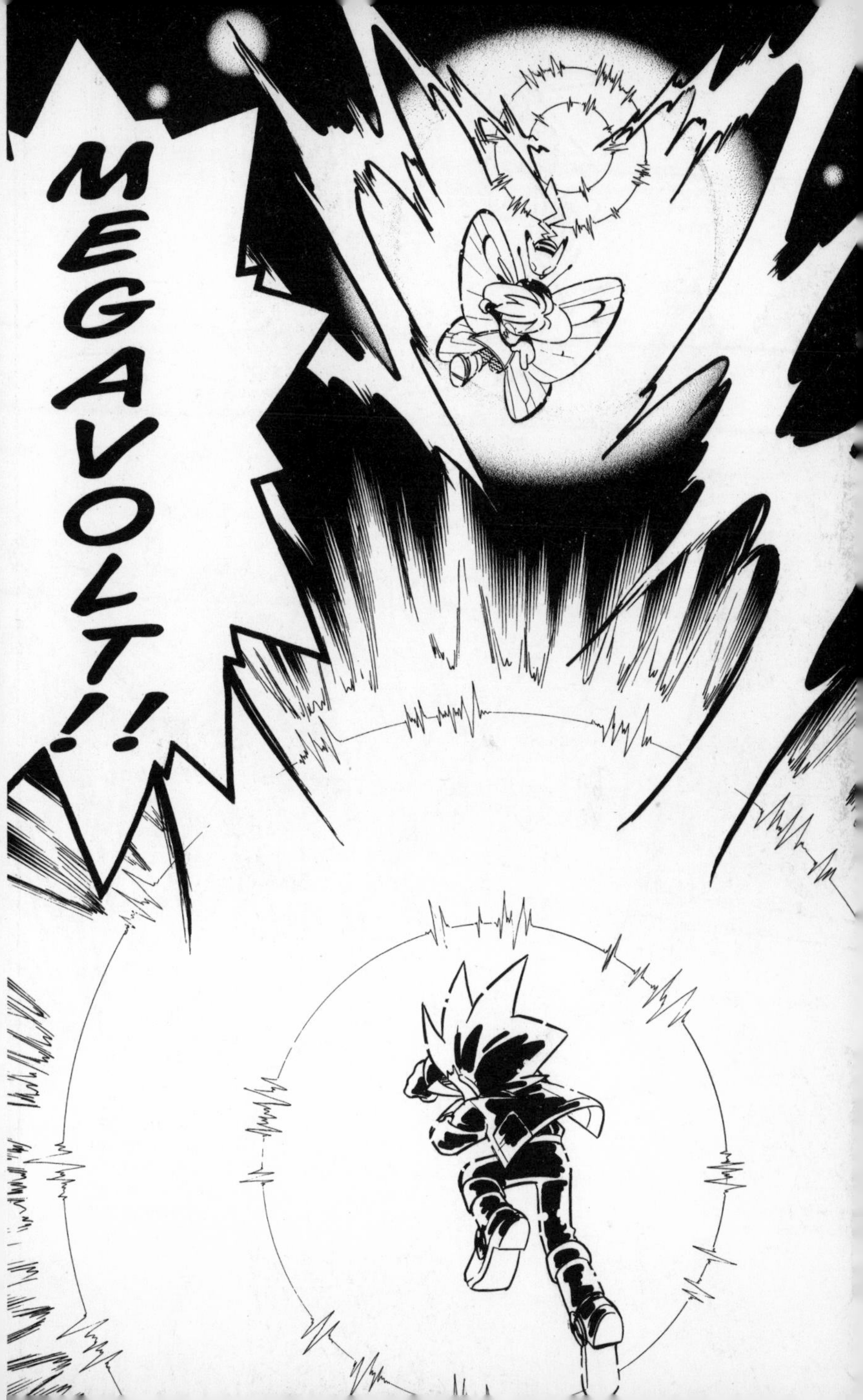
MEGAVOLT!!

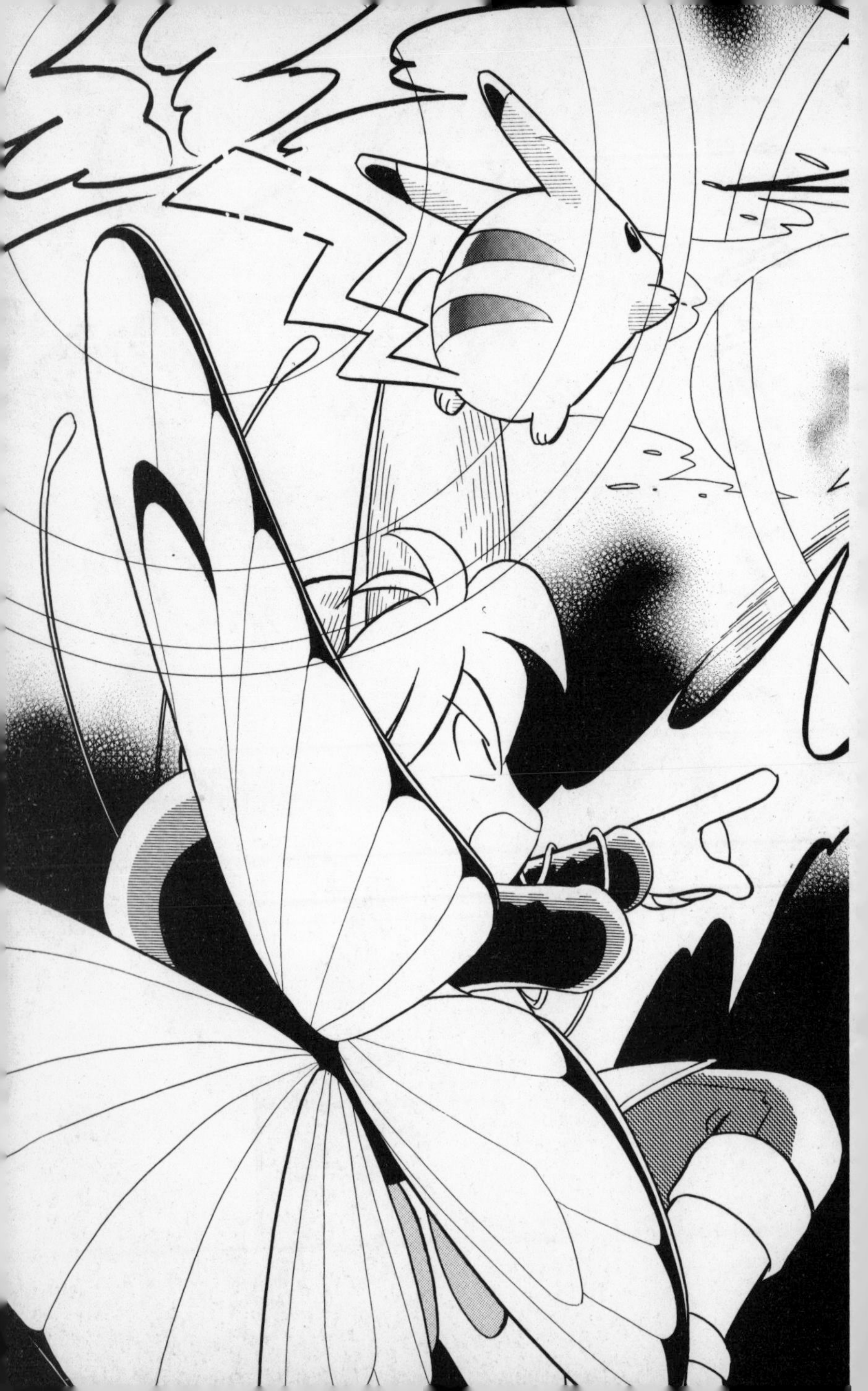

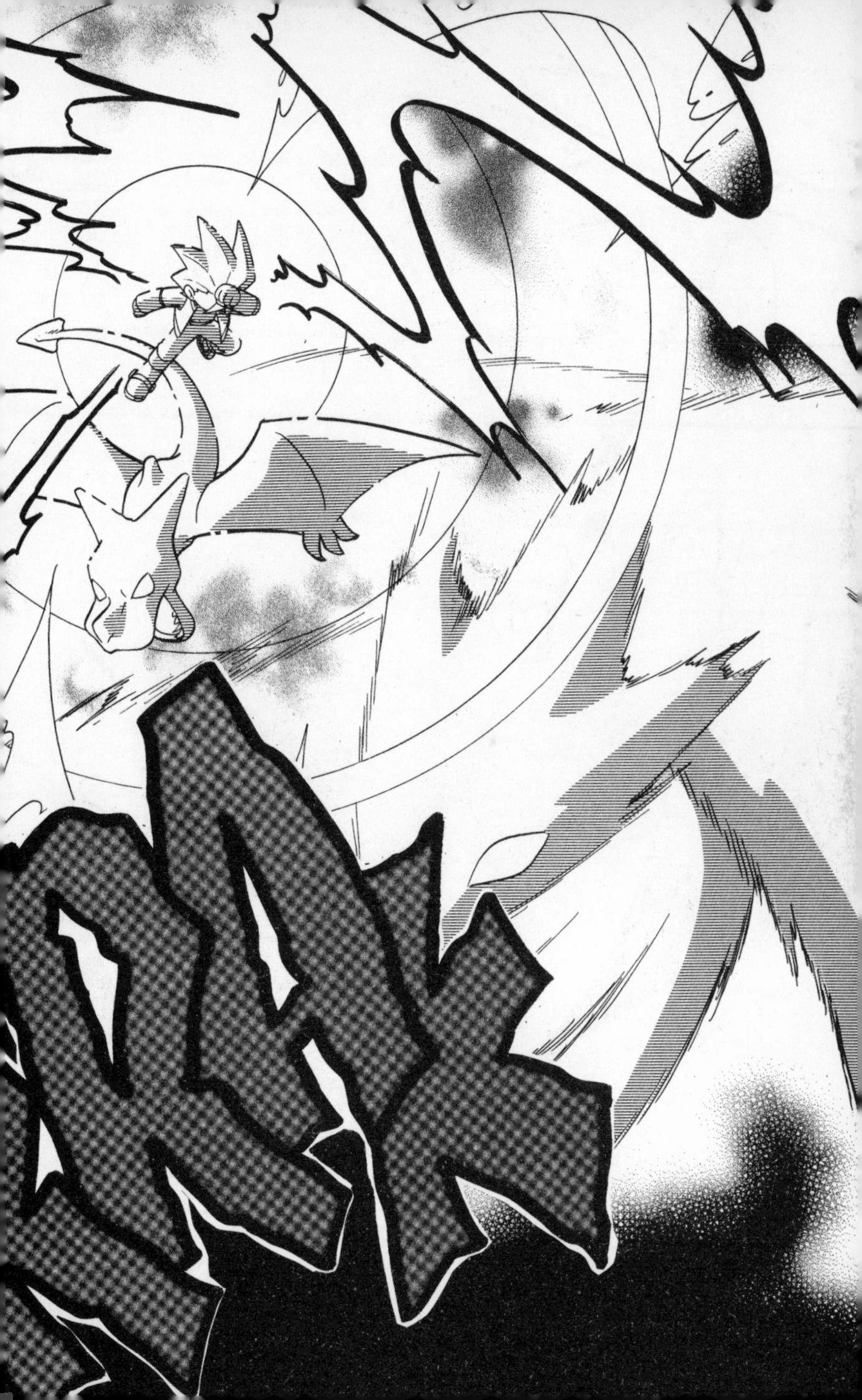

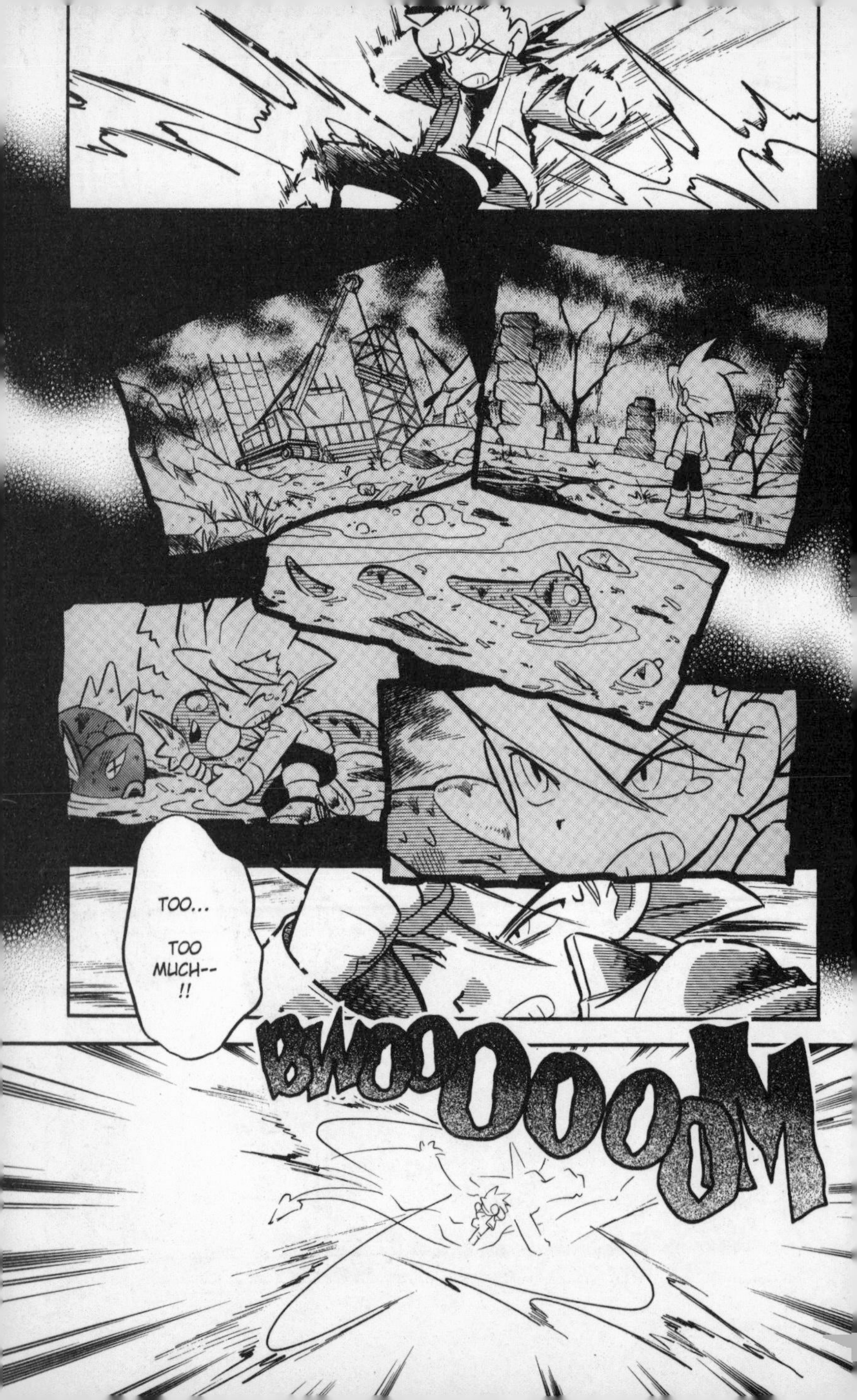
TOO... TOO MUCH-- !!
BWOOOOOOM

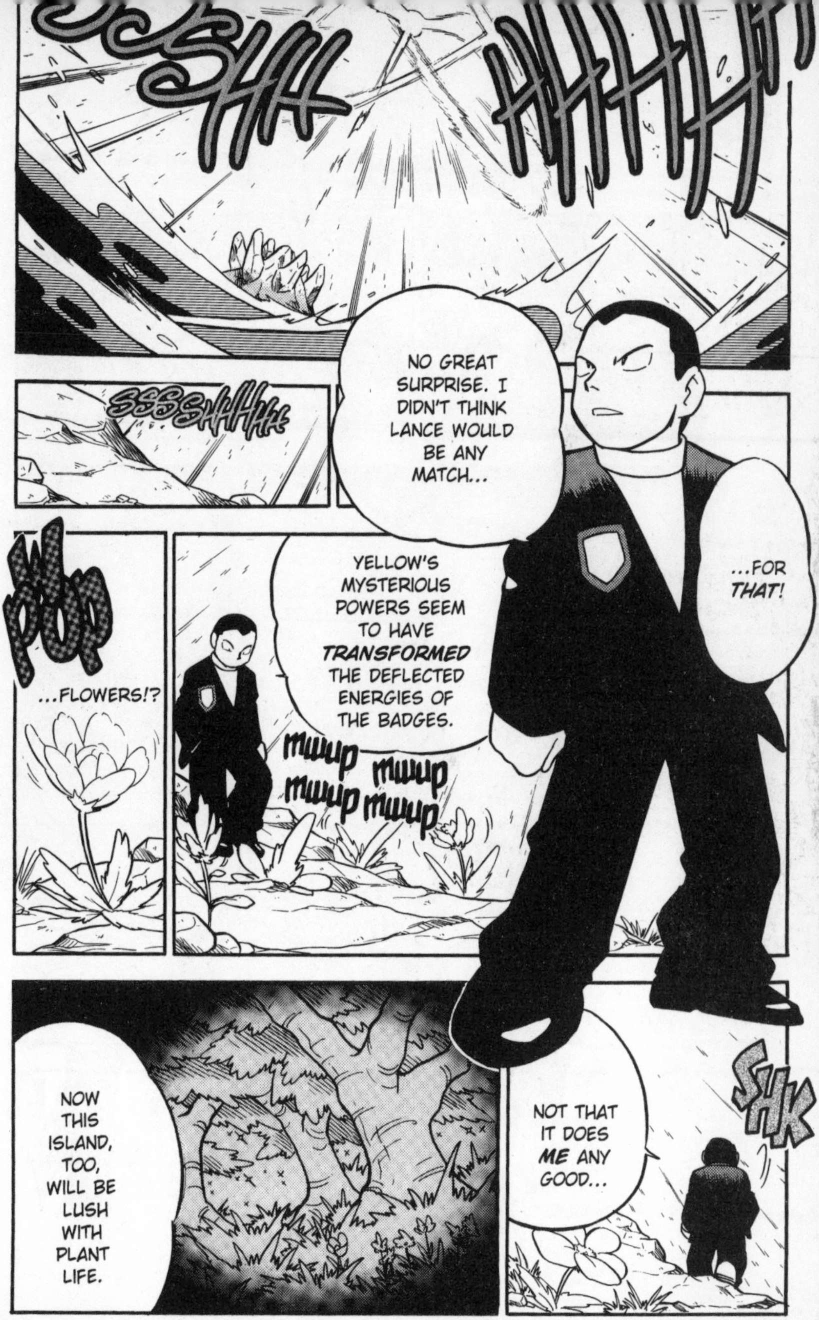
SHAAAHHHHHH
SSSSHHHHH
NO GREAT SURPRISE. I DIDN'T THINK LANCE WOULD BE ANY MATCH...
...FOR THAT!
POP
...FLOWERS!?
YELLOW'S MYSTERIOUS POWERS SEEM TO HAVE TRANSFORMED THE DEFLECTED ENERGIES OF THE BADGES.
mwup mwup mwup mwup
SHK
NOT THAT IT DOES ME ANY GOOD...
NOW THIS ISLAND, TOO, WILL BE LUSH WITH PLANT LIFE.

BOSS!! WAIT!!

I KNEW WE'D MEET AGAIN, BOSS!

AS YOU CAN SEE, WE'VE BEEN GETTING THINGS READY FOR THE ORGANIZATION TO RISE UP AGAIN! NOW'S THE TIME TO STRIKE BACK-- TOGETHER!

LT. SURGE... AND SABRINA. I TAKE IT KOGA IS AFRAID TO SHOW HIS FACE.

AND DOES GETTING READY FOR THE RESURRECTION MEAN SEEKING HELP IN DEFEATING *CHILDREN!?* ...FROM THE ELITE FOUR...

B-BUT BOSS--!!

I'M STILL IN THE MIDDLE OF A TRAINING JOURNEY, SEEKING TO BUILD UP MY OWN STRENGTH ENOUGH TO REALIZE MY PLANS.

I SUGGEST YOU GO HOME FOR NOW. TEND YOUR OWN GYMS!

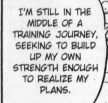

THE MEGA-THUNDERBOLT... TEN TIMES MORE POWERFUL THAN THE THUNDERBOLT.

IS THERE EVEN ONE AMONG US WHO CAN PRODUCE AS MUCH POWER AS RED OR YELLOW?

LOOK. THE DEFLECTED ENERGY EVEN REACHED THE MAINLAND.

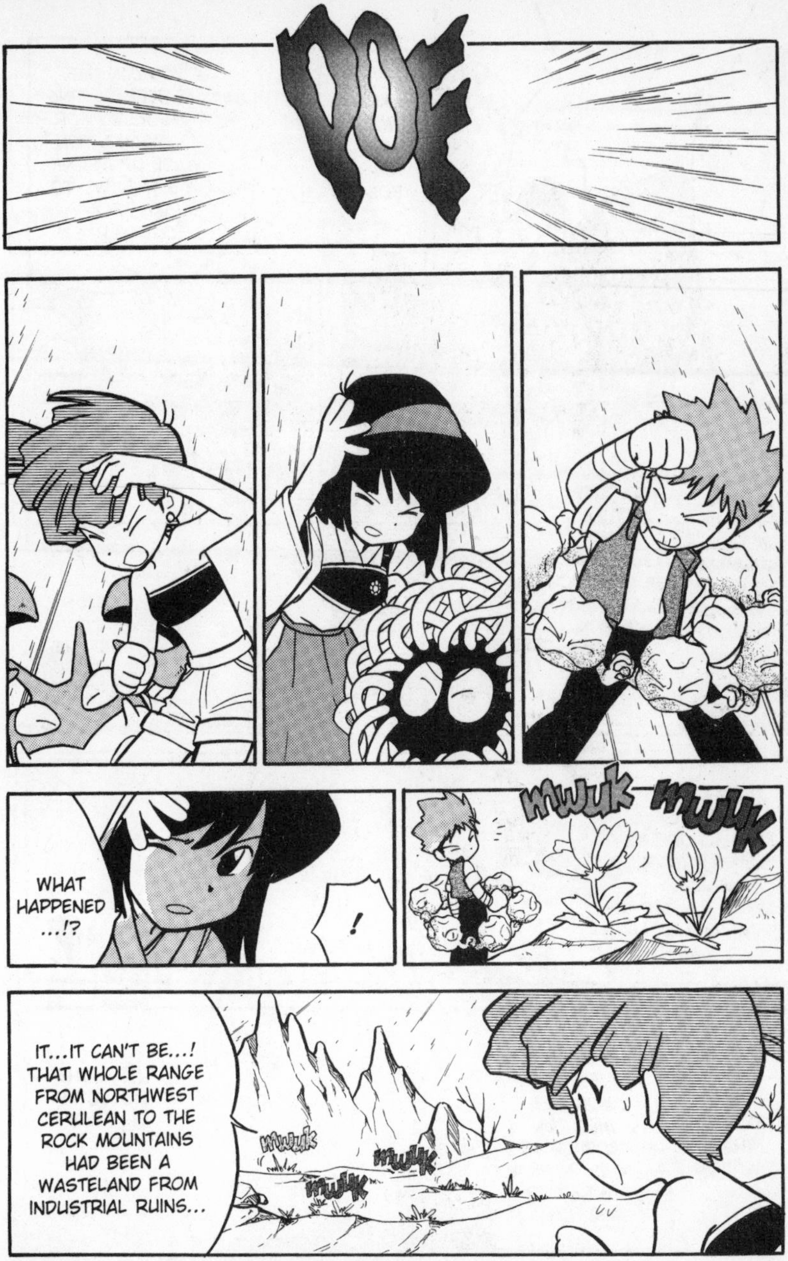
DOF
WHAT HAPPENED ...!?
!
MWUK MWUK
IT...IT CAN'T BE...! THAT WHOLE RANGE FROM NORTHWEST CERULEAN TO THE ROCK MOUNTAINS HAD BEEN A WASTELAND FROM INDUSTRIAL RUINS...
MWUK
MWUK
MWUK

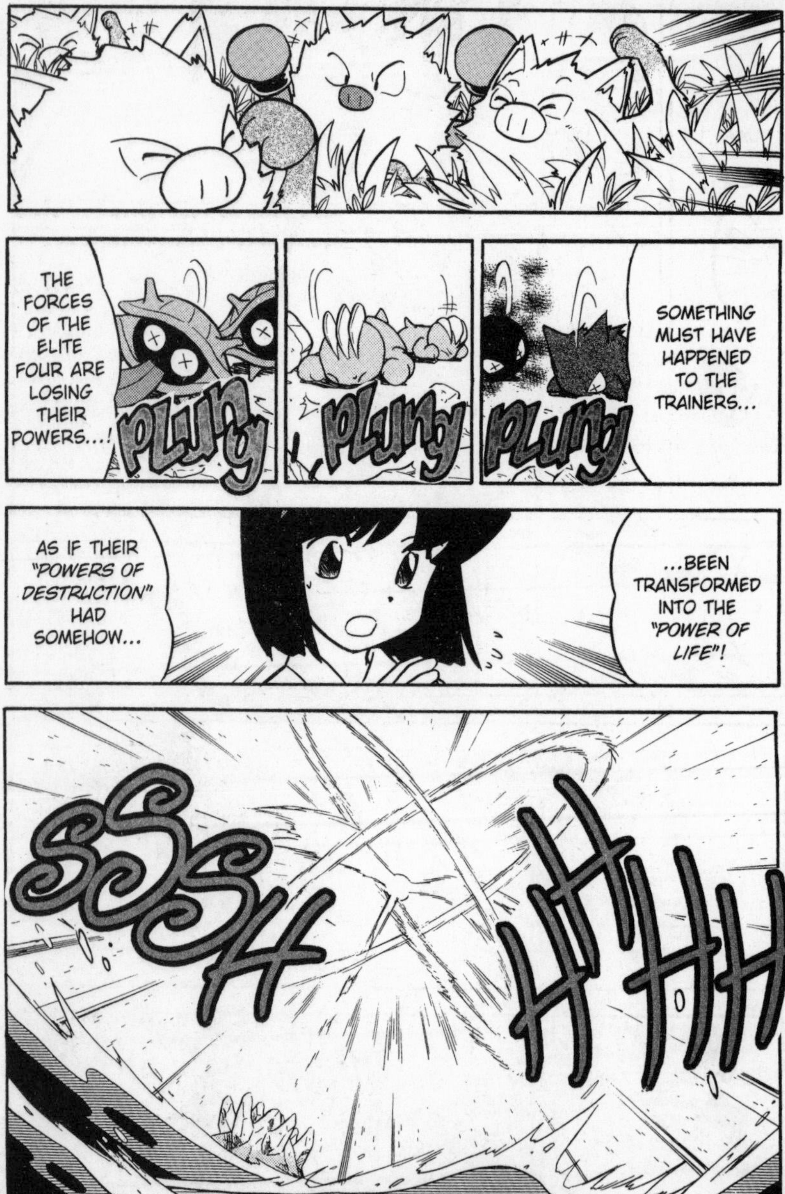

THE FORCES OF THE ELITE FOUR ARE LOSING THEIR POWERS...!
PLUNG
PLUNG
PLUNG
SOMETHING MUST HAVE HAPPENED TO THE TRAINERS...
AS IF THEIR "POWERS OF DESTRUCTION" HAD SOMEHOW...
...BEEN TRANSFORMED INTO THE "POWER OF LIFE"!
SSSHHHHHH

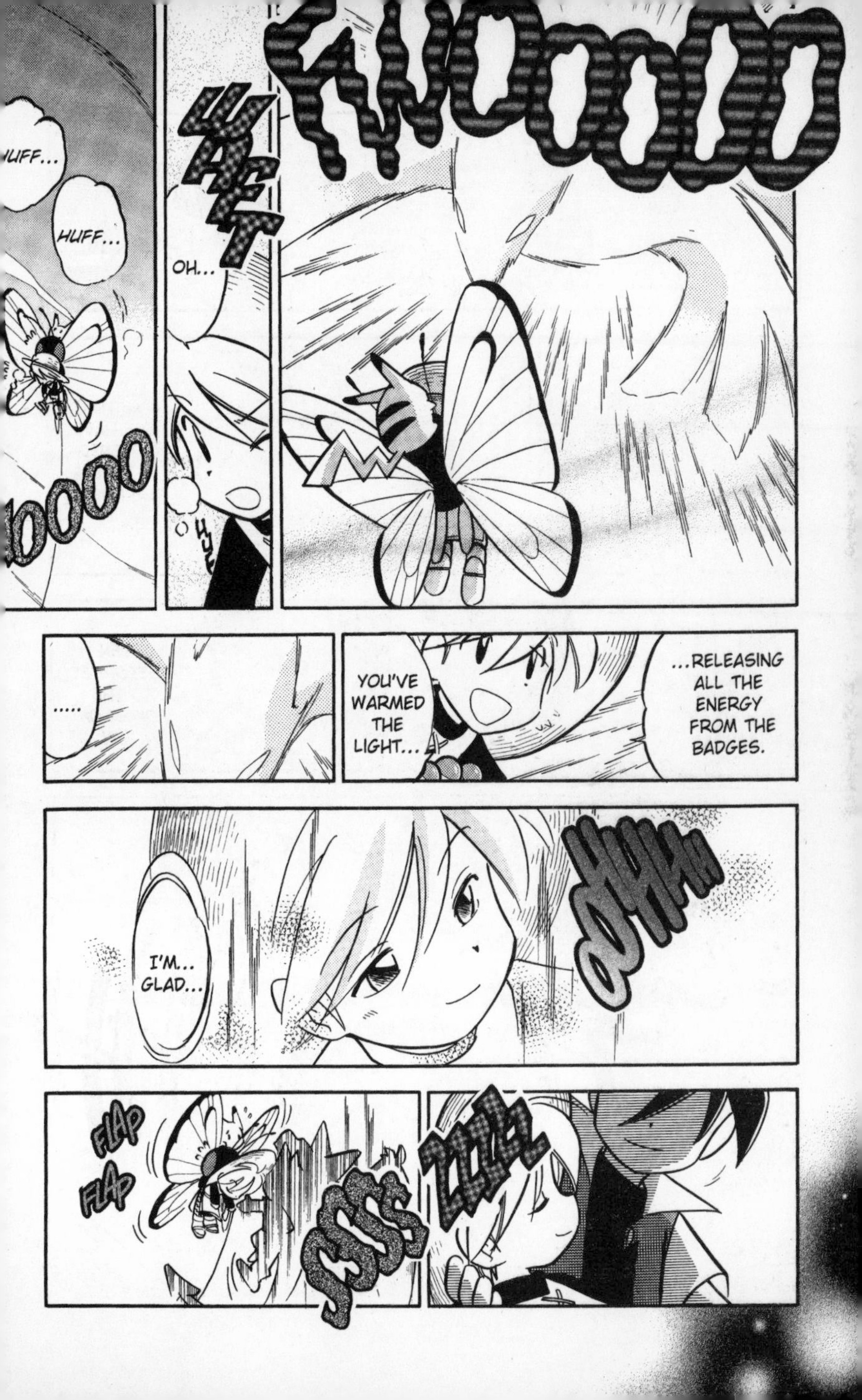

WAFT
OH...
HUFF...
HUFF...
YOU'VE WARMED THE LIGHT...
...RELEASING ALL THE ENERGY FROM THE BADGES.
.....
I'M... GLAD...
FLAP
FLAP

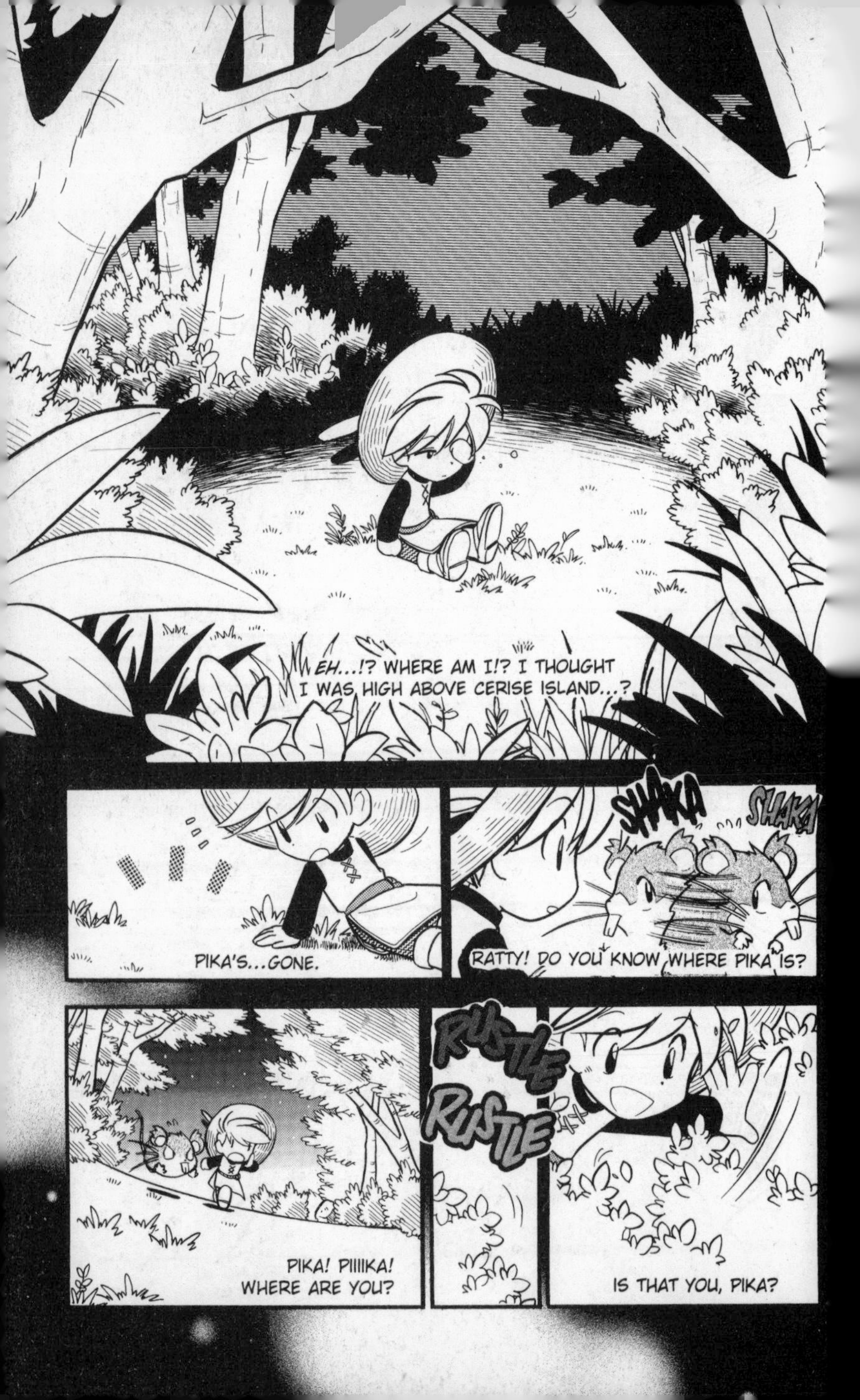
EH...!? WHERE AM I!? I THOUGHT I WAS HIGH ABOVE CERISE ISLAND...?
PIKA'S...GONE.
SHAKA SHAKA
RATTY! DO YOU KNOW WHERE PIKA IS?
PIKA! PIIIIKA! WHERE ARE YOU?
RUSTLE RUSTLE
IS THAT YOU, PIKA?

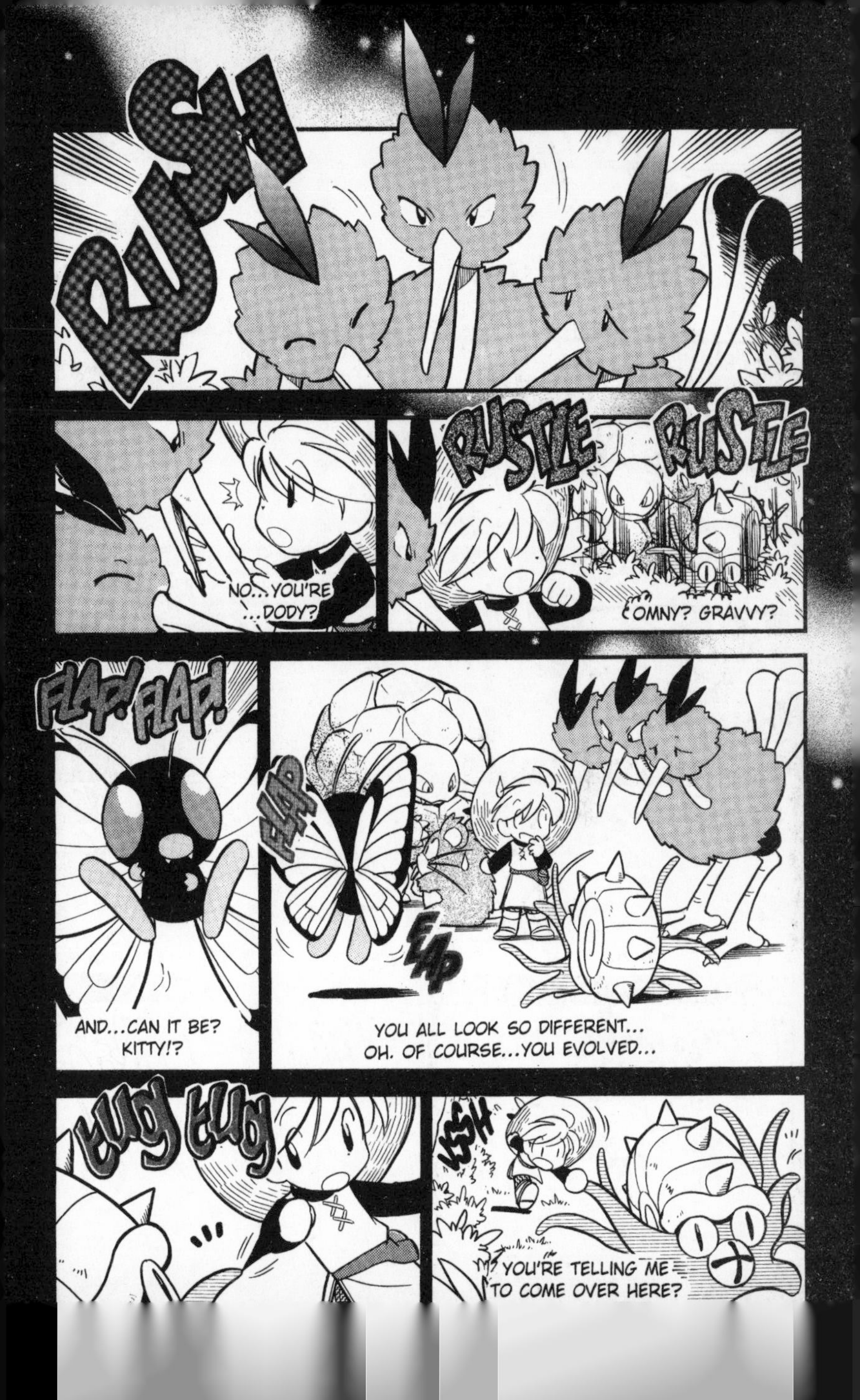
RUSH
NO...YOU'RE ...DODY?
RUSTLE RUSTLE
OMNY? GRAVVY?
FLAP! FLAP!
AND...CAN IT BE? KITTY!?
FLAP
FLAP
YOU ALL LOOK SO DIFFERENT... OH. OF COURSE...YOU EVOLVED...
tug tug
...
YOU'RE TELLING ME TO COME OVER HERE?

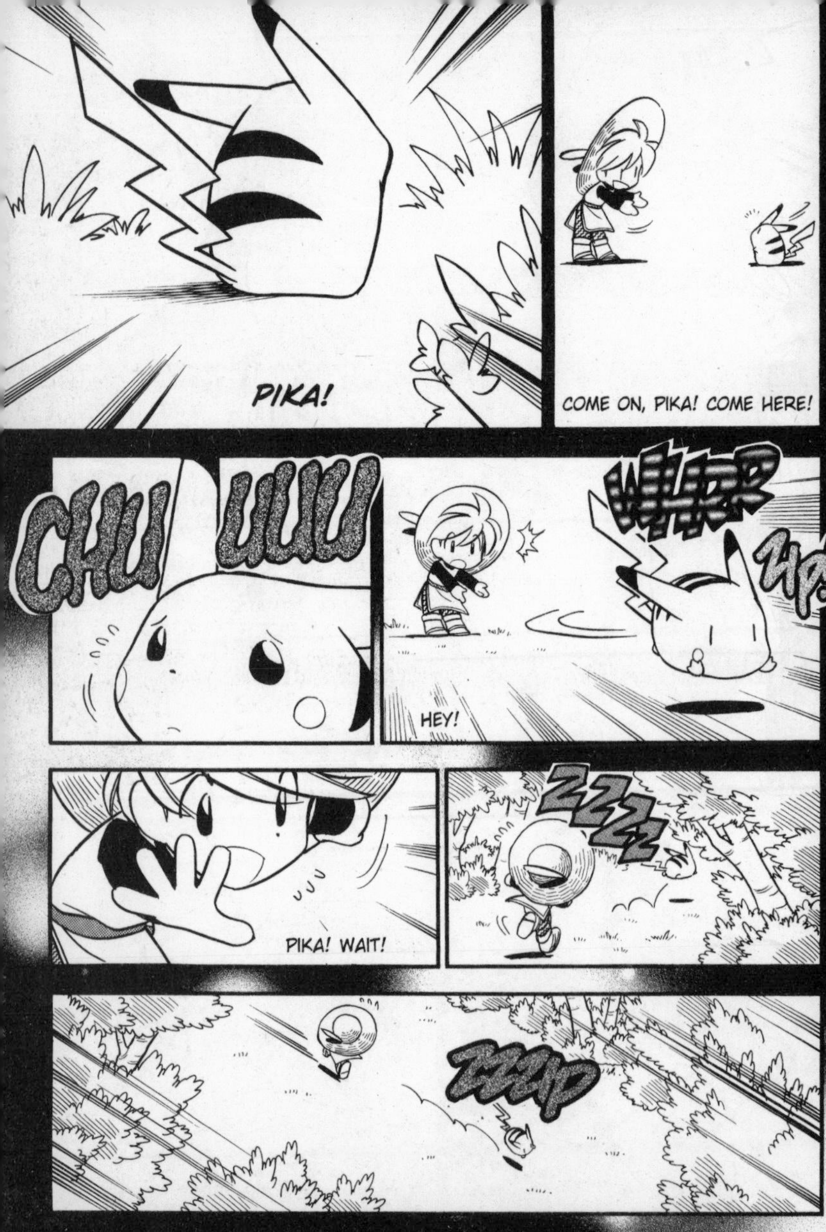
PIKA!
COME ON, PIKA! COME HERE!
CHU UUU
WHRR
ZIP!
HEY!
PIKA! WAIT!
ZZZZ
ZZZIP

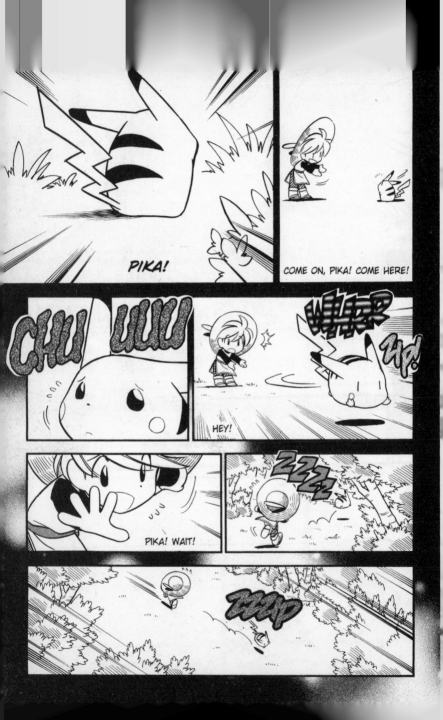

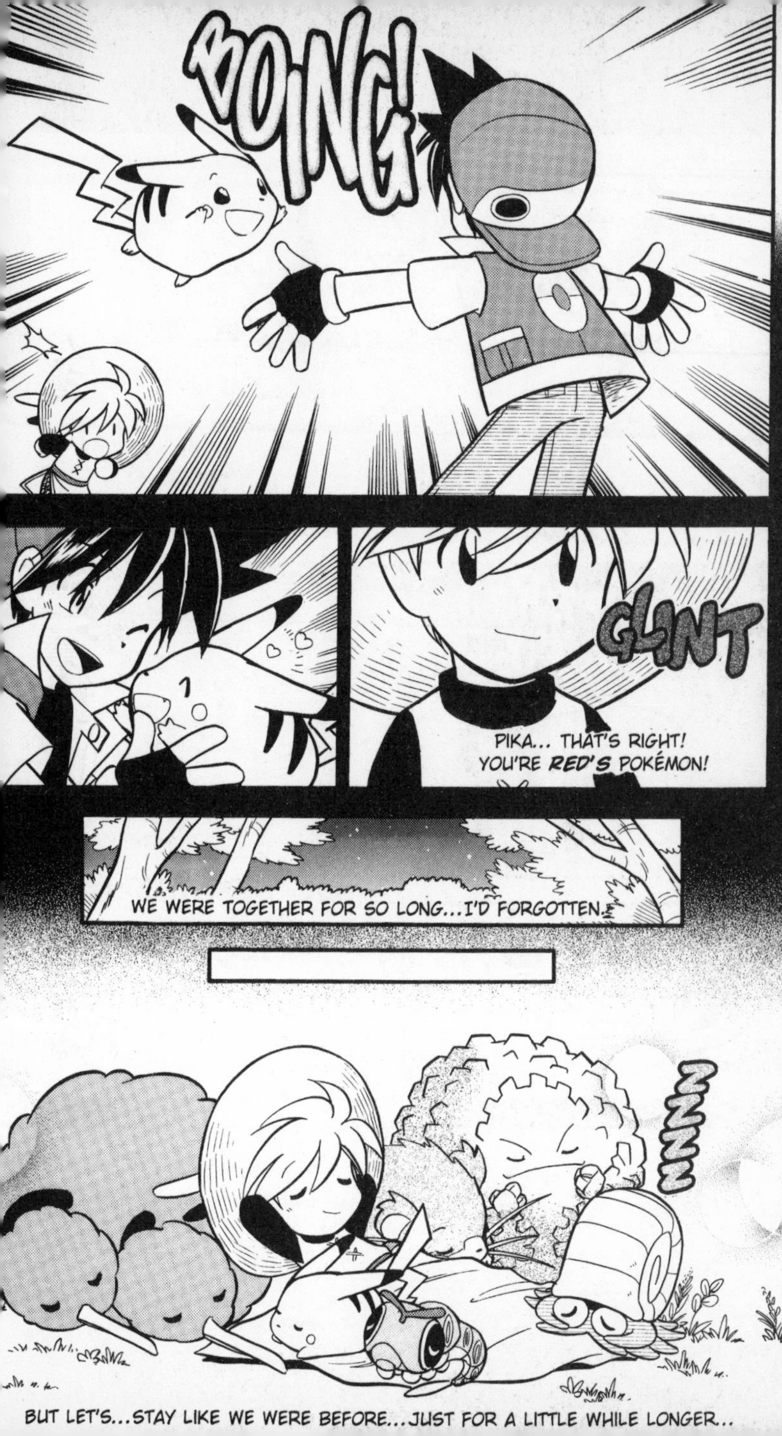
BOING!
GLINT
PIKA... THAT'S RIGHT! YOU'RE RED'S POKÉMON!
WE WERE TOGETHER FOR SO LONG...I'D FORGOTTEN.
ZZZZZ
BUT LET'S...STAY LIKE WE WERE BEFORE...JUST FOR A LITTLE WHILE LONGER...

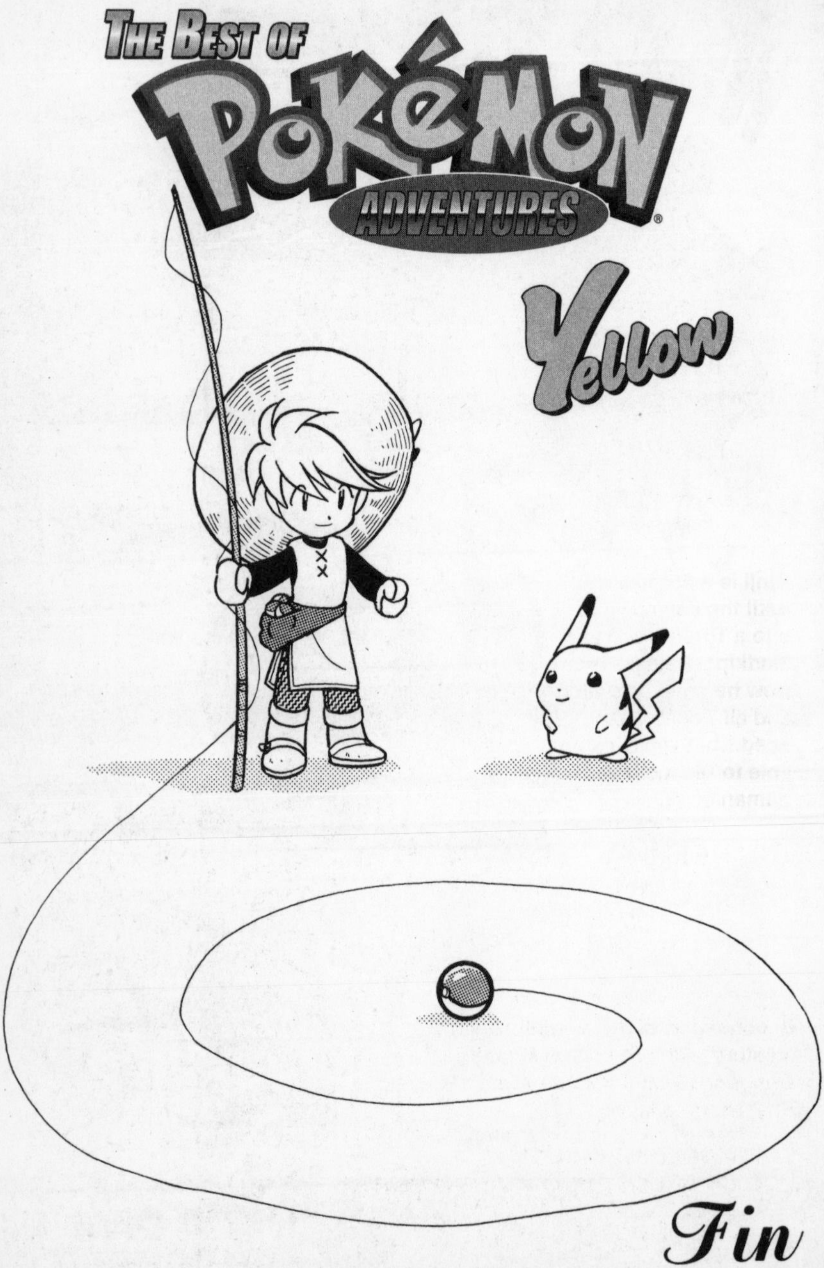
THE BEST OF
POKéMON
ADVENTURES
Yellow
Fin

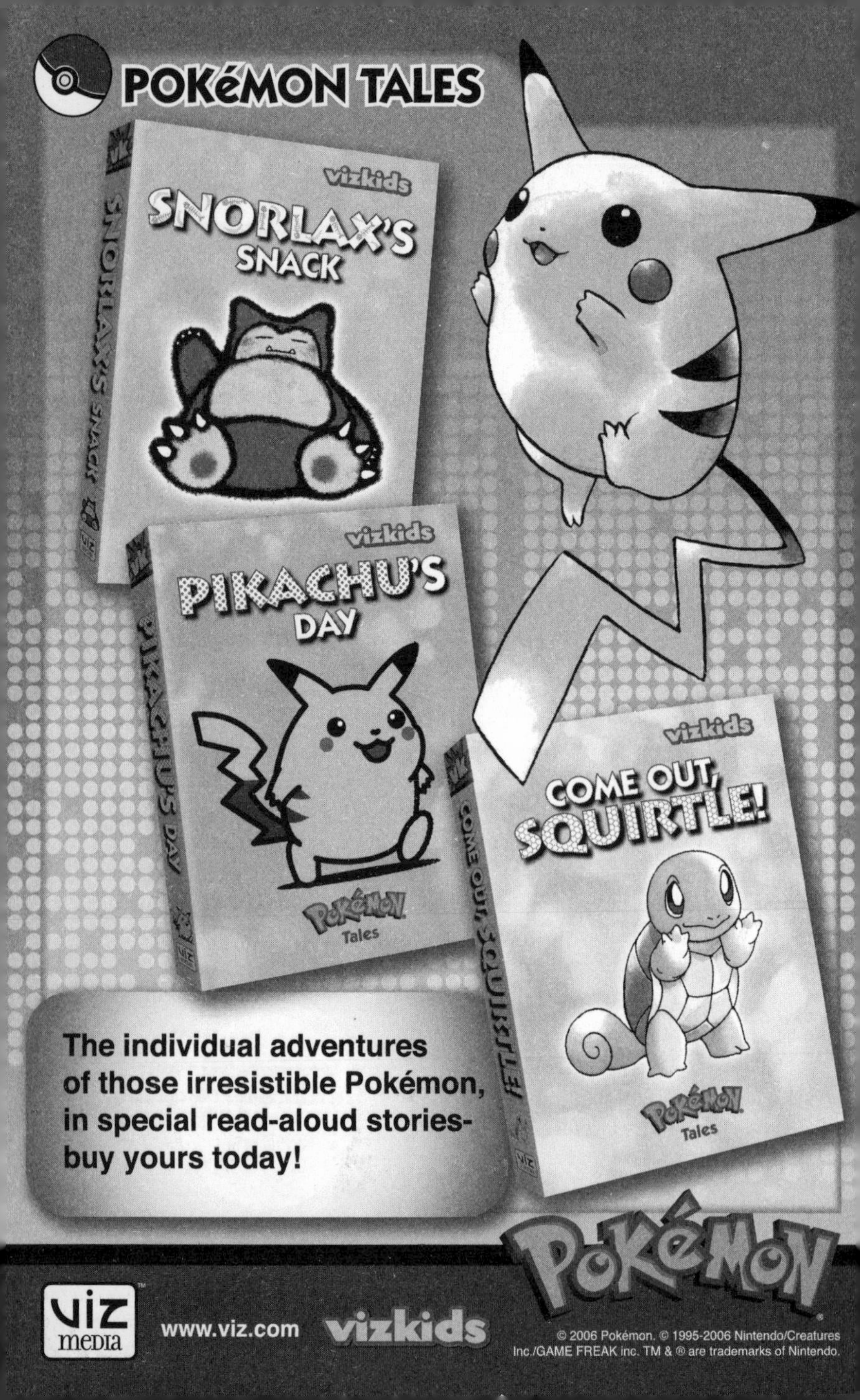
POKéMON TALES
vizkids
SNORLAX'S SNACK
vizkids
PIKACHU'S DAY
Pokémon Tales
vizkids
COME OUT, SQUIRTLE!
Pokémon Tales
The individual adventures of those irresistible Pokémon, in special read-aloud stories- buy yours today!
Pokémon
viz media
www.viz.com
vizkids
© 2006 Pokémon. © 1995-2006 Nintendo/Creatures Inc./GAME FREAK inc. TM & ® are trademarks of Nintendo.